The Shout

STEPHEN LEATHER

The Shout

HODDER &
STOUGHTON

First published in Great Britain in 2018 by Hodder & Stoughton
An Hachette UK company

1

Copyright © Stephen Leather 2018

The right of Stephen Leather to be identified as
the Author of the Work has been asserted by him in
accordance with the Copyright, Designs and Patents Act 1988.

A CIP catalogue record for this title is available from the British Library

Hardback ISBN 978 1 473 67178 2
Trade Paperback ISBN 978 1 473 67179 9
eBook ISBN 978 1 473 67182 9

Typeset in Plantin Light by
Palimpsest Book Production Ltd, Falkirk, Stirlingshire

Printed and bound in Great Britain by Clays Ltd, St Ives plc

Hodder & Stoughton policy is to use papers that are natural, renewable
and recyclable products and made from wood grown in sustainable forests.
The logging and manufacturing processes are expected to conform
to the environmental regulations of the country of origin.

Hodder & Stoughton Ltd
Carmelite House
50 Victoria Embankment
London EC4Y 0DZ

www.hodder.co.uk

For Thorne

I

He smiled as he looked down at the body sprawled across the bed. Her name was Emma Fox and she was in her early thirties, a natural blond with shoulder-length hair splayed across the pillow. She had been dead for twenty minutes so she was still warm. Her eyes were wide and staring, the whites flecked with pinpricks of red. That was what happened when people were strangled. Petechial haemorrhages they were called, ruptures of the capillaries.

It had taken Emma the best part of forty minutes to die. He had wanted it to be longer but strangulation was an inexact science. He had tied her hands to the bedhead but left her legs free. She couldn't struggle much because most of the time she was unconscious, but when she did struggle it felt so much better. He'd used a length of cord to restrict her air supply, looped twice around her pretty neck. It was a delicate balance, cutting off her air. He wanted her conscious, but if she was conscious she could scream and that would spoil everything, so he used pressure on the cord to keep her precariously balanced between being awake and being out cold. He had ejaculated inside her, and that was when he had pulled the cord too tight for too long and the life went out of her.

The cord lay coiled at her feet. The fire would destroy it, the way it destroyed all the evidence of what he had done.

He dressed. He could smell her scent on him and he wouldn't shower or bathe for two or three days, not until it had faded completely. He went over to the sash window and opened it a few inches. A fire needed three things to burn efficiently – heat, fuel and an oxidising agent. It was what they called the Fire Triangle. Oxygen was the perfect oxidising agent. The heat would come from the book of matches he had in his pocket. And the room was full of fuel. The bedding, the mattress, the carpet, the curtains, her clothes, all of it would burn nicely.

There was a nightdress lying across a chair in the corner of the room, pink and frilly and quite long. It would burn, but it was polyester so it would leave a residue, which meant she had to be wearing it. He picked it up and carefully pulled it over her head. It took him a while to get her arms through the armholes, but he took it slowly. Eventually he pulled the nightdress down her long, lithe legs. He found himself getting hard again and wondered if he had time to have sex with her one more time. He found himself growing harder as he pictured himself on top of her. He looked at his watch. It was eleven o'clock, the time that she usually went to bed. And sex with the dead was never as satisfying as sex with the soon-to-be dead. Better to set the fire and go.

He knew pretty much everything about Emma Fox. He had befriended her on Facebook with a fake profile and chatted to her on Twitter under another identity. He had watched her apartment from the cafe across the road and followed her to and from her work. She was a shop assistant in Top Shop in Oxford Circus. Early on in his stalking he had approached her in the store and asked her advice on buying a pullover for a non-existent sister. That was one of the most exciting things he had ever done. To stand next to her, to breathe in her fragrance and look into her eyes, knowing that one day he would own her. He had thanked her and walked away, almost shuddering with anticipation. That had been two weeks ago. And now she was dead.

He pulled the duvet from under her, then placed it on top of her. He took out a toilet roll and a plastic spray bottle he'd filled with diesel. He pulled a length of ten pieces of toilet roll and laid it on the floor, then repeated the process six times. He lined the lengths up so that they were touching and then sprayed them with diesel. Diesel in its natural state was almost impossible to ignite, but when sprayed over tissue it became deliciously flammable. He put the spray bottle into his backpack and then laid the strips of toilet tissue over the duvet. They would burn quickly and hotly and would be totally destroyed in the fire.

He took out a pack of cigarettes and a book of matches from his jacket pocket and placed them on the bed. In his backpack he had a small can of lighter fluid. He poured a little of the liquid over the foot of the bed and watched it soak into the quilt. It was important not to use too much as that might leave a trace for investigators to find. He put the can back in the backpack and took a final look around the room, making sure that he would be leaving nothing behind.

Satisfied, he lit a cigarette with one of the matches, took two drags on it and then clipped the cigarette into the book of matches so that the burning end was about two inches from the first match. It was a Benson and Hedges, the same brand that Emma smoked, but they were counterfeits that he had bought at a car boot sale in south London, almost certainly manufactured in the Far East. Since November 2011, all cigarettes sold in the UK and the European Union had to be reduced ignition propensity cigarettes, designed to go out if not drawn on regularly. The RIP cigarettes had been designed to cut down on the number of fires started by smokers but the counterfeiters weren't bound by the EU regulations and would burn down to the filter. He carefully placed the book of matches on the bed and stood up to admire his handiwork. The cigarette would take at least ten minutes to burn down to the matches by which time he would be long gone. The matches would ignite, the lighter fluid-soaked duvet would catch fire, boosted by the diesel-impregnated tissue and within minutes the room would be ablaze.

He shouldered his backpack, left the bedroom and headed for the front door. There was a smoke alarm in the hallway but he had taken care of that. By the time anyone realised the flat was ablaze the fire would have reduced the bed and the body to ashes. He took a final look around the hallway and left. He didn't plan on waiting around to see the fire brigade arrive. Most arsonists were caught eventually because they stayed to stare at the flames. He wasn't an arsonist. He took no pleasure from watching things burn. The fire was a means to an end, and that end was for him to continue to kill. That was what gave him pleasure, the taking of human lives. But not just any lives. He had a type. He knew that was a weakness, and that having a type was as likely to get him caught as watching the buildings burn. He knew that as well as he knew that night followed day, but he couldn't help himself. It was in his nature. Or his genes. He wasn't sure which, but then it didn't matter, all that mattered was that he loved taking lives and he had found a way of doing it and getting away with it.

A cold breeze blew down the street as he stepped out on to the pavement. He turned up the collar of his jacket and walked away, whistling softly to himself.

2

The blue flashing lights were reflected off the shop windows either side of the fire engine, and the noise of its sirens cut through the night as the eleven-ton vehicle sped along the city streets. What little traffic there was had pulled over already and Dom Laffy was able to keep their speed close to forty miles an hour. There was a red traffic light ahead of them but just as Laffy was preparing to go through it changed to green and he pressed his foot down on the accelerator. He grinned. 'I love it when that happens,' he said.

'What's the story, Vicky?' asked Gary Jones from the back. He was the oldest member of the crew, coming up to fifty, grey-haired and cheeks peppered with red veins, the result of his love for sailing.

Vicky Lewis scanned the printout she had torn from the printer before jumping on to the fire engine. She was crew manager and had taken the front passenger seat as usual. Vicky was approaching thirty, though she looked five years younger, with her upturned nose sprinkled with freckles and her blond hair cut short in a functional bob. She was still sometimes asked for ID in the pub, much to the delight of the guys on her shift. 'Fire in an abandoned building,' she said. 'No alarm but a passer-by called it in.'

'Probably another fucking hoax,' said Laffy.

There had been more than a dozen hoax calls over the past week, all made from phone boxes. It was probably kids getting a kick out of wasting the fire brigade's time, but it was close to midnight and most of the hoax calls had come in within an hour or so of the schools closing. With Jones in the back were Colin Noller – a thirty-something recent arrival at the Kilburn station – and Mark Beech, a beefy West Indian with almost twenty years' experience under his belt. All were wearing full gear and had their yellow helmets on.

Laffy was driving a Mercedes-Benz Atego fire engine. It was equipped with a thirty-foot ladder, more than a thousand feet of hoses – though firefighters referred to them as lines – breathing apparatus, chemical suits and pretty much anything that might be needed to rescue people from burning buildings or crashed cars. About fifty yards behind them was another fire engine, this one a pump ladder carrying everything that was on Vicky's vehicle but with a ladder that was fifty per cent longer. The driver of the pump ladder was Billy Moore, a veteran firefighter who had been a keen kick-boxer in his youth and who spent most of his down time in the station's well-equipped gym. With him were Frank Westworth, Andy Mitchell and Mike Wells, who when they weren't putting out fires ran a very profitable landscaping company. London firefighters worked two ten-and-a-half-hour day shifts followed by two thirteen-and-a-half-hour night shifts, and then four days off. Many firefighters put their off-days to good use and the station gossip was that Westworth, Mitchell and Wells were now making more from doing up gardens than they were from their LFB salaries.

Like Vicky, Westworth was a crew manager, his rank shown by the two black rings around his yellow helmet. Whoever got to the shout first would be incident commander and in charge. Vicky's pump was in the lead partly because she'd switched Westworth's boots around in the station, costing him a few extra seconds in the rush to pull on their protective gear.

Laffy indicated left and the tyres squealed as the truck took the corner at close to thirty miles an hour. A young couple walking arm in arm stopped to watch them hurtle by. Ahead of them a black cab switched on its hazard lights and pulled over.

The shout was the sixth Vicky had attended since she had started the night shift at 8pm. Three had been malfunctioning fire alarms, two in shops and one in an office block, one had been a kitchen fire caused by an elderly women pouring water on to a burning frying pan, and the last one had been a burning skip, probably caused by a passer-by tossing in a lit cigarette.

A set of traffic lights resolutely refused to change from red so Laffy slowed and looked left and right as they rolled through. The road was clear to the left but half a dozen cars had stopped to their right. Laffy accelerated. Vicky leaned forward and looked at the nearside wing mirror. The pump ladder was about a hundred yards behind them now.

The next lights were on green, then Laffy took a left and slowed. 'Here we go,' he said. A group of half a dozen onlookers were gathered on a street corner staring up at a building. Smoke was billowing up from the ground floor. Laffy parked at the side of the road opposite the building, making sure there would be enough room to unload the ladder. Vicky climbed out and surveyed the scene. She could see immediately that it was definitely more than a two-pump fire. Four appliances would be needed, possibly six. There was a bar on the ground floor of the four-storey hotel building. It had its own entrance to the left and to the right was the main hotel reception. The doors and windows were boarded up and there was an estate agent's sign announcing that the property had been sold. The bar was clearly on fire, smoke was seeping out through the boarded-up door and around the sheets of plywood that had been nailed over the windows. There were no other buildings next to the hotel, which meant that its chances of spreading were limited. There were flats opposite the hotel and lights were on in many of the windows as the occupants looked out to see what was going on.

She looked up at Laffy. 'Dom, get on to control. Make pumps four.'

Laffy grabbed for his transceiver to call for two more fire engines as Jones, Noller and Beech climbed out of the pump and joined Vicky on the pavement. 'Let's get two lengths of forty-five on it asap,' she said. The pump had two sizes of hose – 45mm and 70mm. Vicky figured the smaller diameter would do the job and it was much more manoeuvrable than the 70mm version. 'One of you do a three-sixty and let me know what's happening around the back.'

Jones and Noller hurried to the pump and started pulling out the seventy-five-foot lengths of hose while Beech went around to the rear of the building to see what the situation was there.

There was a fire hydrant on the other side of the road

so water wasn't going to be an issue. The pump carried 300 gallons of water but that wouldn't last more than a minute when it was pumping flat out and to deal with anything major it had to be connected to a water source.

Vicky looked around for the police but they didn't appear to be there so she headed over to the crowd of onlookers. 'Ladies and gentlemen!' she shouted. 'I know everyone wants to watch a fire, but you're a bit too close for comfort! Can I ask you all to please move away a good hundred feet. For those of you using the metric system, that's about thirty metres.'

No one moved.

'I won't ask you twice!' she shouted. 'If you're still on this corner in ten seconds, I'll get those nice men over there to spray you with freezing cold water. Your call.' The onlookers were already moving away like startled sheep as she strode back to the pump, just as the Kilburn pump ladder arrived. Frank Westworth climbed out of the pump ladder and jogged over to her. 'Don't think I don't know it was you who fucked with my boots,' he said, wagging a finger at her face.

'No idea what you're talking about, Frank,' said Vicky, straight-faced. 'Anyway, I've made pumps four.'

Westworth nodded and looked up at the building. 'I might have gone for six.'

'The building's abandoned so I'm assuming most combustibles will be out. It's a standalone building so there's no immediate risk of it spreading. And no risk of casualties.'

Westworth nodded. 'Yeah, I hear you,' he said. He looked over at the hoses being prepared. 'Do you think two lines of forty-five is enough?'

'It could do with a covering jet as well,' she said. 'It seems to be confined to the bar. We get the boards off the windows and open the door, then attack it front to back. Can you handle the covering jet?'

'Sounds like a plan,' said Westworth. 'Cops not here?'

'Probably too busy handing out speeding tickets and hassling people on social media.' Just as she spoke a police car arrived, siren off but blue lights flashing. 'Speak of the devil,' she said. She went over to talk to the cops as Westworth walked quickly to the pump ladder.

The driver of the police car was an overweight West Indian woman who was having trouble getting out of the front seat. Vicky tried not to grin as the officer swung her legs out of the vehicle and then used the door to pull herself up. The cop in the front seat was younger and considerably thinner, but looked to be barely out of his teens and his stab vest was a couple of sizes too big for him. 'The fire looks as if it's confined to the downstairs bar,' said Vicky. 'Can you block off the road and stop all traffic coming down? Also, there's a crowd of rubberneckers over there, it'd be great if you could move them away.'

'No problem,' said the cop. He turned to his colleague. 'Mary, maybe use the car to block the road, yeah?'

Mary sighed and began lowering herself back into the vehicle as Vicky hurried over to the pump. Mitchell and Wells were dragging hoses out of the fire engine, while Moore was pulling out a Halligan bar. The Halligan bar was a souped-up crowbar, designed and named after a New York fire chief. Hugh Halligan came up with a design back in 1948 that could be used for a multitude of tasks. It was the Swiss Army knife of firefighting kit with a claw,

a blade and a tapered pick. It could be used to break
open doors and windows, as a crowbar or an axe, and
was strong enough to smash through a wall. The claw
was perfect for shutting off valves and the pick could
bust open any padlock in seconds. Moore was planning
to use it to rip off the wooden boards covering the
windows and door.

Noller had connected the pump to the hydrant while
Beech and Jones were fitting nozzles to the hoses.

Two more police cars arrived and they helped block
off the road. The onlookers had been moved back to a
safe distance, though there were now more of them, several
dozen men and women, most with their smartphones out.
Vicky looked back at the building. Smoke was billowing
out through the wooden boards over the ground-floor
windows but there were no flames that she could see.

'Where is Stefan?' shouted a man behind her. Vicky
turned around. A bearded man in his fifties was standing
with his hands on his head. 'Stefan!' he shouted. 'Stefan!'
He was wearing a heavy leather jacket over stained brown
cargo pants.

'Sir, you have to move away from the area,' said Vicky,
but he didn't seem to hear her.

'Stefan!' he shouted again.

'What's wrong?' Vicky asked him.

'I think Stefan is inside,' he said, waving at the building.
His accent was Eastern European and from the state of
his clothes he was homeless. His nails were bitten to the
quick and those teeth that weren't missing were stained
yellow.

'Why do you think that?' asked Vicky. The man frowned
and so Vicky repeated the question, slower this time.

The man pointed up at the top floor. 'We sleep there.'

'You sleep there? How do you gain access?' The man frowned again. 'How do you get inside?' asked Vicky.

'We break window, round back,' said the man. 'Please, you have to find Stefan.' He pointed at the top floor. 'Stefan is inside. I know it.'

'And how many people sleep up there?' asked Vicky.

'Five. Six.' The man shrugged. 'Sometimes more.'

Vicky waved Westworth over. 'Frank, we've got people in there, top floor,' she said, before turning back to the man. 'What is your name, sir?' she asked.

'Alexandru.'

'Okay, Alexandru, I need you to think very carefully. Are you sure Stefan is inside?'

The man nodded. 'He didn't feel well. We were working and he came home.'

Vicky frowned. 'Working? You have a job?'

'Selling *Big Issue* is job. That is how we earn money.'

'Does he have a mobile phone?'

'Yes. But he not answer.'

'And you say there are five or six people sleeping up there?'

He nodded again.

'Is it five?' asked Vicky. 'Or six? We need to know for sure.'

'Sometimes five. Sometimes six. Me. Stefan. Maria. Maria is Stefan's wife. They have two children.'

'Are Maria and the children up there?'

'No, they are working.'

'It's after midnight,' said Vicky. 'Why are they working so late?'

'They sell more magazines at night.'

'And you're sure Maria and the children aren't up there?'

'Sure. They stay out until one o'clock every night.'

'And who else sleeps up there?'

'Silviu. But he is staying with his friends tonight. Cristian and Clara, but they went back to Romania.' His eyes widened. 'Oh, one of Stefan's friends went back with him. Dorian. Dorian is probably up there.'

'So there are two people up there?'

The man nodded. 'I think so. But it is difficult to be sure. People come and go.'

Vicky went over to the cab of the pump and shouted up at Laffy. 'Persons reported, Dom,' she said. 'Call it in. And make pumps six.'

'Will do,' said Laffy, reaching for the transceiver.

Vicky turned to Westworth. 'We need to clear the upper floors. If they're not out by now they're either trapped or overcome by smoke.'

'We're going to be short-handed on the lines,' said Westworth.

'Four more pumps are on the way,' she said.

'Okay, that makes sense' said Westworth. 'But I'd advise against sending in a BA team until the rest of the pumps are here.'

Alexandru put a hand on Vicky's shoulder. 'You will help?' he asked.

'Of course,' said Vicky. 'Do you have electricity in there?'

He shook his head. 'No. But there is still water.'

'So how do you cook food? What light do you have?'

'We have a gas stove. And candles.' He shrugged. 'It is not easy but at least we do not have to pay rent.'

'And you sleep on the top floor?'

'We have a room each,' said the man.

'But no one sleeps on the floors below?'

'Only the top floor.'

'And where is Stefan's room? The front or the back?'

The man frowned as he considered the question. 'Back,' he said eventually.

'Would Dorian stay in the same room as Stefan?'

'I don't know.' He looked up anxiously at the top floor of the hotel. 'Please, you have to help them.'

'We will,' said Vicky. Two pumps from Paddington arrived and Vicky hurried over to the lead vehicle. Watch Manager Tony Abbey climbed out. He was a big Mancunian who had inherited his Jamaican father's build and burnished brown skin and his Irish mother's sharp tongue. As a senior officer he was wearing a white helmet and had two pips on his shoulder. 'We have possibly two trapped on the upper floor, guv,' Vicky said. As senior officer, Abbey was now incident commander in charge of the fire and the first order of business was for Vicky to brief him on the situation. 'The fire seems to have started on the ground floor but the occupants have been using candles and gas stoves. I've two lines ready to attack the seat of the fire and Frank is setting up a covering jet. I'd like to send teams in with breathing apparatus now that you're here.'

Abbey looked up at the hotel. 'You think it's safe to send BA teams in now?'

'The fire seems to be confined to the pub,' said Vicky. 'The stairs to the hotel floors are to the right with its own entrance. There's some smoke but no fire.'

'But if the fire moves across, any BA team would be trapped.'

'We'll have all the lines up and running in a minute or so. That should hold the fire back. Sir, there are two men possibly trapped here. Now that you're in charge I'd like to take a team of four in. That would mean your guys operating my hoses.'

Abbey frowned. 'You're sure about this?'

'Two men trapped. I don't see we have a choice.'

'We're light on manpower.'

'Two more pumps on the way. I've called it six pumps.'

Abbey rubbed his chin thoughtfully. 'Always leading from the front, huh, Vicky? Have you called in persons reported?

'Yes, guv.' The 'persons reported' message would automatically trigger an ambulance being sent, along with a command unit and a station manager.

He nodded. 'Okay, go for it,' he said. 'I'll send my guys over to your pump. Who's going to be entry control?'

'I was going to use Dom Laffy.'

Abbey shook his head. 'It'll have to be a stage two entry control, which means you'll have to use a crew manager.'

Vicky wrinkled her nose. 'Frank is overseeing the jets on the bar.'

'I'll send you Dave Potter, he's crew manager on the Paddington pump ladder.'

'Thanks, guv,' said Vicky, throwing him a mock salute.

'But at the first sign of the fire spreading to the hotel, I'll be pulling you out. When did you ask for the extra pumps?'

'Just now.'

'Euston is closest but they're attending a burning skip on the Charing Cross Road and a possible false alarm in an office block down the road from them. False alarm or not they're going to be tied up for a while. I think it'll be Soho that attends. They'll be a few minutes yet. Five. Six, maybe.' He looked back at the hotel. 'Only two persons in there? You're sure?'

'They're sleeping rough, so there's no way of being sure how many, but I'm told two.'

'There are a lot of rooms, Vicky. A BA team could be searching all night if there's smoke up there.'

'I'm told they're in the top-floor rooms, at the back. A team of four should do it.'

Abbey scrunched up his face. 'Thing is, if we are going to need lines in the hotel we might have to move up to eight pumps.' He looked over at Vicky. 'Take two teams of two. That way I only need a two-man crew on standby.'

'Will do. Two two-man teams it is.'

Abbey nodded. 'Okay. Get your teams ready. But you're not to go in until there's an emergency crew in place.'

'Yes, guv,' said Vicky. She hurried over to the pump where Beech and Noller had finished preparing their hoses. 'Colin, Mark, prepare your BA gear.' She waved over at Jones. 'You too, Gary.'

'What about our lines?' asked Noller, holding up his hose.

'Paddington will take over,' said Vicky. 'Colin, bring the thermal-imaging camera.'

The hand-held thermal-imaging camera was a relatively new piece of kit and all the firefighters were impressed with it. They had all been trained to search smoke-filled rooms by touch, but the camera enabled them to find casualties no matter how bad the visibility. 'Righto,' said Noller. He dropped the hose and went over to the pump where Beech was already pulling out his breathing apparatus from the cab.

Andy Mitchell and Mike Wells were running hoses from the Kilburn pump ladder. The pump was already connected to the hydrant and another hose connected the pump ladder to Vicky's pump to supply it with water.

Abbey began shouting commands to the Paddington firefighters but they were a well-drilled team and were already setting up their hoses and connecting to the hydrant water supply. Two of the firefighters hurried over to the Kilburn pump to take over from Beech and Noller. Abbey spoke to Dave Potter who went over to his pump ladder to retrieve the control board from the crew cab. The electronic control board was a relatively recent piece of brigade equipment – in the past clocks and pens were used to keep track of who was where in a breathing apparatus operation, and how much air they had left. Now it was all done by computer. Sensors on the firefighter's equipment sent data on the amount of air in the tank and the firefighter's breathing rate, and was used to transmit man-down alarms and evacuation acknowledgements. All the firefighters wore man-down alarms – automatic distress signal units – which activated a loud warning after fifteen seconds of no movement and a full alarm after thirty seconds. The ADSU warning would also sound on the board and a light flash, letting the entry control officer know that a firefighter was in trouble.

Vicky joined Noller, Beech and Jones at the side of the cab and grabbed an air cylinder. She slung it on to her back, bending forward as she fastened the straps that kept it in place. She hung her mask from a strap around her neck.

The Paddington firefighters had two of the hoses ready to go and Billy Moore used the Halligan bar to attack the plywood sheets covering the windows so that they could get water inside.

Potter came over, carrying the entry control board. Vicky nodded at him. 'Good to go, Dave?'

'Always happy to bail out Kilburn in their hour of need,' said Potter with a grin.

Vicky looked over at Abbey who was busy supervising his men. Strictly speaking, the incident commander was supposed to brief the BA team, but Vicky had worked with Abbey enough times to know that he'd let her get on with it. 'Okay,' said Vicky. 'We'll use the hotel main entrance as the one and only entry control point. We're heading to the top floor, we believe there are two people trapped there, probably in rooms at the back. All good?'

The firefighters nodded as Potter noted their names on the board with a black marker.

'There's no fire in the hotel, right?' asked Noller.

'Not so far, it's confined to the bar,' said Vicky.

They took off their helmets and pulled on their masks, checked that the air supply was working and that Potter could hear them on their radios, then replaced their helmets.

Potter pulled the yellow plastic tally tags from the ADSUs of the four firefighters and slotted them into the side of his board. Immediately the board began displaying the data from the individual units.

Billy Moore had removed the wood covering the windows and the Paddington firefighters began to spray streams of water into the bar. Vicky pointed at the door to the hotel. 'Get ready to gain access, Billy,' said Vicky. Moore nodded and headed towards the door.

'Right, let's all check our gauges,' said Vicky.

One by one, Noller, Beech and Jones read out their air readings from their Bodyguard warning and monitoring units. Potter checked that they matched with the numbers he was seeing on his board. The BA sets were charged on average to between 290 and 300 bar. Any lower than 240 bar and the firefighter would not be allowed in. Vicky looked at her air gauge. It was showing just under 300 bar. She did the calculation for her turnaround point in her head. Halfway would be 150 bar. The safety margin was 60, so she needed to halve that for the return. Adding the 150 bar to 30 bar gave 180 bar. When the air gauge read 180, it was time to get out. 'Three hundred,' she said, and Potter gave her a thumbs-up.

'All right, guys?' she asked.

The three men nodded and flashed her okay signs.

'Okay, Dave?' she asked Potter.

'Ready when you are,' he said.

'As soon as we get an emergency crew in place, we're good to go.' Just as she finished, two more pumps arrived. As Abbey had predicted, they were from the Soho station. They parked up and the crew managers hurried over to Abbey. Vicky watched as Abbey gave instructions to the two crew managers. 'Come on, come on,' she muttered as the two crew managers hurried back to their pumps.

Jones and Beech had a hose connected to the pump and had fixed a branch – what civilians called a nozzle – to the end. Beech was holding the branch and Jones was looking after the hose.

Vicky watched as the Soho pumps were connected to a hydrant and hoses were connected. Two of the Soho firefighters were putting on BA equipment as another firefighter stood ready with a control board. She looked over at Abbey. 'Okay, guv?' she shouted.

Vicky looked over at the emergency crew, then back to Abbey. She could tell from the look on his face that he would have preferred to wait until the emergency crew was ready at the door so she flashed him an okay sign. 'Okay?' she repeated.

Abbey sighed and waved for her to go in.

'Let's go,' she said.

They fitted their facemasks, then pulled fire retardant hoods over their heads before fastening their helmets. Potter checked them one at a time to make sure there was no exposed flesh. 'Good to go,' he said eventually.

Moore attacked the boarded-up door with his Halligan bar. The plywood split and shattered with just a couple of blows but the door was solid oak and took half a dozen hits before it sagged on its hinges. He put the Halligan bar down and ripped the door away with his gloved hands. 'Nice one, Billy,' said Vicky. She patted him on the shoulder and stepped into the reception area. There was some smoke leaking out from the bar but visibility was still good. The reception desk was ahead of her, with a stairway to the right. Two double doors to the left led to the bar but they were fire doors so were capable of holding the flames back, for a while at least.

Vicky led them up the stairs. There had once been carpets but they had been ripped out to reveal the bare boards and the gripper strips.

The stairs turned to the left and they headed up to the next landing. The smoke was thicker and she figured it must be finding its way up from the bar. She looked down the first-floor corridor and after the third door it was too hazy to see much. 'Crew now on first floor. Just reached the first floor. Some smoke logging, no fire apparent,' she said.

Vicky headed up the stairs. The three firefighters followed behind her in single file. Jones was carrying the hose.

The visibility was no worse as she climbed, it was easy enough to see ahead, though when she reached the second-floor corridor there was smoke feathering from under some of the doors.

'Crew now on the second floor and heading up,' she said into her radio.

'Vicky, have you seen this?' It was Jones, at the rear. Vicky turned around. The stairwell behind them was filling with smoke.

'We've got smoke coming up behind us, what's going on down there?' Vicky asked over the radio.

'They're still attacking the fire in the bar,' said Potter. 'Should be under control soon. I'm not seeing much smoke in reception.'

'Well, there's smoke here,' said Vicky. 'A lot of it.'

Vicky stared at the thickening smoke for several seconds, then continued up the stairs. Most of the corridor's ceiling was obscured in smoke and she couldn't see much beyond the fourth door. She looked behind her and grey smoke was billowing up the stairs.

'Crew now on the third floor. Heading up to the fourth now.'

'Be careful,' said Potter.

'The smoke is getting worse. What's it like on the ground floor?'

'There's smoke but not much,' said Potter.

Vicky turned to check that Noller, Jones and Beech were ready to go but frowned when she saw how thick the smoke was behind them. 'Let's go,' she said.

She walked up slowly, taking it one stair at a time, until she reached the top floor. The smoke was slightly thicker than it had been on the third floor, and she could only see as far as the second door.

The rooms at the back of the hotel were to her left and she headed across the corridor and stood in front of the first door. She touched it with the back of her glove and when she was satisfied that the wood wasn't hot, she turned the handle and pushed it open slowly. The smoke was thicker in the room than it was in the corridor, which suggested it was coming up through the floor. There was no furniture and there were marks on the walls, which suggested that fitted cupboards had been ripped out. As in the corridor there were no carpets or floor coverings, just bare boards. She stepped to the side and motioned for Noller to check the room. He did a quick walk around, then looked into the bathroom. 'All clear,' he said.

She held the door open for him as he came back into the corridor, then she pulled it closed.

The second room was also empty, as was the bathroom, though there were two sleeping bags on the floor and a collection of empty pizza boxes.

Vicky went over to the window and looked down at the back alley behind the hotel. Two firefighters were dragging a hose along the ground to the rear of the building.

'Vicky, how's it going in there?' Abbey's voice crackled in her earpiece.

'No joy so far, sir,' said Vicky. 'We've cleared two of the rooms. I'm just looking out of the window. I see a line at the back.'

'That's from the Soho pump. The fire's still burning so be quick.'

'Will do, sir.' She headed back on to the corridor. The smoke had grown thicker and Noller, Beech and Jones were crouching by the wall. Noller had his hand against Beech's back. Beech was holding the branch with both hands but there was no fire source to douse with water.

Vicky motioned for Noller to do the third room He opened the door and almost immediately a ball of flames billowed out, sending them all staggering back. Noller hit the door on the other side of the hallway and pushed against it to regain his balance.

Vicky gritted her teeth, Noller should have checked the door for heat before opening it. It was a rookie mistake, but even through his mask she could see from the look in his eyes that he knew what he'd done so she let it go. She looked through the doorway. Most of the floor was alight and flames were licking around the floor. A thick layer of combustible gases covered the ceiling and was inching closer to the floor, rippling like a living thing. She was about to yell at Beech to turn on the water but he beat her to it and yanked the branch lever to send a water jet spraying high into the room. He aimed high and started a pulsing jet, aiming at the combustible gases at the top of the room. It wasn't the burning fixtures that were the danger – it was the gases. If they were to catch fire the whole room would ignite. The short pulses of water dissipated the gases quickly and efficiently. Once he was satisfied they had been neutralised he aimed a steady jet at the burning wood. The fire was soon extinguished though the steam produced decreased the visibility markedly.

'Sir, we've got fire up here in one of the bedrooms,' said Vicky. 'We need another line up here asap.'

'I'm on it,' said Abbey. 'How bad is it?'

'It's under control,' she said.

'You need to get out of there, Vicky!'

'We've still got rooms to clear, guv.'

'I understand that, but I don't want your team at risk,' said Abbey.

'The fire is confined to the one room at the moment,' said Vicky. 'There's only smoke in the corridor.'

Abbey paused for a few seconds before speaking. 'It's your call, Vicky. Just be careful.'

'Will do.' She went over to Noller. 'Are you okay, Colin?'

He nodded. 'Just caught me by surprise, that's all.'

'The fire must have come from downstairs,' she said. 'These old places are all wood, pretty much.'

Flames flared up again by the bathroom and Vicky moved behind Beech as he continued to douse the room with water. When all the flames were out, Vicky stepped inside. Like the previous rooms there was no furniture but through the smoke and steam she saw an old suitcase and a nylon kitbag against one wall, next to a rolled-up sleeping bag that had been singed by the fire. The floor to her right was ablaze as if the fire had come up from the floor below and the curtains were burning. She hurried over to the bathroom, confirmed that there was nobody there and went back into the corridor, pulling the door closed behind her. The smoke was thicker now and her three colleagues had gone down on their knees where the visibility was slightly better.

'Everyone okay?' she asked.

They all flashed her 'okay' signs.

'The smoke's getting worse, that's for sure,' said Jones.

'Let's press on,' said Vicky.

She bent down and peered through the smoke but couldn't see more than a few feet. She shuffled forward, running her right hand against the wall as she worked her way along to the next door, holding her left hand out in front of her. She placed the back of her hand against the door to see how hot it was. They were taught the back-of-the-hand technique in training. Generally, it was more sensitive to heat than the palm, but it was also to reduce the risk of electrocution if they touched a live wire or electrical source. With a palm-forward approach, there was a danger that the hand would contract around the electrical source. By using the back of the hand, any contraction would be away from the danger. The door was only warm to the touch so she grabbed the handle and opened it slowly. The room was thick with smoke but she didn't see any flames so she pushed the door wider. Almost immediately she saw the man on the floor. 'Casualty!' she shouted. She hurried across the floor and knelt down. The man was lying on a bare mattress. Next to him was a canvas kitbag full of clothes and a stack of copies of the *Big Issue* magazine. Vicky put a gloved hand on the man's chest. He was still breathing. 'Colin, Gary, over here!' Noller and Jones hurried over. 'You guys get him downstairs, asap.' She held out her hand to Noller. 'Let me have the camera.'

Noller unclipped the thermal-imaging camera from his tunic and gave it to Vicky, then the two firefighters grabbed the man and between them carried him to the door.

'We have a confirmed casualty, probable smoke inhalation, but still alive,' said Vicky into her radio. 'Colin and Gary are bringing him down now.'

'Vicky, we've got fire on the first floor now,' said Abbey over the radio. 'The line I sent in is dealing with that so he can't get up to you. You need to come on out now.'

'Colin and Gary arc on their way down with the casualty,' said Vicky. 'Can you send someone up to meet them?'

'Will do,' said Abbey. 'But I want you out of there now.'

'We've just a few more rooms to clear,' said Vicky.

'How bad is it in there?'

'Visibility isn't good but other than the one room on fire, it's only smoke.'

'How many more rooms have you to check?'

'Two at the rear. That's where I was told they were sleeping. We haven't checked the rooms at the front.'

'Just do the two and then get out of there,' said Abbey.

'Will do,' said Vicky. She nodded at Beech and pointed at the door, then headed out. The smoke was much thicker now and she had to crawl on all fours to see ahead of her. She held the thermal-imaging camera in her left hand and looked at the screen but there were no signs of any heat signatures on the floor or walls below the smoke. Noller and Jones were heading down the corridor towards the stairs, holding the casualty between them, the beams of the torches on their tunics lancing through the smoke.

Vicky scurried along to the next door, then sat back on her heels and tested it for heat. It wasn't especially hot so she slowly turned the handle and pushed. The door wouldn't move and she realised it was locked from the inside. She stood up and hit it with her shoulder. Beech joined her and together they threw their weight against the door. The jamb splintered on the second attempt and the third time they hit it the door collapsed inward and crashed to the ground. The smoke was as thick as it was in the corridor and the floorboards to their left were smouldering.

Vicky moved to the side to allow Beech to play pulses of water around the ceiling before spraying the walls. The water hissed and steamed and clouds of thick grey smoke billowed over their heads. When she was sure that any fire had been extinguished she shouted for Beech to shut off the water, then she dropped down on all fours and crept forward. Beech dropped the hose and followed her. Vicky used the hand-held camera to check the room. Her heart pounded when she saw a greenish blur on the floor. A body. 'Casualty!' she shouted.

Beech crawled over to her and they both grabbed at the body. It was a man. Unconscious. As Vicky reached out to him, flames erupted up through the floor by the window, so hot that she felt the heat through her mask.

'Let's get him out of here,' said Vicky. 'We have another casualty,' she said into the radio. 'We're coming out now.'

Vicky grabbed the man's legs and Beech put his hands

under the man's arms. They stayed on their knees and dragged him out into the corridor. Vicky pulled the door closed.

'Vicky?' It was Abbey.

'Yes, guv. We're on our way down.'

'There's a man in the far corner of the building at the front. He's just broken a window. Our ladder isn't long enough.'

'I'll go.'

'What's it like up there?'

'It's okay. I'll send Mark down with the casualty and I'll check the corner room.'

'That's a negative, Vicky,' said Abbey. 'You're not to go solo. BA teams stay together, you know that.'

'You're breaking up,' said Vicky.

'Don't fuck around, Vicky. Get down here now.'

Vicky clapped Beech on the shoulder. 'Can you manage him on your own, Mark?'

'Sure,' said Beech. 'But it's not standard procedure, you know that.'

'There's a man trapped in there. If we both go down now, he'll die.'

'Then I'll stay with you.'

She pointed at the casualty. 'If you don't get him down now, the smoke will kill him.' Even through the mask she could see the confusion on Beech's face and she patted him on the shoulder. 'You start down. I'll catch you up. I won't be more than a couple of minutes. I'll be right behind you.'

Beech nodded reluctantly. He grabbed the man by the arms and pulled. The man was heavy but he could manage. The BA equipment meant he couldn't use the traditional fireman's lift so he dragged the man down the corridor, keeping as low as he could to avoid the worst of the smoke.

Vicky turned to look back down the corridor. The smoke was now halfway down the walls. She got down on her hands and knees, picked up the branch with her left hand and moved along the corridor, pulling the hose behind her. The corridor was in darkness but the torch fastened to her tunic illuminated the corridor ahead of her.

'Vicky, I'm ordering you to come down now,' said Abbey over her radio as she reached the door. She checked it with the back of her hand. It was warm, but not hot, so she grabbed the handle and turned it, then pushed the door open. That was when she heard the man shouting in between fits of coughing. The room was thick with smoke but there didn't seem to be any flames. There was a yellowish patch among the smoke. The window, she realised, and the street lights beyond it. She walked towards the light, holding her hands out in front of her. As she got closer she made out a dark figure. 'Help me! Help me!' he shouted, then doubled over, coughing.

Vicky hurried over to him. The window was open and smoke was pouring out. The man's idea had been to lean out of the window and breathe fresh air but there was just too much smoke. 'Stay down!' she shouted at him. 'Keep your face as close to the floor as you can.' She dropped the hose and pushed him down to the floor. 'Stay there, and try to stay calm!'

She stood up and leaned out of the window. She looked down at the street below and saw Abbey standing on the pavement by his pump ladder. She waved and flashed him a thumbs-up. A few feet away from Abbey was a yellow and green ambulance with two paramedics standing at the rear doors. 'I've got him,' she said.

'Is Mark okay?' asked Abbey.

'He's on the way down with the other casualty,' she said.

'Get out of there now, Vicky,' he said.

'On my way.'

'How are you for air?'

She looked at her gauge. It was showing 160, which meant she was eating into her safety margin. But she would be going straight down whereas outbound she had stopped off at several rooms. 'I'm good.'

'Come on, then. I'll send a BA team up to meet you.'

'On my way.'

She crouched down and shook the man on the floor. 'Come on, sir, it's time to go!' she shouted. He didn't react. She shook him again but he'd clearly passed out. She was going to have to carry him out. He wasn't big, five feet eight maybe, and probably didn't weigh much more than 180 pounds, but Vicky was tired and her energy reserves were low. She gritted her teeth, bent her knees and grabbed his arms. She grunted as she pulled him along the corridor.

She leant back as she pulled, trying to let her legs do most of the work, but it was tiring and she was soon gasping for breath, which meant she would be getting through her air at a much faster rate than normal.

The smoke was much thicker now but she could see that the door to her right was ablaze, though all she could make out was a red and orange glow through the smoke. She kept count of the doors she passed. When she reached the final door she slowed and carefully slid each foot backwards, feeling for the stairs. Left. Right. Left. Then there was only air. She pulled the casualty as she went back down the stairs, taking care not to bang his head. Visibility was now close to zero, it was as if her mask had been painted grey. The beam of her torch only penetrated the smoke for a couple of feet then faded out. The lack of vision meant she was more aware of the sounds around her. The static of the radio, her laboured breathing, the crackle of burning wood. Her heart was pounding and she made a conscious effort to try to breathe slowly.

She went down the stairs one at time and it seemed an age before she reached the third-floor landing. She looked down the corridor but couldn't see more than a few inches. There was no red glow of fire, though, which was a good sign.

She continued down the stairs. Every muscle in her body was aching and her spine was in agony. She gritted her teeth and forced herself to ignore the pain as she pulled the man with her. 'Heading to the second floor now,' she said.

'Good girl,' said Abbey.

'That's sexist, guv,' she grunted, and she heard him chuckle.

'Colin and Gary are down and the paramedics are dealing with their casualty,' said Abbey.

'What about Mark?'

'No sign yet. But I have the emergency team in already. You should see them on the way down.'

'No problem,' she said. 'Two more floors and I'm there.'

As Vicky stepped into the second-floor hallway a wall of heat stopped her in her tracks. Most of the floor ahead of her was burning and flames were licking up the walls. She crouched down, panting for breath.

'I've got a problem on the second floor,' she said.

'What's happening, Vicky?'

'The floor's burning. The stairs are alight. Can you get a line up?'

'We've got a line working up to the first floor but it's taking time.'

'Shit,' said Vicky.

One of the bedroom doors collapsed inwards and the rush of air fed the flames. She ducked down as fire flared up to the ceiling and flashed in her direction. She could feel the heat through her tunic and leggings.

'Can you get through?' asked Abbey.

'I don't think so,' said Vicky, trying not to sound as worried as she felt.

'You've still got the casualty?'

'Yes, guv.'

'Can you get to a second-floor window? We can get a ladder to you.'

Vicky looked at the wall of flames ahead of her. The only way to the second-floor corridor was to go through the fire, and even if she could get through there was no guarantee that the corridor wasn't also burning. 'That's not an option,' she said.

'What about getting to a window on the third floor? We can reach the third floor, just about.'

Vicky turned to look back up the stairs. The smoke was almost impenetrable now but there was no glow to indicate flames. 'I'll give it a go.' She turned around and began pulling the casualty up the stairs. It required a huge effort with each pull and by the time she had moved up half a dozen stairs she was exhausted and drenched with sweat under the protective clothing. She forced herself to ignore the pain and concentrated on dragging the unconscious man up the stairs, one stair at a time. When she got to the third floor she laid the man on the floor and edged out into the corridor. 'I'm in the third-floor corridor,' she said.

'Good girl,' said Abbey, and this time she didn't correct his sexism. 'Get into a room at the front, we're getting the ladder in position.'

Vicky dragged the casualty along the floor until she reached the first door. She laid him down in the middle of the corridor, then grabbed the handle, hoping that it wouldn't be locked. It was, and she cursed. She had a decision to make, to try to force the door, or to move on and try the next one. She decided to press on. She grabbed the man's arms and dragged him slowly along the floor to the next door. The corridor was full of smoke now and she knew that every second the man spent in the foul air was putting his life at risk.

She laid him down and felt her way towards the door, groping for the handle. She grabbed it and twisted and her heart fell when she realised it was also locked.

She looked back at the stairs. There was a red glow amid the smoke. The fire was moving towards her. The skirting board to her right was smouldering but hadn't yet ignited. She felt the door. It was warm but not hot. She took a step back and hit it with her shoulder but she was tired and made barely any impact on it. She took a step back and kicked the door, just under the handle. It held but the jamb splintered a little. 'Come on, you bastard!' she shouted and kicked it again, this time with her full weight behind it. The door slammed inwards and almost immediately fire flashed from the stairs as the air from the room billowed out. Vicky ducked down and gasped as the fire raged above her head. It passed within seconds and she crawled over to the casualty. She grabbed him and pulled him into the smoke-filled room and then kicked the door shut.

She pulled the man over to the window, then stood up. She fumbled for the window catch but it wouldn't budge so she smashed the glass with her gloved fist.

There was a roar behind her as the fire flashed through the room in search of the fresh air supply and she dropped down and held on to her helmet until it had passed. She stood up and smashed what glass there was left in the frame and looked out.

Abbey was still on the pavement looking up at her and he waved. 'Well done, Vicky,' he said over the radio. 'Hang on in there, we'll get a ladder to you.'

Four men from the Paddington pump ladder were manoeuvring the ladder towards the building.

The fire was raging in the corridor behind her and the door was smoking and even through her insulated tunic she could feel the heat. Smoke was coming up from between the floorboards and flames were licking around the skirting board, left and right. She wanted to tell Abbey to hurry but she didn't want him to know how worried she was.

She bent down and looked at the unconscious man on the floor. His chest was moving, but barely. She crawled over to the bathroom. There was a bathmat on the floor

and she grabbed it and held it under the tap. Alexandru
had said the water was still connected but she was still
surprised when she turned the cold tap and water gushed
out. She soaked the mat under the torrent of water then
crawled back to the window. She wiped the man's face
with the wet mat then draped it over his body in an
attempt to cool him down.

When she stood up and looked out of the window the
ladder was closer, only a few feet away from the side of
the building. Two firefighters from Paddington were
standing either side of Abbey and they were all looking
up at her. Jones and Beech were at the rear of the ambulance and one of the paramedics was examining the man
they'd carried down. Jones looked up at her and gave her
a thumbs-up.

'Hang on in there, Vicky, we'll be up there in a minute
or two,' said Abbey.

Vicky looked over her shoulder. The whole room was
ablaze now. She bent down and checked on the unconscious man. He was still breathing, just. She hastily undid
her helmet and took it off, then held her breath and
removed her mask. She pressed it against the man's face.
It was totally against regulations, but she felt she had to
do something to help him. She kept the mask over his
face until her lungs began to burn and then she slipped
it back over her head and stood up.

The ladder was close to the window now. It juddered
against the wall and moved closer, so close that she could
reach out and touch it.

'We're coming up, Vicky,' said Abbey.

Vicky knelt down and grabbed the man under the arms,
bent her legs and then hauled him up, grunting with the

effort. She pushed him against the windowsill and the top half of his body bent over it. He was a dead weight but his chest was still moving. The ladder was shuddering as one of the Paddington firefighters climbed up. Vicky's arms were screaming in pain but she blocked it out. Her back was burning from the flames and her face was bathed in sweat under the mask.

She looked down and saw the yellow helmet of the firefighter moving towards her. She hauled the casualty over the sill as the firefighter reached the top of the ladder. He tilted back his head and she saw his face. It was Mick Mackie, one of the Soho crew managers. Mackie was a former Gordon Highlander with a greying moustache and piercing eyes that always gave Vicky the feeling that he was about to grab a bayonet and charge. She'd been on several shouts with him that year, though none had been as dramatic as this.

'Room service,' he said, and she laughed despite the seriousness of her situation.

'You took your time,' she said.

'Better late than never,' said Mackie. 'Can you pass him through or do I have to come in and get him myself?'

'Fuck you, Mick,' she said, grabbing the casualty by the back of his trousers and hauling him up.

'In your dreams, darling,' laughed Mackie. He reached over and grabbed the man's arm and Vicky helped him manoeuvre the man over his shoulder. Taking an unconscious man down a ladder was one of the toughest things a firefighter had to do but Mackie was big and strong and made it seem easy. A paramedic pushed a trolley towards the pump ladder, ready to take charge of the casualty. The ladder shook as Mackie headed down.

The room was totally ablaze now, and sweat was pouring off her. Vicky was just about to grab hold of the window to pull herself through when there was the sound of tearing wood and the floor gave way beneath her. Her arms flailed but there was nothing to grab hold of and she screamed as she fell into the darkness.

3

Tony Abbey's jaw dropped as the ball of flame exploded from the window where Vicky had been standing. 'What the fuck?' Abbey turned to John McNally, the Paddington pump crew manager. 'What the fuck just happened?'

The question was rhetorical but McNally shrugged. 'Flashover,' he said. 'Then she went down.'

'Vicky, can you hear me?' Abbey shouted into his transceiver. 'What's going on in there?'

There was no response.

Mackie was heading down the ladder with the casualty over his shoulder. He was so focused on getting down the ladder that he hadn't seen the explosion above his head.

Abbey hurried over to the hotel door where Dave Potter was staring at his control board. The Kilburn crew had gathered around Potter and the firefighters turned to Abbey, concern written all over their faces. A light was flashing and Abbey knew immediately what it was. Vicky's Automatic Distress Signal Unit.

'Any radio contact?' asked Abbey, but Potter just shook his head. 'Fuck, fuck, fuck,' said Abbey.

He looked over at the two teams directing jets into the

bar. As far as he could see there were no flames, just smoke. The emergency BA crew had gone in but were fighting a fire on the stairway between the second and third floors. Abbey swore again as he stared up at the building. Smoke was pouring out of the window where he'd last seen Vicky. He called over to Carl Hankinson, crew manager on the Paddington pump ladder. He pointed up at the window. 'Get a jet in there now, Carl! And call control, make pumps ten. And tell them we've a man down.' He looked up at the open window and corrected himself, his voice a hoarse whisper. 'Woman down.'

Hankinson radioed in they needed ten pumps, and notified control there was a firefighter in the hazard zone. Calling in a firefighter emergency would automatically trigger a range of extra resources including six extra fire engines, two fire rescue units, three station managers, a group manager, and a deputy assistant commissioner.

'Yes, guv,' said Hankinson and he ran over to the pump ladder.

'We're going in,' said Beech.

Abbey shook his head. 'Not until I've completed a risk assessment. Otherwise you'll just be putting more lives in danger.'

'Tony, that's Vicky in there. Fuck the risk assessment.' Beech swung his air tank on to his back and buckled the harness. Gary Jones joined him.

Abbey nodded. 'Okay. Fine.' He called over to Frank Westworth. 'Frank, get your arse in gear. I'm sending in three teams. I need you on entry control.'

'Right, boss,' said Westworth. He hurried over to the Kilburn pump ladder to retrieve the control board from the cab.

Abbey nodded at Beech and Jones. Colin Noller ran over but before he could speak, Abbey raised a hand. 'I know, I know.'

'Me too,' said Andy Mitchell, coming up behind Abbey.

'Each team takes a hose in with them,' said Abbey.

The four firefighters hurried to put on their equipment. 'How is she?' Abbey asked Potter.

Potter grimaced as he looked at the man-down warning. It was still flashing, though he had muted the audible warning. 'No change,' he said. 'Sorry.'

Abbey waved over at McNally and the crew chief hurried over. 'John, I'll need another emergency crew. Can you put that together? Get Bob Beveridge to handle the control board.'

'Will do,' said McNally.

Abbey went over to the Kilburn pump ladder where the BA team was getting kitted up. Frank Westworth was checking their gear. 'Frank, I need you overseeing this while Dom handles communications. We're sending in two two-man teams now with another two men on standby.'

'We're ready to go now,' said Jones, buckling his harness.

'I know, but we play this by the book, guys. I know it's Vicky in there, I know she's in trouble, but I'm not sending more guys in until we know we can do it safely. There's fire up there so all three teams are going in with hoses.'

Jones opened his mouth to protest but Westworth glared at him and shook his head. Jones nodded. 'Okay, okay,' he muttered.

'Guys, listen up. I know that the first instinct when we have a man down is to pile in to help them, but that can so easily lead to further casualties. We get water in through the window and when we have an emergency crew set up we'll put you in with jets. Your safety is paramount, do you understand me? You do not put yourselves at risk.'

Beech and Jones stared over Abbey's shoulder and he turned to see what they were looking at. A Paddington firefighter was heading up the ladder with a hose, watched by Carl Hankinson. Two other firefighters were holding the bottom of the ladder and a third was keeping the hose free.

The two firefighters making up the emergency crew ran over, wearing full BA gear and pulling a hose between them. The Paddington Pump 2 crew chief, Bob Beveridge, was holding the control board. Beveridge and Abbey were old friends and had been best man at each other's weddings and Abbey was godfather to Beveridge's elder son. 'Any news?' asked Beveridge.

'Radio's quiet and her ADSU is still flashing,' said Abbey. 'She's not moving.'

'What the fuck happened?' asked Beveridge. 'The fire should be confined to the bar, how the fuck did we get a flashover up there?'

'It must have travelled up and across,' said Abbey. 'It's an old building. Edwardian. Wooden joists everywhere, all sorts of crap between the floors.' He turned to look at the BA team. 'Bear that in mind, guys. This is an old building, listed, so it's not got the sort of stairwells and fireproofing that we have these days. Be careful. One step at a time. It's a potential deathtrap.'

'Can we go?' asked Jones impatiently.

Abbey looked up at the hotel. The Paddington firefighter was aiming his jet into the window where Vicky had been. 'Yes,' said Abbey. 'Go!'

The two firefighters ran to the hotel door and went inside. Abbey went over to Westworth and looked at the control board he was holding. Vicky's ADSU continued to flash accusingly.

A command support unit drove slowly through the cordon and parked. The CSU was about the same size as a pump but it had no firefighting capabilities. It was sent to any scene attended by more than four crews and was used as a base from which the senior officers could control the incident. A big man with a neatly trimmed moustache and horn-rimmed spectacles climbed out, then put on his helmet. It was the Kilburn station manager, Rick Blackwell. Like Abbey, his helmet was white, but the black stripe running around it was thicker than the one on Abbey's helmet and Blackwell had three pips on his shoulder. He walked quickly over to Abbey. 'What's happening, Tony?' he asked. As senior officer Blackwell was now in charge.

'The fire has spread from the bar to the hotel, no idea how that happened because we've had jets on it from the get-go,' he said. 'Crew Manager Lewis took in a BA team to rescue persons trapped on the top floor. We got all the people out but then the fire turned and her ADSU has been activated. We've called in a firefighter emergency.'

'What the fuck was she doing up there on her own, Tony?'

'She was with a BA team. They came down with the casualties.'

'Who was she partnered with?'

'Colin Noller.'

'And Colin came down and left her there?'

'They had a casualty overcome by smoke. Then we

had a person trapped in the far corner. Vicky went to get him. That was on the top floor so the ladders wouldn't reach. Colin brought his casualty down; she was supposed to be right behind him.'

Blackwell shook his head. 'They shouldn't have separated.'

'I told her to stay with Colin,' said Abbey.

'So she disobeyed an order?'

Abbey looked pained. 'She said her radio was playing up. Look, guv, you know what Vicky's like. She's a terrific firefighter, one of the best, but she always leads from the front and sometimes . . .' He shrugged.

'Doesn't think ahead?' Blackwell sighed. 'I know what you mean. But they're going to be looking at your risk assessment very carefully after this, Tony. You need to make sure your ducks are in a row.' He looked up at the third floor where the firefighter was still pouring water through the window. 'I just hope to God she's okay.'

4

Vicky Lewis wasn't okay. She was a long way from okay, but at least she was alive. When she fell through the hole in the floor she broke her wrist on a burning floorboard. The blow ripped the glove off her left hand. She fell to the floor below, and landed awkwardly, snapping her left ankle and fracturing her left leg just above the knee. Her leg gave way when she hit the ground and she fell to the left, slamming into the floor. The impact knocked off her mask and she breathed in the choking smoke that filled the room. She was still conscious, just about, and rolled on to her back, her chest heaving as she gasped for breath. She could barely see the gaping hole she'd fallen through and her eyes were streaming with tears. She didn't know it then but she'd ruptured her spleen and broken two ribs. One of the ribs had speared her left lung and it was slowly filling with blood.

She tried to get up but pain lanced through her side. As long as she didn't move the pain was almost bearable, the result of the body flooding itself with natural pain-killers. She tried to move her left hand to get to her transceiver but it was trapped under a piece of burning wood. Breathing was getting harder. Every breath was an effort. She looked up at the hole above her head, now a patch of red and orange in the smoke. There was the sound of tearing wood and a roar and she realised that the rest of the floor was collapsing on top of her. She tried to put her gloved right hand up to protect her face but it made little difference and the burning debris hit her hard in a shower of sparks.

5

It was Colin Noller who found Vicky first, but Mark Beech was close behind. She was lying under a pile of smouldering debris on the second floor. Pretty much all of the floor above had fallen down during the fire and they had to pull away more than a dozen floorboards to get to her.

The jet through the window had done its job and the firefighters had fought and beaten the blaze in the stairwell, but it had taken almost twenty minutes until the BA team had been able to reach the second floor.

The air was still thick with smoke and ash so they had to keep their masks on, but Noller took off his glove and felt for a pulse. As he did he pushed her head to the right and his eyes widened when he saw what the fire had done to her face. He pulled his hand away as if he'd been stung. 'Bloody hell,' he muttered. Her flesh had been burned black, through to the bone in places, and the damage continued down her neck into her jacket.

Beech knelt down next to him. 'We've got her!' he shouted into his radio.

Noller carefully moved her head to the left. The right side of her face and neck was nowhere near as damaged and he felt for a pulse. Nothing. He moved his fingers but still couldn't find any evidence that her heart was still beating. He shook his head, but Beech took off his glove and pushed Noller to the side. Beech pressed his fingers into the side of Vicky's neck. Nothing. He swore under his breath, then moved his fingers fractionally. His heart leapt when he felt something, a faint beat. Barely there but there nonetheless. 'She's alive!' he said.

Mitchell and Jones came into the room and rushed over to pull away the rest of the debris that covered her legs.

Beech went to lift her up but Noller grabbed his arm. 'No mate, there's no way of knowing what state's she's in. We need a stretcher, and a neck brace.'

Beech nodded and stood up. 'We need a stretcher, asap,' he said into the radio.

'Vicky!' shouted Noller. 'Vicky, can you hear me?'

Her eyes stayed closed. Her chest didn't seem to be moving but the heavy jacket could account for that. Noller felt for a pulse and again he couldn't find one. He looked up at Beech and Beech nodded. He was sure she was alive.

Noller ran his hands down her legs. He couldn't feel any obvious breaks but again the insulated leggings could conceal a multitude of sins. He winced when he saw the damage that had been done to her left hand. She'd lost a glove and burning debris had been lying on it, the flesh had been cooked like barbecued steak, black streaked with red.

He looked at Beech and grimaced. 'She's a fucking mess, all right.'

'She's alive, Colin. That's enough. After what she's been through, she's lucky.'

Noller pointed at her mangled face. 'You call that lucky?'

'Leave it, mate. Let's just get her to hospital and they can sort it out.'

The basket stretcher arrived within minutes. It was made of lightweight aluminium with plastic padding. The firefighter who brought it was from the Soho Fire Rescue Unit, and he also had a neck brace with him. Beech undid her tunic and fitted the brace, then he and Noller gently lifted her onto the stretcher. They carried her downstairs with Mitchell and Jones and rushed her over to a waiting ambulance.

Abbey and Blackwell ran over. 'How is she?' asked Abbey, just beating Blackwell to the question.

'She's got a pulse,' said Beech. 'Faint but it's there.'

A paramedic wearing green overalls went over and he winced when he saw the burns to her face and neck. 'Get her in the back of the ambulance,' he said, his voice a low monotone.

The firefighters were used to handling casualties and they got Vicky into the ambulance quickly and efficiently and then piled out to give the paramedic room to move. The paramedic spoke to the driver, slammed the back door shut, and the siren and lights kicked in as the ambulance drove away.

As the siren faded into the distance, a red Volkswagen fire investigation unit drove slowly through the police cordon and parked behind one of the Soho pumps. A grey-haired man in his fifties climbed out, wearing a fluorescent jacket over his uniform. Blackwell waved over at him. His name was Willie Campbell, one of the brigade's most experienced investigators. 'The early bird, Willie?'

said Blackwell as Campbell walked over. Investigators wore the same uniforms and boots as regular firefighters as more often than not they entered premises that, if not actually burning, were still smouldering. Fire was an efficient destroyer of evidence so the investigators tended to move in quickly.

'It's been a quiet night up until now,' said Campbell, pulling on his white helmet with its black comb and thin black horizontal line that denoted his watch manager rank. 'So what's the story?'

'The fire started in the bar,' said Blackwell, pointing to the left of the building. 'Spread across to the hotel and has now moved into the top floors. We've had to pull out. The stairs are pretty much gone and it's just too dangerous in there. There's a turntable ladder en route from Soho and another from Old Kent Road. Soon as they're here we can attack the top floor. The first floor is under control but we've had to move back from the second. As you can see we're putting water in through the windows we can reach. The difficulty is it's all wood and plaster, and God knows how many layers of wallpaper.'

Campbell nodded. 'It's an old building, all right. Should have been torn down years ago.'

'It's listed,' said Blackwell. 'Of architectural interest or whatever they call it.'

'A bloody death trap, that's what I call it,' said Campbell. 'Who phoned it in?'

'Anonymous passer-by saw smoke. By the time we got here the bar was burning. There were persons inside so we sent in a BA team. Two casualties were retrieved but Vicky was injured. She was in that ambulance that just left.'

'Vicky? Your Vicky Lewis?'

Blackwell nodded.

'Shit. Sorry to hear that. How is she?'

'Badly burnt. The third floor collapsed underneath her and she fell down to the second.'

There was a crashing sound from the top of the building and several slates smashed to the pavement.

'It's going to be a while before you can get in there, Willie,' said Blackwell.

Campbell nodded. 'No problem, I'll be in the van getting started on the paperwork.' He headed back to his vehicle as Blackwell looked up at the burning building.

6

The first time Vicky woke up she was fairly sure she'd only just arrived at the hospital because she was in a lot of pain, mainly down the left-hand side of her body. An Asian woman was looking down at her, the bottom of her face hidden behind a pale blue mask. The woman was either a doctor or a nurse and she knew Vicky's name, her first name at least. 'You're okay, Vicky, you're in hospital. Don't worry, we're going to take care of you, just stay calm and breathe slowly and evenly. You're going to be fine, Vicky. Don't worry.'

Vicky didn't believe the woman. She doubted that she was fine. All the strength had gone from her limbs and it was only the pain that convinced her she wasn't dead already. Doctors and nurses lied. They had to, because sometimes the truth was too brutal and people couldn't deal with it. Firefighters lied too, sometimes. They had to. Vicky had lied to a ten-year-old girl once, trapped under a bus as her life blood drained away into the gutter. The ambulance had been on its way but there was no way it was going to get there in time. Vicky had been just six weeks into the job and it was her first fatality. The little girl's name was Sara and she had been going to school, tapping away on her smartphone as she stepped in front of the bus. The bus had gone right over her and then stopped and the car behind had rammed into it.

The pump had arrived before the ambulance, but after the police. The two police officers had no medical gear and were clearly out of their depth and Vicky had been left to deal with the injured child. Except there was nothing she could do, the injuries were just too severe, the wheel had gone over her midsection and crushed her internal organs. Vicky had started carrying out emergency medical care procedures but she realised that it was pointless. Sara didn't seem to be feeling any pain, though she kept saying she was cold even though it was a hot summer's day. Vicky had taken off her helmet and her tunic and she had lain down next to the little girl and held her and hugged her and told her that everything was going to be all right. It was a lie, and one that Vicky repeated over and over again until the little girl had given a final shiver and died. So when the nurse or the doctor or whoever she was told Vicky that she was going to be fine, she didn't believe her and when she closed her eyes she truly thought it was going to be for the last time.

The second time she opened her eyes there was a nurse standing over her, red-haired with round spectacles and a kindly smile. 'Can you hear me, Vicky?' she asked. She had a Newcastle accent. A Geordie. Vicky tried to talk but her throat was red raw, 'It's okay, Vicky, you just relax,' she said. 'The operation went well, you're going to be fine. You just relax now and get better.' Then Vicky felt something warm flow through her left arm and she closed her eyes and slept a dreamless sleep.

The third time she woke up her father was standing

at the side of her bed, in full firefighting gear and with his yellow helmet on his head. He smiled down at her. 'Look at the state of you, sweetheart,' he said. 'You've been in the wars.'

'I saved that man though,' she said. 'I got him out.'

Her father nodded. 'Yes you did, sweetheart.'

'Are you proud of me, Dad?'

He chuckled. 'Of course. As proud as punch.'

His uniform was wet, she realised, as if he'd just come from a shout. And there were dirty smears across his face.

'I love you, Dad,' she said.

'I love you, too, sweetheart.'

'Do you want me to come with you now?'

He smiled and shook his head. 'No, sweetheart. You stay where you are.'

'I'm so tired, Dad.'

'I know.'

'But I saved him. I got him out.'

'And that's what's important.'

'Yes. And you're proud of me?'

'I said I was, sweetheart. And I am.'

She sighed and closed her eyes. She had no way of telling how long she kept them closed, but when she opened them again he had gone and her mum was there, sitting at the side of the bed, reading a book.

'I saw Dad,' said Vicky, and her mum jumped.

'You're awake,' she said.

'Dad was here,' said Vicky.

'They're pumping you full of all sorts of painkillers and drugs,' said her mum.

'He said he was proud of me.'

Her mum smiled tearfully. 'We all are, honey,' she said. 'You did a very brave thing. You saved that man's life.' She wiped away tears. 'I thought I'd lost you, Vicky. They said . . .' She sniffed. 'I don't know what I would have done . . .'

'I'm sorry, Mum.'

'No need to be sorry. You and your dad, peas from the same bloody pod.'

'Mum . . .' Vicky tried to say more but she felt as if she was wrapped in warm, cosy, cotton wool and consciousness slipped away again. She lost all sense of time as she lay in the hospital bed. Sometimes when she opened her eyes there was someone there, usually her mum, sometimes she was alone. She never saw her father again. There was a constant beeping noise and there was always a drip connected to her arm. She presumed the drip was feeding into her veins whatever it was that was keeping her feeling all warm and cosy.

After a week she was moved out of intensive care and they cut back on her medication. She was still weak and couldn't get out of bed and she hated the fact that she wasn't able to get to the bathroom. But the nurses were friendly and helpful and her mum was there most of the time.

The surgeon who had removed a big chunk of her spleen came around most days, always with the same message: she was getting better and he was pleased with her progress.

There was a dressing on her left hand and arm and her left leg was in plaster. And there were dressings on her face and neck. They were the ones that worried her the most. Whenever she asked the doctor how bad the burns were on her face he would just smile and say it was early days, that she would take time to heal. She realised he was avoiding answering the question but at least he wasn't lying to her.

7

'Miss Lewis?' The voice seemed to be coming from a long way away, as if whoever was speaking to her was at the end of a tunnel. 'Miss Lewis, are you awake?'

Vicky opened her eyes. There were two men standing at the side of her bed. They both wore dark suits, pale blue shirts and striped ties. One was older with grey thinning hair, the other was in his early thirties with a tan that looked as if it might have been sprayed on. She couldn't tell which one had spoken. She frowned up at them. 'Yes?'

'My name is William Goldberg,' said the older of the two. 'I represent the company that owns the building where you were . . .' He hesitated before finishing the sentence. 'Where you had your accident.' He nodded at the man standing next to him. 'This is my colleague. Mr Allsop.' The younger man smiled and nodded. Goldberg held out a business card to her, then realised that she couldn't take it with her bandaged arms and hands. 'Sorry,' he said. He put it on the tray next to her bed. 'I'll leave it here. It has all my office details and my mobile number.'

'What is it you want, Mr Goldberg?'

'We want you to know that our clients are horrified by what happened and want you to know that they will do whatever they can to put this right.'

Vicky frowned. 'What do you mean?'

'Compensation, Miss Lewis. We are in the process of putting together a substantial compensation package for you. After what has happened . . . your injuries . . . my clients want to make sure that you are looked after.'

'Looked after?'

'My clients will take care of all your medical bills, and will compensate you for your injuries.'

'Medical bills?' she repeated. 'This is an NHS hospital.'

'Of course it is, yes, but it might be that you will get a better standard of care in the private sector. Then there is the plastic surgery.'

'Plastic surgery?'

'I'm told that extensive cosmetic surgery will be required and it might be quicker if it was done privately.' He grimaced. 'I know the NHS does its best, but they are over-stretched at the best of times.'

'Who said I'd need cosmetic surgery? Have you been talking to my doctors?'

'We needed to know what surgery will be required in order to put together your compensation package, that's all. Miss Lewis, please, we're here to help. We just want to make sure that you are taken care of.'

'Because you're scared I'll sue, is that it?'

'Why would you sue us, Miss Lewis? You are a fire-fighter who was injured in the course of performing her duties. The premises had been adequately secured and were in the care of a reputable security firm. So far as anyone knew the building was unoccupied. If at

any time the security company had been made aware
that someone had gained admittance, they would surely
have done something about it.' Goldberg had been
speaking quickly, as if he was delivering a prepared
speech. He stopped, and smiled, though his eyes were
cold and calculating and not in the least bit friendly.
'We're here to help, Miss Lewis. To make good what
has happened. You're a hero. You went into a blazing
building to rescue a homeless person, and you paid a
heavy price. We want to help you get through this as
best we can, that's all.'

'Thank you,' said Vicky coldly.

'We'll get an official proposal drawn up and you can
have a look at it. But I can assure you it will be a generous
settlement. The company I represent is very well aware
it has obligations to you and they are committed to
fulfilling those obligations.'

'Who are the owners?' asked Vicky.

'The building is owned by an investment vehicle,' said
Goldberg. 'They purchase properties and redevelop them.
The company is in a very healthy state financially so
making good on their commitment to you won't be an
issue, Miss Lewis.'

The door to the room opened. It was Zachary Khan,
the surgeon who had operated on her. She had called
him Dr Khan the first time he had introduced himself
but he had reminded her quite forcefully that doctors
were 'doctor' and surgeons 'mister'. He'd been in to see
her more than a dozen times and wasn't one for small
talk. She knew he was from Scotland from his accent but
other than that and his name and the fact that he'd saved
her life, she knew nothing about him.

'I'm sorry, gentlemen,' he said. 'I need a few words with my patient. You can wait outside if you want.'

Goldberg smiled without warmth. 'No, we're finished here.' He looked back at Vicky. 'We'll be in touch, Miss Lewis,' he said.

Vicky nodded and smiled.

The two men left the room. 'Lawyers?' asked the surgeon.

'How did you know?'

'The suits. The briefcases. The cold dead eyes.' Vicky chuckled. 'One thing is for sure, they're not firemen,' said the surgeon.

'That's the truth,' said Vicky. 'They represent the company that owns the building.'

'Worried that you're going to sue them?'

'Actually no. They were talking about compensation.'

He looked at her over the top of his spectacles. 'Sounds as if they're getting their defence in first,' he said. 'You should talk to a lawyer. Your own lawyer.'

'I'm not going to sue, Mr Khan. I made the decision to go in, no one forced me.'

'I'm surprised you haven't had ambulance chasers queuing up in the corridor. Bloody parasites.' He looked at the iPad in his hand. 'Anyway, I just wanted to pop in and say that all's good. You're making tremendous progress. As you know we removed a large section of your spleen but what is left is functioning nicely. As I explained, you can live quite happily without a spleen but it's better to have one if you can.' He looked up from the iPad. 'And you still have one, so that's good. Your broken bones are all healing nicely. The big issue now is your hand. It's healing but we have to deal with the motor issues, and for that I'll be handing you over to another specialist.' He clasped the iPad to his chest. 'So my work here is pretty much done. It's been a pleasure working with you. I wish all my patients were as easy to deal with as you.'

'Thanks for all you've done,' she said. 'You saved my life.'

The surgeon shook his head. 'You're the hero, Vicky. I just patched you up.'

'The lawyers were talking about cosmetic surgery.'

'Yes, well, they could probably do something to improve their looks,' said the surgeon. 'The older one would definitely benefit from a facelift.'

Vicky laughed. 'They were referring to me.'

'Ah,' said the surgeon.

'So are they right? Am I going to need cosmetic surgery?'

'That's not my field, Vicky. I'm more internal.'

'I understand. But I'm going to need plastic surgery, right?'

'If you do, then it's for down the line. The important thing now is that we get you up and about. As I said, the work on your spleen has gone well and your fractures are healing. I can understand you are worried about the damage to your face, but on a positive note your eyesight is fine and your hearing in your left ear hasn't been affected.'

'What does it look like, Mr Khan?'

He frowned. 'I'm not sure I follow you.'

'I haven't been able to see for myself. I'm told that the dressings have to stay on, and when the dressing gets changed I'm told that there isn't time for me to take a look at it. So I don't know how bad it is.'

'Vicky, it's early days. Healing takes time. What it looks like now will bear no relation to what it will look like in a month's time. Or a year.'

'You've seen it, right? You've seen the damage?'

'I saw you when you were brought in, of course. But since then it's Dr Adams in our burns unit who has been managing the damage to your face and neck.'

'He's the same. I keep asking for a mirror and he says I should wait. I'm fed up with waiting. I want to see for myself.'

'All I can do is repeat that it would be a pointless exercise. Your reconstruction will take time. It's your long-term prognosis that matters, and that is good. I'd say excellent.'

'But going back to my original question. I'm going to need plastic surgery, yes?'

The surgeon sighed. 'Yes. I would think so. But it's early days.'

'How bad is it?' Vicky could see the hesitation in the man's eyes. 'Tell me,' she pressed. 'I need to know.'

'I'll talk to Dr Adams. Next time he has the dressing changed, I'll get him to show you.'

'I appreciate it. But I want your opinion. Your professional opinion.'

The surgeon swallowed nervously, then nodded. 'It's pretty bad,' he said.

'How bad? I'll need to cover it with make-up bad? I'll need to grow my hair long bad? Or Phantom-of-the-Opera bad?'

'Vicky, please. We've only just started on this journey. New techniques for skin grafts are being developed every day, stem-cell research is making great strides. All that matters is that you get well and regain your strength.'

'So it's Phantom-of-the-Opera bad?' said Vicky. She lay back and stared up at the ceiling. 'Shit.'

8

She was his type even though he knew it wasn't a good idea to have a type. A type meant there was a pattern and that was what the police looked for when they had a serial killer. But the whole point of doing what he did was that he was attracted to his type. He didn't want to kill men, or children, or old people. He wanted to kill his type. Not too young. Not too old. And they had to be blond. Definitely blond. They didn't have to be a natural blond. Dyed was okay. And with pale skin. And a good figure.

Her name was Diana Hewson, and he'd first spotted her sitting outside Starbucks drinking her latte as she checked her phone. She was in her late twenties, maybe thirty. She had a good figure. Her breasts were 34C, he'd bet money on that. He was good at judging bra sizes. After the killing, he always checked their underwear and he was always right about the size. He took pride in that.

She was a secretary. She was ambitious and had a LinkedIn page that gave away her entire work and education history. He'd checked that after he'd followed her home the first time. He'd waited until she had finished her coffee and then followed her to the Tube station and got on the train with her. She lived in Camden, in a small terraced house. His heart had fallen when he had seen the house because a house usually meant more than one person. His type had to live alone because he needed to spend time with them while he did what he had to do. If there were flatmates or a relative or a spouse then the degree of difficulty increased exponentially. He had almost given up there and then but he had a feeling that it was worth sticking with her so he had hung around and watched the house all evening. It looked as if she lived there alone. Perfect. The following day he had checked the electoral roll and, yes, she was the only occupant.

Her Facebook page showed that she enjoyed horse-riding and tennis and that she spent most weekends with her parents, who owned a large house in Norfolk. The parents clearly had money so they were probably paying the rent on the house for her, or maybe they had even bought it.

He lit a cigarette and smoked as he watched the house. The downstairs lights went off at just before eleven o'clock. The bathroom light went on for half an hour so he figured she was taking a bath. Then the light went out and the bedroom light was on for just over five minutes. Then the house was in darkness.

It was the fourth time he had watched the house. Preparation was everything. The more he knew about her routine, the less likely he would be to make a mistake. He had to stay one step ahead of the fire investigators and the police. They were experts at spotting fires that had been deliberately set. He smiled to himself. But he was an expert himself. At setting fires.

9

'Are you up for a visitor, Firefighter Lewis?' said a voice.

Vicky opened her eyes. It was Rick Blackwell, her station manager. He was wearing grey slacks and a dark-blue blazer and looked more like a holiday rep than a firefighter with more than twenty years' service.

'Hello, guv,' she said. She tried to sit up but pain lanced through her left side.

'Don't move,' said Blackwell, pulling up a chair and sitting down next to her. 'How are you?' His hair was dyed a deep chestnut brown, the same colour his wife used, but the roots were already showing grey. He used to wear glasses but had gone through laser surgery to correct his vision, and there were rumours that he'd had cosmetic surgery to reduce the bags under his eyes.

'I'm good,' she said. 'They're discharging me in a couple of days. My leg is still healing and there's work to do on my hand and face but that can be done as an out-patient.' She forced a smile. 'I'll be glad to get out of here. Lying in bed all day does my head in.'

'I'm sure it does.' He gestured at her bandaged arm. 'How's the hand?'

'It's getting better. They'll arrange physiotherapy for

me. A few weeks and it'll be back to normal, they say.'

'And the leg?'

'I can walk on it, just about. It'll be a while before I can do star jumps, but I'm healing.'

'That's good.' He nodded and looked away.

He hadn't mentioned her face. None of her visitors did. They'd happily chat away about the damage to her hand and her leg and what life was like with only half a spleen, but it seemed that nobody wanted to discuss what had happened to her face. In a way Vicky was relieved, because she had seen the damage and it wasn't pretty. It wasn't pretty at all. Her neck and face were badly burnt from the ear down to her shoulder and across to her nose. It was still red and bloody and festering under the dressings, but according to Dr Adams it was improving day by day. Even Dr Adams wasn't prepared to say what it would look like once it had fully healed but he had conceded that she'd need extensive cosmetic surgery to look anywhere near normal.

'I'll be back at work as soon as I can,' she said.

'All that matters is that you get fit and well. What do the doctors say?'

'That it's going to be a few months, but what do the doctors know?'

'You take your time,' said Blackwell. 'The guy you rescued is out of hospital and has been talking to the press. You're a hero, he says.'

'I was just doing my job.'

'You saved his life, Vicky. And the lives of the other two guys that your crew rescued. You made the decision to go in when a lot of firefighters would have played wait and see.'

'There wasn't time,' said Vicky.

'Yeah, well, you made a tough call and you saved lives,' said Blackwell. He nodded at the bed. 'It's just a bugger you ended up here.'

She shrugged. 'It could have been worse. So how's the station?'

'Same old,' said Blackwell. 'We're still getting those hoax calls. Bloody kids.'

He sat in silence for a while. Then looked at his watch. She could see how uncomfortable he was. 'Actually, guv, I'm feeling a bit tired,' she said. 'Doc says I need to rest.'

'Are you sure?'

'I'm fine. It was really good of you to visit.'

He stood up. 'The guys will be around at some point,' he said.

'Most of them have already been in,' Vicky said. She heard a noise at the door and turned to see her mum, holding a pile of magazines and a carrier bag that almost certainly contained fruit.

'Oh, I'm sorry, I didn't know you had a visitor,' said her mum.

'You know my boss, Mum. Mr Blackwell. He's station manager at Kilburn.'

Blackwell nodded at Vicky's mum. 'Nice to see you again, Barbara. You take care of Vicky, she's very important to us.'

'And to me,' she said.

Blackwell headed out.

'He's such a nice man,' said Barbara, putting the fruit on a table.

'I know.'

'Does he dye his hair?'

'Yes, I think so.'

'Why do men do that, do you think?'

'He wants to look younger, I guess.'

'Men should grow old gracefully,' said Barbara. 'Look at that George Clooney. He's not scared of going grey or having the odd wrinkle.' Barbara sat down on the chair next to the bed and reached over to take hold of Vicky's right hand. 'That lawyer has been in touch. Mr Goldberg. The one representing the building owners.'

'He shouldn't be bothering you, Mum.'

'He wasn't bothering me. He's going to give you three million pounds.'

Vicky wasn't sure she'd heard right. 'What?'

'I know it won't make up for what you've been through, but that's what they are offering. Mr Goldberg said it'll be in your bank by the end of the week. And he said if you decide to have the plastic surgery done privately, they'll pay for that too. I said that was the least he could do.'

Vicky was speechless.

'I told them that it was their fault that you got hurt and they didn't argue with me. I think they are genuinely sorry about what happened and they said they wanted to make it right. I know they can't turn back time, but at least you'll never have to worry about money again.'

'I don't care about the money.'

'But three million pounds is three million pounds. Just think of what you can do with that money.'

'Like what?'

'Buy a house, for instance.'

'I like living with you, Mum.'

'A new car. You've always wanted a BMW.'

Vicky smiled. 'Well, yes, I could go for a BMW i8, that's for sure.'

'There you are then. And you could set yourself up in a business. Or buy-to-let. Get some apartments and rent them out.'

'Mum, I'm a firefighter, not a landlord.'

'Oh now, don't be silly. You're not going back to work. Not after this.'

'I am, Mum,' said Vicky, firmly.

Barbara shook her head and patted Vicky's hand. 'We'll talk about it later.'

10

SIX MONTHS LATER

A young secretary with long blond hair and too-high heels showed Vicky into the meeting room, doing everything she could to avoid looking at Vicky's scarred face. 'Firefighter Lewis,' she mumbled and hurried out.

'Crew Manager Lewis, actually,' said Vicky to the departing secretary. 'But that's okay.'

She had grown her blond hair long so that it covered most of her burnt ear and neck, though there was nothing she could do about the scars on her left cheek.

There were three men and one woman sitting at a polished wooden table. One of the chairs had a higher back than the others and that was occupied by Harry Linklater, president of the Fire Brigades Union. He was in his fifties with steel-grey hair cut short and pale blue eyes that always seemed to be squinting. He had been president for just three years but had earned a reputation as a hard negotiator who put the interests of the 44,000 men and women he represented above all else. He pushed back his chair and walked around the table to shake her hand. 'Crew Manager Lewis, it's a pleasure to meet you,' he said.

'Thank you, sir,' she said.

He looked her in the eyes as he shook and didn't seem at all put out by her scars.

Linklater headed the FBU, which represented pretty much all the country's firefighters. Their HQ was based in Kingston-upon-Thames, in a three-storey brick-built office block sandwiched between an Italian restaurant and a line of suburban semi-detached houses.

'You found us all right?'

'Satnav did, I just followed instructions,' said Vicky.

'Have you met Carol Horton? She's in charge of our female section.'

Horton was a dumpy thirty-something with short permed dyed hair and a square chin. Vicky's first thought was that there was no way she could have passed the brigade's fitness test, but she knew that appearances could be deceptive.

The two women shook hands. Horton's grip was weak as if she wasn't happy about the physical contact. 'Crew Manager Lewis,' she said, as if committing the name to memory.

'And you know Martin Greaves, your local officer.'

'Of course I know Greavsie,' she said.

Greaves walked over and hugged her. 'How the hell are you, Vicky?' he said, squeezing her tightly. Greaves had been a crew manager at Kilburn when Vicky had first been assigned there, though he had left shortly afterwards to work for the union.

'All good, Greavsie,' she said. 'I just want to get back in harness.' Vicky saw a look of distaste flash across Horton's face and she realised the woman didn't approve of the hug.

Greaves stopped hugging her, but put his hands on Vicky's shoulders and looked into her eyes. 'I'm glad you're okay,' he said.

Vicky loved him for the fact that he didn't seem the least bit fazed by her scarred face. 'Me too,' she said. He squeezed her shoulders, then sat down. Horton sat on his left and Linklater took his place in the high-backed chair. There was a jug of water and six glasses on a tray in the middle of the table.

There were five chairs facing them and Vicky took the centre one. She smiled but felt suddenly uncomfortable, as if she was attending a job interview. Or a trial. Horton had an iPad on the table in front of her and she began to tap on it.

Linklater put his hands down on the table and smiled at Vicky. 'So, we're here to discuss your career options now that you're ready for active service. My understanding from Mr Greaves is that you have asked to return to duty but that no slot has been opened up for you?'

Vicky nodded.

'The accident occurred six months ago, is that correct?'

'Yes, sir.'

'But your original station has refused to reinstate you on their rota?'

'That's correct, sir.'

'What exactly have you been told?' asked Linklater.

'Officially, nothing,' said Vicky. 'Headquarters won't answer my letters or my emails and when I phone there's no one available to talk to me.'

'What does your station manager say?'

'He says that until he hears otherwise I'm not fit for duty. And they've already replaced me.'

'Who is your station manager?'

'Rick Blackwell.'

Linklater looked over at Greaves. 'Have you spoken to him?'

Greaves nodded. 'He wants Vicky back. They already have a new crew manager but he'd have her back as a firefighter at the drop of a hat. But citywide, there are a dozen vacancies for crew managers. It's not about staffing levels.'

'Has Station Manager Blackwell applied to have Crew Manager Lewis reinstated?'

'He's sent more than a dozen memos. They're stalling, clearly.'

Linklater scratched the back of his neck as he stared at Vicky. 'You've been medically assessed?'

Vicky shook her head. 'I can't get an appointment.'

'Why not?'

Vicky shrugged. 'I phone the LFB Occupational Health department and I'm told someone will get back to me. They never do. When I phone, there's never anyone available to talk to me. Sometimes they put me on hold and forget about me.'

Linklater nodded thoughtfully. 'What about your fitness?'

'I'm good to go,' said Vicky. 'I'm in the gym every day. I'm as fit as I ever was.'

Linklater gestured at the black glove on her left hand. 'What about your hand?'

'It's stiff still, but there's nothing I can't do with it. It's scarred, obviously. And there's tendon damage, but I don't need medication and the physio has given me exercises to do.'

'And the prognosis is what?'

'As I said, I'm good to go. There's no equipment I can't operate, my grip is good. Mobility is pretty much as it was before the accident. And I don't seem to feel any pain. The doc says the burn probably damaged the pain receptors. It may or may not fix itself in time. But my hand is perfectly serviceable.'

'You can operate a branch?'

'Absolutely.'

Linklater looked over at Greaves. 'I think the first thing we have to do is to get Vicky a full medical assessment,' he said. 'Then put her through a fitness test.'

Greaves nodded and scribbled a note.

'Sounds to me as if your reappointment is being blocked somewhere up the food chain,' said Linklater. 'I'll put out some feelers.'

'I wonder if there's a sexist element involved,' said Horton, looking up from her iPad. 'Perhaps we could get the media involved? Get some sort of campaign going?'

'This is nothing to do with the fact I'm a woman,' said Vicky.

'Are you sure about that? I can't help thinking that they wouldn't be making it so difficult for a male firefighter to get his job back.'

'I don't want my job back because I'm a woman,' said Vicky. 'I want my job back because I'm a firefighter and a bloody good one.'

'No one's saying you should play the sex card, Vicky,' said Linklater.

'But it's fair to say that with women making up only seven per cent of the LFB workforce, we need every female firefighter we can get,' said Horton.

Horton poured herself a glass of water. 'According to the papers, you received a pay-off of three million pounds,' she said.

'Not from the brigade,' said Vicky. 'That was an out-of-court settlement from the company that owned the building.'

Horton nodded. 'I guess my question is, with that much in the bank, why would you want to go back to work? If it was me, I'd go off and buy a cottage by the sea and kick back.'

'I'm too young to retire,' said Vicky. 'And this isn't about money. It's about them letting me do the job I was trained for. I'm a firefighter. I want to fight fires. They can't throw me out just because I was injured, can they?' She looked at them, one by one. 'Well, can they?'

'No, they can't,' said Linklater. 'And we won't let them.'

11

Simon Reid sipped his white wine, grimaced, and looked around the room. It was filled with familiar faces, politicians major and minor, assorted bureaucrats and NGO officials, PR executives and journalists. A feature writer from the *Guardian* tried to catch his eye but Reid turned his back on her. He was no fan of the *Guardian* and the paper took every opportunity to highlight what it considered his failings. It was the *Guardian* that had first referred to him as the Gatekeeper, the man who controlled access to the Mayor. No one got to see the Mayor without first going through Reid, claimed the paper, which was pretty much true. The Mayor also used Reid to pass on bad news. Reid spotted the London Fire Commissioner at the far end of the room, talking to an earnest young man in a double-breasted grey suit. The commissioner was in day-to-day control of the London Fire Brigade but he answered to the Mayor who ultimately set the brigade's budgets and decided its strategy. Reid walked over. Another journalist, this one from the *Independent*, smiled at Reid and held out his hand but Reid pretended not to see him and walked straight by. Reid was no fan of the *Independent* either, and once it had discontinued its newsprint edition and become a website-only publication he ranked it even lower than the *Guardian*. The *Independent* liked to refer to Reid as the Mayor's Rottweiler, which Reid actually took as a compliment.

As Reid walked up to the Commissioner, the man in the grey suit pulled his mobile phone out and began to talk into it. Reid took the opportunity to shake the Commissioner's hand and lead him over to a quiet corner. 'I was hoping I'd catch you here,' said Reid. 'The Mayor is very keen that I have a word with you.'

'That sounds ominous,' said the Commissioner. He was a big man who had run to fat in his years behind a desk and his stomach was straining the buttons of his uniform tunic.

Reid raised his glass. 'Some things are best said in private.'

Reid was a good six inches shorter than the Commissioner, even with the hidden lifts in his shoes. He had to tilt his head back slightly to look the Commissioner in the eyes.

'Even more ominous.' The Commissioner looked around as if trying to identify an escape route.

Reid smiled his most winning smile and put his hand on the Commissioner's shoulder. He moved his head closer to the Commissioner's ear. 'The Mayor is very concerned about the Vicky Lewis situation,' he said.

'Ah,' sighed the Commissioner.

'The Mayor is insistent that you can't sack her, Bill. You really can't. She's a hero and so was her dad. She was one of the first responders at Grenfell Tower and helped bring a family down from the tenth floor. Her picture was in all the papers, remember?'

'She isn't being sacked,' said the Commissioner. 'She's unfit for duty. She's being let go for medical reasons.'

'The girl's a hero, Bill. An honest-to-God hero. And so was her father. He saved half-a-dozen people at King's Cross.'

The Commissioner's eyes narrowed. 'Don't you go lecturing me on the King's Cross fire,' he said. 'Or Grenfell Tower. I was at both.'

'And I was on the street on the day of the funerals, Bill. It was a sad day for all of London. But if it hadn't been for Jim Lewis and the hundred and fifty other fire-fighters who risked their lives at King's Cross, the death toll would have been a lot higher than it was. Which is why you can't go throwing his daughter on the scrap heap just because she got burned.'

'Have you seen her?' whispered the Commissioner, fearful of being overheard. 'The whole side of her face melted.'

'Are you telling me that you only hire firefighters good-looking enough to be in a calendar? You're no oil painting yourself, Bill.'

'She was very badly burnt and she's going to carry those scars for the rest of her life. Having her on an appliance is the worst possible PR for the brigade. Every time she attends a fire someone is going be snapping away on their mobile and the pictures will be all over the tabloids.'

'How is that a problem?'

'She got burned, and that means she fucked up, which-ever way you look at it. But it's not just the publicity issue. What about the other firefighters who'll be with her? Her burns are a constant reminder of what can go wrong, and that's got to be bad for morale.'

'Has any firefighter ever said that to you?'

'Of course not.'

'They're a tough bunch,' said Reid.

'You're making it sound as if I'm personally responsible for rehiring her.'

'It's not a question of rehiring. She's still on the books, she's still being paid.'

The Commissioner sipped his drink. 'It's not as if she needs the money, is it? The owners of the building gave her three million quid in an out-of-court settlement.'

'That was to pay her medical bills,' said Reid.

'The NHS took care of her. And they'll do whatever plastic surgery is necessary. All that money is sitting in her bank account.'

'Is that what's going on?' asked Reid. 'She got a pay-off so you're letting her go?'

'It's not about the money,' said the Commissioner. 'But with that sort of cash in the bank, why doesn't she just go off and enjoy herself?'

'Because she's a firefighter, Bill. The same as her father was. Don't tell me you can't relate to that? You've been in the brigade for what? Thirty years? You could have gone into the private sector ages ago, made more money and incurred a lot less grief.'

'That's the truth,' admitted the Commissioner.

'But you stayed. Because it's in your blood.'

'But I wasn't injured. The army does the same, it medically discharges troops when they're no longer fit to carry out their trained role. It doesn't matter how many medals they've won.'

'But Vicky is perfectly capable of being a firefighter. She'll pass any fitness test, that's what I'm told.'

'She's got the heart of a lion, I'm not disputing that.

But as I said, there are PR and morale considerations. Plus, let's not forget she broke the rules.'

Reid frowned. 'She what?'

'She was in the building on her own when she got burned, and she shouldn't have been. That's one of the rules of breathing apparatus operations. You are always paired up. You never leave a man – or a woman – alone. She knew that.'

'Why was she on her own?'

'That's not the point. The point is that standard operating procedure is always to be paired up. Always.'

'She split up the team to save a guy's life. Right?'

'She broke the rules. End of. And she removed her helmet and mask. Also against the rules.'

'She was giving air to a casualty.'

'She took off her helmet. If she hadn't, maybe her injuries wouldn't have been so severe.'

Reid sipped his drink and winced. 'This is crap,' he said. 'Why is the wine at these things always so bloody awful?'

The Commissioner smiled thinly but didn't say anything.

'Look, Bill, this isn't going away. She's not going to go willingly and I can't say I blame her. The union is backing her, and if push comes to shove the Mayor will be giving her his support and so will the London Fire and Emergency Planning Authority.'

'You're putting a gun to my head,' said the Commissioner.

'No, but I'm telling you the Mayor has a gun in his pocket and it's loaded,' said Reid. 'Look, how about this? Keep her on the payroll but find her something else to do, something where she won't be visible. How does that sound?'

'That could work, I suppose,' said the Commissioner. 'Let me take it under consideration.'

Reid smiled and clinked his glass against the Commissioner's. 'The Mayor will be grateful, Bill,' he said. 'Very grateful.' His smile widened as he saw the Deputy Prime Minister looking in his direction. He raised his glass and the Deputy Prime Minister waved him over. 'Catch you later,' said Reid.

12

Dowgate Fire Station, on Upper Thames Street at the bottom of Dowgate Hill, was the only station in the City of London, known colloquially as the Square Mile. The only other station in the Square Mile had been the Barbican, which was closed in cost-cutting measures in 1999. As another cost-cutting measure the Dowgate station also covered most of Southwark in south London, which meant its pump ladder was forever racing back and forth over the Thames.

Vicky parked in the street a short walk from the station. The pump was parked up and two firefighters were busy checking the breathing apparatus. In most stations the offices were on the upper floors so she looked around for the stairs, but before she spotted them a black spaniel ran over and started pawing at her legs. 'Hello, fella,' she said and knelt down and patted the dog's neck. It yelped excitedly.

'Hey, Watson, keep your mind on the job,' called a firefighter walking in from the training yard behind the pumps. He was wearing a tunic and leggings and holding a yellow tennis ball. He was in his thirties with ginger hair and pale white skin peppered with large freckles.

The dog licked Vicky's face enthusiastically, oblivious

to the scars. Vicky loved the way that animals didn't care how she looked. She rubbed her cheek against the dog's fur. 'You're a good boy,' she said.

'He always goes crazy for a pretty girl,' said the man. Vicky was wearing LFB gear, with a fleece over it, and carrying a black nylon backpack and her helmet. He nodded at the helmet. 'You're the station's new crew manager?'

As she stood up she saw his eyes widen. It was a look she'd seen hundreds of times but that didn't make it any easier. She didn't blame the man, it was instinctive, and he quickly smiled and concentrated on her unmarked cheek. 'Vicky Lewis,' she said. 'I've been assigned to the Fire Investigation Unit.'

'Oh my God, you're Vicky Lewis.'

'I just said that.'

'*The* Vicky Lewis?'

Vicky laughed. 'I guess so.'

'No one said you were coming to Dowgate.'

'Yeah, I don't think they're advertising the fact. You are . . .?'

The man looked shamefaced and held out his hand. 'Sorry. Yes. Jamie Hughes. I'm with fire investigation, too.' He gestured at the dog. 'Obviously. He's supposed to be sniffing out the accelerant swabs I've hidden around the yard.' He held up the tennis ball. 'This is the love of his life, though the way he's fawning over you might say otherwise. He gets this as a reward when he finds the swabs.'

The dog was still scrabbling at her thighs and Vicky laughed and knelt down again, letting him lick her face. 'He's lovely,' she said.

'Like I said, he likes the ladies. Actually, we both do. Especially blonds.'

Vicky looked up at him. 'I thought dogs were colour blind.'

'Watson seems to manage okay. So you're going to be an investigator?'

'Yeah. Apparently. I'm here to see Watch Manager Desmond Farmer.'

'The Grouch? He's in the main building. Third floor.'

Vicky laughed. 'Is he hard work?'

'I'll take the fifth, as the Americans would say,' said Hughes. 'Reception is through there, they'll point you in the right direction.' He pointed at a door to the right-hand side of the station. 'Maybe see you for a drink one day after your shift. The guys often pop into the Steelyard for a quick one.' He whistled at the dog. 'Come on, Watson, that's enough of a break.' Watson wagged his tail and ran over to him. Hughes nodded at the stairs. 'Good luck with the Grouch.'

'Thanks,' said Vicky. She headed to the door as the man went back into the training yard. There was an intercom to the left of the door and she pressed it. She could see a young man in dark-blue LFB shirt and trousers sitting at a desk and he buzzed her in. 'Crew Manager Vicky Lewis,' she said. 'I'm here to see Desmond Farmer.'

The man pointed at the stairs. 'Third floor.'

Vicky shouldered her backpack and headed up the narrow flight of stairs. On the third floor was a long corridor with piles of cardboard boxes against one wall and a line of doors to the left. The first door was open and appeared to be an equipment store. The second door was ajar, and Vicky caught a glimpse of a man in shirt-sleeves talking into a telephone. To the left of the door was a small white plastic sign with DANIEL MAGUIRE, FIRE INVESTIGATION in black capital letters. The third door was also ajar. The sign on the wall said the office was Farmer's. Vicky knocked and when there was no reply she knocked again and then pushed it open. A grey-haired man in his fifties was sitting behind a desk piled high with files and papers. He looked up and squinted at her. 'What do you want?' he growled.

'I knocked.'

'Nobody knocks here,' he said. 'You open the door, you tell me what you want, then you fuck off.' He looked down at the file he had propped on his lap and chewed a biro. He was wearing a white LFB uniform shirt with two circular pips on his black epaulettes denoting his rank: watch manager. To his left was a metal filing cabinet and two more shirts were hanging from the handle of the top drawer. The blinds had been pulled down and the over-head fluorescent lights were on. The walls were covered with official notices, health-and-safety memorandums and charts of various sizes. There didn't seem to be anything of a personal nature on the walls or on his desk.

'I'm Vicky Lewis.'

'I know who you are,' he said, not looking up.

'You're Desmond Farmer?'

'No one's called me Desmond since I was an altar boy, and I've got bad memories of those days.'

'Mr Farmer?'

'Are you taking the piss?'

'I'm not sure what I'm supposed to be calling you? Guv? Boss?'

He sighed. 'You choose. I couldn't care less either way.'

Vicky forced a smile. 'Guv, then. And they call me

Vicky. Or Crew Manager Lewis.' She approached him and held out her hand.

He ignored it and concentrated on the file he was holding. 'This isn't going to work,' he said.

'What isn't? You sweet-talking me?'

He looked up from the file. 'Your dad was a hero, no question. By all accounts, so are you. But I'm not Batman and I don't need a sidekick. I investigate fires, you put them out. The two activities are in no way related.'

'You were a firefighter once.'

'A long time ago.'

'But you made the transition.'

Farmer sighed. 'Yes, I did. But I'm not a teacher and I don't want to be one. I told them I didn't want to hold your hand, but apparently my opinion counts for nothing these days.' He tossed the file on to the desk. 'This isn't personal, sweetheart. I'm just not cut out to be Yoda.'

'That's all right, guv. I never saw myself as Luke Skywalker. So I understand that my mentor you cannot be.'

He waved his hand in the air dismissively. 'Forget it. What I'm saying is you shouldn't be here. You should be putting out fires and charging into burning buildings.' She saw his eyes widen as he realised what he'd said. 'Sorry,' he said. 'No offence.'

She turned so that her scarred cheek was towards him. 'Don't worry about this.' she said. 'I've come to terms with it. It's part of me now.' She nodded at a chair. 'Can I sit?'

'Of course. Yes.' He ran a hand through his hair. 'Look, you seem like a nice girl but I've raised it with my guv'nor and you're not staying.'

Vicky sat down. 'Just so we're clear, I wasn't thrilled

to be sent here,' she said. 'I want to fight fires, not investigate them. I want to pull people out of burning buildings, not visit their bodies on a slab. They want me out of the brigade, there's no question of that.' She pointed at her scarred face. 'Because of this, obviously. I've been burned twice. Once by the fire and now by the brigade. That's why I'm here. Not because they want me to be your assistant, but because they want me out. I'm not going to let them win. If they want to stick me in fire investigation, fine. I'll do the best job I can, and when the time comes I'll move back to fire-fighting. But the one thing I'm not going to do is quit.'

Farmer put up both his hands. 'I understand. Hell's bells, I empathise, I know what shits management can be. I'm sure they'd have pushed me out years ago if they had the chance. But you can understand why I'm not thrilled to have someone assigned to me who doesn't want to be here.'

Vicky shook her head. 'That's not what I said. Don't get me wrong. I want to be out fighting fires, but while I'm here I'll work any hours you want, you'll never hear me complain. If you want me to get you coffee in the morning or pick up your dry-cleaning then I'll do it. I'll work my balls off for you. I swear.'

Farmer tried to suppress a smile. 'I assume you're talking metaphorically.'

Vicky ignored the clumsy attempt at humour. 'I've read the fire investigation manual three times. I'll make this work because I don't have any choice. If I fuck up here then they win and I'm out.'

Farmer tilted his head on one side as he looked at her. 'You've read the manual, have you?'

Vicky nodded enthusiastically. 'Front to back and back to front.'

'There's no such thing,' said Farmer. 'The brigade doesn't have a manual.'

'I meant NFPA 921 and Kirks Fire Investigation.'

'And you read them both?'

Vicky nodded.

'Really? So you'll know the five steps of risk assessment at a fire scene?'

She nodded earnestly. 'Sure. Step one: determine the hazards present in the working area. Step two: determine who may be exposed to the hazards. Step three: evaluate risks and decide if existing precautions are adequate. Step four: record the risks and any actions taken to eliminate or mitigate these risks. Step five: review the risks regularly.' She smiled, knowing that she'd nailed it.

Farmer didn't appear to be impressed. 'And if you determine that it is safe to proceed, what questions are we looking to answer?'

'Where did the fire start? What caused it? How did it spread? Was it accidental or deliberate?'

'Anything else?'

Her eyes narrowed as she tried to remember what she'd read. 'The people in the fire. What did they do? And how did the fire precaution measures perform?'

Farmer stared at her thoughtfully for a few seconds, then nodded and stood up.

'Okay,' he said, reaching for his tunic and helmet. 'Dump your bag in the corner and come with me.'

13

They went downstairs into the station and Farmer handed her a set of keys and nodded at a red Volkswagen Transporter with a yellow stripe around it and Fire Investigation Unit markings. 'I assume you can drive,' he said curtly.

'Yes, guv,' said Vicky, unlocking the door and climbing into the front seat. She reached for the satnav. 'Where are we going?'

'Don't use that thing,' he said. 'I'll talk you through it.' He slammed the door and fastened his seatbelt.

She drove out of the station and he told her to head east to Whitechapel. The traffic was light and it took them less than half an hour to reach their destination. Farmer didn't say anything during the drive, or while she parked in a side street of terraced houses. As soon as she climbed out of the van, Vicky saw the reason for their trip – one of the houses had clearly been damaged in a major fire. Plywood panels had been nailed across the downstairs window and two planks had been nailed across a badly burnt door. The brickwork was streaked with soot, but only on the ground floor.

'This was a fire two days ago,' said Farmer. 'Four pumps. No one hurt but it could have very easily turned nasty.'

'Arson?' asked Vicky.

'You tell me,' said Farmer.

Vicky walked up to the front door and peered through the gap between the planks. Someone had sprayed capital letters in red paint across the wood. 'ASYLAM SEEKERS OUT'.

'Spelling wasn't their strong point,' said Vicky. 'Was the graffiti done the same time as the fire?'

'Apparently. Right, we can go in the back way. I just wanted you to see the damage to the front. Any initial thoughts as to the seat of the fire?'

'Downstairs, obviously,' said Vicky, pointing at the scorch marks. She peered at the burnt door, then looked at the boarded-up window. 'Was the window smashed?'

'It was, but by the firefighters. The front room was well alight so they put water in through the window.' He started walking down the street and Vicky hurried to catch up with him.

'Does this happen a lot around here?' she asked.

'Fires? No more than anywhere else.'

'I mean attacks like this? Are there racist groups locally who would do something like this?'

'There's racists everywhere,' said Farmer. He turned left and took her to an alley that ran behind the houses. Wooden doors led off the alley, left and right, and they walked along to the one that led to the burnt house. There was police tape across the door and Farmer pulled it away. The door had been kicked in. Farmer pushed it open. 'More brigade damage,' he said. 'They sent two men in the back just to make sure no one was trapped there.' The door led to a paved garden the width of the house and about ten feet deep. There was no fire damage and two plastic rubbish bins stood against the wall. Plywood had been nailed across the back door and Farmer ripped it away. The door was lying on the kitchen floor. There was a strong smell of smoke but there didn't appear to be any fire damage in the kitchen. There was no water damage in the kitchen either. 'So they didn't bring a line around the back?'

'They were able to deal with it at the front,' said Farmer. He pulled open the door that led to the hallway. The side away from them was burned black but it had obviously held the fire back. 'Shows the value of closing all doors at night, if nothing else,' said Farmer. 'Be careful here, it's a wooden floor and it's been compromised in several places.'

She moved into the hallway. The smoke smell was much stronger now and she stopped. She gasped as she pictured the hallway in flames. The vision was so strong that she could almost feel the heat on her face and she took a step back.

'Sweetheart, are you okay?' asked Farmer.

Vicky took a deep breath. 'Yes, guv.'

'You looked like you'd seen a ghost.'

'Yeah, I don't know what happened. But I'm okay. Really, I'm okay.'

'Come on, then, have a look around and tell me what you see.'

There had been a carpet covering the hall floor but much of it had been destroyed in the fire. Most of the floorboards were charred and around the bottom of the stairs they had burned through in places. By the look of it the fire had spread up the stairs, charring the walls and covering the ceiling with soot. The firefighters had soaked everything to stop the fire reigniting and there was a thick layer of sooty mud across the floor and stairs.

Vicky watched where she was putting her feet as she walked up to the front door. Farmer was right: the floorboards had burned through completely in places. The inside of the front door was much more damaged than the side facing the street, and there was a V-shape of more serious damage spreading up from the bottom of the door, suggesting that the fire had started at the floor and moved up.

She knelt down and looked at the floorboards in front of the door. It looked as if they were more damaged than the boards at the sides of the hall. The charring was more severe. There was also a semicircle of darker charring spreading out from the door that looked as if a doormat had once been there, but which Vicky assumed had been produced by an accelerant being poured through the letter box. She straightened up and turned to see Farmer watching her expectantly. 'So what do you think?' he asked.

'Arson,' said Vicky.

'Because?'

'I think the petrol poured through the letter box is a bit of a giveaway,' she said.

Farmer smiled. 'So who was the perpetrator?'

'Presumably racists,' said Vicky.

'And you say that because?'

'The racist graffiti on the door.'

He smiled and shook his head. 'Wrong.'

'Wrong how?'

'Well, let's see if you can work it out,' said Farmer. 'Yes, we have racist graffiti on the front door and we have petrol apparently poured through the letter box. So tell me how the fire spread.'

Vicky frowned, wondering why she was being asked to state the obvious. 'The petrol was poured through the letter box. Then ignited. So the fire spread from the door along the hall and to the stairs.'

'Ignited how?'

'A match, maybe.'

'We didn't find a match.'

'It could have been completely destroyed in the fire. Or the firefighters could have moved it.'

Farmer nodded. 'That happens. But suppose I were to tell you that there was a higher concentration of accelerant at the base of the stairs than there was at the door.'

Her eyebrows shot up. 'That's not possible,' she said. She went over and examined the bottom of the stairs. He was right. The charring there was more severe than it was in the middle of the hallway.

He wagged a finger at her. 'The evidence is what it is,' he said. 'You start with that and you use it to tell you what happened. You're approaching it the other way, you only want to accept the evidence that backs up your theory.' He wagged his finger again. 'Forget your preconceptions and stick with the facts. It is a fact that there was more accelerant at the base of the stairs than there was at the doorway. We sent samples to the lab and they confirmed it. So what does that tell us?'

'That means the fire was set from the inside.'

'Exactly.'

'But the fire started at the letter box and spread down the hallway.'

'Yes. That's what the evidence suggests. Which means what?'

Vicky frowned. 'That whoever set the fire wanted to make it look as if it had been started from outside.' She could hear her own uncertainty in her voice.

Farmer smiled. 'There you go.'

'So the racist graffiti is separate from the fire?'

'Let's leave the graffiti for a moment. Let's go back to the facts. We know where the fire started. We know what caused it. We know how it spread. We know that it was deliberate. What do we ask next?'

Vicky frowned as she tried to recall what was in the manuals she had read. 'The people in the fire. What did they do?'

'Well, I can tell you that Mr and Mrs Qadri and their five children were out on the street when the first pump arrived. Safe and sound.'

'What time was the fire?'

'Two o'clock in the morning.'

She wrinkled her nose. 'How did they get out?'

'According to Mr Qadri, he heard a noise and came downstairs, saw what had happened and managed to get his family out through the kitchen before the fire spread.'

'They came down the stairs?'

'According to Mr Qadri, yes.'

'That's not possible.'

Farmer smiled. 'Because?'

'Because there was accelerant at the base of the stairs. It would have spread from the door to the stairs in seconds. The chimney effect would have filled the stairs with smoke and hot gases so quickly that there wouldn't have been enough time for the family to escape that way.'

'Well, that's what Mr Qadri says happened.'

'But the evidence says otherwise.'

He smiled. 'Exactly.'

She wrinkled her nose. 'So Mr Qadri set fire to his own house?'

'That's what the evidence suggests. So why would he do that?'

She looked up the stairs. 'How many bedrooms are there?'

'Two, but there's a box room, as well.'

'So a family of seven are living in a three-bedroomed house?'

'They have bunk beds in the box room. The three girls sleep there. The two boys are in the second bedroom. And Mrs Qadri is pregnant.'

'And this is a council house?'

Farmer smiled. 'They've been here for two years since the family fled from Iraq.'

'Have they by any chance been asking the council for a bigger house?'

Farmer's smile widened. 'Pretty much from the first day they arrived in this country. And they want to be nearer their friends in Holland Park. Mr Qadri calls around to the council offices every Monday to plead his case. The house is too small for his needs, he says, and he doesn't like the area.'

Vicky bit down on her lower lip.

'So now what do you think happened?' asked Farmer.

She sighed. 'He set the fire himself. Did the graffiti himself. His English isn't great so he gets the spelling wrong. Probably got his family out before he lit it. Then blames it on a racist attack knowing that the council is duty-bound to find him alternative accommodation.'

'They did that within twenty-four hours. They're already in a four-bedroom house, only a couple of Tube stops from their relatives.'

Vicky frowned. 'But you told the council what happened?'

Farmer flashed her a cold smile. 'I gave them my report and I told them what I'd found. But I think they preferred the scenario that Mr Qadri gave them.'

'But they realise what happened? He set fire to the house to get what he wanted.'

'If that is what happened and he ends up in court, how does that make the council look? The evidence is circumstantial so a good lawyer might get him off. But if he is found guilty then he'll claim that he was pushed to the end of his tether by a council that refused to do right by his family. The more he plays the victim, the worse the council looks. Better to just move him to a bigger house. And there's the money. If he goes to prison, that's forty grand a year for his keep. Plus his wife speaks almost no English, so there's a chance the kids would end up in care. That's another hundred grand at least. So the council is probably thinking that the most cost-effective way of dealing with this is to keep the family together.'

'You're serious?'

'About what?'

'He set a fire. His family could have died. So could the neighbours. What about the police? Do they know what happened?'

'They've seen my report as well, but because it was logged as a racist incident they have to investigate, no matter what.' He shrugged. 'But that's not the point. The point is that we know how the fire started. That's all our role is in this. We don't prosecute, that's up to the police. We just investigate, and that's what I did.'

His mobile phone rang and he answered it. He listened, muttered a reply and put the phone away. 'Vehicle fire they want us to have a look at,' he explained. 'Not far from here.'

'Anyone hurt?'

Farmer shook his head. 'Probably an insurance job.'

'So much for your policy of not letting your preconceptions affect your judgement.'

'That's not what I said,' replied Farmer gruffly. 'You have to go into every fire investigation assuming there is a possibility that it was deliberate. You're looking for evidence either way. But cars are a bit special because the stats show us that half of all vehicle fires are down to the owners trying to put in a dodgy insurance claim. And in this case the car is in a car park and the owner's nowhere to be found, so that's a red flag right there. Two red flags, as it happens. If the car's parked where it's normally kept and the owner has dialled three nines, then there's a good chance it's down to mechanical failure. Otherwise we go with the stats which means there's a fifty per cent chance the owner did it.'

14

The burnt-out car was in a pub car park. A pump was parked nearby and the crew manager hurried over to talk to Farmer when he climbed out of the van. The two men shook hands.

The crew manager was an old friend, Terry Jenner. She'd worked on numerous shouts with him and he had been a regular visitor when she was in hospital. He grinned when he saw her getting out of the van. 'No fucking way,' he said. 'They put you with the Grouch?'

'Guilty as charged,' said Vicky.

Jenner hugged her and patted her on the back. 'Haven't seen you for donkey's,' he said. 'They said you'd left.'

'They're not going to get rid of me that easily.'

Jenner gestured at the burnt vehicle. 'We'll leave that in your capable hands,' he said to Farmer. He flashed Vicky a thumbs-up. 'Good to see you again.'

'You too, Terry.'

Jenner climbed back into the pump and it drove off. The burnt vehicle was soaking wet and there were pools of water around it. It was far enough away from the pub that the building hadn't been in any danger of catching fire but the pump had obviously got there early because only the front half of the car was damaged. It was a blue

Ford Mondeo. The bodywork was badly burnt but didn't seem dented. 'It doesn't look as if there has been a collision,' said Vicky. 'So vandalism, maybe?'

'Vandalism tends to happen where cars are parked in the street or in driveways,' said Farmer. He looked around. 'I don't see any CCTV cameras. So we're probably not going to be able to ID the driver.'

'You think the driver torched the vehicle?'

'It's an option. Tell me what you see.' Farmer took out a pack of tobacco and a piece of cigarette paper. He turned and rested against the van as he rolled a cigarette.

Vicky put her head on one side as she stared at the wreckage. The bonnet was blackened and the windscreen had cracked. The front tyres had burned away completely and the car had sagged forward on its metal rims. The driver's door was ajar.

'The fire started at the front,' she said.

Farmer didn't turn around as he continued to roll his cigarette. 'And?'

'The driver's door is open.'

'Any other doors open?'

Vicky walked around the car. All the other doors were closed. 'No,' she said.

'Which means?'

'It might just mean the firefighters opened the door and left it that way. Or that the driver left the door open.'

'What condition was the car in before the fire?'

'Difficult to say,' said Vicky.

'Try,' said Farmer. He turned around, slipped the roll-up between his lips and lit it with a disposable lighter. He blew smoke as she slowly worked her way around the car. Most of the paintwork was burned and blistered from the fire and streaked with dirty water.

'I don't see any signs of damage other than the fire,' she said.

'And it's what, ten years old?'

She checked the rear licence plate. 'Eight,' she said.

'So probably not worth much, insurance-wise,' he said.

Vicky frowned. 'So it's not arson.'

'Strictly speaking, it's only referred to as arson if there's a human life at risk,' said Farmer. 'If no one is in danger then it's a malicious firing. The question is whether or not the fire was deliberately set. And to determine that, we need to know the cause. Now, from the look of it, we can assume the fire wasn't external.' He blew smoke up at the greying sky. 'So let's look inside the vehicle. Check for the seat of the fire.'

Vicky pulled open the passenger door and peered inside. The floor carpet had burned as had the plastic seats. The plastic panels in the doors had burned, and so had the roof. The seats at the back had been scorched but not burned and the roof was less damaged there.

Vicky straightened up. 'It spread from the front.'

'The engine bay?'

'I think so. I don't see any ignition sources here.'

'Any smell of petrol? Oil? Brake fluid? Smell anything that shouldn't be there?'

Vicky put her head back inside and sniffed. All she could smell was burnt plastic and rubber. 'No, nothing,' she said.

Farmer dropped what was left of his roll-up on to the ground, stamped on it, then went over to the car and pulled on a pair of green nitrile gloves. He then put a second pair on top of the first. Vicky followed his example. The bonnet had been forced open by the firefighters. Farmer touched it gingerly to reassure himself that it wasn't still hot, then opened it. Vicky joined him and peered into the engine bay. It was blackened from the fire and the underside of the bonnet was thick with wet soot. Farmer put his head down and sniffed, then carefully inspected the sides of the engine. The cover of the battery had melted and he had to twist it to pull it off. The connections to the terminals showed no signs of sparking. The cover to the fuse box had also been damaged by the fire but when he removed it there was no apparent electrical damage. He examined the covers. Both were damaged on the outside and relatively unmarked on the undersides. He showed them to Vicky.

'So probably not an electrical fire,' she said.

Farmer nodded. 'But from the look of the damage to the underside of the bonnet, it clearly started in the engine compartment.'

'The damage looks worse on this side,' she said, pointing to the left.

'Agreed,' said Farmer. He peered down into the left-hand side of the compartment. 'Ah-ha!'

'Ah-ha?' repeated Vicky.

Farmer took a pen from his pocket and poked it down the side of the engine. 'Down on your knees, sweetheart,' he said.

'Excuse me?'

'With an evidence bag.' He handed her a clear plastic bag and then pushed the pen down into the gap between the engine and the bodywork. Vicky knelt down on the tarmac. 'Here it comes,' said Farmer. He prodded again and a burnt piece of rag tumbled to the floor.

Vicky put it into the bag and stood up, frowning. 'That started it?' she said. She sniffed it and smelt a mixture of burnt cloth, oil and grease.

'Looks like it,' said Farmer.

'So it's a deliberate fire?' said Vicky. 'Someone set fire to the rag and shoved it on the engine?'

Farmer grinned. 'That's a pretty haphazard way of setting a fire,' he said. 'I think we're looking at accidental damage.'

'How does a burning cloth accidentally get on to an engine?' asked Vicky.

'We need to talk to the owner,' said Farmer. 'The car was obviously running and the bodywork was in fairly good nick prior to the fire, doubtful he'd have anything to gain by torching it. In fact, from the look of it he took pride in his vehicle. Maybe even worked on it himself. The key is still in the ignition so we need to check if it was stolen from outside his house and if he was working on it at the time.'

Realisation dawned and Vicky smiled. 'Got it,' she said. 'The owner was working on the car, steps inside for a moment and an opportunistic thief sees the keys in the ignition and drives off. What he doesn't know is that there's an oily cloth on the engine. It catches fire, the car burns and the thief bales.'

'You can make some calls when we get back to the office,' said Farmer. 'But yes, that's what the evidence suggests.' He looked at his watch. 'Right, how about lunch?'

'I could eat,' said Vicky.

Stephen Leather

'That's good because you're paying,' said Farmer.

'Why am I paying?'

'It's tradition,' he said. 'First day on the job, the assistant buys lunch.'

Following Farmer's curt directions, Vicky drove the van to an East End pub and found a parking space across the road. It was a Wetherspoon's and Farmer ordered steak and kidney pie and chips and Coke and Vicky asked for fish and chips and a coffee. The girl who took their order did a double take when she saw the scars on Vicky's face, then stared studiously at her notepad and refused to look up until she left the table.

'Can I speak frankly, without you bursting into tears and going running to the bosses?' said Farmer when the waitress finally left.

'Sure,' said Vicky.

'I'm serious, sweetheart. I'll put my cards on the table, but if I do that, I don't want you alleging constructive dismissal or whatnot.'

'I don't think you can sack me, guv.'

He waved a hand. 'I don't want you blabbing, that's what I'm saying. But I want to tell you the way things are.'

'I'm all ears. And I'd rather you were straight with me.'

Farmer nodded. 'Good. Okay, here's the thing. Fire Investigations isn't a dumping ground. Never has been and never will be. I don't understand why my boss allowed it, but I'm guessing he wasn't given a choice. It's bloody hard to get into investigations. There's a waiting list of highly qualified men and women who deserve a place in the unit. There's an intensive selection procedure to get through, and a lot of studying to be done. And yet you were dropped into the unit like an unwanted turd.'

'Thanks. That image will stay with me for a long time. But I take your point. I was foisted on you and I get that no one is happy about that.'

'Okay.' Farmer nodded slowly. 'And you were serious, you've read the manuals back to front?'

'Like you said, I'm a firefighter not an investigator. So when they told me I was being assigned to the investigation department, I figured I should at least be prepared.'

'It's a different job completely,' said Farmer. 'And not everyone can do it. It's not just about the manual. It's about understanding fire and how it operates. Fire can be like a living thing: sometimes it follows the rules, sometimes it doesn't.'

'I understand,' said Vicky.

He squinted at her. 'That's easy to say, but do you really?'

'Guv, with the greatest of respect I've been a firefighter for almost ten years. I was at Grenfell Tower. I've seen what fires can do.'

'Fighting fires and understanding fires are two different things,' said Farmer. 'The big difference with what we do is that we are working backwards, whereas firefighters are working forwards. Firefighters arrive and make predictions. They look forward. I get there when it's all over, and I have to work backwards. I have to work out how the fire started. And why. We need to know why the fire happened. Because a big part of this job is to make sure that future fires don't happen. We're always looking for causes so that we can prevent the same thing happening again. We're looking for links, for patterns of behaviour that can lead to fires, for faulty products, for materials that increase the risk of a fire.'

'Fire prevention?'

'That's the end result, yes. It partly explains why the death toll from fire is down forty per cent in London over the past ten years. That's what we do, Vicky. We save lives.'

A bearded waiter brought their food over. He approached from Vicky's right side and he gave her a beaming smile until she turned to face him. The movement pushed her hair away from her cheek and revealed all her scar tissue and he grimaced and almost dropped the plates he was carrying. 'Oh God, sorry, sorry,' he muttered, putting the plates on the table and rushing away.

'Does that get to you, the way people react?' asked Farmer.

'It's not their fault,' she said, picking up her knife and fork. She tilted her head down so that her hair swung over her face. 'It's not as if they're being deliberately hurtful. I'm probably the same. You see something you don't expect and you react instinctively.' She shrugged. 'I probably react the same way when I see something that takes me by surprise. It's what you do afterwards, that counts. Some people just can't look at me again, like the waiter. Others just accept it for what it is and ignore it. Or at least they pretend to ignore it. It's impossible to not see it, obviously.' She grimaced. 'What can I do? My face is a mess, I just have to deal with it.'

She raised her eyes and saw that he was looking at her scarred cheek. He shrugged. 'I've seen worse,' he said. He dug into his steak and kidney pie. 'So, back to the manual. Tell me about the Fire Triangle.'

Vicky put down her knife and fork and poured ketchup over her food. 'Are you serious?'

'I need to know how much you know about the mechanics and chemistry of fire. I know you know how to fight fires, but I need to know if you really understand them.'

Vicky sighed. 'The fire triangle or combustion triangle sets down the three elements that a fire needs to ignite. Heat, fuel and an oxidising agent.'

'The most common oxidising agent being?'

'Oxygen.'

'Other examples being?'

'Nitrates. Chlorine. Iodine. Peroxides.'

Farmer nodded. 'Okay,' he said. 'But the triangle model is now regarded as old school, correct?'

Vicky nodded. 'They talk about a fire tetrahedron now. The fourth element is chemical chain reaction.'

'Which means what?'

'There has to be enough exothermic reaction energy to produce ignition. Without the chain reaction there is no fire.' She grinned mischievously. 'Though actually, on the pump we always thought it was more of a fire pentagon.'

He frowned. 'How so?'

'We always reckoned there were five elements to a fire. Heat, fuel, an oxidising agent, a chemical reaction and senior officers. Remove any of the five and the fire would go out a lot quicker.'

Farmer chuckled. 'Nice one.' He popped a chip into his mouth. 'So take me through the stages of a fire.'

'Incipient stage, smouldering stage, and flame.' Vicky grinned. She knew that Farmer was testing her, and on one hand she was offended that he had so little faith in her abilities. But she also knew how well prepared she was and she was fairly sure there was no question that he could ask that she couldn't answer. She was serious when she had said she had read the manuals front to back and back to front. She had gone through Kirks Fire Investigation manual from the front to the back, then reread it from the last chapter to the first. It was a trick she'd learned at school, changing the order she read things helped her memorise them.

Framer nodded as he hacked away at his pie.

'Any more questions, guv?'

He shook his head. 'Not at the moment, no.'

15

Vicky drove the van back into Dowgate station. The station's pump had gone and Farmer spotted Vicky's car. His jaw dropped. 'What the fuck is that?' he said, gesturing at the blue two-door coupé with a massive downward wedge on the sloping bonnet and bulbous buttresses over the rear wheels.

'That's mine,' she said. 'A BMW i8.'

'You bought it?' He climbed out of the van, took a roll-up from his tobacco pack and lit it as he looked at the car.

'You think I stole it?'

'How much does a car like that cost?'

'I didn't ask. A hundred grand or so, I guess.'

'How can you buy a car and not know how much it cost?'

'I just gave them the credit card and said I wanted it.'

He blew smoke at the car. 'How fast does it go?'

'I don't know. I haven't really driven it fast. It's just a great car. It's a hybrid, and there's no congestion charge, which is a bonus.'

'I'm in the wrong job,' said Farmer. 'I'd never be able to afford a car like that, no matter how much I saved.'

'I got the car because of this,' she said, turning her scarred cheek towards him. 'I'd give up the car in a heartbeat if it meant I could get my face back.'

'A hundred grand?'

'Give or take.'

Farmer shook his head and took another drag on his roll-up. 'So you sued the bastards did you? The bastards that owned the hotel.'

'No, they gave it to me. Paid me the money while I was still in the hospital.'

'How much?'

'I can't say. There was a confidentiality clause. I'm not supposed to talk about it.'

'But it was a lot, yeah?'

'I didn't want the money and I didn't ask for it. I just wanted to be a firefighter.'

'You're a funny one, Vicky Lewis. If someone gave me a shed-load of cash you wouldn't see me for dust.'

'Seriously?'

He took another drag on his cigarette. 'Seriously.'

'Somehow I don't believe you. I think you enjoy what you do, same as I enjoyed being a firefighter. It gets in your blood.'

'Yeah,' said Farmer. 'Like hepatitis.' He dropped the remains of his cigarette on to the ground and stamped it out with his boot.

As she and Farmer walked over to the main building, Watson the spaniel ran over to them. 'Get away from me you flea-ridden mutt,' scowled Farmer.

'You don't like dogs?' asked Vicky.

'Only between a roll with mustard on it,' said Farmer.

Vicky knelt down and let the dog lick her face.

Farmer grimaced. 'You know what else they lick, right?' He walked away in disgust.

Vicky carried on petting the exuberant dog until she heard an urgent whistling from behind her. She stood up and turned to see Jamie Hughes. He waved at her and walked over. 'How is your first day?'

'I'm on a steep learning curve,' she said.

'Just don't tell him I called him the Grouch.'

Vicky grinned. 'Your secret's safe with me.'

'Cool. Anyway, hopefully we'll be working together sooner rather than later. If you need a dog, give me a call.'

'I'll do that.' She looked down at Watson who was still pawing at her knees.

Hughes whistled and bounced Watson's ball and he went running over to him, tail wagging.

Vicky headed up the stairs. Farmer was already at his desk. 'Sorry about that,' she said, but he waved her apology away with an impatient wave of his hand. 'Before you get settled, pop along to the tea room and get me a coffee, will you? Milk, two sugars. And if there are any Hobnobs, a couple of them.'

'Right, guv.' She went back along the corridor. There was a kettle so she switched it on and took two mugs from a cupboard and a jar of Gold Blend. There were several packs of biscuits in a cupboard, including Hobnobs, so she took two and put them on a plate.

The man in the next office popped his head around the door. 'I thought I heard the kettle,' he said. He was in his mid-thirties, with close-cropped dark-brown hair. He was wearing a white shirt with the sleeves rolled up and a fire brigade tie that was loose around his neck. 'Black. One sugar.'

'I'm sorry,' said Vicky.

'Coffee. Black. One sugar.' He had a soft Yorkshire accent.

'And you are . . .?'

He stuck out his hand. 'Sorry, Danny Maguire. I'm in the office next to the Grouch. You're his gofer, right?'

'I suppose so, yes,' said Vicky.

She turned to shake his hand and for the first time he saw her scarred face and he flinched. 'Fuck,' he said.

Vicky shook her head. 'I'm happy enough to make you coffee but I draw the line at a fuck.'

'Oh God, I'm sorry. Des didn't say anything and I . . . I'm so sorry.'

She frowned. 'Sorry about what? That I was injured in the line of duty?'

'He just said he had been given a new assistant. That was all he said.' His jaw dropped as realisation dawned. 'You're Vicky Lewis.'

'He didn't tell you?'

'The Grouch isn't one for chit-chat,' said Maguire. He held out his hand. 'Pleasure to meet you, Vicky. Hell, it's an honour.'

They shook hands.

'And forget about the coffee. I can make my own.'

Vicky shook her head. 'Nah, I'm the new girl, I'm happy to make the coffees. I'm here to learn the ropes.'

'Well, Des knows his stuff, that's for sure,' said Maguire. 'It's just the social skills that he's missing.' He shook his head. 'Vicky Lewis. Bloody hell. You deserve a medal for what you did, pulling that guy out of the building.'

'I was just doing my job. Same as any firefighter would have done.'

'And the whole building fell on you?'

'Not quite,' she said. 'The floor collapsed under me.'

'You were lucky,' said Maguire.

Vicky put her gloved hand up to her scarred face. 'Yeah, I suppose I was.'

'So now you want to try fire investigation?'

She shook her head fiercely. 'I want to be a firefighter, but they won't put me back on a pump, so here I am.'

He leaned towards her and smiled conspiratorially. 'If you get fed up with Des, I'd be more than happy to take you under my wing.' He winked. 'I know how difficult he can be.'

'Thanks,' said Vicky. 'I'll bear that in mind. Black, one sugar?'

'Thanks.'

'Hobnob?'

He laughed. 'Why not? But don't tell the Grouch, he thinks they're his personal property.'

Maguire went back to his office and Vicky made three coffees. She took Maguire's into his office with a couple of biscuits. Maguire's office was much tidier than Farmer's, but again there was nothing of a personal nature other than a gym bag on the floor by the door with a pair of running shoes on top. He thanked her and nodded at a row of reference books on a shelf by the door. 'I know Des isn't one for the manuals, but I've got some books there you might find useful. Feel free to borrow anything you want.'

'Thanks, guv,' said Vicky.

Maguire grinned. 'I'm not one for "guv" or "boss", just call me Danny.'

'Will do, Danny, thanks.' She went back and picked

up the coffees and biscuits and took them along to Farmer's office. She put them on his desk and he grunted in thanks. He gestured down the corridor with his thumb. 'Willie Campbell retired a while back and his old office is still empty, you can pitch your tent there. Two doors along.'

'And what do I do?'

'Log on to the system, have a look around. I've got some admin to take care of and we'll see what happens. We're busy most of the time.'

'Thanks.' Vicky left Farmer and went into the corridor. The office door still had WILLIAM CAMPBELL, FIRE INVESTIGATION in the slot to the left of the door. The door was closed so she knocked just in case but there was no answer and when she opened it the room was empty. It was pretty much identical to Farmer's office, a desk with a computer terminal on it and a high-backed chair behind it, a metal filing cabinet and a steel-framed chair. There were various rectangular areas on the walls where pictures had been hanging, and on the filing cabinet was a potted rubber plant with yellowing leaves.

She put her coffee mug on the desk and opened the filing cabinet drawers. They were empty, except for two dog-eared books of Sudoku puzzles, most of which had been completed. The desk drawers were empty and there was nothing but dust on the shelves. 'Home sweet home,' she said, then carried the rubber plant along to the tea room. She half-filled the sink with cold water and stood the plant in it. She heard a dog bark and she looked through the window to see Jamie encouraging Watson to play with his tennis ball. The dog was clearly having fun, its tail whipping from side to side like a metronome on speed.

Jamie took the ball from the dog and threw it across the yard. The dog ran after it, barking happily. Vicky smiled. Both Jamie and the dog seemed to enjoy their work. Watson brought his ball back to Jamie and was sitting in front of him, his tail twitching along the ground, his tongue lolling between his teeth. Jamie looked up and saw that she was watching and he smiled and waved. Vicky smiled and waved back, tilting her head so that her hair swung over the left side of her face.

16

Vicky had barely opened the front door when her mum called from the kitchen. 'Is that you, honey?'

'No, Mum, it's a serial killer, come to wreak havoc.' She closed the door behind her. It had taken her almost an hour to drive from Dowgate and she was exhausted.

'Now why do you always say that?' said Barbara, walking out of the kitchen and wiping her hands on a tea towel.

'Why do you always ask me if it's me? Who else has a key?'

'Mrs Evans next door, for a start.'

'Yes, but she'd ring first. I live here, Mum. Remember.'

'Of course I remember, honey. I'm not senile yet.'

'Is the kettle on? I'm parched.'

'Come on and sit down. You can tell me all about your day.'

Vicky followed her mum through into the kitchen and sat down at the table. She had been living with her for more than two years. Before that she'd lived with her boyfriend Tim in a rented flat in Kensal Green. His name had been on the lease and when they broke up she'd moved out and back in with her mum. It was the house that Vicky had grown up in, a three-bedroom semi in

Peckham, and she always felt comfortable there. Even before the accident she'd had no plans to move, and now she was grateful to have her mum close at hand.

There was a scratching sound coming from the back door and Vicky opened it. Their dog Baxter, an eight-year-old Labrador, bounded in, tail wagging. Vicky bent down and rubbed his chest and the dog woofed excitedly.

Barbara busied herself making tea as Vicky told her about her day – and about the Grouch.

'He sounds like he might be challenging,' said Barbara when Vicky had finished.

'He's just a bit rough around the edges. Old school. A dinosaur.'

'Your father was old school, but he always treated women well. He treated me like a queen and you like a princess.'

Vicky laughed. 'Dad was married to you. At work it's different. We want to be treated just like the men. That's the whole point of equality. We don't want special treatment.'

'Nonsense,' said Barbara brusquely. 'You want doors opened for you and you want a man to give up his seat on the Tube.'

Vicky laughed even louder. 'Mum, the days of men giving up their seats on the Tube are long gone.'

'You make it sound as if that's a good thing,' said Barbara, pouring tea into two cups.

'We have to be treated as equal. Otherwise there's no point.'

'You can be equal and still be treated with respect,' said Barbara. 'Would he be treating you so rudely if you were a man? I don't think so.' She added two spoons of sugar to Vicky's tea before giving it to her.

'I was forced on him. He's not happy about having to teach me.'

'He doesn't know what a quick learner you are,' she said. 'In a couple of months, you'll be running the show.'

'Thanks, Mum, but it doesn't work like that.' She sipped her tea. 'I don't like the way he talks to me, but back in his day women were treated as second-class citizens and they didn't want them on the pumps. Things have changed, but dinosaurs like Des are still around.'

'You could report him.'

'What for? He's not going to change, and if I go to Human Resources, I'd get branded as a troublemaker and end up in some back office somewhere.'

Barbara sighed. 'I wish you'd just leave and find something else to do. It's not as if you need the money.'

'It's what I want to do, Mum. I've been a firefighter for almost ten years, I don't want to do anything else.'

Barbara sighed again, but she was smiling. 'I know, honey. You're just like your dad.'

'The apple doesn't fall far from the tree.' She sipped her tea again. 'So what's for dinner?'

'I have some lovely sea bass. I was going to oven bake it with some ginger and lime. And garlic mashed potatoes. How does that sound?'

'Brilliant,' said Vicky. Barbara had retired as headmistress of a local primary school five years earlier and spent a lot of time watching TV cookery shows and replicating the recipes herself in her kitchen. She had always been a good cook but in retirement had started producing dishes that would do credit to a Michelin-starred restaurant. It was one of many reasons why Vicky was in no rush to leave home.

'And I've got something special for dessert.'

Vicky laughed. 'Mum, you're going to have to go easy on me. Fire investigation isn't as active as firefighting. If you keep overfeeding me I'll be as big as a house.'

'What a ridiculous thing to say,' said Barbara, opening the fridge. 'You need your strength.'

The fridge was an expensive Samsung; Vicky's father had insisted on buying it because it was one of the safest on the market. Like all firefighters, her father had been a stickler for fire safety measures at home. There were carbon dioxide detectors and a foam fire extinguisher in the kitchen, two fire blankets mounted on the wall by the cooker, and smoke detectors in the hallways upstairs and downstairs. When she was a child there had been a fire rehearsal every year, always on her birthday. After her father had passed away her mother had continued the tradition. They still did the fire rehearsal every year, more as a tribute to her father than a genuine need to go back over an escape route.

Vicky put down her cup and headed for the stairs. 'I'll shower first.'

'I could smell smoke on you.'

'The guv took me to a couple of fires.'

Barbara's eyes widened. 'He what?'

'They were out, Mum. That's what we do. We visit the aftermath of fires and try to work out what caused them.' She could see the concern in her mum's eyes so she went over and gave her a hug. 'I'm not putting out fires.'

'Yet,' said Barbara.

'It's practically an office job,' said Vicky. 'So don't go overboard on the mashed potatoes. This job is nowhere near as physical as what I used to do.' She kissed her on the cheek and went upstairs.

She stripped off her jacket and trousers in her bedroom, then stood in front of the mirror. When she had first left the hospital, she had avoided looking at herself and had hung a scarf over all the mirrors in the house. But after a few weeks she had realised that the only way to deal with the scars was to confront them head on, and now she checked herself in the mirror every day.

Vicky pulled back her hair, turned her head and examined her scarred cheek in the mirror. Dr Adams had explained that the wounds had healed and the scars were there to stay. Hypertrophic burn scars, they were called, a vivid purple and raised above the normal level of the skin. They were caused by full thickness burns, the most serious type, where the skin had been burned right through. Dr Adams had explained how the fire had damaged the dermal layer and it was that damage that produced the scars. When healthy skin repaired itself, the cells produced collagen, which was laid down to produce new tissue. But when the dermal cells were damaged the collagen got thrown together in a haphazard fashion giving the scars a completely different texture and appearance. Vicky reached up with her right hand and ran her fingertips across her cheek. It felt like plastic.

Dr Adams said that the scars would settle down over the next eighteen months or so, that they would fade in colour and became flatter and softer and more like her regular skin. But they would always be there, and they would always be noticeable. He wanted to wait at least a year before suggesting skin grafts. Until then she was going to have to learn to live with the irritation and the attention.

The fire had destroyed most of the oil glands in her

skin that usually prevented the skin from getting too dry. That meant she was constantly having to moisturise the scar tissue with a high-water-content moisturiser that Dr Adams had given her. She had to avoid the sun, too. Immature scars burned easily, so she needed to apply a factor 50 sunscreen every couple of hours when she was outside.

She took off the glove on her left hand and removed the silicone gel sheets that she wore as extra protection. The gel sheet reduced the itching and dryness and Dr Adams said they would improve the rate of healing. There were half a dozen small blisters across the back of her hand but there were no fresh wounds or bleeding. The scar tissue was fragile and easily damaged and the slightest touch would make the skin blister. It was less of an issue on her face and neck, but her hand was a constant source of problems. If she knocked or banged it there would often be lesions, and even when she was careful there were almost always blisters.

The blistering and tearing would lessen with time, Dr Adams had promised, but the scarring would always be visible. They could try skin grafts but again, they would never be a perfect match to the original.

Vicky picked up a bottle of TCP, took off the cap, and dipped in a needle before piercing them one by one and dabbing them with sterile gauze. She then smeared a little antibiotic ointment on each one. It was something she had to do several times a day and had done it so often that she now performed the task on autopilot. If the blisters were really bad she would cover them with a non-stick dressing but generally it was just a matter of popping them before they got too large.

Just as she was finishing, Barbara called up from the kitchen. 'I'm just putting the sea bass in the oven now, honey. Don't be long. And I've a lovely bottle of Chardonnay to go with it.' Vicky smiled at her reflection. There were definitely benefits in being close to thirty years old and living at home with her mum.

17

Weekends were always the best time to go trawling for victims. People worked during the week and often stayed in at night. Weekends were the time for shopping and eating out, for going to the cinema and clubs. But that didn't mean that the perfect victim wouldn't present herself midweek.

It was his day off and he'd been walking around aimlessly, just passing the time. He went to Oxford Street and down Regent Street. They weren't great places for spotting victims because there were so many tourists around and there was no way he could ever get away with rape, murder and arson in a hotel. He needed locals, local women who ideally lived alone. But he enjoyed the feeling of being a predator on the prowl, of knowing that everyone he saw, every young woman at least, was a potential victim.

Mobile phones had made being a predator so much easier. When people went out on their own they usually held their phones and more often not they would be looking at them rather than at their surroundings. Young women seemed to be the most attached to their mobiles, often texting or scanning their Facebook pages as they walked through the crowded streets. That was what she was doing when he spotted her. Blond-haired, pale white skin that contrasted with her bright red lipstick. She had her head down and was smiling as she looked at the screen of her smartphone. She was wearing a blue jacket over a white dress that was short enough to make the best of her long, lithe legs. Her dress was open at the top revealing a thin gold chain and a nice cleavage. Lovely, he noticed. Almost certainly 32B.

He spotted her in Regent Street and followed her to Carnaby Street. She spent an hour going in and out of various boutiques and not once did she even look in his direction. The moment she stepped out into the street she was glued to her phone. She bought a pair of jeans in Diesel and some make-up from Urban Decay and a coffee from Starbucks and then she walked back to Oxford Street and spent half an hour walking around Top Shop but didn't buy anything there. She dropped her Starbucks cup in a bin and went down Oxford Street Tube station, taking the escalator down to the Bakerloo line. He waited on the platform so close to her that he could smell her perfume. Miss Dior, almost certainly. When the train arrived she got on first and sat to the left, he went right. She spent the whole journey to Charing Cross station looking at her phone. That's where she got off and transferred to a southbound train on the Northern line. He didn't sit in the same carriage this time but stood in the one next to it, making sure he had a good view of her. She got off at Clapham Common station. All the way up the escalator she was staring at her phone.

He followed her through the ticket barrier and out on to the street. She nearly bumped into an old lady with a walking stick and mumbled an apology without looking up. She appeared to be walking on autopilot, holding her carrier bags in her left hand and her phone in her right. He was sure he could have walked next to her and she wouldn't have noticed but he held back.

Most people looked up from their phones when they reached their destination so he didn't want to be too close. The other side of the road was usually best, and as she turned into a street of small terraced houses he crossed over and kept pace with her. She stopped outside a house, put her phone in her mouth and fished a set of keys from her handbag.

She let herself in and closed the door behind her. He made a note of the number and the name of the road in his phone, then walked away. Terraced houses were always difficult. With a detached or a semi-detached house it was usually easy to get access to the rear of the house. Getting access to the back of terraces was problematical. He'd have to do something more creative if he was going to get into her house. Ideally, he'd get her to invite him in. He smiled to himself. It wouldn't be a hardship. Far from it. Getting up close and personal to the victim before he struck always made the kill that much more exciting. But he was getting ahead of himself. Maybe she lived with her parents. Maybe she had a husband or a live-in boyfriend. Or rented a room. He had to check and check again, to make sure she was a suitable victim. Preparation was the key to a successful kill. Preparation and patience.

18

Vicky woke to the sound of her mobile ringing and she groped for it. It was six thirty in the morning and it was Des Farmer calling. 'Yes, guv,' she said, trying not to sound as tired as she felt. Baxter shifted on the bed next to her.

'Sweetheart, I'm going to need a lift this morning. My car was playing up last night and I now can't get it started.'

Vicky sat up and ran a hand through her hair. 'No problem. What's the address?'

'Good girl. I'll text it to you.'

The line went dead and Vicky glared at the phone. 'Do you have to be so bloody sexist all the time?' she muttered. Baxter turned to watch her go but made no move to get off the bed.

Vicky padded across the carpet and down the hall to the bathroom. While she showered Farmer sent her an SMS with his address. She pulled on her LFB shirt and trousers, then carefully placed a gel sheet over the back of her left hand before pulling on a black cotton glove.

Barbara was already in the kitchen when Vicky went downstairs. 'Tea and toast?'

There was already bread in the toaster and the kettle

was boiling. Baxter woofed at the back door and Vicky let him out into the garden.

'I can't, Mum. The guv wants me to pick him up.'

'So he's treating you like a chauffeur, is he? You need to put a stop to that.'

Vicky grinned. Barbara was always the first to run to her defence. Always was and probably always would be.

'It's more important to keep him sweet.' She kissed her on the cheek. 'See you tonight.'

Vicky went through the connecting door that led to the garage and disconnected the i8 from its charging point. She climbed in and ran her hands around the steering wheel. She really did love being in the car, though she never drove above the speed limit or took the vehicle to anywhere near its full potential. She pressed the remote to open the garage door and then she pressed the starter before programming Farmer's address into the satnav.

19

Farmer lived in Bethnal Green in a quiet tree-lined road. Vicky parked and walked along to his house. It was semi-detached with a small paved area separated from the pavement by a low brick wall. There were two doorbells marked FLAT 1 and FLAT 2 and she realised the house had been subdivided and she didn't know which flat her boss lived in. She pulled out her phone and called his number. 'I'm outside, guv.'

'I'll be right down.'

A couple of minutes later the front door opened. Farmer was wearing a green parka over his uniform. He grunted at her and walked towards the car, swinging a battered brown leather briefcase.

'You're welcome,' she said quietly enough that he wouldn't hear her. She caught up with him as he was climbing into the front passenger seat.

'What's the postcode?' she asked as she slid behind the wheel.

Farmer frowned. 'Postcode?'

'So I can set the satnav.'

'You don't need the postcode, sweetheart. Just drive to Soho. I'll show you where it is.' He sighed and shook his head. 'How did people manage before satnav?'

'People got lost a lot. And kept asking for directions.'

'Satnav turns you into an idiot,' said Farmer putting his briefcase under his legs. 'Once you rely on it you stop being aware of your surroundings.' He pointed ahead. 'Just drive to Soho. We'll be fine.'

'We don't need the van?'

'This is off the books,' he said gruffly as he settled back in his seat and folded his arms. Vicky pulled away from the kerb and concentrated on driving. It was rush hour and the roads were busy.

Farmer kept sniffing as if he had the start of a cold.

'You okay?' she asked eventually. There was a cyclist in her blind spot so she kept having to move her head from side to side to keep him in view.

'What's that perfume?' he asked gruffly.

Vicky frowned. 'Perfume?'

'Your perfume. Chanel, right?'

'Coco Mademoiselle, yes.'

He sniffed again, louder this time.

She looked across at him. 'Something wrong?'

He avoided her stare, but nodded. 'There is, yeah. I'd prefer you didn't wear it. You'd be better off au naturel. Pardon my French.'

'What?'

He shrugged but didn't say anything.

'Guv?'

He looked away from her, out of the side window. 'It's just not a good idea, you wearing perfume.'

A bus stopped in front of the BMW so Vicky braked. The cyclist whizzed by, his bag clipping her wing mirror. 'Arsehole!' she shouted, even though she knew he couldn't hear her. She looked across at Farmer. 'Not you, obviously.'

'I should hope not,' he said.

They rode in silence for a while. Farmer continued to sniff until Vicky couldn't take it any more. 'Just what is your problem with my wearing perfume?' she snapped. She gestured at her scarred cheek. 'A face like this and I shouldn't wear perfume, is that it? With the greatest of respect, guv, you can go fuck yourself.'

The bus braked in front of her again and she cursed and put both hands on the wheel. She stopped inches from the bus and pounded on her horn. 'Fucking moron!' she screamed. 'Did you see that?'

Farmer shrugged. 'You should have kept your eyes on the road,' he said quietly.

'What is your problem?' she said, glaring at him.

A car beeped its horn behind them and Farmer pointed ahead. She grunted and edged the car forward. She drove in silence, silently fuming.

'Most fires are accidental,' Farmer said eventually, his voice a dull monotone. 'But some aren't. Some are deliberate. Accelerants are used. Petrol. Lighter fluid. Oil. Accelerants have an odour, most of them. Even after a fire you can often smell them. So your sense of smell is important. Wearing perfume is going to blunt it.'

Vicky nodded. 'Okay,' she said quietly.

'Plus, if you're with me at a fire scene, I need my sense of smell. What I don't need is Coco Mademoiselle clogging up my nostrils.'

'I get it. No more perfume.'

'So no need to bite my head off, then?'

'Sorry.'

'No problem.' He pointed at the dashboard. 'Does this have a radio?'

'Sure. What do you want to listen to?'

'Radio Five,' he said. 'Let's find out what's going on in the world.'

Vicky found her way to Soho without a problem and Farmer gave her curt directions to a street lined with restaurants. Just as they arrived a delivery van pulled out and Vicky nipped into the parking space. 'What's the story?' asked Vicky as they climbed out of the BMW. 'Why aren't we using the van?'

'Favour for a friend, sort of,' said Farmer.

'Sort-of favour or sort-of friend?'

'Bit of both,' said Farmer. 'There was a fire here last week, and the insurance company has asked a guy I know to do his own investigation. He wants a chat.' He nodded at a blackened storefront festooned with police tape and with sheets of plywood nailed across the windows. The front door was battered but intact, and a thick metal hasp had been fitted so that it could be secured. The hasp was unlocked and the door was ajar.

Farmer handed Vicky Tyvek overshoes and green nitrile gloves. She put on the overshoes and two pairs of gloves and followed him inside. She wrinkled her nose at the acrid burnt smell as she looked around. Fire flashed into her mind, flickering flames and heat and smoke, and she gasped. She took a step to the side so that Farmer wouldn't see her discomfort and she took slow deep breaths to calm herself down. The vision went as quickly as it had appeared, though her heart was still racing.

'Paddy!' shouted Farmer. 'You've got visitors!'

The door opened into the main dining room. The once-carpeted floor was burned and the drapes on the windows had been destroyed. Metal frames that had once been chairs were stacked against one wall and there was a stack of fire-damaged tables near the window. Everything was streaked with soot and there was a thick layer of sludge covering the floor. There were sooty cobwebs all over the ceiling. Usually near invisible, once coated with soot they became clearly visible, showing just how many spiders called the restaurant home.

There had once been double doors that led to the kitchen but they were badly burnt and had been ripped from their hinges, probably by the firefighters. A man in his forties wearing a white hard hat and a bright yellow fluorescent jacket and waterproof trousers walked out, holding a metal briefcase. Like Farmer and Vicky he had blue protective covers over his work boots. 'Des,' he said. 'How the hell are you?'

He had a northern Irish accent, Vicky realised. He was tall, well over six feet, thin and wiry and had a thick black moustache.

Farmer shook hands with the man and then turned to introduce him to Vicky. 'Vicky, meet Paddy. You wouldn't know to look at him but he used to be a bloody good firefighter and I've heard tell he was a decent enough fire investigator. He cut his teeth in Belfast, but decided he'd had enough of terrorist bombings and arson attacks so he went private and moved over the water.'

'Paddy O'Neill,' said the man, holding out his hand. 'Well, it's Patrick, but there's bugger all chance of them calling me that.' There was the merest flicker of unease in his eyes when he saw the damage to the left side of Vicky's face but he shook her hand firmly and smiled at her.

'Paddy works for all the big insurance companies,' said

Farmer. 'It's his job to find a reason for them not to pay out.'

'I do exactly the same job as you, Des. We're both trying to find out how the fire started.'

'Yes, but I'm not doing it to save my client money.'

O'Neill sighed. 'It's always a pleasure working with you, Des,' he said, his voice loaded with sarcasm.

'Hey, let's not forget I'm the one doing you a favour by agreeing to see you,' said Farmer.

'You might take the view that I'm helping put you straight on the cause of this fire,' said O'Neill. 'You've said it was an accident so of course the cops have agreed with you. But I'm pretty sure it was deliberately set.'

Farmer raised his eyebrows. 'So now you're saying I'm not doing my job properly?'

'When have I ever suggested that you've been anything other than the consummate professional?' said O'Neill. He grinned over at Vicky. 'You know they call him the Grouch, right? Because of his sunny disposition.'

Farmer looked pointedly at his watch. 'Paddy, I've got work to do, you know. Real work.'

O'Neill held up his gloved hands. 'Okay, fine. Let's get into it. There's a couple of things you don't know about this case that I need to highlight. The big red flag is that less than a year ago, the owners almost doubled their insurance coverage. And that at a time when business was slumping. The restaurant was set up three years ago. The one that was here prior to that lasted two years. The one before that went out of business in eighteen months.'

'Bad feng shui?" asked Farmer.

'There's a lot of competition here,' said O'Neill, ignoring Farmer's sarcasm. 'With a lot of very good restaurants in the area you really need something extra to succeed.'

'Or appeal to the gay market,' said Farmer. He shrugged at the look of disdain that flashed across O'Neill's face. 'I'm just telling it like it is, Paddy. Big gay area, the bars and restaurants that go after the pink pound tend to do better than those that don't. But you're not telling me anything I don't know. One of the owners showed me the books.'

'And the insurance policy?'

'They were underinsured. The original policy was taken out before they did the refit.'

'And you believe that?'

'It's reasonable,' said Farmer.

'His business was going down the toilet, he ups his insurance, the place burns down. That doesn't strike you as suspicious?'

'Circumstantial rather than suspicious. You know the situation, right? It's a group of investors and they own four restaurants. Two are doing well, one is breaking even, and this one was going downhill. But overall the group is in profit.'

'They'll be showing a much bigger profit if they get the payout on this place,' said O'Neill.

'Again, circumstantial,' said Farmer. 'The fire itself looks accidental. Well, I say accidental, the fact that the chef was an idiot didn't help, but I don't think you can refuse to pay on the grounds of stupidity, can you? It would revolutionise the motor insurance industry if you could.'

'That's what I wanted to talk through with you,' said O'Neill. He gestured towards the kitchen. 'Through here, yeah?'

'Lead on, McDuff,' said Farmer with a theatrical wave.

'You said O'Neill,' said Vicky.

Farmer sighed. 'It's Shakespeare. *Macbeth.*'

'Actually it's a misquotation,' said O'Neill. 'What Shakespeare wrote is "Lay on, MacDuff", which means attack vigorously. Act five, scene eight.'

'No one likes a smart-arse, Paddy,' said Farmer.

'Isn't that the truth,' said O'Neill. He took them through the damaged double doors to the kitchen. There was a preparation area to the right, and a large metal refrigerator door set into the wall. The stoves were to the left, three of them against the wall. Most of the shelving on the walls was fire-damaged. If anything, there were even more sooty cobwebs than there had been in the dining room.

O'Neill motioned for them to come into the middle of the kitchen. 'There's no doubt that the fire started in here,' he said. 'Because the kitchen is at the back and the back isn't overlooked. By the time someone called three nines it had spread to the dining area.'

Vicky looked up at the smoke detector in the ceiling. 'Didn't the alarm go off?'

'It did, but it's a standalone and no one reported it,' said O'Neill. 'It was when the fire was at the front that the brigade was called. They were here within minutes, but by then it had taken hold. That was another red flag. The call was received at just after four o'clock in the morning, and that's another signal that there's something not right.'

'Because?' asked Vicky.

'Most fires are set in the early hours,' said O'Neill. 'Fewer witnesses, fewer people around to phone it in.'

'Again, circumstantial,' said Farmer, folding his arms.

'Fine,' said O'Neill. 'But this isn't.' He went over to the row of ovens and stood by the side of the one closest to the doors. There was a misshapen lump of ash-covered plastic that had once been a rubbish bin. On the wall behind it was a black V-shaped wedge of scorching on the wall. 'We have a fire seat here, obviously. The fire started in the bin, spread to the grease on the ovens and then up to the ceiling.' He pointed at a fire-damaged extractor fan on the wall. 'All the plastic here burned, but clearly it started in the bin and moved up.'

'Sounds good to me,' said Farmer. 'Exactly as I said in my report.'

O'Neill walked away from the stoves to a line of food preparation tables with metal shelving on one side and storage cupboards underneath. All were covered in ash and debris that had fallen down from the ceiling. O'Neill went over to the wall at the end and pointed to another V-shaped charring pattern on the wall. 'And here is a second seat. There was another fire source here, twenty feet away from the rubbish bin. Now in my book, that's fire-starting one oh one.'

'What does that mean, anyway?' asked Farmer. 'One oh one?'

'It's what they call their introductory courses in America,' said O'Neill.

'Yeah, well, the last time I looked we weren't in America, Paddy. Try to speak English.'

'What are you now, the grammar police? You know what I'm saying. We've got two seats for this fire. One by the rubbish bin. Another seat is twenty feet away at the far end of the kitchen. Both show typical V-shape charring. Two seats, that means the fire was set.'

'Not necessarily. That rule isn't carved in stone.'

'So do you want to explain to me how the fire moved from there . . .' O'Neill nodded at the remains of the rubbish bin. 'To there.' He pointed to the fire-damaged wall at the end of the long steel counter.

'I can give it a go,' said Farmer. 'Though I suppose I'll have to speak slowly so that you can follow my logic.' He indicated the remains of the rubbish bin. 'The fire started there. The chef was pretty lazy, according to the owner. They were thinking of getting rid of him. The fridges were in a mess, he'd let the cleaning slip, his staff had lost respect for him. It's a chicken-and-egg thing, I guess. The restaurant was doing badly so he let standards slide. Or he got lazy and they started losing customers. Either way there was grease everywhere, the hoods were filthy, it was a firetrap. All it needed was an ignition source.' He pointed at the remains of the plastic bin. 'The rubbish was supposed to be emptied every night, but if it wasn't full it was left. There was food in there, but that's also where he threw his dirty rags and paper towels. The bin was next to the stove so it would have been hot all the time.'

'So you're saying spontaneous combustion?'

'It happens all the time. Oil- and grease-soaked towels, paper or cloth, if they get hot enough can start to smoulder. They can smoulder away for hours and then if there's enough air you get combustion. And a plastic bin is going to burn quickly.'

'Or someone could have dropped in a match,' said O'Neill. 'But that doesn't explain how the fire jumped across the kitchen.'

'Flameover,' said Farmer. 'It would have got very hot, what with the plastic bin and all the grease over the stove. The hot gases rise and move across the ceiling.' He turned to look at Vicky. 'You know the difference between flame-over and flashover?'

'Sure,' said Vicky. Farmer smiled expectantly and she continued. 'Flameover is when the flames literally roll across the ceiling. There isn't enough oxygen around the fire so it moves up to the ceiling in search of more. That gives you incomplete combustion so you don't get flash-over. Flameover can lead to flashover, but not always.'

'And flashover is . . .?'

'The transition between a fire that is growing, to the point where all the combustible contents of a room ignite at the same time.'

'And how long does it take between ignition and flash-over?'

'It's variable,' said Vicky. 'It's sometimes said that flash-over occurs four minutes after a fire breaks out but research has shown that flashover depends on a host of factors, but mainly on the type of combustibles, the size of the room, and the type of ventilation. In a well-ventilated room, you shouldn't get flashover at all.'

'And at what temperature does flashover occur?'

'Six hundred degrees centigrade.'

Farmer grinned at O'Neill. 'She's read the manual. Back to front.'

'Yeah, well, it's not all about the manual, is it?' said O'Neill. 'No one's saying there was a flashover. What I'm saying is there were two seats to this fire which means it was deliberately set.'

'And that's where we disagree, Paddy.'

'That there are two seats? You can see them for your-self.' He pointed at the charring around the rubbish bin. 'One,' he said. Then he pointed at the far wall, which showed a similar V-shaped charring. 'Two.'

Farmer walked over to the wall. There had been three wooden shelves on the wall but they had been destroyed by the fire. There were ashes and charred chunks on the floor, along with pots and pans that had been damaged by the fire. To the side was a stainless-steel workspace covered in a thick layer of ash, and behind two metal racks.

'You know what this station was?'

'Salads,' said O'Neill. 'And cold side dishes.'

'And the fire appears to start under the shelving here?'

'There was an upturned plastic bucket there,' said O'Neill. 'The chef used to sit down on it during quiet periods.'

'And you think that someone set light to the bucket?'

'You don't?'

'I think that the fire started in the bin. Spontaneous combustion of oil- and grease-soaked rags. It burns, it rolls over, and the fire spreads across the ceiling here.'

'Yes, well the last time I checked, salads weren't inflammable,' said O'Neill.

'Then you don't know what the chef's special is. Bacon, Gorgonzola and pear salad with a brandy vinaigrette.'

'Brandy?'

Farmer grinned. 'Brandy.'

'But wouldn't the brandy be stored with the oils in the back room?'

'He used to put the bottle in the storage room overnight but once the chef started to let standards slip, he didn't bother.'

'And you know that how?'

'I interviewed him. I interviewed everyone who worked in the kitchen.'

O'Neill looked at the remains of the bin, then the ceiling, then the wall. He nodded slowly. 'So the fire rolls over the ceiling, heats up the wall, the bottle breaks and the brandy drips down to the floor. The brandy ignites the plastic bucket and we have a second source of fire. Shit.' He pointed at the pile of ash and burnt shelving on the floor. 'You found glass in there?'

Farmer nodded.

O'Neill walked up to the wall, squatted down and ran a hand through the muddy ash. His probing fingers found a shard of glass and he picked it up. 'Shit,' he said again.

'Satisfied?' asked Farmer. 'If I'd known you were misreading the scene I'd have sent you a copy of my report.'

O'Neill dropped the shard of glass on to the ash and stood up. He forced a smile. 'Like I said, it's always a pleasure doing business with you, Des.'

'Glad to be of service,' said Farmer.

The two men walked outside. Farmer took off his gloves and overshoes, then fished out his tobacco pack, opened it and popped a pre-rolled cigarette between his lips. He lit it as O'Neill locked the door to the restaurant, then walked over to Vicky's car.

O'Neill's jaw dropped when he saw Farmer standing next to the BMW. 'What the hell is that?' he asked.

'A BMW i8,' said Farmer. 'It's a hybrid.'

'Yeah, I know what it is,' said O'Neill, walking around it. 'This is yours?'

'Thought I'd treat myself,' said Farmer, patting the roof as if it was a favoured pet.

'How the fuck did you afford a car like this?' asked O'Neill.

Farmer shrugged. 'The pay's better than it was,' he said. 'The brigade has realised the value of its investigators.'

'Do you still want me to drive?' asked Vicky.

Farmer looked over at her and caught the twinkle in her eyes. 'Yes, sweetheart,' he said. 'But go easy on the accelerator, you were over-revving it on the way here.'

'Sorry, guv,' said Vicky, opening the door and climbing into the driver's seat. Farmer took a last pull on his roll-up and then ground it out with his shoe. He climbed in and pulled the door shut, then waved a cheery goodbye to O'Neill as Vicky drove off.

20

Vicky drove Farmer back to Dowgate and parked. 'Get me a coffee, will you, sweetheart,' he said as they headed up the stairs. 'I'm parched.'

'Yes sir, no sir, three bags full, sir,' Vicky muttered under her breath as Farmer disappeared into his office. She was getting fed up with being treated as the office junior, though deep down she knew that was exactly what she was. She had been shoehorned into the job with next to no training or experience, and until she could carry her weight she really didn't have any choice other than to suck it up.

She dropped her tunic and helmet in her office and headed for the tea room. She was waiting for the kettle to boil when Farmer popped his head around the door. 'Change of plan,' he said. 'There's a fire in Brixton we need to check out. See you downstairs in five.'

'Right,' said Vicky. Farmer disappeared back into his office. She grabbed her tunic and helmet and went downstairs to the van. She had the engine running by the time Farmer appeared in his uniform. He climbed in and put his helmet on his lap.

The van was equipped with sirens and lights but there was no emergency and it took just over forty-five minutes to get to Brixton.

'So I read that more than a quarter of all fires are deliberately set,' said Vicky as she drove across the river.

'That's about right,' he said. 'But that figure is skewed by the small fires set by kids and the fact that half of car fires are insurance jobs. But yes, overall it's about one in four. But the one we're on the way to see is a restaurant, and despite what the insurance companies think, restaurant owners aren't queuing up to set fire to their own businesses.'

'It happens, though.'

'Sure. But it's a big step to take, setting fire to a business. It's against the law; people might get hurt. Plus, if there's a reason for torching your business then the cops are going to be all over you. It's like murder. Almost all murders are committed by someone the victim knows. And it's usually a family member. So when a murder happens, the first thing the cops do is look at friends and family. It's the same with a fire in a restaurant. If it does look like it was deliberately set then they look at the owner. And the competition. So if you're an owner and you know that, you'd be pretty stupid to set fire to your business.'

'Or desperate?'

Farmer pulled a face. 'I'm not saying it doesn't happen, but it's rare. It tends to happen more in the States. Maybe one in ten restaurant fires are deliberate. Here's it's maybe one in a hundred. And if a guy is stupid enough to set fire to his own business, he's probably going to be stupid enough to do it in a way that he gets caught.'

'What about professionals?'

'Professionals?"

'You know. Pay someone to do it.'

'It happens,' said Farmer. 'But for every professional there are a thousand enthusiastic amateurs. Thankfully, most of the amateurs are stupid so they get caught sooner rather than later.'

Farmer settled back in his seat. 'Thing is, restaurants are fire traps, just because of the nature of what they do. You've got people packed into rooms full of combustibles, and you have chefs cooking with oil and fat over naked flames. Cooking is the number one cause of fires in restaurants and in forty per cent of cases it's the food that flames first. A chef takes his eyes off the stove, something catches fire and they don't deal with it properly. It happens all the time.'

They arrived at Brixton and Farmer gave her directions to the restaurant. 'You really don't like satnavs,' she said.

'They make your brain lazy,' he said. 'You concentrate on the screen and not your surroundings and that means you miss things.'

'Don't you get lost, though?'

'Sure. But not for long. And each wrong turn you make teaches you something.' He pointed ahead. 'Park there, on the left.' There was a parking space at the side of the road and Vicky reversed in. She twisted around in her seat and looked at the equipment in the back. 'What do we need?' she asked.

'Gloves and boot covers,' he said. 'We'll have a look around first, see what there is to see.' He went around to the back of the van and pulled it open. Vicky joined him on the pavement. He handed her shoe covers and gloves. 'And we'll need the camera, too,' he said. He pulled open the side door of the van and took a small digital camera from a plastic drawer. He showed her how to operate it and then gave it to her. 'You need to photo-graph everything,' he said. 'Start with the outside and anything we see inside. General shots, specific shots, just keep shooting. More is always better. That way in the unlikely event that we miss anything we have the pictures to fall back on.'

The restaurant was in the middle of a line of shops including a dry-cleaners, an off-licence and a pound shop. The brickwork was stained with soot and the windows were broken. The door was open and the frame splintered as if it had been kicked in. There were two floors of what appeared to be apartments above the shops. Vicky saw that most of the brickwork above the restaurant was coated in soot, which suggested the fire had spread up rather than down. As she photographed the brickwork, Farmer went over to the door and knocked on it. 'Hello? Is there anyone there?'

Vicky went to join him. The acrid smell of burnt wood and plastic assailed her nostrils and she wrinkled her nose. The floor was awash with a thick black sludge.

'We're not open!' shouted a man from inside.

'We're coming in,' said Farmer.

'Hey man, I told you, we're not open!' A large black man walked out of the gloom. He was wearing a yellow, green and gold knitted cap over long dreadlocks, a multi-coloured tie-dyed shirt and baggy combat trousers. 'We're gonna be shut for a while.'

'Are you the owner?' asked Farmer.

'Who wants to know?'

'We're with the fire investigation unit,' said Farmer.

'The police have already been,' said the man.

'We're with the Fire Brigade,' said Farmer. 'We visit

every unusual fire to see what happened. Hopefully we can stop it happening to anyone else.'

The man's eyes narrowed. 'Nah, man, you think I torched my own place, don't you? That's what the cops seem to think.'

'Did you?' asked Farmer.

'Hell no,' said the man. 'This is my livelihood. This place burns and I got nothing.'

'But you've got insurance, right?'

Vicky was clicking away with the camera, starting at the corners and covering every inch of the floor and ceiling.

'Some,' said the man. 'But this place was always busy. Every day I'm shut I lose money.'

'There you go then,' said Farmer. 'So you are the owner?'

The man nodded. 'Moses Miller.' He grinned showing a gold tooth at the front of his mouth. 'They call me M&M.'

'I'm Des Farmer.' He gestured at Vicky. 'This is Miss Lewis.'

Moses grinned at Vicky but his smile hardened when she lowered the camera and he saw the scars on her left cheek. 'Hey, baby, what happened to you?'

'I got burned,' said Vicky.

Moses nodded. 'That must have hurt like hell, baby.'

'It did,' said Vicky. She tilted her head so that her hair fell across her ear and started photographing the fire damage again.

'So this is what, an Ital restaurant?' said Farmer, looking around.

Vicky turned to look at him. 'Guv, it's clearly not an Italian restaurant,' she said.

'Not Italian,' said Farmer. 'Ital. Comes from the word Vital, if you must know. It's a Rastafarian way of cooking. No salt, no meat, no preservatives, no colourings, no artificial flavourings. It's as natural a way of cooking as you can get.'

Moses was staring at Farmer in astonishment. 'You know your Ital,' he said.

'I get around,' said Farmer. 'What's your signature dish?'

'I'm famous for my curried lima beans,' he said.

'I bet you are.'

'Lots of turmeric, coriander and cumin, plus my own special curry powder,' said Moses proudly. 'Ain't nothing like it outside of Jamaica.'

'I'm a big fan of curried lima beans,' said Farmer.

'Get out of here,' said Moses. 'So how do you know so much about Ital food?'

Farmer grimaced. 'My second wife was Jamaican.'

'Get out of here!' said Moses, louder this time.

'It's true. She came over as a nurse in the nineties. She was a great cook. I was married to her for three years and I put on twenty pounds.'

Moses laughed. 'Yeah, man, rice and beans will do that.'

'I miss her jerk chicken more than anything,' said Farmer. 'It was her grandmother's recipe and she never told me what was in it.'

'Did she do it in the oven or original style, roasted on coals and pimento wood?'

'If the weather was good, yes, she'd do it on the barbecue in the garden.'

Moses laughed and slapped his thigh. 'There'll be

pimento, scallion, thyme and onions in the sauce,' said Moses. 'But it's Scotch bonnet that makes it special.'

Vicky frowned. 'Scotch bonnet?'

Moses grinned and tapped the side of his nose. 'Yeah, that'll be the secret ingredient,' he said. 'It's a Caribbean chilli pepper, shaped like those hats that Scotsmen wear.'

'Tam-o'-shanters?' said Vicky.

'That's right,' said Moses. 'Scotty bons, or bonny peppers they call them. Nothing else tastes like a Scotch bonnet. That's what she'll have used.'

'So I'm guessing you're also the cook?' said Farmer.

'You got that right,' said Moses. 'They're all my recipes, too.'

'And you were working last night?'

'Every night,' said Moses.

'Do you sleep above the shop?'

Moses shook his head. 'I live a couple of miles away. I got the call to say the restaurant was on fire about two o'clock in the morning.'

'Not too much fire damage,' said Farmer, looking around the restaurant.

'It's mainly in the kitchen,' said Moses. 'The firemen did most of it with their water,' said Moses.

'They had to move fast,' said Vicky. 'They couldn't risk it spreading to the flats upstairs.'

'But even when the fire was out, they kept going back in to spray more water.'

'They have to,' said Vicky. 'It's called dampening. If they don't keep everything wet, the fire can start up again.'

Farmer pointed at double doors at the far end of the restaurant. 'That's the kitchen?'

'What's left of it,' said Moses. He took them across the

muddied floor and pushed the doors open. The burnt smell was much stronger and the stains on the wall were much darker. The kitchen was in darkness.

'Electricity's off,' said Moses.

Farmer nodded at Vicky. 'Grab a couple of torches from the van,' he said. Vicky hurried outside. 'And the portable LED lights. Let the dog see the rabbit.'

Vicky headed out to the van.

'She your assistant?' asked Moses.

'For the moment.'

'That burn is something.'

'Yeah.'

'She a fireman?'

'A firefighter? She was, yes. Dragged a guy out of a burning building. Saved his life.'

'I didn't know they had women firemen.'

'Yeah. They do.'

Moses shook his head. 'No job for a woman, that.'

Farmer smiled thinly. 'You're preaching to the converted there, Moses.'

Vicky returned with torches and handed one to Farmer. She was carrying a rack of LED lights and she assembled them. They operated on their own batteries and she switched them on so that the kitchen was illuminated with a bright, clinical white light. It was about ten feet wide and fifteen feet long with two stoves to the left and storage cupboards and a fridge-freezer to the right. Vicky clicked away with the digital camera.

'How many staff do you usually have in the kitchen?' asked Farmer as he looked around the room. Most of the fire damage seemed to be in the far corner where there was a metal rubbish bin.

'Three cooking,' said Moses.

'Including you?'

'I'm head chef.'

'Waiting staff?'

'Two girls.'

'So a staff of five?'

'We have a busboy to clean.'

Farmer looked around, then went over to the two large metal hoods over the stoves. He shone his torch inside them. 'How often do you clean these?'

'Every night,' said Moses.

'I mean inside.'

'Inside?' Moses frowned.

'Yeah, they need to be steam-cleaned on a regular basis. They get coated in grease over time. Sometimes cooking alone can set them alight. From the look of the burn patterns on the wall, they caught fire last night.'

'But no one was cooking,' said Moses. 'The place was empty last night.'

Farmer nodded. 'The hoods didn't cause the fire, but they helped the spread. So where do your staff smoke?'

'Outside. There's a yard where we keep our rubbish.' He frowned again. 'You think one of my staff caused the fire?'

Farmer grinned. 'Let's see what my young assistant thinks. Vicky, over here.'

Vicky stopped photographing and joined them.

'Right, let's put your investigative skills to the test.' He grinned at Moses. 'She's read all the manuals. Back to front.'

'Does that help?' asked Moses.

'Apparently,' said Farmer. He nodded at Vicky. 'Right,

you've been snapping away but have you been using your eyes and ears?'

'I think so, guv.'

'What do you think caused this fire?'

Vicky smiled at Moses. 'It was raining last night, wasn't it?' she asked.

'It had stopped by the time we closed up.'

'Sure, but I'm guessing your staff don't smoke in the rain,' said Vicky. 'So when it rains, where do they smoke?'

'They open the back door and stand there.'

'So they smoke in the kitchen?'

Moses nodded. 'They're not supposed to. But, yeah.'

Vicky tried the door. It was burnt but locked. She looked at the metal bin. It was on its side and he lifted it up. 'This is for rubbish, right?'

Moses nodded.

'Is it emptied every night?'

'It's supposed to be.'

'Was it last night?' she asked.

'I don't know, man. Maybe.'

Vicky examined the wall above the metal bin. There was a dark V-shape of soot that went up to the ceiling. 'See that, Moses? That tells me the fire started in the bin. With the grease and stuff on the ovens and hoods the whole place would be burning within a few minutes.'

Vicky photographed the marks and Farmer nodded his approval.

'But how would the bin catch fire?' asked Moses.

'That's why I was asking about the smoking,' said Vicky. 'I'd say one of your staff took a quick smoke without opening the door and popped the butt into the bin. Thought he'd extinguished it but hadn't and it smouldered away happily without anyone noticing. Where do you normally empty the bin?'

'I don't. It's the busboy's job.'

'And where does he empty it?'

'There's a skip in the alley.'

'Did you check that he emptied it into the skip?'

Moses sighed. 'No.'

Vicky nodded. 'There you go,' she said. 'The rain stops them smoking outside. Someone puts a lit cigarette end in the bin. It smoulders. It's still raining so your busboy decides not to take out the rubbish. It catches fire late in the night. Bob's your uncle.' She looked over at Farmer and he smiled and flashed her a thumbs-up.

'Shit,' said Moses. 'That's some freaky detective work there.'

'It's just common sense,' said Farmer. He handed his torch to Vicky. 'Well done. Now pop the gear back in the van and we'll do the paperwork.'

'What about my insurance?' asked Moses. 'They'll still pay out, won't they?'

'It was an accident, Moses,' said Farmer. 'It was stupid but it wasn't deliberate. They'll bitch and moan but they'll pay out. And don't worry about the cops. I'll talk to them.'

Moses slapped him on the back. 'As soon as I'm back in business, you come back and see me,' he said. 'You can try my jerk chicken. The restaurant is vegetarian but I'll make an exception for you.'

'I'll hold you to that,' said Farmer as he headed to the door. Before they drove back to Dowgate, Farmer sat with Vicky at a fold-down table in the back of the van and went through the twenty-four-page A4 booklet that had to be filled in each time an investigator went to a fire. On the front page were the words FIRE INVESTIGATION SCENE CONTEMPORANEOUS NOTES with the incident number, the date and the name of the lead investigator. 'That would be me, obviously,' said Farmer.

'Right,' said Vicky, writing in his name in capital letters.

The booklet required them to fill in details of who was doing the investigating, details of the weather, and a comprehensive risk assessment. They had to list any witnesses to the fire, and full details of the property including the types of alarms and sprinklers, details of the mains gas and electricity supplies. There were several pages left blank for witness statements.

Vicky looked up at Farmer. 'Witnesses?'

'Not needed at this stage,' he said. 'If the police SOCO team comes up with anything then we might start interviewing, but this looks open and shut.'

Page 12 was devoted to possible sources of ignition with a list including electric supply, electrical appliances, gas appliances, naked flames, and smoking materials. The final section was Deliberate Ignition. Each possibility had Y/N next to it and a space to be filled in under REASON DISCOUNTED. 'Okay, so we're pretty sure it was a stray cigarette, but we need to discount every possibility with a reason,' he said. 'That way if it ever went to court and a QC asks you how you can't be sure it was a rat chewing through a wire that caused the fire, you can point to the fact that we saw no evidence of a rodent infestation.'

'Rats cause fires?'

'Not maliciously,' said Farmer. 'They like to chew and if they chew through a live wire they can start a fire. I had one crawl into the back of a freezer and cause a short circuit.'

The final section of Page 12 was for the investigator's conclusion. 'You can write "accidental ignition of rubbish in bin by discarded cigarette" or something like that,' said Farmer.

There were then several pages of grids so that the investigator could draw a map of the premises and Vicky did it from memory. Farmer nodded his approval.

The subsequent pages were a log of all the photographs that had been taken. Farmer watched as Vicky took the number of each photograph and a brief description of what it showed.

When she had finished she turned to the next page, which was where casualties were listed. 'Obviously doesn't apply here,' said Farmer.

The page after that was for details of vehicle damage, and again this didn't apply. There was then a summary of the material forming the investigation, and a final page to be filled in if there had been a fire involving appliances or equipment. 'That's so we can chase up similar cases, say if we had a fridge malfunctioning,' said Farmer. 'Doesn't apply in this case.'

Vicky finished the paperwork and she and Farmer signed it. 'There you go,' said Farmer. 'It can be a pain at times but it has to be done. Everything we do has to be detailed and recorded. Partly because sometimes our evidence ends up in court, but also because the damage is usually made good pretty quickly, so we need a full record of what happened. Right, let's head off.'

21

As they pulled into Dowgate, Danny Maguire was heading out, carrying his tunic and helmet. 'What's the story?' asked Farmer as he climbed out of the van.

'Meth lab in Hackney.'

'Are you single-handed?'

Maguire nodded. 'Tom got called in to an inquest today.'

'Why not take Vicky with you? Be good for her to see a meth lab at first hand.'

'I've seen meth labs before,' said Vicky.

'But not as an investigator,' said Farmer.

'Happy to have her along,' said Maguire. He nodded at Vicky. 'Do you want to drive?'

'Sure,' said Vicky. She put her helmet, tunic and boots in the back of the van and climbed into the driving seat as Farmer headed upstairs.

Maguire took the passenger seat, pulled the door shut and tapped the address into the satnav. Vicky laughed and Maguire looked over at her. 'What's wrong?'

She nodded at the satnav. 'Des refuses to use it.'

'Yeah, the Grouch has his own way of doing a lot of things. Rank has its privileges.'

'You've worked with him for a while?'

'Three years, but it feels longer.'

'What station were you at before? I don't remember seeing you around.'

'I transferred down from Leeds. More action down here.' Vicky drove off. 'Don't get me wrong,' said Maguire. 'Des is one hell of an investigator. He's just a bit tetchy sometimes. That's why all his wives end up leaving him.'

'How many wives has he had?' asked Vicky.

'Three that he admits to, but I suspect there might be more.' He laughed. 'His maintenance payments must be a nightmare. I told him it would be cheaper to just bump them off, but he didn't seem to think that was funny.'

Vicky looked across at him. Maguire caught the look and flashed her a shamefaced smile. 'I was joking.'

'It's not that funny, Danny. I can see why Des might take offence. What about you?'

'Do I kill my ex-wives?' He chuckled. 'I've never been married.'

'How come?'

He shrugged. 'No rush,' he said. 'It's not as if I have a biological clock ticking away.'

'I guess it's not easy meeting people in the brigade,' she said. 'The ratio of men to women isn't in your favour.'

'Whereas you've got plenty of hunky men to choose from? I think my problem is that I'm too fussy. I see plenty of girls in the gym but none of them take my fancy.'

'Yeah? What's your type, then?'

He opened his mouth to speak but then seemed to check himself. 'Difficult to say. I guess I'll know when I see her.'

As Vicky followed the satnav's instructions, Maguire

studied a written report. '*Breaking Bad* has a lot to answer for,' he said eventually.

Vicky frowned. 'The TV show?'

Maguire nodded. 'It glamourised methamphetamine production. That and the Internet meant all sorts of idiots started messing around with chemistry kits. If they were lucky they'd start a fire and lose their eyebrows. Unlucky and . . .' He shrugged. 'Luckily we haven't had many deaths yet in London. Just a few fires. The firefighters found glassware and tubing in the attic. That's usually a pretty good indication that someone has been going all Walter White. Pretty small scale and they put the fire out quickly.'

They arrived at the fire scene. The traffic had been cleared from around the house that had burned and police bollards placed along the pavement fifty feet either side. There was a lone uniformed policeman standing in front of a door criss-crossed with police tape. He was in his twenties, stick-thin with a wispy moustache, and was playing with his smartphone when Vicky drove up and parked.

Vicky opened the rear of the van. 'SOCO are here already so we won't need the lights,' said Maguire, nodding at a police van.

'Right,' said Vicky, handing him gloves and overshoes.

'We need full fire-fighting kit,' he said. 'There can be all sorts of hazardous stuff in there.'

She put on her kit, grabbed the camera and flashlights, and slammed the door. The policeman looked up from his smartphone as they approached.

Maguire looked up at the top floor and shielded his eyes with his hand. There was a pitched roof and parts of it had fallen in to reveal jagged burnt beams. Both windows on the top floor had been smashed. There wasn't much broken glass on the pavement, which suggested that the firefighters had broken them to get water in.

'Officer, I'm a bit light on details,' said Maguire. 'Was anyone hurt?'

The policeman nodded at Maguire. 'Your guys pulled out two men, both very badly burnt. They're in the burns unit at Chelsea and Westminster.'

'They were on the top floor?'

'One was, the other was in the attic.'

'Is it known as a drug den?'

'Not specifically, but this whole area is rife with it. If they're not making speed they're growing marijuana or cooking crack. The ones that don't make it, sell it. It's a cottage industry around here.'

'Good to see the spirit of enterprise isn't dead,' said Maguire, his voice loaded with sarcasm.

He took Vicky over to the door. It had been kicked in, probably by the firefighters. The building had once been a single house but had been converted into small flats, two per floor. There was no smoke or fire damage in the stairway but there was the stench of burnt wood and plastic and the carpets were soaked. The doors were closed on the first floor but on the second floor the door to the right had been broken in.

'Right, first rule of any drugs den, be it crack, or meth or marijuana, is to watch out for booby traps. They set them for the cops and other gangs but they're just as dangerous for firefighters or investigators. Sometimes they wire doorknobs up to the mains or put razor blades in the floorboards. Just be careful what you touch, okay?'

'Got it,' said Vicky. 'I've attended my fair share of drugs labs over the years.'

'Just be careful, that's all I'm saying. If anything happens to you, I'll get the blame.'

They heard a scuffling sound and a man in a white overall appeared. He was in his early forties. His hood was up so Vicky couldn't see his hair but he had a neatly trimmed goatee. The man smiled when he saw Maguire. 'How's it going, Danny?' asked the man.

'Busy, busy, busy as always,' said Maguire. 'This is the new member of the team. Vicky, Garry Harding.'

Vicky smiled. 'Hi, Garry.'

'So you're Robin to Danny's Batman?'

'She's been assigned to the Grouch,' said Maguire.

Harding grinned. 'My sympathies, then.'

Maguire smiled. 'Okay, let's check out the scene,' he said to Vicky. 'I've no doubt Des has already told you we photograph everything, distance shots first and then close-ups. Can you pay particular attention to the burn marks on the ceiling?' He looked at Harding. 'We don't need masks?'

'The air's fine,' said Harding.

Maguire stepped into the flat and Vicky followed him. There was a small hallway with a bathroom at the end of it, and directly opposite the door was the sitting room. There were burnt remains of a plastic sofa, a table and chairs, and a melted flat-screen TV. There was a soaking wet carpet covered in a thick sludge and the walls were black with soot. The ceiling was charred and blackened. There was broken glass on the floors that suggested the windows had been broken from the outside. Maguire bent down and picked up a piece of charred cardboard.

He held it out for Vicky to look at it. It was part of a package of lithium batteries. He bent down again and lifted up a piece of melted plastic. There was enough of the label left intact to see that the bottle had once contained sodium hydroxide drain cleaner. He found several more melted bottles with similar labels. 'I'm thinking this was the storage area,' said Maguire. He pointed at a hatch in the ceiling above a metal stepladder. 'They probably did the cooking in the attic. You know how to make methamphetamine, right?'

'Not really.' She snapped away with the camera, though there wasn't much to see.

Maguire grimaced. 'It's not rocket science, or the scumbags around here wouldn't be making it in their attics. Basically, you start with ephedrine or pseudoephedrine, which you have to separate out from cold medicine tablets. That's why Boots won't let you buy more than a couple of packs. You grind them into a powder and mix them with any number of solvents, all of which are highly inflammable. The scumbags forget all the warnings and let the solvent near a naked flame and whoosh, game over. But if they get past the first stage, they have to filter out the pure pseudoephedrine which is then mixed with red phosphorus and hydriodic acid. You can make your own red phosphorous from match heads but you've got to be careful because it can burst into flames just from friction. You filter out the red phosphorous and neutralise the remaining acid with sodium hydroxide and after a bit more jiggery pokery you end up with crystal meth. The problem is that a lot of the stuff used in the process is highly inflammable, not to say toxic.'

'Garry, are we okay to go upstairs?' asked Maguire.

'Help yourself,' said Harding. 'It's pretty bad but the floor is stable.'

Maguire pointed at the ladder. 'Ladies before gentlemen.'

He held the ladder steady as Vicky climbed up and hauled herself into the attic space. Maguire followed her and pulled himself through the hatch. There was a metal table at the far end of the attic around which was a lot of broken glass and smashed laboratory equipment. Vicky snapped away with the digital camera. There was plenty of light coming in through the holes in the roof so Maguire switched off his torch.

He walked the length of the attic, staring at the parts of the roof that hadn't fallen in, then checked the floor-boards. Then he examined the broken glass and ashes under the table. 'I'm not seeing much in the way of specialist glassware or metal tubing,' he said. 'This has the look of a Shake and Bake operation.'

Vicky frowned. 'How does that work?'

'It's a small-scale meth-manufacturing method,' said Maguire. 'It uses one container for the mixing. A two-litre plastic pop bottle will do the trick. You put in your ground-up tablets, the beads from a gel cold pack, hydro-chloric acid, lighter fluid, sodium hydroxide – that's caustic soda drain cleaner – and lithium strips from inside an AA battery. You've got to be careful that you don't get any moisture on the lithium because it'll burst into flames. You put everything but the cough tablets in the bottle and give it a shake. Then you add the ground-up tablets and shake again. Any air inside the bottle and the whole thing can blow up in your face. It takes about an hour for the reaction to take place but there's an increase in pressure and if you don't release it you get an explosion. Looks to me like that might have happened here.'

'Causing all this damage?'

'Probably stored their chemicals downstairs and did the mixing up here. Rookie mistake. They should have done the mixing downstairs and kept the windows open for ventilation.' He pointed at the charring around the hatch and the blackened roof above it. 'That's where most of the heat was,' he said. 'I'm guessing he was doing the mixing and had an explosion. He drops the bottle down the hatch and it ignites the flammable materials down there. He manages to get out with his pal while the fire rages upwards.'

Vicky was scanning the floor as Maguire was speaking. She stiffened as she spotted a small melted piece of metal. She went over and picked it up and carefully sniffed it. 'Lithium battery, what's left of it,' she said.

'Well spotted,' said Maguire. 'Photograph everything and then I'll go through the contemporaneous notes with you. I'll go and have a chat with Garry. No need to put anything in evidence bags, Garry'll do that.'

22

As Vicky left her office at just after eight o'clock she saw Farmer and Maguire heading down the stairs.

'We're off to the pub, fancy a jar?' asked Maguire.

'She's driving,' said Farmer.

'I can leave the car here,' said Vicky. 'I could do with a drink.'

'Thirsty work being Mr Farmer's bag-carrier?' asked Maguire.

Farmer threw him an annoyed glance but Vicky wasn't sure if he was upset at the jibe or the invitation. She smiled brightly. 'He keeps me on my toes.'

'And did Des explain that the newest member of the team buys the drinks?'

Vicky laughed. 'No, he said lunch. But I can stand my round.'

'Nice one,' said Maguire. 'Lagers it is.' He patted Farmer on the back. 'You've got a keeper here, Des.'

The Steelyard pub was next door to the station, set under the arches of Cannon Bridge, which ferried trains to and from Cannon Street. There was a printed notice on the front door warning that drugs weren't allowed, which

struck Vicky as overkill as drugs weren't allowed anywhere. 'What's the story?' asked Vicky, nodding at the sign.

'It's a nightclub when the sun goes down,' said Farmer.
'Different sort of clientele.'

There was a long bar to the left, with tables, chairs
and low black sofas to their right. The walls and vaulted
ceilings were bare brick. Judging from the number of
nods and smiles they got, the two men were clearly regu-
lars. Maguire and Farmer commandeered a table by the
wall while Vicky went to the bar. Most of the drinkers
were men and heads turned as she ordered the drinks.
The men to her right smiled at her, the ones to the left
looked away as soon as they saw the damage to her face.

The barman who served her was in his twenties with
gelled hair and designer stubble. He grinned as he put
two pints of lager down in front of her. 'You with the
fire brigade, darling?'

'What was it that gave it away? The burns?'

His jaw dropped in surprise and he took half a step
back. 'What? No. Fuck, no. Shit. Sorry.' He looked around
as if searching for an escape route, then moved closer to
the bar and put his hands on it as he leaned towards her.
'I meant that you came in with Danny and Des, that's
all. I'm so sorry if it came out wrong.'

Vicky felt her cheeks flush. 'It didn't, it was my fault.
I'm sorry. I just get so used to being . . . you know . . .
stared at.'

'I wasn't staring,' he said. 'I barely noticed it.'

'Oh, come on . . .'

'Seriously.' He held out his hand. 'Can we start again?
I'm Matt.'

She smiled. 'Vicky,' she said. 'And yes, I'm with the

Fire Brigade.' They shook hands and if anything she felt even more embarrassed. 'I'm sorry I overreacted. Really.'

'Water under the bridge.' He grinned. 'Now I've forgotten what you wanted.'

'Lager,' she said.

Matt laughed. 'You really are a fireman,' he said.

'Firefighter,' she corrected him.

'Whoops. Firefighter. Another pint of lager it is.' He went over to the pumps and poured her pint. 'It's on the house,' he said as he put the glass down in front of her.

'You don't have to do that,' she said.

'Only yours,' he said. 'I'm not giving Danny and Des free drinks. That'd be the road to ruin.'

She laughed and paid him, then took the drinks over to the table.

'So, Danny says you impressed him at the meth lab,' said Farmer.

'I'm still on a learning curve,' said Vicky.

'She's got a good eye, Des,' said Maguire. 'She spotted a bit of a battery that I'd missed. And she knows her way around a fire scene.' He grinned. 'And all her pictures were in focus, which is more than can be said for yours.'

Farmer scowled at him and sipped his pint.

'The world would be a safer place if they'd stick to marijuana. The worst that can happen there is an electrical fire.'

Des grinned. 'And a lot of grinning firefighters.'

Vicky frowned, not getting the joke.

'The fumes,' Maguire explained. 'If a marijuana factory goes up in flames, anyone in the area tends to get a little high.'

'Is there much marijuana growing?'

'Bloody hell, yeah,' said Maguire. 'It's an easy business to get into. You just need lights and water and seeds. But you have to get the wiring right or things start overheating. But meth production is a whole different animal. If something goes wrong, the whole building can go up in flames and the idiots doing it get badly burnt. Or worse.'

'It's a bugger of a drug,' said Farmer. He sipped his pint, then took a couple of gulps before continuing. 'You know the history, right?' he asked Vicky. 'Bikers were the first to make it for recreational use in the States. They got their ephedrine from farm feed. They used to hide the drug they made in their crankcases, which is why it got called crank.'

'Now it's got hundreds of street names,' said Maguire. 'Speed, fast, cinnamon, tweak, crystal, glass, ice – seems like there's a new name for it every week. Google it and you'll get dozens of recipes. The powers-that-be keep making it harder to get the raw materials but you're up against the Internet so it doesn't take long to find a way around it.'

'It's a losing battle?' said Vicky.

Farmer shrugged. 'People take mood-altering drugs. They always have done and always will. Methamphetamine is a bitch of a drug but alcohol causes far more deaths every year.'

'Are you saying they should be legalised?'

'Did I say that?' Farmer snapped. 'Did you hear me say that?'

'I was inferring from what you were saying, that's all. If meth is less dangerous than alcohol, why make it a criminal offence to have it?'

Farmer sighed and looked across at Maguire. 'See what

I'm up against? See what they've sent me?' He looked back at Vicky and sighed again. 'The point I was trying – and obviously failing – to make is that alcohol kills a lot more people each year than methamphetamine. More than eight thousand, every year. That's disease, not accidents. Drug-related deaths? About a third of that, and they're mainly heroin deaths. But far more people drink than take drugs.' He raised his glass. 'And it's possible to drink socially for decades with no ill effects. You start taking methamphetamine and you'll be dead within three years. There's a world of a difference between the two. And legalisation would be a disaster for the country. So don't start misquoting me, sweetheart.'

'Point taken,' said Vicky.

'So how are you enjoying investigations?' asked Maguire. 'Other than the public bollockings.'

'Like I said, I'm on a learning curve.'

'And a bloody steep one it is,' said Farmer.

'Think you'll stick at it?' asked Maguire.

'I don't have any choice.'

Maguire frowned. 'You didn't ask for the job?'

'Fuck no!' said Vicky quickly. Then she held up her hand. 'No offence.'

Maguire laughed. 'None taken. So if you didn't ask for the job, what are you doing here?'

'They sent her, under duress,' said Farmer. 'She wants to be out fighting fires. But the powers-that-be want rid of her, so they sent her to me.' He gulped down more lager.

'Is that true?' Maguire asked Vicky. 'You didn't go through the selection process?'

'Pretty much, yeah.'

'I don't follow their logic,' said Maguire, looking at Farmer. 'How does she go from firefighter to investigator without any training?'

'Basically they hope she'll get so pissed off with me that she'll quit.'

Maguire grinned. 'Who could possibly not love working with you, Des?' he said. 'Misogynistic, sexist, bad hygiene, what's not to like?'

'They're bastards,' said Farmer. 'They're too lily-livered to do their own dirty work so they expect me to do it for them.'

'I'm still sitting here, guv,' said Vicky.

'Don't be coy, sweetheart,' said Farmer. 'You know as well as I do what they're up to. I didn't want an assistant, you didn't want to work in fire investigation. But here we are.'

'And how's it working out for you both?' asked Maguire, who was clearly enjoying winding them up.

'So far, so good,' said Vicky while Farmer sipped his drink.

Farmer put down his glass and sniffed. Maguire looked at him expectantly. Eventually Farmer shrugged. 'Yeah,' he said. 'So far so good.'

Vicky couldn't help but smile. It was the closest he'd got to paying her a compliment.

'But it's early days yet,' added Farmer. He took out his pack of tobacco. 'I need a smoke.'

'I'll join you,' said Maguire, taking out a pack of Rothmans and a lighter.

'Don't you get enough smoke on the job?' asked Vicky.

The two men stood up. 'It's not about the smoke, it's the nicotine,' said Maguire. 'I've been a pack-a-day man for years.'

Farmer shook his head. 'It's the smoke I like.'

'It's about control, guv,' said Vicky. 'You've got fire in your hand and you're in control of it.'

Farmer threw her a withering look. 'The last thing you want to be doing is psychoanalysing me,' he said, jabbing his finger at her. He looked as if he wanted to say more but he just glared at her and followed Maguire out of the bar.

23

When Farmer came back after his smoke, he seemed in a better mood. Maguire left after just one pint. Vicky looked at Farmer expectantly, wondering if he was about to call it a night. He hadn't mentioned her driving him home, but she assumed that's what he'd want. 'Are you in a rush?' he asked.

'I'm fine,' said Vicky. She nodded at his empty glass. Hers was half full, she was still planning to drive home. 'You want another?'

Farmer got to his feet. 'The newbie buys the first round, you don't have to keep buying my drinks,' he said gruffly, and headed over to the bar.

Vicky looked around the bar. It was clearly the station's local as there were half a dozen off-duty firefighters at the far end of the bar. As she'd been chatting to Maguire and Farmer she'd noticed them glancing over in her direction and she was pretty sure they were talking about her.

Farmer returned with his pint and sat down. 'Checking out the talent?' he asked, nodding at the firefighters.

'There don't seem to be many females at Dowgate,' she said.

'There's a few,' he said. 'More's the pity.'

'What do you mean?' asked Vicky.

'You know what I mean, sweetheart. Don't go goading me.'

'So it's not just me you have a problem with? You're against women firefighters in general?'

'The plain fact is that women aren't cut out to be firemen,' said Farmer, folding his arms. 'And the clue is in the name. Fire*men*.'

Vicky grinned. 'The correct term since the seventies has been firefighters.'

Farmer shook his head. 'It's a man's job, and you can't say otherwise.'

'Girton Ladies College had an all-women's fire brigade from 1878 to the 1930s,' said Vicky.

'It's sad that you would know that,' said Farmer.

'And during the Second World War there were seven thousand women in the National Fire Service.'

'Yeah, well all the men were away fighting the bloody war,' said Farmer. 'What do you expect?'

'There have been women firefighters in the London Fire Brigade since 1982.'

'And you know how many have actually put in thirty years' service? Five. They leave because they can't hack it, or because they want kids.'

'Is that any surprise when you see how they're treated?'

'Sweetheart, they're treated exactly the same as the men, which is how it should be. And answer me this. If you were in a smoke-filled room on the top floor of a house, who would you want kicking down the door and dragging you out? A strapping six-foot rugby player or a five-foot-two blond with painted nails?'

'Are you serious?'

'Yes, I'm serious. The LFB had to cut back the fitness and strength tests so that women can be allowed in. That's an admission that women just aren't as strong or as fit as men. And dropping standards puts lives at risk. How is a slip of a girl going to pull a fully grown man from a burning building? Answer me that?'

Vicky didn't say anything, but slowly turned her scarred cheek towards him. He grimaced. 'Okay, I apologise, no offence,' he said. 'I'm not talking about you here. You're clearly as fit as a butcher's dog but a lot aren't.'

'I've never come across a female firefighter yet who was less capable than a male officer,' said Vicky. 'But I've met a hell of a lot of overweight and unfit men who couldn't keep up with me.' She leaned across the table towards him. 'I tell you what, guv. How about this? I'll throw you over my shoulder and run a hundred yards down the street and back. Then you do the same with me. Quickest time wins.'

Farmer chuckled. 'You think you could lift me? I'm what, sixteen stone?'

'I'd say closer to eighteen. But yes, I can lift you. And run with you. And carry you out of a burning building if I had to.'

Farmer settled back in his seat. 'This isn't me saying you're not cut out to be a fireman.' He smiled and corrected himself. 'Firefighter. I'm just staying that standards are standards and lowering them is never a good idea. Look at what happened to the police. They lowered their fitness and height standards to allow in more women and guys from ethnic minorities. You only have to look at the cops on the beat these days to see how that's worked out. Some of them couldn't run to save their life. And I swear last week I saw a midget in uniform and even with the pointy hat I don't think he came up to my shoulders. Now they want to do that with the brigade. Lowering fitness standards in the LFB is the thin end of the wedge.'

'You're saying that the LFB should allow in women but only if they're built like brick shithouses?'

Farmer picked up his glass and drank slowly. Vicky figured he was playing for time so she picked up her own glass and followed suit. Eventually he put down his glass and shrugged. 'I guess I am, yes. Doesn't mean they can't be pretty shithouses and wear make-up, but yes, I'd want them as strong as men. Or stronger.'

'Yeah, well, my bet stands. Happy to throw you over my shoulder whenever you want.'

'I'll pass,' said Farmer. 'Look, I'm not saying you're not up to the job. You clearly are, and when the chips were down you proved that you're as good as any man and probably better than a lot of them. I'm talking about your sex in general and when push comes to shove men are always going to be stronger than women – on average.'

'Everyone knows that women are tougher than men, when it matters,' said Vicky. 'Maybe not physically, but mentally, and that's where it counts.'

Farmer sipped his drink again and didn't say anything.

'A while back MI6 were looking to recruit assassins, to do all the dirty work the government needed doing,' said Vicky.

Farmer looked at her over the top of his glass. 'This is a joke, right?'

'Just let me tell my story, will you? Okay, so they have narrowed their selection process down to three. Two men and a woman. And they set up a final test to see if they've got what it takes to be an assassin. They get the first applicant and they give him a gun. Now he doesn't know it but they've put blanks in the gun. They tell him to open a door and kill the person who is sitting in the next room. So the guy opens the door and sees his wife, sitting on a chair. "I can't do it," he says, and gives them back the gun. He's sent on his way. They do the same thing with the second guy. They give him the gun and send him into the room. He comes out a couple of minutes later, tears in his eyes, and says he can't kill his wife. They send him on his way. So then it's the turn of the third applicant. The woman. They give her the gun and tell her what to do. She opens the door and sees her husband. She goes inside and closes the door. For the next two minutes all they hear are screams and shouts and banging and crashing and more screams. Eventually the door opens. It's the woman, covered in blood. "There were blanks in the gun," she says. "I had to beat him to death with the chair." She got the job, obviously.' Vicky grinned, raised her glass and then drained it.

Farmer smiled. 'So what are you saying? That you'd beat me to death with a chair if you were told to?'

Vicky grinned. 'Without a second thought,' she said. She stood up and held out her hand for his glass. 'Another drink?'

24

Farmer was on his third pint when he mentioned Vicky's father for the first time. 'I knew your dad. He was a good guy.'

'I didn't know that.' She smiled. 'I mean, I know he was a good guy. I didn't know you knew him.'

Farmer nodded. 'I met him on a training course, not long after I joined. How to fight fires on the Tube. He came to talk to us about King's Cross. He was a real hero, your dad.'

'I know.'

Farmer continued as if he hadn't heard her. 'He was on the fourth pump to arrive and they went straight down, just before the flashover in the ticket office. If they'd got there five minutes earlier . . .' He shrugged. 'He was lucky.'

'He always said that,' said Vicky.

Farmer was in full flow. 'He led five commuters to safety then went down again. Came back with three more and by then the smoke was so thick they couldn't see their hands in front of their faces. But he went back down a third time. He was a brave man, all right.'

Vicky nodded. 'They all were. There were a hundred

and fifty firefighters attending. All because of one match. One stupid match.'

'That's all it takes, sometimes,' said Farmer. 'They'd never had a fatal fire on the Tube system, so the staff weren't trained for it. And who the hell thought wooden escalators were a good idea? And because of that thirty people died.' He drained his glass. 'But it would have been a lot worse if it hadn't been for your dad and the rest of them.' He tried to get to his feet but it was too much of an effort and he sagged back into his chair. 'Get me another drink, sweetheart.'

'What is it with you and "sweetheart"? Do you call all women that, or just me?'

Farmer sighed. 'Don't get all PC on me, darling. It's a term of endearment, not sexual harassment. Not that I'm capable of sexually harassing anyone at the moment.' He sat back in his seat and burped loudly.

'That's what my dad used to call me. Sweetheart.'

'Really? I didn't know.'

'How could you have known?'

'God, I'm sorry.'

'No, it's okay. It's not that.'

'Not what?'

She sighed. 'It might be nice if you called me by my name sometimes, that's all.'

'You don't use my name. It's "guv" this and "guv" that.'

'That's a sign of respect. Calling me "sweetheart" is . . . well, it's sexist.'

'Was it sexist when your dad did it?'

'You're not my dad, guv.' She sighed. 'Maybe we should call it a night?'

His eyes narrowed. 'Are you saying I can't handle my drink?'

'I'm saying it's late, that's all.'

He looked at his watch. 'It's not as if I'm driving, is it?'

'Fine,' said Vicky. She stood up and went over to the bar and bought Farmer a pint.

Matt was waiting for her and he grinned. 'You don't want to be trying to match Des drink for drink, he can consume alcohol for England.'

Vicky laughed. She had been about to order herself a coffee but she had second thoughts and asked for two pints of lager. 'I could put a couple of vodkas in his,' said Matt.

'You'd do that?'

'Hell, yeah,' said the barman, grinning.

'I'm going to have to watch you,' said Vicky, and he laughed.

She took both drinks back to the table. 'I thought you were my designated driver?' Farmer said, gesturing at her glass.

'Fuck it,' she said. 'I'll call a cab.'

'What about me?'

'I'll get a cab for you, too.' She picked up her glass. 'Cheers.'

Farmer grabbed his glass and clinked it against hers. 'Good to have you on board.'

'Are you serious?'

He looked her in the eyes as he nodded. 'I am,' he said. 'I think you're going to be okay.'

'As a fire investigator?'

'Yeah. I know you don't want to be investigating, that

you'd rather be out fighting fires, but I think you've got a flair for it. I wasn't going to say that in front of Danny, obviously, but that's the truth.'

'Thanks, guv.' They toasted each other and drank.

'When did your dad pass away?' he asked as he put his glass down.

'End of nineteen ninety-nine,' she said.

'How old were you then?'

'Just turned ten,' she said.

'That must have been hard.'

She nodded. 'Yeah, it was worse because it happened so quickly. He was doing some decorating work. That's what he did on his off-days, him and a few mates ran a painting and decorating company on the side. He was painting a window and he had a stroke. Just one of those things. He'd always been fit, sailed through every medical, he just had this weak blood vessel that could have gone at any moment. I didn't even see him that day; he left before I woke up. I came back from school and my mum was crying and my uncle and aunt were there and . . .' She shrugged. 'Just one of those things. You survive one of the worst fires London has seen and your own body lets you down.'

'It's a rough old world,' agreed Farmer. 'But at least you had a father you can be proud of. My old man kicked the bucket when I was twelve and all I remember of him is the hidings he used to give me.' He smiled ruefully. 'If he hadn't drunk himself to death I'd probably have topped him myself.' He drank more and wiped his mouth with the back of his hand. 'What about your mum?'

'Never remarried. Fusses over me. I live at home so she has plenty of opportunity to spoil me.'

'She was okay with you being a fireman?' He grinned and corrected himself. 'Firefighter.'

Vicky laughed. 'Hell, no. Fought me tooth and nail. Actually used the phrase "no job for a girl" at one point.'

'But you talked her into it?'

Vicky shook her head. 'No, but she couldn't stop me.'

'And she came around eventually?'

Vicky laughed again. 'No. Don't get me wrong, she's proud of me. But when she first came to the hospital I could see it in her eyes. It's no job for a woman, that's what she was thinking.'

Farmer raised his glass to her. 'I'd like to meet your mum.'

'Don't even think about it,' she said.

'What?'

'I'm not fixing you up with my mum.'

Farmer frowned. 'How do you know I'm not married?'

'Just a hunch,' she said. 'You've never mentioned a wife. Plus you're almost always working. Plus no one seems to be ironing your shirts.'

His frown deepened. 'Who irons shirts? You put them on a hanger wet and they dry just fine.'

'Good luck with that,' said Vicky. 'So you're not married?'

Farmer grimaced. 'Well, strictly speaking I am, but I haven't seen her for a couple of years.'

'Topped her, did you?'

Farmer was just about to drink and he spluttered as he laughed. He wiped his mouth again. 'No, I didn't top her. The shoe was on the other foot, as it happens. She kicked me out.' He smiled shamefacedly. 'She was wife number three so the last thing I want is another one, thanks but no thanks. Your mum is safe with me. I just meant I'd like to discuss the suitability of women as firemen with her, that's all.'

'Firefighters,' she said, correcting him.

He nodded. 'Firefighters.' He drained his glass and waggled it in front of her. 'You still buying?'

'I guess so,' she said. She stood up and headed for the bar.

25

It was just before eleven when Vicky and Farmer left the pub. She'd drunk three and a half pints, Farmer had put away half a dozen. She'd planned on ordering two cabs, one each, but Farmer was unsteady on his feet and she decided to take the one cab and drop him off before heading home.

'I'm okay,' said Farmer. 'I've only had six pints.'

'It's no bother,' said Vicky. She was surprised at how drunk he was; he didn't seem to be a man who couldn't hold his alcohol.

She called for an Addison Lee cab because generally she found the drivers were more professional than the run-of-the-mill minicabs and it was worth paying the extra. The guy at the wheel of the cab that arrived in front of the pub was called Mohammed and was wearing a dark blue suit. 'Vicky?' he asked as she opened the back door.

'That's me,' she said. 'We're going to Bethnal Green first then I'll send you the final address.' She helped Farmer on to the back seat. Farmer burped loudly and slumped back in his seat.

'He's not going to throw up, is he?' asked Mohammed nervously.

'He's fine,' said Vicky. 'He's tired, that's all.' She climbed in next to Farmer and pulled the door shut.

'If he throws up, I'll have to clean the car,' said the driver.

'Mohammed, mate, if he throws up I'll give you a hundred quid, cash,' she said. 'But the sooner you get us to Bethnal Green, the less the chance of him barfing.'

Mohammed nodded reluctantly and headed off. Farmer burped again, then appeared to fall asleep. Vicky didn't try to wake him, figuring he was less likely to throw up if he was asleep. After a few minutes he began to snore softly. The driver kept glancing nervously in his mirror but Vicky flashed him a smile. 'He's all right, mate, he's sleeping it off.'

Mohammed muttered under his breath.

Vicky turned to look at Farmer. He appeared to be fast asleep. After half an hour they pulled up outside Farmer's home. She shook him. 'We're here.' His eyes stayed firmly closed so she shook him again. 'Guv!' He opened his eyes, smiled, then closed them again.

Vicky cursed under her breath. 'I'm sorry about this, Mohammed, I'm going to have to get out with him. I don't think he can walk.'

'I'll help you,' said the driver, obviously eager to get Farmer out of his car. He climbed out and opened the passenger door. Vicky got out of her side and hurried around the back. Together they managed to get Farmer out. He was blinking slowly and mumbling to himself. 'Which is his house?' asked Mohammed.

'It's okay, I can handle it from here,' she said.

For the first time he saw her scarred face and his jaw dropped.

'Really. You can go,' said Vicky.

Mohammed nodded and hurried back into the car, slammed the door and drove off. Vicky threw Farmer's arm around her shoulder. 'Are you okay?' she asked.

Farmer stared at her glassily for a few seconds, then burped.

'I'll take that as a no,' she said. 'I thought you could handle your drink better than this.' She grabbed his belt with her right hand. 'Lean on me,' she said. He burped again. She took a step towards the house and almost immediately his legs buckled and he sagged to the ground. She managed to keep him in a sitting position, then she patted his trouser pockets until she found his door keys. She held the keys in her left hand, then grabbed him under his arms and pulled him to his feet. Then she bent down and put her shoulder against his chest. She bent her knees, put her right arm under his backside and took his weight on her shoulders. She grunted as she straightened up. It was a perfect fireman's lift and she was annoyed that he wasn't sober enough to appreciate it. He burped as his arms brushed her back. 'You throw up over me and you're paying for the dry-cleaning.'

She carried him across the pavement, found the front-door key and transferred it to her right hand and unlocked the door. It opened into a narrow hallway and she stepped inside, turned around and closed the door. As she turned back to the stairs his head banged against the wall. 'Sorry,' she said. She flicked a light switch before heading up the stairs. She knew from experience it was easier if she kept up the momentum so she kept her left hand on the bannister and went up with a steady rhythm. At the top of the stairs was a small landing with another door. There was a Yale lock and she found the right key and used it to unlock the door and stepped through into a narrow hallway with four doors leading off it. The door at the far end of the hall was open and there was enough light to illuminate a double bed with a rumpled duvet. Farmer groaned, and then coughed. 'Nearly there,' she said. She couldn't find a light switch so she carried him over to the bed and lowered him down before going back to the door. The switch was lower than usual and she flicked it. There was a three-bulb light fitting in the middle of the ceiling but two of the bulbs had died. There was a built-in wardrobe to the left of the bed. One of the panels was a mirror and she winced at her reflection. It still affected her when she caught sight of herself unexpectedly.

Farmer began to cough and splutter and she went over to the bed, but by the time she'd reached it he had quietened down. She looked down at him and shook her head. 'I can't believe I'm doing this,' she said. She undid his shoelaces and pulled off his shoes and socks, then unbuckled his belt and carefully took off his trousers. She tossed them on to the chair by the door, then undid his tie and unbuttoned his shirt. She had to roll him from side to side to get the shirt off and it took several minutes but eventually he was lying on the bed wearing only his Marks and Spencer boxer shorts, which she figured was as far as she could go. He was snoring heavily but then he stopped and burped. She wrinkled her nose at the sour odour emanating from his mouth. He burped a second time and she decided to roll him on to his side and into the recovery position. At least that meant if he threw up he wouldn't choke on his own vomit.

'Water,' he murmured.

'What?'

'Water,' he said. His eyes were still closed.

She stood up and went out into the hallway. She opened the door to her left and flicked on the light. She gasped involuntarily when she saw the state of the room. It looked like the spare room. There was only one piece of furniture – an armchair under a bare light bulb. A whiteboard had been nailed across the window and like the walls to her right and left it was covered in photographs and type-written reports and newspaper cuttings, most of which were dotted with scribbles. In the centre of the whiteboard was a map of the United Kingdom with pins in it, most of them in London. Threads of different colours ran from the pins to information pasted to the walls.

'What the hell is this?' she muttered to herself. She shivered. It wasn't the cold, it was a feeling that she had stepped into something that just wasn't right. She moved to her right and looked at one of the newspaper cuttings. MODEL KILLED IN FREAK CANDLE FIRE. She read the story. A catalogue model by the name of Samantha Stewart had fallen asleep on the sofa and a candle had ignited a curtain. By the time the Fire Brigade had got there she had burned to death, though the jour-nalist speculated that she had died from smoke inhalation before the fire had engulfed the room. There was another picture of the woman that appeared to have been taken from a Facebook page, smiling and holding a large glass of wine. Underneath it was a post-mortem photograph and Vicky grimaced as she looked at it – there was nothing more than burnt bones and a blackened leering skull. There was a red thread running to the map and she followed it. It was attached to a pin in south London.

There was another pin in north London, Camden, and a blue thread led off to the left. There was another photograph at the end of the blue thread, also pulled off social media. A younger woman, in her twenties maybe, riding a horse. And below it a post-mortem photograph, a corpse that had all been destroyed by fire. There was a newspaper article containing just five paragraphs. Her name was Julia Silk, she'd been a secretary, which Vicky figured was why there had been less media attention. A model dying was a story for the tabloids, a secretary not so much.

There was a brief description of what had happened that appeared to be a screenshot of an LFB report. Julia had been in bed, asleep, when a fire had started in the sitting room below. An investigation had concluded that her TV had been left on and a faulty plug had started an electrical fire. There were fitted carpets and rugs that had burned quickly, and a leather sofa that had apparently been imported from China and was not up to British safety standards.

Vicky stood back and looked at the map. She counted eight pins in London, with eight threads leading off to eight sets of photographs, notes and clippings. All of them women. All of them dead. There were another three pins in Leeds. And two in Manchester. Thirteen pins in all.

'Water!' The shout made her jump and she put a hand up to her throat. She switched off the light and opened the other door. There was a string to pull to switch on the light and it illuminated a small bathroom that didn't appear to have been cleaned in years. There was a white plastic beaker in a stainless-steel bracket and she filled it full of cold water and took it to Farmer. He was still in the recovery position, snoring softly. Spittle had dribbled from his mouth and smeared across the pillow. She shook him but he was fast asleep. She put the beaker of water on the table next to the bed then pulled the duvet over him. She switched off the light and went downstairs. She let herself out of the front door, pulled it closed behind her and ordered another minicab.

26

He smiled as he studied Jayne Chandler's Facebook page. He lit a cigarette and took a long pull on it as he looked through her photographs. It had taken him just seconds to get her name from the online electoral roll after tapping in the address of the house in Clapham. There were more than a hundred Jayne Chandlers on Facebook but most were in America and anyway the profile picture was just the way he'd seen her in the street and on the Tube. It took him only a few minutes to find her. She had her privacy settings configured such that he couldn't see her postings or photographs but he sent her a friend request from an account he'd set up more than a year earlier. He had more than a dozen accounts, all women but with varying interests and backgrounds. The account he used was a pretty redhead who claimed to work for a bank in Croydon. The friend request was accepted within hours. Once he started reading her posts it became clear she worked in the human resources department of the London department store where he'd first spotted her. It hadn't taken long to find her LinkedIn profile. Her interests were fashion and badminton. She had a degree in marketing from the University of Brighton.

She wasn't in a relationship and most of her friends were like her – single girls in decent jobs. Most of the Facebook photographs were of her and her friends eating at restaurants or drinking cocktails. There were several pictures of her playing badminton. It didn't take him long to discover that she played every Wednesday evening. Most of the cocktail photographs were taken on Fridays and Saturdays.

He went back through four years of posts. There were no pictures of her with pets, which was good news because dogs were a nuisance. Cats not so much. But her house seemed to be a pet-free area so there was nothing to worry about. There were no pictures of her smoking.

There was a boyfriend two years ago. A balding guy with a beard and glasses and a tendency to wear turtle-neck sweaters. She had gone on holiday with him to Marbella. He was at one of her birthday parties and had gone horse-riding with her but in the few pictures of them together, they didn't seem close.

There was a picture of her celebrating her mother's birthday, and she spent every Christmas with her parents and her brother at their house in Norfolk.

There were a dozen or so photographs taken inside her house, usually when friends were visiting. The sitting room had a large sofa that looked as if it would burn easily, and there were fitted carpets and thick curtains that would add to the inferno. There were fitted wooden cabinets in the kitchen and a pine table, and more carpets running up the stairs. There was just one photograph of her bedroom but in it he could see more curtains, a wooden wardrobe and a collection of soft toys. There was a battery-operated smoke detector in the hall. He smiled to himself. He had found his next project.

27

Vicky was woken from a dreamless sleep by the ringing of her mobile. She squinted at her bedside clock. Seven o'clock. Her mouth was dry and her head was throbbing. It was Des Farmer and he got straight to the point. 'Did you bring me home last night?'

'Yes, guv. You were a bit tired.' She sat up and ran a hand through her hair. She swallowed and coughed. Her tongue felt too big for her mouth.

'And you put me to bed?'

'I helped you. Is there a problem?' She looked over at her bedside table. She usually took a glass of water to bed with her but she'd obviously forgotten. She desperately wanted a drink. Baxter was awake and watching her, his tail twitching on the off-chance she would pay him some attention.

'No problem, sweetheart, I'm just trying to fill in the gaps. So, are you okay to collect me? My car's still playing up and we've got a job early doors.'

'Bit of a snag there. My car's at the station, remember? I had to take you home in a cab last night.'

'That's not an issue, is it? Just get a cab to the station, pick up the car and then come and collect me. Easy peasy.'

'Okay,' she said.

'Soon as you can, yeah?'

'Right, guv.'

'I'll have breakfast waiting,' he said.

'I'm sorry? What?'

'Breakfast. The most important meal of the day.'

The line went dead. Vicky stared at the phone in disbelief. What Farmer wanted made no sense. All he had to do was call a cab and make his own way into Dowgate. Instead he wanted her to get a cab to the station, pick up her car and then collect him? What the hell was he thinking? She had half a mind to call him back and tell him that she wasn't his bloody chauffeur but then she remembered what she'd said when she'd first met him. She'd do whatever it took to prove herself and that was what he was doing. He was testing her.

She groaned and rolled out of bed. She brushed her teeth, then took a quick shower in lukewarm water. Showers were better than baths, her doctors had told her. The scars had to be kept clean but soaking in a hot bath actually dried the skin out, which would slow down healing. She moisturised her scars and then spent five minutes exercising her left hand and arm. When she had first left the hospital she could barely use her left hand but over the months she had followed the exercise programme that the physiotherapist had given her and it had improved to the point where it was almost as good as it had been before the fire. But at night the hand still seemed to tighten up and lose its flexibility and it took several minutes to take the stiffness out of it. When she'd finished she put a silicone gel sheet over the back of her hand and pulled on a black cotton glove before dressing.

When she went downstairs, Baxter followed her, tail wagging. Her mum was up and making toast. There was a cup of tea already on the kitchen table. 'Eggs?' asked Barbara.

'The guv's giving me breakfast,' said Vicky. She opened the back door so that Baxter could go out into the garden. Vicky sipped her tea and looked at the clock on the wall above the cooker. 'I'd better go.' She used the Addison Lee app on her phone to order a taxi. There was one just a couple of minutes away.

'Your boss is cooking you breakfast?'

'That's what he said.'

'Well, that's a first.'

Vicky took another sip of tea, pulled on a coat, kissed her mum on the cheek and headed out. A taxi pulled up and she climbed into the back. Her mind flashed back to the strange display in Farmer's spare bedroom and she shivered.

The driver dropped her outside Dowgate station and she collected her BMW and drove to Bethnal Green. She parked and sat for a few minutes with her hands on the steering wheel, wondering what she should do. Was he going to rip into her for letting herself into his house? Did he know that she'd gone into the spare bedroom? He had been out for the count, and he hadn't moved while she'd been out of his bedroom, but had he picked up on the fact that she'd been in the spare room? She got out and rang his doorbell. It had a buzzer system so he didn't have to come downstairs to let her in, the front-door lock simply clicked and she pushed it open.

She went upstairs and found that he'd opened the front door for her. She stood on the threshold, frowning. 'Guv?''

'In here!' shouted Farmer.

She stepped into a narrow hallway. To her right was an open door and she saw a sofa and a coffee table piled high with hardback books. She went in and saw Farmer at the far end of the room in a kitchen area. He was wearing a bright orange apron over his uniform and standing in front of a stove. 'How do you like your eggs?' he asked, without turning around. There was a carbon dioxide fire extinguisher on the floor by the fridge. And a fire blanket attached to the wall by the cooker. Like most firefighters, Farmer obviously believed in practising what he preached. Vicky had never yet met a firefighter who didn't have fire extinguishers, smoke alarms and carbon monoxide detectors in their homes.

'My what?' she asked.

'Eggs? Fried? Scrambled? Poached? Please say fried because that's the easiest and that's what I'm having.'

'Fried is good, thanks.'

'Grab a seat and butter some toast.'

There was a table by the window, just big enough for two people. On it was a plate of toast and a jar of marmalade and a pack of Lurpak butter. Vicky sat down and buttered two slices of toast as Farmer cracked two eggs into a frying pan. 'So what's the job this morning?' asked Vicky.

'Unexplained fire last night,' said Farmer. 'A garage near Waterloo station. No one hurt but a lot of motors written off. The crew that attended thought it was an accidental fire but the insurance company investigator has thrown up a few red flags so we need to prepare an LFB report in case it ends up in court.'

Vicky looked around for a plate to put the buttered toast on. 'Plates?' she asked.

Farmer pointed at a cupboard with his spatula. She stood up and opened it. She was surprised at how neat and tidy it was. There were two sizes of plates, small and large, and above it three lines of upended mugs and three lines of wine glasses, and on the top shelf were neatly stacked serving dishes. She took two small plates over to the table and put the toast on them before cutting them diagonally.

Farmer put two filled plates down on the table – bacon, sausage, black pudding slices, button mushrooms, tinned tomatoes and fried onions. 'Bloody hell,' said Vicky. 'That's a heart attack on a plate.'

Farmer laughed and went back to the cooker, returning with the frying pan. He put a fried egg on her plate and another on his. 'You need to stoke the furnace every morning,' he said. He dropped the frying pan into the sink and joined her at the table with two mugs of coffee that he had apparently produced from thin air.

'I'm sorry about last night,' he said. 'Usually I handle my drink better than that.'

'It was a long night,' she said, spooning two sugars into her coffee.

Farmer shrugged and bit into a slice of toast. 'Well, thanks for bringing me back,' he said. 'And for leaving my boxer shorts on.'

'No problem,' said Vicky.

He held her look for several seconds as if he was trying

to read her thoughts, then he nodded and smiled and attacked his sausages.

It was one hell of a breakfast, Vicky had to admit, but she didn't have much in the way of an appetite. She made small talk with Farmer but all she could think about was the room down the hallway and the pictures and cuttings plastered over the walls. What the hell was he up to? And did he know what she'd seen? Was that why he'd invited her into his flat, to see how she would react?

She sipped her coffee, watching him over the top of her mug. He seemed relaxed, happy even, just two colleagues sharing a meal before heading out to work. But she could see that he was watching her, too. She put the mug down and smiled. 'You're a great cook,' she said.

'I can do breakfasts,' he said. 'But that's about it.'

'My dad was always a big one for breakfasts. He did great fried eggs. The yolks not too hard, not too runny.' She was talking too much, she realised. It was a sign of nerves. Why was he so interested in women who had died in fires? And why were the cases on his bedroom wall and not back in the office, where they belonged? Did Farmer have a personal interest in the deaths? Something that he wanted to keep hidden from the brigade?

'Are you okay, sweetheart?' asked Farmer.

She jumped. 'Sorry, what?'

'You were miles away.' He picked up a slice of toast. 'Penny for your thoughts?'

Vicky forced a smile. There was no way she could tell him what she was thinking about so she just shrugged and lied. 'Just missing my dad, that's all.'

Farmer nodded. 'Can't have been easy. He died too young.'

'What about you, guv? You got any kids?'

'Never wanted them,' said Farmer. 'In my experience, they tend to fuck up marriages.' He smiled ruefully. 'Mind you, I seem to have no problems managing that on my own.'

28

Farmer had Vicky drive to Dowgate where they collected one of the fire investigation vans and they drove in it to Waterloo. The garage was around the corner from the main railway station. There was a small forecourt with three second-hand cars festooned with stickers announcing that they had very careful owners and were being offered at the cheapest possible price and that finance was available. All the cars had suffered fire damage on the sides nearest the main building, a single-storey brick structure with a flat roof. To the left was an office with a large window overlooking the forecourt and to the right was the main workshop area. Most of the damage had been done to the workshops. Large sliding metal doors had been pulled back and the interior was a mess of mangled, burnt vehicles and equipment. Blackened water had poured out over the forecourt and run along the pavement to the nearest drain.

As Vicky parked the van by the side of the road, a ginger-haired man in a pin-striped suit and a garish tie hurried over. He was in his fifties with greying hair swept back and a suspiciously smooth forehead that suggested Botox. 'Are you with the police?' he asked.

'Fire Brigade,' said Farmer, gesturing at the liveried van.

'Sorry,' said the man. 'I suppose the van is a clue.' He held out a hand festooned with gold rings. 'Brendan O'Hara.' He pointed at the name of the garage: BRENDAN O'HARA MOTORS.

'Looks like you've had a bad night, Mr O'Hara,' said Farmer.

'Tell me about it.'

Vicky had gone around to the rear of the van and opened the door. Farmer and O'Hara walked to the entrance of the workshop and looked in. Most of the cars to the left had been completely destroyed, the ones to the right had burned but less severely.

Vicky came over. She had put on her overshoes and gloves and was carrying the digital camera.

'They said we had to leave everything as it was until you'd had a look,' said O'Hara.

'Yeah, we need to photograph everything,' said Farmer. He nodded at Vicky. 'Start on the left and move across, it's going to be a complicated one so fill in the report as you go.'

'Right, guv,' said Vicky. She headed to the wall on the left where there were metal racks that had once contained tools. All the wood and rubber had been destroyed by the fire leaving misshapen chunks of metal on the floor.

Farmer looked up at the blackened ceiling. 'No sprinkler system,' he said, a statement rather than a question.

'I looked into it a few years ago but the cost was just crazy.' O'Hara saw the look on Farmer's face and raised his hands in surrender. 'I know, I know, hindsight is a wonderful thing. But I never expected anything like this to happen.'

'In the words of Tom Jones, it's not unusual,' said

Farmer. 'Park a lot of cars together in an environment full of fuel and electrical equipment and it doesn't take much for it to all go tits up.'

'This is the first time we've ever had anything like this happen,' said O'Hara. 'And if the insurance company don't pay up, it'll be the last.'

'What's the problem?' asked Farmer.

'The assessor said something about original points or something.'

'Points of origin,' said Farmer. 'It means that the fires started at several places at the same time. That can be a sign that someone set the fire.'

'Yeah, that's what he said. He didn't come flat out and accuse me of setting fire to my own place, but that's what he seemed to think.'

Farmer nodded. 'Multiple points of origin can be a sign that something is not right, but you would get that with vandalism as well. He'd have needed more than multiple points of origin to reject your claim.'

O'Hara winced. 'Business had been well down, and I increased my insurance a few months back.'

'Yeah, two red flags there,' said Farmer.

'We're still making money,' said O'Hara. 'Just not as much as last year. The insurance thing is just an unhappy coincidence. My broker got me a better deal, is all. We're getting more coverage for a lower premium. It was saving us money. Win–win. That's what my broker said.'

Farmer nodded as he looked around. The doors to the workshop had obviously been prised open at some point. He showed the marks to O'Hara.

'The doors were locked when the fire engines turned up. They did that.'

'You weren't here?'

'I'd been gone about an hour. When I locked up everything was fine. I was at home with the wife and kids when I got a call saying the place was in flames.'

'Let me get kitted up,' said Farmer. He took some gloves and shoe covers from the back of the van, put them on and picked up a torch before joining Vicky. O'Hara started to follow him but Farmer told him to stay put. Vicky was still photographing the tool racks and the remains of the tools on the floor. 'Any thoughts?' he asked.

Vicky pointed to the corner to her right. 'There's a power socket over there with V-shaped charring above it,' she said. 'I'd say it started there.'

Farmer went over to where she had pointed. It was a double socket and both had adaptors plugged in. The adaptors were almost destroyed but he could make out wires running away from the sockets, the plastic insulation burned away in the fire. Farmer shone his torch around the walls and eventually found a large fuse box, about six feet off the ground. He stood up on tiptoe and used his pen to flip it open. Several of the fuses had tripped. 'Sweetheart, do me a favour and photograph this, and the sockets.'

O'Hara walked over but Farmer raised a hand to stop him. 'Can you wait outside, Mr O'Hara,' he said. 'We don't want the scene contaminated.'

'I think your fireman did a pretty good job of contaminating the scene,' said O'Hara. 'Breaking down my doors and then spraying water like there's no tomorrow.'

'To be fair, that is how you put out fires,' said Farmer. 'But seriously, if you can just stand at the doorway until we've finished. It'll make our job a lot easier and we can get out of your hair.'

He went over to the car nearest the tool racks. The tyres had burned away and the vehicle was resting on its rims. The fuel tank had caught fire and the windows had all shattered. The inside was a charred mess. The vehicle next to it was in a similar state. There was a large piece of equipment next to the second car that had been reduced to melted plastic and blackened metal.

The cars in the middle of the garage were also fire damaged, the tyres burned and the roofs blackened, and their petrol tanks had also ruptured and ignited. Farmer checked the filling caps but all were sealed. Car fuel tanks were designed not to explode – giving a lie to most film and TV car crashes – but they did split if the temperature got high enough. It looked to Farmer as if it was the heat of the fire that had caused the cars to burn, rather than vandalism or deliberate fire-setting.

A rubbish bin next to the far wall had been reduced to a misshapen clump of plastic. Farmer bent down to examine it. From the way the plastic had melted it appeared that the heat had been above the bin rather than inside it. He straightened up and called over to Vicky. 'Sweetheart?' When she looked over he pointed at the remains of the bin.

'Will do,' she said.

When he had walked around the whole garage, Farmer went back to O'Hara. 'You've got a lot of electrical equipment in there, obviously,' Farmer said.

'It's all about electronic testing, these days,' said O'Hara. 'In my day you could fix most things with a hammer, a spanner and screwdriver. Now it's all chips.'

'Looks like you overloaded a circuit or two,' said Farmer. 'Your guys were running too much equipment off two sockets over there and from what I can see they were using it to run a small fridge. The fridge motor probably malfunctioned. The fuses tripped eventually, but I'm guessing that a wire had already started to smoulder. Then at some point last night the smouldering became a fire. Plenty of combustibles around so it would have spread quickly.'

'So it was an accident?'

'An accident caused by stupidity,' said Farmer. 'Overloading circuits is asking for trouble.'

O'Hara nodded. 'The mechanics are always complaining about not having enough sockets, but then they complain about everything.'

'We'll start following the various circuits to nail down where it started, but it looks pretty cut and dried to me.'

'So why was the assessor telling me that he thought there was something suspicious about it?'

'He'd probably seen that several of the cars had ignited separately, even those some distance away from where the fire started. Now, that could mean that someone had set fire to them, but I don't see any signs of that. It's much more likely that they were caused by flameover. And that rubbish bin, at first sight you might think a fire had started there.' He pointed at the fuse box, where Vicky was standing on tiptoe and photographing the inside. 'But it looks to me that the fire initiated there, probably caused by an overheated circuit. There was plenty of wood and plastic over there and it would have started burning quickly. Lots of heat, lots of combustible gases.' He pointed at the scorched ceiling. 'The gases rise to the ceiling, and because you've no ventilation up there, the gases would spread out across the garage. Eventually they would have covered the entire ceiling and then they'd start to move down. At some point, those gases would start to burn, which is what we call flameover. That would mean a sheet of fire right across the ceiling, burning at five hundred degrees or more. At two hundred degrees, any nearby wood will start to ignite and at five hundred the tyres will start to burn. So even those cars that are far away from the source of the fire will burn.' He pointed off to the right. 'I think the one that probably worried him the most was the Toyota Prius over there,' he said. 'It's a lot more damaged than the others around it. He probably figured that's a sign that accelerant was used, but I think he didn't take into account that the Prius has a lithium-ion battery. They burn vigorously and at a higher temperature than petrol, so when the flameover ignited it the damage was much more severe, just because of the battery.' Farmer pointed over at the melted rubbish bin. 'I'd bet money that he thought the melted bin was a red flag and that someone had set a fire there, but again that's typical flameover damage. So in my opinion, he added two and two together and got five.'

'So it's definitely an accident, in your opinion?'

'Don't worry, Mr O'Hara, the SOCO team will back me up. We see this a lot.'

'And the insurance company will pay out?'

'I don't see why not.'

O'Hara sighed with relief. 'Thank God for that. When can I start clearing the place up?

'We'll be here for a couple of hours, but you'll have to wait for SOCO to go over the place as well.'

O'Hara scowled. 'This is a bloody nightmare.'

'Sure, but look on the bright side. At least no one was hurt.' Farmer took out his pack of tobacco. 'Do you mind if I . . .?'

'Sure,' said O'Hara. He took out a pack of Rothmans. 'I'm a smoker myself.' He offered the pack to Farmer but he shook his head.

'I prefer to roll my own,' said Farmer. 'Too many chemicals in the mass-produced ones.' He pulled out a pack of cigarette papers. 'Volvos are usually pretty reliable, right?' asked Farmer as he rolled a cigarette.

'Sure,' said O'Hara. 'Why?' He slid a Rothmans between his lips and lit it.

'I've got one but it's been playing up. Sometimes it starts, sometimes it doesn't. Any idea what the problem might be?'

'Electrics, maybe. What model is it?' O'Hara blew smoke up at the sky.

'A V40.'

'Petrol or diesel?'

'Petrol.'

'Could be electrics. Could be the fuel pump. Difficult to say without having a look at it.' He waved an arm towards the devastation behind him. 'And it's going to be a while before we're able to look at anything.' He blew smoke at the ground and then nodded over at Vicky. 'Your sidekick?'

'Sort of a trainee.'

'She's okay with you treating her like that?'

'Like what?'

'Calling her "sweetheart". The women who work here, if I tried that I'd get a spanner thrown at me.'

Farmer grinned. 'It's a term of affection.'

'It sounds like sexual harassment.' He shrugged. 'Just saying.'

Farmer leaned towards O'Hara. 'That girl there, she's a bloody hero,' he said, punctuating the words with jabs of his cigarette. 'She saved lives at Grenfell Tower and those burns, she got them rescuing a guy in a burning building. Literally picked him up and carried him out before she got trapped. I've got nothing but respect for her, and so when I call her sweetheart, it's because I like her. And if she thought otherwise then yeah, I'd expect her to hit me over the head with a Halligan bar.'

O'Hara frowned. 'What the fuck is a Halligan bar?'

'It's like a spanner,' said Farmer. 'But bigger.'

29

It was midday before Vicky had finished photographing everything and they were back loading their gear into the van. 'So it was an accident?' she asked.

'Accident is a funny term,' said Farmer. 'Most accidents aren't accidents, not using the word with its true meaning.' He grinned. 'Pop test. What's the definition of an accident?'

She frowned. 'Something that happens unexpectedly,' she said hopefully.

'Close enough,' he said. 'Me, I'd go with an event that happens by chance or that is without apparent or deliberate cause. But yeah, "something that is unexpected" is okay. Now here's the thing, how often in life do things happen without a cause? It's very rare. As any traffic cop will tell you, the vast majority of what are called road accidents aren't accidents at all. They're people driving stupidly, or aggressively, or simply not paying attention because they're on the phone or staring at their satnav. They used to call them RTAs, road traffic accidents, but a while back they stopped referring to them as accidents, now they're RTCs, road traffic collisions.'

'So you're saying accidents don't happen?'

'I'm saying that true accidents are very rare.' He

gestured with his thumb at the garage. 'Like I said to O'Hara, it was an accident caused by stupidity. The mechanics overloaded the circuit. Did they mean to? Of course not. Did they realise they could cause a fire? No, obviously not. But from the look of it, the wiring wasn't in great shape to start with. I'm sure it was up to code but it was old and could have done with being replaced. If the wiring had been better then the circuit probably wouldn't have overloaded.' He shrugged. 'What we've got is a chain of events. The wiring wasn't in great condition. The mechanics were running too much equipment off a single plug. Someone had put combustible materials close to the plug. If any one of those steps hadn't been in place, there wouldn't have been a fire. Or at least the fire wouldn't have been as bad as it was. The insurance will pay out because it wasn't a deliberate fire, but it certainly wasn't what I'd call an accident.'

Vicky nodded. 'And what about the assessor? Why didn't he see what you saw?'

'Oh he did, he just read it differently. Multiple seats of a fire is often a sign that the fire was set. But not always. I know that because I've been to thousands of fire scenes over the years. But for insurance assessors and SOCO investigators, fire is just a small part of what they look at, probably less than ten per cent of their workload. A SOCO investigator is more likely to be investigating an assault or a rape or even a murder, so unless someone dies a fire is pretty low down their list of priorities. Most insurance assessors are chasing up water damage, theft, weather, they maybe only get to see fire damage a few times a year. But we see fires every day, they're our bread and butter.'

They climbed out of the side door, Vicky slammed it shut, then they got into the front. Vicky started the engine, but then she turned to look at Farmer.

'Guv, can I ask you something?'

'Sure.'

'What you were saying to Mr O'Hara there. And what Paddy was saying about two seats of a fire meaning it's arson.'

'Sweetheart, as I've already told you, it's only arson if there's potential loss of life. You need to remember that because one day you'll be in court giving evidence and you'll say arson when it isn't arson and a barrister will tear you a new one.'

'Got it. Sorry. But what he was saying, if you have two seats of a fire then it's usually malicious.'

Farmer grinned. 'You heard what I said. It doesn't mean that at all.'

'No, with respect, you showed Paddy that in that case an accidental fire could look like it had been set deliberately. But what he said made sense too. If a fire has two points of origin then that can't be a coincidence, it has to be a sign that the fire was deliberate.'

'Okay, yes. If you have two ignition sites, two places independent of each other, at the same location, then yes, it's probably a fire-setting. The problem is that sometimes it can appear that a fire started in several places when in fact there is a chain reaction in play. That's what I told Mr O'Hara there. Things aren't always what they seem. I'll give you an example. Say you've got curtains either side of a window, and a valance linking them over the top of the window. The fire starts on the left, and climbs up the curtain. It moves across the valance and sets fire to the curtain on the right. The burning curtain falls to the ground and continues to burn. Once it's all over, it could well appear that there were two seats to that fire, one on the left of the window and another on the right.'

He frowned as he realised she wasn't listening to him. 'What's on your mind?'

'I'm not sure.'

'Spit it out, girl.'

She sighed and gripped the steering wheel with both hands. She stared at her gloved left hand, and shuddered at the thought of what the skin looked like underneath the black material and protective gel sheet. 'Okay, it's that whole seat-of-fire thing,' she said. 'The fire that I was at, the hotel, looking back it feels to me that there was more than one point of origin.'

'How so?'

She looked across at him. 'When we got there, the fire was confined to a bar, on the ground floor, to the left. The hotel entrance was to the right, and there were rooms above. The BA team went into the hotel. There was smoke. Initially not much but it got thicker the higher we went.'

Farmer frowned. 'So there was more smoke on the upper floors than on the ground floor?'

Vicky nodded. 'By the time we were on the top, visibility was close to zero.'

'But no fire?'

'We found fire in one of the rooms, on the top floor. It looked like it had come up from the floor below.'

'It's possible it moved up from the bar.'

'But the room was at the back of the hotel. The bar was at the front.'

'How old was the building?'

'I don't know. More than fifty years. Maybe closer to a hundred. They said it was listed.'

'So brick-and-wood construction, lathe and plaster. Fire can move in all sorts of directions.'

'Yes, but when I took the casualty downstairs, there was fire in the stairwell on the second floor. I took the casualty back up to the third floor because there was no fire there. They got a ladder to a window and I got the casualty out, then the floor burned through.'

'So the room below you was burning?'

Vicky nodded. 'And that was at the front.'

Farmer's frown deepened. 'So you had a fire on the top floor at the back? And a fire on the second floor on the front?'

'And fire in the stairwell on the second floor. You can see what I'm thinking? There was fire at the back, and fire at the front. But when we got there on the shout, the only fire that was burning was in the bar.'

He shrugged. 'Like I said, it can move with a life of its own in an old building.'

'Sure, but if it was the wooden floor supports that were burning, they burn at three-quarters of an inch an hour.'

'That's charring, not burning,' said Farmer. 'Fire can move a lot faster than that across surfaces. And there are lots of variables. The condition of the wood, ventilation, contamination. Who knows what they used for insulation between the floors. Plus decades of dust and whatnot.'

'The floor must have collapsed because the floorboards and joists burned through,' said Vicky. 'That must have taken time. But the BA team was only in for twenty minutes at the most. I don't know. It's been playing on my mind, that's all. I hadn't given it much thought until

I heard what you said to Paddy.' She nodded at the garage. 'And then when you explained all that to Mr O'Hara.'

Farmer nodded. 'Okay, I'll tell you what, I'll pull the file when we get back to the station and let you know what I think.'

'Thanks, guv.'

Farmer pointed ahead. 'Now let's get going, time's a wasting.'

30

As soon as they arrived back at Dowgate station, Farmer asked for a coffee. Vicky did the honours, then took her own coffee back to her office. She spent the next hour filling out the report on the garage fire, attaching a dozen of the most relevant photographs and putting the rest in a separate file.

When she'd finished, she stared at her screen thoughtfully for the best part of two minutes before tapping a name into the database's search engine. SAMANTHA STEWART. That was the name of the model who had died in the south London fire and whose picture and details had been up on the wall of Farmer's spare room. She called up the initial fire report and read through it. The newspaper cutting she had read had got the story right. Samantha had fallen asleep on the sofa, a candle had set fire to a curtain and she had burned to death. The investigating officer was Danny Maguire. Vicky frowned, wondering why Farmer would have one of Maguire's cases on his wall.

She tapped in the second name she remembered. JULIA SILK. In Julia's case, the investigating officer had been William Campbell, her predecessor. She read through his initial report. Julia had died in an upstairs bedroom when a faulty plug had ignited downstairs. The fire had spread quickly because a sofa wasn't up to British safety standards and the living room had been full of combustibles.

'It's not going to pull through,' said Farmer.

Vicky jumped. She hadn't seen him appear in her doorway. She fought to regain her composure and forced a smile. 'Sorry, what?' He couldn't see her screen from where he was standing but he had only to take two steps and he'd be able to see everything. She wanted to clear her screen but worried that he might wonder if she was hiding something.

Farmer nodded at her rubber plant, which was now on one of the filing cabinets. 'I think you're flogging a dead horse.'

'It takes time,' she said.

'You could just buy another one.'

'I like this one. It deserves a chance, right? We all do.'

'Plants aren't people,' said Farmer. He gestured at her terminal. 'Are you all done?'

She nodded. 'Yup.'

'Excellent,' he said. 'Grab your gear and I'll see you down at the van. We've got a fire in Kilburn.'

'Be right there,' she said, and switched off her screen.

31

'What's the story?' Vicky asked as she drove the van north to Kilburn.

'Fire in a hostel, one fatality,' said Farmer. He pointed ahead. 'Next left.'

'You really never use the satnav?'

'Never,' he said. 'The one day when you rely on it is the day it'll let you down. Trust me.'

'Sounds luddite-ish to me, but you're the guvnor.'

'Indeed I am,' said Farmer. 'Next right and that's us. Park where you can.'

Vicky found a parking space down the road from the hostel. A pump from West Hampstead was double-parked outside the building, its blue lights flashing. Several fire-fighters were rolling up hoses and packing them away. There were a dozen men standing around outside, middle-aged and older and wearing cheap clothes. Most were unshaven and smelled of drink.

Vicky and Farmer climbed out and put on their helmets. Grant Parker – a thirty-five-year-old former soldier who had served in Afghanistan – was crew chief. He was talking to the pump driver but jogged over when he saw Vicky and Farmer.

Parker punched Vicky gently. 'How the hell are you, Lewis?'

Vicky grinned. 'All the better for seeing you, Granty. Managed to put this one out, did you?'

Parker laughed. 'We did our best. So what the bloody hell are you doing in fire investigation? I thought you always wanted to fight fires, not write reports on them.'

Vicky shrugged. 'You'd have to ask the powers-that-be about that.'

'Maybe I will, you're wasted in fire investigation, you need to be doing a real job.' He grinned at Farmer. 'No offence.'

'Yeah, fuck you too, Parker,' said Farmer. 'So what's the story?'

'Fire on the second floor, confined to one room. One fatality, male, hard to tell the age. The cops are treating it as a crime scene. They got here about ten minutes after we did and they've called for SOCO.'

'Cheers. Safe to go up?'

'We haven't dampened everything down because we wanted to preserve the scene as much as possible, but you're good to go. You might get an earful from the manager, he's banging on about compensation.' He punched Vicky again. 'You're looking good, kid.'

The thought that flashed across her mind was that he was only saying that because the helmet covered most of her injuries, but she and Parker went back a long way and she knew that his heart was in the right place. 'You too, Granty.'

Farmer and Vicky crossed the road. There was a locked glass door and next to it a uniformed PC. He pressed the intercom button for them and spoke to whoever was inside. The door buzzed and he pushed it open for them. 'Any idea when SOCO will be here?' asked Farmer.

'They tell me nothing, sir, just to stop anyone going in,' said the PC. 'Sergeant Rowling is inside. He'll be able to fill you in.'

Farmer thanked him and went inside. The lights were off and it was gloomy and there was a strong smell of smoke. There was a linoleum floor showing dirty boot marks and there were marks all over the walls. Firemen were generally big guys carrying a lot of equipment and usually in a rush. A bearded man in his early thirties was standing by a counter above which was a sign saying RECEPTION – PLEASE TREAT OUR EMPLOYEES WITH RESPECT. He was talking into a mobile phone and rubbing the back of his neck with his left hand. He ended the call and came over to them. 'Hi,' he said. 'I'm Clive Morrison, one of the managers here.' He was wearing a green turtleneck sweater and camouflage pattern cargo pants.

Farmer shook his hand. 'Des Farmer. I'll be handing the investigation for the fire brigade,' he said. 'I'm told there has been a fatality.'

Morrison nodded, then pushed his thick-framed spectacles higher up his nose. 'Yes, up on the second floor.'

'What was the victim's name,' asked Farmer.

'Anthony Lawson.'

'How old was he?'

'Mid-fifties, I think. I can check.'

'Please.'

The man went around the counter and tapped on his computer. He cursed and slapped his forehead theatrically. 'I'm sorry, the power's off, obviously. He came back around to their side of the counter. 'Anthony was fifty-seven, fifty-eight maybe. He moved in three months ago.'

'Any problems?'

'Good as gold. He was a bit upset that social services took away his cat but other than that he's been one of our quieter residents.'

'They took away his cat?' asked Vicky.

'We don't allow pets, unfortunately.'

'So what happened to the cat?'

'I think social services gave it to the RSPCA.'

'Vicky, let's stay on point, shall we?' said Farmer. 'Did Mr Lawson have any problems? Drugs? Alcohol?'

'No more than usual,' said the man. 'As I said, he was one of our better-behaved residents.'

'Mental health issues?'

The man shrugged. 'He seemed okay. Muttered to himself a bit, but anyone who has spent any time on the streets tends to do that.'

'Who called the fire brigade?'

'I did. One of the residents came running down saying that he could smell smoke. I went up to the second floor to check and as soon as I saw how bad it was I called nine nine nine.'

Farmer pointed up at a smoke detector in the ceiling. 'How come they didn't go off?'

'It's an old building so we don't have a central system,' said Morrison. 'There are individual smoke detectors in the rooms but some of the residents disable them so they can smoke.' He shrugged. 'They're not supposed to, but there isn't much we can do about it.'

'And he was a smoker?'

Morrison nodded. 'He was. Big time. When he wasn't

smoking he was rolling up his next one. To be honest, I've never seen smoking as a problem, not compared to drink and drugs. He was a nice guy, kept himself to himself.'

Farmer looked across at Vicky. 'Can you request a fire safety officer? We'll need a risk assessment done to check that the detector was working. If it wasn't, LFB Fire Safety might well prosecute.' Farmer looked around. 'The officer outside said there was a sergeant here who was in charge.'

Morrison pointed down a corridor. 'He was down there, where the stairs are.'

Farmer nodded. 'Okay, we'll head on up.'

'Can I ask you a question?'

'Sure. But I can't promise I'll be able to answer it.'

'All the damage your guys did. Who's going to pay for it? There's water pouring into the first-floor rooms, they broke the door to the room. They sprayed water every-where.'

'Well, to be honest, that's how they put out fires,' said Farmer. Outside the West Hampstead pump drove off. The driver blipped the siren for show as they went.

'I know, I know,' said Morrison. 'And obviously it's great that they put it out and that the fire was confined to the one room, but we're on a really tight budget, we don't have the money for redecorating and replacing the furniture. Plus the electrics are probably shot and the last time I checked an electrician charges one fifty an hour.'

'Are you council run? They'll usually pay for any damage caused by firefighters.'

'We're funded by the council and we get government

grants, but we're actually a quango so we run our own budget.'

'Then your insurance will pay,' said Farmer.

'You're sure? I was wondering if the Fire Brigade would put right the damage?'

'They won't. But like I said, your insurance will cover it.'

'And another question?'

'Go ahead.'

'All the residents were told to evacuate the building when the fire was spotted, but no one has said when they can come back in.'

'I'll talk to the police and let you know,' said Farmer. 'The fact the appliances have gone means the fire risk is over, but the police might have issues.'

Morrison thanked him and Vicky followed Farmer down the corridor. There was more damage to the walls and the floor was wet from where water had come pouring down the stairs.

Two policemen were standing by the stairs, drinking Starbucks coffee. The older of the two was a grey-haired sergeant who nodded at Farmer. 'You with the fire brigade?'

'What was it gave us away?' asked Farmer. 'The uniforms or the helmets?'

The sergeant frowned, not getting the joke. Farmer sighed. 'Des Farmer, fire investigation.' He nodded at Vicky. 'This is my colleague. Vicky Lewis.'

The sergeant looked at Vicky and nodded, then back at Farmer. 'Brian Rowling, we got here not long after your guys. They put out the fire but there's a casualty so we're not touching anything until SOCO gets here.'

'We were told one deceased,' said Farmer. 'Was anyone else hurt?'

The sergeant shook his head.

Farmer moved to get by the police officer but the sergeant held out his coffee to stop him. 'It's a crime scene,' said the sergeant. 'We think Mr Lawson was robbed and beaten to death and the fire was used to cover it up.'

'Do you now?' said Farmer. 'What makes you think that?'

'You'll see when you get up there,' said the sergeant.

'Did he have much to steal?' asked Farmer.

'We don't know what was taken. But we think robbery was the motive.'

Farmer nodded. 'Okay.'

'So you'll be waiting for SOCO?'

'I think we might just have a quick look around,' said Farmer. 'Get the lie of the land.'

'Suit yourself,' said the sergeant gruffly. 'But you'll need to be wearing protective gear, we don't want any evidence transfer.'

'Good idea,' said Farmer, and it was clear from the sergeant's satisfied look that he hadn't heard the sarcasm in Farmer's voice. He grinned at Vicky. 'Sweetheart, pop out and get us the overshoes and nitrile gloves will you? Plus oversuits and dust masks. Torches and the camera, obviously.'

'Yes, guv.' Vicky headed outside to the van. She opened the back and took out gloves and overshoes, the camera and two torches under the watchful eye of the dozen or more men standing on the pavement. Two of them were drinking cans of lager.

As she was closing the door, a West Indian in a long

coat and dreadlocks tied back with a strip of red, yellow and green cloth ambled over. 'Miss?' he said. 'Can I talk to you?'

She was taken aback by his politeness and had already taken a step away from him.

He realised he had startled her so he held up his hands. 'Sorry, miss. I didn't mean to scare you.' He smiled showing brilliantly white teeth. 'I just wanted to ask you about Anthony.'

'Anthony Lawson?'

He nodded. 'He's a friend of mine. We used to sleep rough together, then he moved in here. He said he was trying to get me in, too.'

'You know there's been a fire?'

The man nodded. 'Sure.'

'I'm afraid you friend was hurt.'

'Hurt? How bad.'

'I'm sorry, your friend is dead. I'm here to carry out an investigation to find out what happened.'

'Yeah, that's what I heard, I heard he was dead.' The man began shifting his weight from side to side. 'So, here's the thing, miss. Who do I talk to about getting the room?'

Vicky frowned. 'The room?'

The man nodded. 'The room. His room. Anthony's room. How can I get his room? I mean, he don't need it no more, right?'

'I suppose not.'

'So who do I talk to?'

'Sir, there's been a fire in there. A bad fire. I don't think anyone is going to be moving in for a while.'

'I don't mind, that's okay, it doesn't have to look good,

I just want a room.' He looked at her pleadingly. 'I need a room, that's all.'

'I understand,' she said. 'Look, they're going to be busy in there all today, why don't you come back tomorrow.' She groped inside her tunic and pulled out her wallet. 'Here, take this,' she said, handing him two twenty-pound notes.

His eyes widened. 'God bless you, miss,' he muttered, then hurried away with the money as if he feared she would change her mind.

Vicky locked the door and headed back inside.

'No sign of SOCO?' asked Farmer.

Vicky shook her head. 'They've got a lot on,' said the sergeant. 'I was told three hours, maybe four.'

'Okay, well we'll have a look-see,' said Farmer. He went up the stairs first and Vicky followed. The stairwell was wet where water had run down from the second floor, and the higher they climbed the more water there was and the stronger the smell of smoke.

The second-floor hallway was tiled and as soon as they walked from the stairs it was clear where the fire had been. The door had been forced in and then ripped out and placed against the wall in the hallway. Police tape had been put haphazardly across the doorway.

Farmer and Vicky put on their overshoes and gloves, then they went into the room. The window had been opened but the smell of burnt wood and carpet was overpowering. They saw the body immediately, lying on its back with the arms and legs bunched in a defensive posture as if warding off blows.

Vicky gasped and took an involuntary step backwards. She put up her hand to cover her mouth.

Whatever clothing the man had been wearing had burned away and the flesh had burst open in more than a dozen places. Vicky couldn't tell if the man had been bald or if the fire had burned off all the hair but the head was a black sphere of burnt flesh with grinning yellowed teeth.

Vicky felt her stomach heave and she began to retch.

'Outside!' shouted Farmer. 'Don't you dare contaminate the scene!'

Vicky turned and bolted out into the corridor, bent double. She threw up over a wall and stood gasping and spluttering.

'For fuck's sake, girl, what's wrong with you?' asked Farmer.

Vicky shook her head but couldn't speak. She spat on to the floor, cleared her throat and spat again. She took several deep breaths and then straightened up. 'Sorry,' she said.

'Have you not seen a dead body before?'

Vicky didn't answer. She had, but never as badly burnt as the one in the room. The smell of burnt flesh had made her flash back to the fire in which she was injured. The stench was the same, the aroma of overcooked meat, of scorched skin and burnt fat. If her colleagues hadn't got to her in time and pulled her out, she could have ended up exactly like the body on the floor. That could so easily have been her and the realisation made her head swim.

'Do you want to go outside?' asked Farmer.

'I'm all right,' she said.

'I can't have you throwing up over evidence.'

'It won't happen again. I promise.'

He stared at her for several seconds and then nodded. 'Okay. But if it does, you can go back to the van.'

'Yes, guv,' said Vicky. She could tell from his tone and the glare he was giving her that if she did have to leave it would be the end of her career with fire investigation.

Farmer went back into the room. Vicky followed him and again the stench made her want to vomit but she forced herself to stay calm as she looked around.

The remains of a broken chair were by the side of the body. The wooden parts had burned away leaving just the metal legs, which had buckled in the heat.

The room was small, barely eight feet wide with a single bed, a small table, and a two-seater sofa by the window. All that remained of the sofa was the metal frame and judging by the black sooty patch above it, whatever it was made of had burned fiercely. The bed had also been totally destroyed by the fire, suggesting the mattress hadn't been fire-retardant.

Vicky looked around the room, taking everything in. There was an open smoke detector on the wall by the door. The battery had been removed. There was a glass ashtray on the table which confirmed that Lawson was a smoker.

'So what do you think?' asked Farmer.

'Cause of death?' said Vicky, trying not to look at the remains. 'I guess we need a post-mortem to be sure.'

Farmer smiled thinly. 'Way to go covering your arse.'

'What do you want me to say?' asked Vicky. She forced herself to look at the body. She threw up into her mouth but forced herself to swallow it. 'Clearly the body has been seriously damaged by the fire,' she said. She swallowed again but the bitter acrid taste was still at the back of her mouth. 'But the position of the arms and the legs looks as if he was trying to defend himself against an attacker. The legs are drawn up and his arms are up over his face. And his hands. They're fists, as if he was fighting.'

Farmer nodded. 'So you think he was fighting someone off before he died?'

She looked at him suspiciously. 'No, now I think you're testing me. What am I missing?'

'Nothing to be ashamed of, sweetheart. The cop downstairs clearly jumped to the same conclusion. You take one look at a body like that and assume he was attacked.'

'It does look like there was a fight, yes.'

Farmer grinned. 'Back in the day investigators did think this pugilistic pose meant the victim was under attack. But now we know that extreme heat alone can cause the muscles and tendons to contract. That tightens them up and flexes the arms and legs.'

'So it all happened after death?'

'That's right. And I don't think he was on the floor when he died, either.' He pointed at the chair. 'I'd say he was sitting on that chair, then had some sort of seizure. A stroke or a heart attack. The post-mortem will hopefully tell us which.' He pointed at the ashtray. 'A smoker, obviously. So there's a chance he was smoking when he had the attack. He drops the cigarette and it lands on the carpet. The carpet looks cheap, imported probably, and not fire resistant. It smoulders and it burns. The old fella was probably dead by then, but if not the smoke would have taken him. The chair's wood, so that burns, and the legs closer to the seat of the fire would burn through first which means he would fall to the side. He hits the floor and rolls on to his back and then the fire takes hold and his arms and legs draw up.'

'So, it's natural causes?' She looked down at the body but she saw herself lying in the same protective position, arms and legs up, her clothing burned away, her flesh burned down to the bone. She could feel herself about to throw up again and she looked away.

'Death by smoking, I'd say. It was probably the smoking that brought on the health issue, and the cigarette that started the fire.'

Vicky looked around the room doing everything she could to avoid seeing the body. 'I wonder what his story was. Nearly sixty years old and he ends up here, in a single room in a homeless hostel.'

'Life can be tough. People make bad decisions. Most people are only a couple of pay cheques away from being on the street.'

'You think so?'

'I know so,' said Farmer. 'Not everyone has the luxury of big chunks of money in the bank.' He saw her lips tighten and held up his hand. 'Sorry, that's not what I meant.'

'No problem.'

'I didn't mean you. I meant, people in general.'

'I know.'

'Your money, that's a whole different—'

'Now you're starting to protest too much,' she said. 'I know what you meant. And I get what you're saying. You get in debt, you miss a few payments and the bank takes away your home. I get that. But people have friends, they have family.'

'You don't see friends for dust when you've got money problems,' said Farmer. 'And as for family . . .' He shrugged. 'They don't always stick around either.'

'But he can't have gone through life alone,' said Vicky. 'If he didn't have a wife and kids he probably had siblings or cousins. His parents might still be alive.' She could see that she was making Farmer uncomfortable so she changed the subject. 'What do you want in the way of pictures?' she asked.

'The works,' said Farmer. 'And I'll let you do the report. Give you a chance to show off what you now know about the pugilistic posture.'

'Thanks, guv, you're all heart.'

They stayed at the fire scene for the best part of two hours. Towards the end, Vicky was able to look at the burnt body without her stomach heaving, but she kept flashing back to her own fire and how close she had come to being burned alive. After half an hour she stopped noticing the smell but the images of the fire that almost killed her kept flashing into her mind no matter how hard she tried to block them out.

Just as she was finishing up two SOCOs arrived in white protective suits and masks. Farmer knew them both and introduced Vicky. They all shook hands.

The more senior of the SOCO men pulled his mask down and wagged his finger at Farmer. 'You know you're supposed to wait for us, Des.'

'I was saving you time,' said Farmer. 'Your guys were about to treat it as a robbery-murder and you know how your detectives hate having their time wasted.'

The SOCO looked down at the body and smiled. 'Ah, the old pugilistic pose,' he said. 'Always throws you the first time you come across it.' He gestured at the door. 'Who was sick out in the corridor?'

Vicky raised her hand. 'Guilty.'

The man smiled. 'We've all been there,' he said.

'To be fair, I've never thrown up at a fire scene,' said Farmer. He looked over at Vicky. 'Hopefully it won't be happening again.'

'At least you made it to the corridor,' said the SOCO. 'First time I threw up it was all over the body.' He pulled his mask back into place. 'Right, let the dog see the rabbit.'

Farmer and Vicky headed out and went downstairs to the van. They put their equipment into the back and Vicky slammed the door. 'Let's leave off finishing the paperwork until we're back at Dowgate,' said Farmer.

They climbed into the front and Vicky started the engine.

'Do you fancy popping around to where it happened?' asked Farmer as he fastened his seat belt. 'The hotel fire? I wouldn't mind having a look.'

'Sure,' said Vicky. 'It's only a few minutes away.' She started the van and drove south. She took a left, then a right, then frowned when she saw all that remained of the hotel was the brick frontage which was held up by scaffolding. The bulk of the building had been demolished and the site surrounded by a hoarding on which were a series of artist impressions of what would replace it – a modern apartment block with shops and restaurants on the ground floor. She parked at the side of the road and wound down her window.

'Didn't you say it was listed?' asked Farmer.

'That's what I was told,' said Vicky.

'The council doesn't usually allow you to knock down listed buildings,' said Farmer.

'I guess the fire must have damaged it so much that it couldn't be rebuilt,' said Vicky. 'They've kept the façade so maybe that's enough to satisfy the planners.'

'Let's have a look around,' said Farmer. He got out of the van and walked over to the hoarding. There was a board stuck to it with the name of the architect, the owners, the contractors and a list of prospective tenants for the shops. Next to it was another board which proudly proclaimed that there had been no accidents on the site for ninety-seven days.

Farmer pointed at the name of the owner of the building. 'Are they the people you spoke to after your accident?'

Vicky frowned. 'I don't think so, no. They were lawyers representing the property firm.' She turned to look at him. 'Whose definition of accident are you using there?'

'That's a very good question, sweetheart.' He nodded at the board. 'It's the same company, though? That owned the building when there was a fire?'

Vicky shrugged. 'I couldn't tell you. Mum had a lawyer check the paperwork and the money went into the bank.'

They got back into the van.

'Have you looked at the file?' asked Vicky.

'It's in storage, I've put in a request to have it pulled. But Willie knew his stuff. He was old school.' He fastened his seat belt again. 'It was one of his last cases, though. He retired not long after. Maybe he took his eye off the ball. What did they say to you about the cause of the fire?'

Vicky frowned. 'To me, nothing. I was in the hospital

and then I was at home. I guess I assumed if it had been deliberate someone would have told me.'

'If there had been proof it was deliberate then there'd have been a court case.' Farmer shrugged. 'Okay, let's see what the file says.' He pointed down the road. 'Home, James.'

Vicky drove off. She wondered what file he was talking about. The file of photographs he kept in his desk? Or did he have another file tucked away?

32

Vicky was making coffee for herself when Danny Maguire walked in. He had rolled up his shirtsleeves and was carrying a Pot Noodle. 'Any hot water going?' he asked.

'Kettle's just boiled,' said Vicky.

Maguire poured water into the noodles and Vicky wrinkled her nose at the chemical smell that filled the room. 'So how's it going?' he asked.

'All good,' said Vicky. 'I'm learning a lot, that's for sure.' She sipped her coffee. 'Danny, do you remember a fatality you handled a while back? Samantha Stewart? She was a model who died when a candle set fire to her room.'

'Why do you ask?'

She shrugged carelessly. 'I'm just going through old cases, getting a feel for the job.'

'But why that case in particular?' His eyes narrowed and she could see that he was assessing her reaction.

'Just random.' She realised as she said it that it sounded weak. She smiled. 'I'm looking at a lot of old cases.'

'Did Des choose it for you?' He was watching her closely and she realised she had made a mistake raising the subject.

'No,' she said. 'As I said, random. I'm looking at cases and seeing what the conclusions were.'

Maguire leaned against the counter. 'What did you want to know?'

'It just seemed strange that she didn't wake up. The sofa was on fire, wouldn't that wake you up. The pain of being burned?'

'She'd been drinking. Big wine drinker was Samantha.'

'Even so . . .'

Maguire sniffed his noodles and stirred them again. 'It's down to the way the fire spread,' he said. 'You're right, if the sofa had burned right away the heat would have woken her up, unless she was blind drunk. But the candle was some distance away, near the window. A curtain blew over the candle and the curtain started to burn. Then pieces of the burning curtain fell on to the carpet and that began to smoulder. That filled the room with smoke and gasses and that's what probably killed her.'

'Probably? You don't know for sure?'

Maguire shrugged. 'Like I said, there was so much tissue damage it wasn't possible to confirm if there was smoke in the lungs or not. But it was pretty clear from the scene what had happened. She'd had a drink or two, there was a half empty bottle on the floor by the sofa, so she didn't smell the smoke. The smoke incapacitated or killed her and then the burning sofa did the rest. You read the report, right?'

Vicky nodded. 'No, I get it. It seems logical.'

'Anything else?'

She shook her head.

'Just let me know if you do have any more questions,'

he said. 'I know there's a lot to take in.' He headed back
to his office, stirring his noodles.

Vicky took her coffee back to her desk, along with a
cup of water for her rubber plant. She poured the water
into the dish under the pot and then sat down at her
terminal.

She called up the Samantha Stewart file and sipped
her coffee as she studied it. The report seemed straightforward and logical and she couldn't find anything to
suggest that it wasn't an accident. She put down her cup.
Except, as Farmer said, most accidents weren't accidents
at all. Samantha had put a lit candle by a curtain. She
had drunk too much wine. The battery in her smoke
alarm had died. If any one of those steps had been missing,
she would probably still be alive.

She closed the file and opened the one on Julia Silk.
She sat back and read through the file again, more carefully than the last time she'd looked at it. Willie Campbell's
report was thorough. A neighbour had called nine nine
nine after seeing flames in a downstairs room in Julia's
house. The house was well ablaze by the time two appliances had arrived from the Euston Road station. They
hadn't been able to enter the house because the fire was
so severe and it had taken the best part of an hour before
they got it under control. They found Julia in her bedroom,
burned almost beyond recognition.

According to Campbell the seat of the fire had been
a faulty plug attached to the television. The television was
badly damaged but Campbell had ascertained that it had
been left on. The plug had been changed for some reason
and was a cheap Chinese version that failed British safety
standards. Campbell theorised that the plug had over-

heated and started to burn, and the fire had spread across the carpets and rugs to a leather sofa that also failed to meet British safety standards.

All the floors and stairs were covered with fitted carpets in a thick pile and the sitting-room door had been left open. The fire had spread upstairs and as her bedroom door was also open it would have quickly filled with smoke. The smoke would have certainly incapacitated her and in all likelihood it would have killed her before the fire reached her. That was why the fire brigade recommended that all bedroom doors were shut at night.

In Julia's case, open or shut, the smoke would have got to her eventually because the smoke alarms weren't working. There were two, one in the kitchen and one in the downstairs hall and the batteries in both had gone flat. Vicky was surprised at how often people went to the trouble of fitting alarms but then couldn't be bothered to put in fresh batteries. The pathologist's report had said that the body was in such a bad state there was no way to confirm the presence of smoke in the lungs. In fact, the damage was so severe that she had to be identified from her dental work.

As she studied the file, Vicky realised that Farmer was right. Accidents more often than not weren't Acts of God, they were a series of decisions that when put together led to something bad happening. And just like Samantha Stewart, if any steps had been missing, Julia Silk would probably still be alive: if she hadn't fitted a cheap plug to her television, there wouldn't have been a fire; if she had switched off the television when she went to bed, the plug wouldn't have overheated; if she had put new batteries in her smoke alarms, they might have woken her before the smoke reached the bedroom. And if she had closed her bedroom door, the fire might have been kept at bay until the firefighters could get in to save her. So many steps, but put together they led inescapably to her death.

Vicky ran her hand through her hair and sighed. But why had Farmer put the details of her death on display in his spare bedroom? And why all the other cases? If he was investigating the deaths, why was he taking the information home with him?

Her door opened. It was Farmer. 'I've got to go see a CPS lawyer. She needs her hand holding on a case they're prosecuting. I don't know how long I'll be.'

'I've got paperwork to catch up on,' she said.

'If Danny catches a good fire, you can hang out with him.' He closed the door and she took another sip of her coffee. After five minutes she went along to his office. She knocked on his door to check that he wasn't still there and when there was no answer she opened it and slipped inside. Her heart was racing because she knew that what she was doing was wrong. She sat down on his chair and eased the top drawer open. There was a diary there and she took it out and flicked through it. There were cigarette papers and a lighter. A small plastic box of LFB business cards. Half a dozen biros.

The second drawer down was full of files, more than a dozen. She flicked through them. None of them were related to deaths, they were all either fires in commercial premises or vehicles. She put the files back in the drawer. She sighed. She wasn't even sure what she was looking for.

There were two old smoke alarms in the bottom drawer

and a handful of batteries. There was a file too, and she took it out and opened it. There were a dozen photographs, all of the same burnt building. She frowned as she recognised it. It was the hotel where she had been injured. What was Farmer doing with them in his drawer? She looked through the pictures and the images made her shudder. She flashed back to the heat and the flames and the smoke and her stomach lurched when she remembered how the floor had given away beneath her. She felt her heart race and she took a deep breath to calm herself as she closed the file.

Underneath the file was a single notebook. She took it out. There was a list of names on the first page. The top name was Diana Hewson. Underneath were eight names including Emma Fox, Samantha Stewart and Julia Silk. Then there was a space and the word LEEDS in capital letters. Underneath were three more names: Eva Hannah; Mary Frear; Catherine Woods. Then MANCHESTER and two names: Angela Griffith and Jill Clarke. Then EDINBURGH with a question mark. And below that, BELFAST and another question mark.

She started as she heard Farmer's voice from down in the yard. She shoved the notebook and file back into the drawer and hurried over to the door. She eased it open, checked the corridor and rushed to her office. She had just reached the door when she heard Farmer at the top of the stairs. 'You all right, sweetheart?'

She turned to look at him and forced a smile. 'Just getting myself a coffee, guv.'

He frowned. 'So where is it?'

She laughed and she could hear the uncertainty in it. 'Forgot my mug,' she said. 'I'd probably forget my head if it wasn't screwed on.' She slipped into her office and closed the door behind her, her heart racing.

She jumped when there was a knock on the door. She opened it. It was Farmer. 'The CPS girl just phoned to reschedule so this afternoon you'll be with me.'

'Great,' said Vicky.

'Are you okay?'

'Sure. Why?'

'You looked flushed. It's not the wrong time of the month, is it? I know how you girls can get.'

Vicky sighed and closed the door in his face.

33

Jayne Chandler was still alive, but she wouldn't be for much longer. He'd met her in a cocktail bar not far from where she worked, bought her a couple of drinks and had been his usual charming self. It wasn't hard. Lots of eye contact, expressing the right amount of interest in her thoughts and opinions, smiling when she said anything funny, touching her occasionally on the arm.

He had his backpack with him and told her that he had just left work. He didn't tell her that it contained everything he would need to rape and kill her. It had the stun gun and pepper spray that he would have used to subdue her if she had proven difficult, but they hadn't been necessary. He'd told her that he worked in the City, he was a metals trader, but at weekends he worked with disadvantaged children. He'd come from a broken home, he'd said, so he wanted to put something back.

All lies. His mother and father were still together and had been perfect parents. It wasn't their fault that he'd turned out to be a sociopathic killer. It was just his nature. He'd started with animals when he was a kid, killing out of curiosity more than anything. Then he'd started to enjoy inflicting pain and he'd moved on to killing women, which was way more satisfying than taking the lives of cats and dogs. He still visited his mother and father every second weekend and at Christmas and Easter. He loved his parents and they loved him, but that's not what he told her as he sipped his drink and looked into her eyes.

He'd slipped the Rohypnol into her third drink as he'd carried it from the bar to their table. Not too much, he didn't want her passing out, just enough to lower her inhibitions. Rohypnol, was the perfect drug for rapists and murderers. Designed to treat severe insomnia, in low doses it was a relaxant and erased short-term memory. He bought his online from a company in Canada, delivered to a PO box in Marylebone. Getting the dose just right was the hard part, but he had had plenty of practice over the years.

He'd told her that he played badminton twice a week and she said that she loved to play and that maybe one weekend they should have a game. He told her that Brighton was one of his favourite places and she said that she had gone to university there. Small world. Except it wasn't a small world, he had just done his research.

At ten he said he had to go home because he had an early morning conference call with Tokyo and he could see that impressed her. He knew where she lived, of course, so when he said he lived half a mile away from her house it was her idea to suggest a taxi. She used her Gett app to order a black cab, and when they pulled up in front of her house she asked him if he wanted to go in for coffee. He'd played hard to get, told her again about the early morning conference call, but then said what the heck, yes, he'd love a coffee. Coffee had turned out to be wine and he'd given her more Rohypnol and soon after that she had passed out. He'd carried her upstairs. She was so light, like a child. She'd moaned when he'd dropped her on to her bed and for a moment he thought she might wake up, but her eyes stayed close and after a while she was quiet again. He'd stripped off her clothes and put them in her laundry basket in the bathroom. He'd checked her bra and smiled when he saw it was 32B. He had been right. Back in the bedroom, he took off his clothes and put them on a chair. He set up his iPhone on the bedside table, leaning it against a lamp so he could record everything he did to her.

He was already hard, anticipating the pleasure that was to come. He adjusted her legs and gasped as he entered her. He could have used a condom, but that would have spoiled the fun. He relished knowing that they died with his life inside them. That made it so much better. Afterwards, he rolled off the bed and dressed. As always, he wouldn't wash for a few days now, and would enjoy her smell on his body for a while longer.

He stood looking down at her. Her breasts were rising and falling. She did have lovely breasts. Soft yet firm and perfectly shaped. 'So how was it for you, Jayne?' he asked, then chuckled to himself. He knew that the logical thing to do would be to let the smoke kill her. The Rohypnol would keep her out while her lungs filled with smoke and then she'd die. But then he'd be missing the best part, the part that made it all worthwhile. He enjoyed the stalking and he enjoyed the raping, but the thing he enjoyed the most was the taking of their lives. To be honest, he would have preferred to do it with a cord around their neck while she was awake but she had neighbours either side and he couldn't take the risk of her screaming.

'Are you ready, Jayne?' he asked.

He got back on the bed and sat astride her, looking down on her face. He put his hands around her throat, softly at first and then harder. It would leave marks, but the fire would take care of them. Fire was the great cleanser. DNA, fingerprints, fibres, fire destroyed them all. He squeezed, tighter. Her head moved, but it was just a reflex. He could feel the blood pounding in her neck, trying to force its way past the blockage. He found himself growing harder as he squeezed the life out of her.

'Is it good for you, Jayne?' he whispered, putting his face closer to hers. Her eyes opened wide and he saw the panic in them. Her mouth worked soundlessly and the fear grew exponentially as even through her drugged state she realised what was happening. His heart was pounding now at the perfection of the kill. She was awake. She was looking at him, right at him. She knew what he was doing to her and that his would be the last face she would ever see. He relaxed his grip on her throat, just enough to allow a little blood up to the brain. She began to struggle but his legs kept her arms pinned to her side. He would have loved to have taken his hands away and hear what she had to say but he couldn't risk her screaming so he tightened his grip again, then bent down and kissed her on the lips. She was bucking underneath him now, trying to throw him off, but he was bigger and heavier and she was drugged up to the eyeballs. 'That's it, Jayne, fight!' he whispered into her ear. 'It won't do you any good, but fight as you die. That makes it so much better for me.'

He squeezed tighter and then suddenly her eyes closed and she went still. He wondered if she was faking it so he kept his grip tight and sure enough after ten seconds had passed her eyes opened and she began to struggle again. He ground himself down against her and felt his fingertips touch behind her neck, and then she went still again and this time he knew she wasn't faking it because the life faded from her eyes. He let go of her neck and shuddered with pleasure.

He realised that he'd ejaculated inside his pants. He sat back, gasping. It had been the most intense experience he'd ever felt. He sighed and looked up at the ceiling and sighed again. Best. Kill. Ever.

He rolled over and sat on the edge of the bed, recovering his composure as his erection gradually subsided. He stood up slowly, then picked up the soft toys that he'd thrown on the floor and arranged them around her. They would burn well. He went downstairs and took a pair of blue latex gloves from his backpack and put them on. He got a chair from the kitchen, then stood on it to open the smoke detector. He took a dead nine-volt battery from his pocket and used it to replace the one that was there. He closed the detector and pressed the red button to check that it wasn't working.

She had left her MacBook Pro laptop on the kitchen table. He took it upstairs. He pulled out the charger and put it in his backpack, replacing it with the one that he had bought at a market stall the previous day, so cheap that it had to be a Chinese copy. He plugged the laptop in and the charging light went on. He put the laptop on the bed next to her, then took a pack of Quavers from his backpack and sprinkled them across the bed. The curly potato snack was almost pure fat, burned easily and left virtually no trace. It was the perfect fire starter.

He made a final check of the room, then took a culinary butane torch from his backpack. He lit it and began to play the flame over the corner of the laptop. The plastic began to melt once it reached 150 degrees Celsius and then it began to smoke. He continued to play the flame across the plastic until it ignited, at close to 500 degrees. Once it had started burning he switched off the blowtorch and put it into his backpack. Thick black smoke was pluming towards the ceiling as he headed for the door. Once the laptop's lithium battery caught fire the heat would be intense and the bed would be consumed in the fire, reducing the body to a charred skeleton in less than an hour. The fire brigade investigators would see the burnt laptop was the seat of the fire and put it down to a malfunctioning computer component. Open and shut. Jayne Chandler's death would be a sad accident, nothing more. It was the perfect crime.

Before he let himself out of the house, he checked that he hadn't forgotten anything, then shouldered his backpack and walked down the road. Her bedroom was at the back of the house and it wasn't overlooked. He doubted that anyone would spot the fire until the house was well ablaze.

He began whistling softly to himself. He was looking forward to replaying the rape on his phone when he got home. He had more than a dozen videos now, and planned to have many more. Playing the video was nowhere near as good as the real thing, but it got him through the quiet times between kills.

34

Farmer opened the door to Vicky's office without knocking. 'Why do you always close your door?' he asked. 'None of us close our doors.'

'I didn't realise it was a thing,' said Vicky. 'Sorry.'

'We have an open-door policy,' said Farmer. 'Literally.' He was holding a manila file.

'No one told me.'

'We probably didn't tell you to flush the toilet after you've used it, but that's policy too.'

'I'll remember that. So how can I help you?'

He held up the file. 'This is everything Willie did on the hotel fire,' said Farmer. He gave her the file, sat down and swung his feet on to her desk.

Vicky flicked through the paperwork and looked at the pictures. She frowned and looked up at Farmer. 'There doesn't seem to be much,' she said.

'The bare minimum,' said Farmer. 'Willie ticked all the boxes, but that's it. And there's no mention of there being more than one point of origin. According to Willie, the fire started in the bar and spread through the hotel.' He gestured at the file. 'He's blaming the homeless people who were sleeping there. He says they'd been taking electricity from the mains and that their wiring overheated and started the fire.'

'The guy I spoke to said they didn't have any power,' said Vicky. 'They had water but they were using gas cylinders for their cooking.'

Farmer nodded. 'Willie mentioned the gas cylinders, he said they added to the fire in the main building.'

Vicky scanned the paperwork. 'He says they tapped the mains in the bar.' She looked up. 'But they weren't living in the bar. They were sleeping on the top floor of the hotel. All their stuff was there.'

Farmer nodded. 'You'll see from the reports that Willie didn't talk to any of the people living in the hotel. There are interviews with the two people who called the fire in but all they confirm is that they saw smoke coming from the bar.'

'He never spoke to me.'

'No, but he interviewed Tony Abbey and Rick Blackwell at the scene.'

'But they both arrived after me and neither was in the building. What about Colin Noller, Shaun Allen, Andy Mitchell and the rest of the BA team?'

'See for yourself,' said Farmer. 'Senior officers only.'

'Is that usual?'

'It is if you're just ticking boxes,' said Farmer. 'Personally, with a fire like that, I would have expected him to be more thorough. But the cause of the fire is backed up by the evidence, so far as I can see.'

'But it spread from the bar to the rooms at the rear of the hotel. And the front.' She flicked through the pages. 'I don't see anything that explains how that could have happened.'

Farmer nodded. 'He was more concerned with the cause of the fire and the point of origin than he was with how it spread.'

'Is that normal?'

'If he was just box-ticking, I suppose so.'

'What do you think, guv?'

'I'm not one for counting chickens,' said Farmer. 'What I will say is that when there's a firefighter injury usually we pull out all the stops. There'd be a health and safety investigation, the FBU would get involved, the police would carry out their own investigation, but in this case none of that happened. According to Willie, the dangerous structures engineer deemed it unsafe so no one could go in. He's got the paperwork to back that up.' He wrinkled his nose. 'I'll reach out to SOCO and see what they have to say.'

'What about talking to Willie?'

'Let me talk to the cops first. No one likes being second-guessed.'

'Whatever you say.'

He swung his feet off the desk and took the file back from her. 'So, I need you to do something for me, by way of quid pro quo,' he said. 'What do you know about human spontaneous combustion?'

'I know there's no such thing.'

Farmer grinned. 'Excellent. You need to talk to a journalist and put her right.'

'A journalist? Me? Why?'

'Because she's been pestering the press office and they don't know what to tell her so they passed her on to me and now I'm passing her on to you.' He gave her a piece of paper on which was written a name – India

Somerville – and a phone number. 'She works for the *Evening Standard.*'

'What do I tell her?'

'I guess she's got questions about human spontaneous combustion so you just answer them. I know how you girls love to natter.' He walked out, leaving the door open.

'Thanks, guv,' Vicky muttered under her breath. She tapped out the number on the piece of paper. It was answered by a man so Vicky asked to speak to India and she heard him shout across the office, asking for her extension. He transferred the call and India answered. Vicky explained who she was and why she was calling.

'Brilliant,' said the journalist. 'Look, I'd really like to show you some photographs I've got, can I pop around and see you?'

'We're not really geared up for visitors and to be honest I've got a stack of work to do here.'

'What time does your shift finish?'

'Why?'

'Thought I could buy you a drink. The Steelyard is still next to the station, right?'

'Yeah, it hasn't moved.'

'I meant it hadn't closed down or anything?'

'No, it's still there.'

'Look, I'm not far away. I'll see you there for a drink.'

Vicky sighed. She was dog-tired and really just wanted to go home and sleep.

'It won't take long,' pressed the journalist. 'And trust me, these are interesting pictures. I've never seen anything like it.'

'Okay,' said Vicky. 'Just one drink.'

35

Vicky walked into the Steelyard and looked around. There was a young woman in a red coat standing by the bar talking to Matt, and she looked over at Vicky and waved. Vicky waved back. The woman walked over and held out her hand. 'India,' she said. 'Thanks so much for this.' She had long, curly blond hair and big green eyes and alabaster-white skin as if she never went out in the sun. Hanging off one shoulder was a Louis Vuitton bag.

'Vicky.'

They shook hands. India's eyes hardened a fraction when she saw the damage to Vicky's ear and face but her smile remained professional. 'What can I get you?' There was a hint of Irish in her accent.

'It's usually lager when the guys are around, but I'd love a glass of wine.'

'Red or white?'

'Surprise me. I'll grab a table.'

Vicky took off her coat and took a free sofa by the bare-brick wall. As she made herself comfortable, India came over with two large glasses of red wine. 'The barman recommends this,' she said.

Vicky looked over at Matt and he flashed her a thumbs-up. She raised her glass to him, tasted it, then smiled and nodded at him. He grinned back at her.

'He's cute, isn't he?' said India, sitting down.

'I guess,' said Vicky.

India held out her glass. 'Well, pleased to meet you, anyway,' she said. They clinked glasses. 'I didn't realise until I googled you that you were *the* Vicky Lewis.'

'The Vicky Lewis?'

'The hero. You went into that blazing building and rescued a homeless man. And you rescued that family at Grenfell Tower.'

'Why would you google me?'

India laughed. 'That's the first thing all journalists do these days. Google and social media is how we do our research. I remember that fire. Didn't you get a huge pay-off afterwards?' She picked up her notepad and opened it.

Vicky shrugged but didn't answer the question.

'I just thought you'd left the fire brigade,' said the journalist.

'I'd never leave,' she said. 'Well, not until I have to retire.'

'You saved that man's life, didn't you? Did he ever thank you?'

'No,' said Vicky. 'I never saw him again.'

'That'd be a great picture, wouldn't it? The two of you together again?'

Vicky smiled. She desperately wanted to change the subject because the last thing she wanted was her picture in the paper. 'Can I ask you a question?'

'Sure.'

'How do you get a name like India?'

She laughed. 'Everyone asks that question. It's where I was conceived.'

Vicky laughed. 'Seriously?'

'Sadly, yes. My parents had their honeymoon in Goa and nine months later I arrived.'

'It's a nice name.'

'Oh yes, but the explanation is always a little embarrassing. So, the reason I'm here. We've had some photographs sent in of a fire in Kensington a few weeks ago. It looks as if it's a case of spontaneous combustion.'

'No such thing,' said Vicky. 'Not with people, anyway.'

'Then explain these,' said India. She opened her bag and took out three colour photographs and spread them over the table. It was a body. It could have been a man or a woman, it was just a vague shape. The skeleton was there but most of the flesh had charred and burned. What was strange was that there was no burning on the carpet of the surrounding furniture.

'When was this?' asked Vicky.

'Two weeks ago.'

Vicky frowned. She wasn't aware of a body being found within the last two weeks, though it could well have happened on another shift.

'You seem surprised,' said India, her pen poised over her notebook.

'If there was a fire, we should have been informed.'

'I think because there was no evidence of a fire, other than the body, the police handled it themselves. There was no damage to the room other than the carpet directly below the body. The man who died had a cleaning lady who had a key and came in at the weekend. She's the one who found the body.'

'Where did you get the pictures?'

'They came into our news desk.'

'They look like police crime-scene photographs.'

'I think they probably are. You can see the outline on the floor. That was a body. But now there's just a small pile of ash. And there's hardly any other damage in the room. It's as if the body just burned away from the inside.'

Vicky nodded. 'I can see that's what it looks like. Yes.'

'Have you ever seen anything like this before?'

'No, but then I've not been in investigations for long. But when I was a firefighter I never saw anything like that. Normally the whole room would have to burn to cause damage like that.'

'So it is spontaneous combustion?'

Vicky laughed. 'No,' she said. 'As I said on the phone, there's no such thing, not with bodies anyway. Some objects, like oil-soaked rags, can spontaneously ignite under the right circumstances, but not bodies. Google would have told you that.'

'Actually, Google is non-committal on the subject. There are plenty of cases where there is no explanation.'

Vicky sipped her drink. 'There have been experiments done that pretty much explain what happens,' she said. 'It's called the wick effect. Something, usually clothing, acts as a wick once the skin has split open. The wick dips into the fat and the fat then vaporises and burns. Most people store fat around the torso and thighs and it burns so slowly that there isn't actually that much heat given off. About the same as if a wastepaper basket was burning. And because it's slow, the oxygen that gets burned is replenished. That means the fire could burn for more than twelve hours without damaging the surroundings.'

'But how do you know the fire didn't start from inside?'

'Because there's nothing inside a human body that can possibly burst into flames. It's all very wet in there.'

'Well, the coroner has put down spontaneous combustion as the cause of death.'

'Really?'

'That's what I'm told.'

'Without an inquest?'

'There's only an inquest if the cause of death isn't known or if it was a violent death. Or if the person died in prison or police custody, which obviously doesn't apply here.'

'Okay, but have you actually seen this, in writing?'

'No, not in writing. But my source is good.'

'The reason I ask is that it wouldn't be the coroner giving the cause of death it would be a pathologist, and no pathologist would ever give spontaneous human combustion as a cause of death.'

'Can I quote you on that?'

'I'd rather you didn't.'

'But you're sure of your facts?'

Vicky nodded. 'Of course. But I don't want to be out there criticising a coroner or a pathologist. Especially when all you seem to have is hearsay.'

'Would you be prepared to say that there is no such thing as spontaneous combustion?'

'No such thing as human spontaneous combustion, yes. But I really don't want my name in the paper, India. My boss just said I should fill you in on spontaneous combustion, that's all.'

'I could just call you a member of the fire brigade's investigation team.'

Vicky sighed. 'I suppose that would be okay. But say something like there have never been any confirmed cases of human spontaneous combustion, an ignition source is always found eventually.'

India nodded. 'Okay, that's cool.' She sipped her drink. 'Can I arrange a photograph of you?'

'Why?'

'Because it's a good story. Firewoman hero turned investigator.'

'Firefighter,' corrected Vicky.

'Firefighter. It's a great human interest story.'

Vicky shook her head. 'I'd rather not.'

'Might help raise your profile.'

Vicky flashed a cold smile. 'I don't want my profile raised. I don't want anyone reading a story about me.' She waved a hand at the photographs. 'I was happy to help with the background you needed, but I don't want to be quoted and I really don't want an article about me. I just want to do my job and hopefully one day get back to fighting fires.'

'That's what you want, to go back to being a firefighter?'

'Of course. That's what all firefighters want to do. To help people, and keep them safe.'

The journalist scribbled in her notebook. 'So why are you investigating fires and not fighting them?'

Vicky shrugged. 'You'd have to ask the powers-that-be about that. But as for a story about me . . . thanks, but no thanks.' She sipped her wine. She looked over at the bar and saw that Matt was watching them. He winked and she smiled.

India reached into her bag and took out a business card. 'If you change your mind, call me.'

'Okay,' said Vicky.

India smiled, gathered up her photographs and put them into her bag along with her notepad and pen, then stuck out her hand. 'It's been a pleasure. Thank you for your time.'

Vicky shook her hand and returned the smile. As the journalist walked away, she stared at the card, wondering if she had said too much.

'You okay?'

She looked up. Matt was looking down at her, holding a tray of empty glasses.

'Yeah, all good.' She slipped the business card into her pocket.

'Drinking alone?'

'I was just heading off.'

Matt nodded at the door. 'Be careful of journalists. You can't trust them.'

'How did you know she was a journalist?'

'She was asking about you before you came in. Did I know you, did you come in here often, what were you like? I felt as if I was being interrogated, to be honest.'

'What did you tell her?'

'I said you were in here every night getting as drunk as a skunk and that most nights we had to carry you out.' He laughed at the look of surprise that flashed across her face. 'Joking!' he said. 'Good grief, girl, you don't think I was serious?'

She laughed. 'Sorry. I've had a hard day.'

He sat down next to her. 'She started asking questions about you, I asked her who she was, she said she worked for the *Evening Standard* and I said she'd have to talk to you because of bartender-customer confidentiality. Then you came in. That's it. End of.'

'Thanks.'

'Have you eaten?'

She shook her head. 'Not yet, no.'

'Fancy a pizza?'

'I'm okay.'

He grinned. 'I don't mean here. I'm finishing now, thought I might drop into Pizza Express.'

'I do like their American Hot,' Vicky said.

'Do you want to come? My treat?' He grinned. 'No ulterior motive, just a pizza and some wine, save me eating on my own.'

Vicky looked at her watch. It was just after eight. If she went home her mother would probably cook something, but a pizza sounded good.

'If you've got something else planned, it's not a problem.'

She smiled at him. 'No, I'm good,' she said.

'Give me five minutes,' he said and headed for the bar.

Vicky watched him put the glasses into the dishwasher and then leave through a staff door. She looked down at her gloved left hand and clenched and unclenched it. She needed to moisturise the skin, it was starting to stiffen. She took out her phone and called her mother. 'Mum, I'll be later than I thought,' she said.

'Work?'

'I'm going for a pizza with one of the guys from the pub,' said Vicky.

'A date?'

Vicky laughed. 'Just pizza.'

'What's he like?'

'What's who like?'

'You know very well who,' said Barbara. 'The mystery man.'

'His name's Matt. He works in the bar next to the station.'

'And?'

'And?' repeated Vicky.

'Tall? Short? Details, please.'

'Mum, we're going for a pizza, that's all.' Her mother didn't say anything and eventually Vicky laughed. 'Fine. He's tall, fit, good-looking. And he's sweet.'

'Send me a picture later,' said Barbara.

'I will not,' said Vicky and she ended the call. As she was putting the phone away, Matt reappeared in a black leather jacket.

Pizza Express was a five-minute walk away and there were plenty of tables. Vicky ordered her favourite American Hot and he ordered a Sloppy Giuseppe – a pizza covered with hot spiced beef, green pepper, red onion, mozzarella and tomato. He asked her if she wanted red wine or white and agreed that red was the better choice. The waitress was so busy smiling at Matt that she didn't even notice Vicky's scars. 'So how long have you been a firefighter?' Matt asked when the waitress finally left them.

'Ten years or so,' she said.

'Did the guys tell you I wanted to be a firefighter?'

'No,' she said. 'Wow. Why didn't you join? You look fit enough.' Her cheeks flushed as she realised what she'd said. 'I mean healthy. Shit, that sounds worse, doesn't it? I mean you're in good condition. Shit.'

He laughed. 'I'm loving all the compliments.'

'You know what I mean. You look like you work out.'

'I do,' he said. 'I'm a bit of a gym rat. You?'

'I used to be,' she said. 'I was always in the gym when I was a firefighter. These days not so much. Too many housewives using their phones and checking their make-up in the mirror.'

The waitress reappeared with their bottle of wine. Again she only had eyes for Matt and waited for him to taste the wine as if his approval was the most important thing in her world. He sniffed, swallowed and smiled. 'Perfect,' he said.

She beamed at him and touched him lightly on the shoulder as she walked by him.

'Looks like you've made a friend,' said Vicky.

He picked up his glass and smiled. 'You're funny,' he said.

'I'm not trying to be,' she said.

He nodded at her glass and she picked it up. They clinked glasses. 'Nice to meet you, Vicky Lewis.' He was looking her right in the eyes and seemed oblivious to the scarring on her left cheek.

She frowned. 'I didn't tell you my name. My surname.'

Matt grimaced. 'Guilty,' he said. 'I was talking to Des about you. Sorry.'

'Why?'

'Why sorry?'

She tilted her head so that her hair swung over her scarred cheek. 'Why were you talking to Des about me?'

He put down his glass and held up his hands. 'Just wanted a briefing on who you are, that's all. The usual questions. Are you married? Are you a bunny-boiler? Lesbian? Free-fall parachutist?'

'None of the above,' said Vicky.

'Good to know. Seriously, I just asked how you were getting on, how long you'd be around, and your name came up. And the fire. He talked about that.'

'Did he now?'

'You're a hero, that's what he said.'

She pulled a face and covered her embarrassment by drinking her wine.

'Sorry,' he said. 'Now I've made you uncomfortable, haven't I? I'm sorry. I'm such an idiot.'

'It's okay,' she said, putting her glass down. 'I'm over-sensitive sometimes.' She shrugged. 'I'm sorry.'

'Let's try not to say that again, shall we?' said Matt. 'Neither of us have anything to say sorry about. So, my failed ambition to be a firefighter? It's down to my knee.' He tapped his left knee. 'I hurt it playing rugby at school and it's never been right since. I'm fine on the flat, I'm on my feet all day in the bar, but I'm no use on ladders. The strength just seems to go really quickly. And I can't crawl. Not for any length of time. I went to see if an operation would help but the doctors said I just have a weak knee. They gave me exercises to do, which is why I'm in the gym such a lot. But at the end of the day if I put it under any sort of pressure it gives way.' He shrugged. 'Luck of the draw, I guess.'

'I'm sorry,' she said, then closed her eyes and shook her head. She couldn't seem to stop apologising. Their pizzas arrived, which cut short her embarrassment.

Matt laughed and reached over and touched her right hand. 'It's okay,' he said. 'I'm the same. Apologising for everything. I blame my mum.'

Vicky nodded. 'Me too.'

'You're blaming my mother?'

Vicky opened her mouth to protest but realised he was joking. 'You're funny.'

'I try my best,' he said.

The both started to tackle their pizzas.

'So how are you getting on with Des?' asked Matt.

'It's all good,' said Vicky.

'You know they call him the Grouch?'

Vicky chuckled. 'Yes. But he's a sweetie.'

'I wouldn't call him that,' said Matt. 'But he's a good customer. And I'm told he was a good firefighter, back in the day.'

'Now that I didn't know.'

'Yeah, he was a watch manager but then, you know . . .' He mimed taking a drink. 'That's what I heard, anyway.'

'Lots of firefighters drink,' said Vicky.

'Yeah, but Des let it get the better of him. That's why he kept getting divorced.'

'How do you know all this?' asked Vicky.

'Loads of firefighters drink in the bar,' said Matt. 'You can't help but hear things.'

Vicky sipped her wine. 'And what did you hear about me?'

Matt shrugged. 'You're a hero. And a first-class fire-fighter.'

'And?'

'And?' Matt repeated.

'I'm just wondering what the office gossip is.'

'I heard Des tell Danny that you were doing a good job.'

'You did not.'

'Day before yesterday. I didn't hear much but it was clear he thinks you're doing well.'

'Good to know,' said Vicky.

They ate in silence for a couple of minutes. 'How was Des that night you took him home.'

She grinned. 'Drunk as a skunk.'

Matt laughed. 'Yeah, I know.'

Vicky's eyes narrowed. 'What do you mean?'

Matt leaned towards her and lowered his voice. 'Just between you and me, I put a couple of vodkas in his lager.'

'You did not!'

'I could see he was getting competitive on the drinking front so I thought I'd level the playing field.'

Vicky sat back in her seat. 'Well that explains why he was so drunk. You're a bad man, Matt.'

'Guilty as charged. But he asked for it. He kept sending you to the bar, it was like he was trying to get you drunk.'

'Isn't that against the bartender's code of ethics?'

He laughed. 'No such thing.'

'Well it should be.'

'Are you mad at me?'

She chuckled and shook her head. 'I guess your heart was in the right place. But spiking drinks? Please don't do that again.'

He crossed his heart solemnly. 'I swear.'

She drank some more wine and he topped up her glass and his own.

'It was a funny night,' said Vicky. 'I ended up putting him to bed.'

'Did you now?'

'He could barely walk.'

'Did you do a fireman's lift?' asked Matt.

'There's no such thing any more,' said Vicky. 'Health and safety insists that there are two firefighters for each casualty.'

'Seriously?'

'Seriously. But of course when the shit hits the fan, health and safety sometimes goes out of the window. If there's a life in danger you do what you have to do.'

'So did you throw him over your shoulder or not?'

Vicky grinned. 'I did.'

Matt clinked his glass against hers. 'You go, girl.' He sipped his wine. 'Don't tell me you undressed him?'

'Only down to his boxer shorts.'

'OMG, you stripped the Grouch.' He sat back in his chair, shaking his head. 'Rather you than me.'

'It wasn't one of my greatest moments.' She sipped her wine. 'That was when it got really weird.'

'Did he try something on?'

Vicky realised she had said too much. Farmer was her boss and she was talking to a civilian. But she liked Matt and she desperately wanted to talk to someone about what she'd seen in Farmer's spare bedroom. 'It's not that,' she said. She shrugged. 'Let's change the subject.'

He grinned. 'Let's not,' he said. 'This sounds far more interesting.'

She shook her head. 'I shouldn't talk out of school.'

'But it wasn't at school, was it? You were in his house, that's what you said. So what happened?'

She shook her head and he laughed out loud. 'Oh come on, Vicky, don't be so mysterious. Did the Grouch pounce on you?'

Vicky giggled. 'No. Of course not.'

'Then what happened? I swear your secret is safe with me, young lady. Cross my heart and hope to die.' He reached over and touched her left hand and the gesture surprised her. It was the first time she'd been out with a man since her accident and she didn't want to misread any signals. She loved the way he seemed totally unfazed by her scars, and didn't react when other people flinched when they looked at her. It was as if he just didn't see the damage. Was it possible that he was really interested in her? Didn't he see the scars? They were the first thing she saw whenever she looked in the mirror.

Vicky sighed. 'Okay, okay,' she said. 'But don't you ever say anything to Des, okay?'

'You have my word,' he said. 'Bartender-customer confidentiality.'

Vicky leaned towards him and lowered her voice. 'He was out for the count. I went to get him a glass of water and I went into the wrong room. He had this display of girls who had been killed in fires. Thirteen of them. He had a map and pins in it and pictures and reports and post-mortem photographs. It was . . . weird.'

Matt pulled away his hand. 'What do you think he's doing?'

'I don't know. I looked up two of the cases and they were accidents. It was really weird, Matt. He'd put a lot of time into it, that's for sure. It gave me the goosebumps.' She shivered and wrinkled her nose. 'Maybe he's planning a book? What do you think?'

'Who would want to read a book about people who died in fires?' asked Matt.

Vicky shrugged. 'I don't know. It was just strange. Like

he had OCD or something. There was all sorts of stuff on his walls, like he'd been collecting it for years.'

'Have you told anybody?'

'Only you. Why?'

'I was just wondering if you'd told his boss. It does sound a bit weird.'

'I don't want to get him into trouble. Besides, it was his home, you know. I shouldn't even have been there.'

'He is a funny bugger, that's for sure. But I never had him down as a nutter.'

'It might be nothing,' said Vicky. She sipped her wine. 'I'm loving this pizza.'

Matt grinned. 'Me too.'

'Anyway, enough about me,' said Vicky. 'You enjoy bar work?'

He nodded. 'Yeah, I do. But I don't think anyone gets into bar work as a career choice,' he said. 'You sort of drift into it if you can't do what you really want to.'

'So what do you really want to do?'

He averted his eyes. 'You'll laugh.'

'You want to be a clown?'

'My feet aren't big enough.'

'That's funny.'

'A poet.'

Her eyes widened. 'Really?'

He nodded. 'I write poetry. But earning a living from poetry is next to impossible.'

'You studied English?'

'BA in Creative Writing and English Literature.' He shrugged. 'Not exactly the path to fame and riches.'

'You do what you want to do,' said Vicky. 'You do what makes you happy. That's why I want to fight fires. If writing poetry is what makes you happy, then that's what you have to do.'

He picked up his wine glass. 'Thank you,' he said. He clinked his glass against hers. 'Thank you for not making fun of me.'

'Well, let's wait until I've heard some of your poems before we decide whether or not I make fun of you.'

36

The taxi pulled up outside Vicky's house. She looked over at the upstairs bedroom window. The lights were off. 'Looks like my mum might be asleep. I'd invite you in for coffee but she'd only come down and start interrogating you.'

'I'm good,' said Matt. 'I've got an early start tomorrow and it's getting late.'

'Thanks for tonight. I had a really good time.' Pizza and wine had turned into drinks at a cocktail bar followed by an hour listening to jazz in a small club in Soho where everyone, including the musicians, seemed to be gay. It had turned midnight before she had realised it, and Matt had suggested he drop her off on his way home. He'd been the perfect gentleman, and she still wasn't sure whether he was interested in her as a friend or a girlfriend.

'Me too. It's been fun.' He smiled and their eyes locked and before she knew what was happening he'd leaned towards her. She opened her mouth for a kiss but he moved to her side and kissed her softly on the cheek. Her right cheek. 'You sleep well, yeah?'

She nodded, wondering if he'd noticed that she was

expecting a full-on kiss and not just a peck on the cheek. 'You too.'

He leaned across her to open the door for her and she was tempted to try for another kiss but before she could act he was sitting back, out of reach. She got out, closed the door and waved as the taxi drove away.

She watched the taxi until it turned left and then she walked to the house. Her mother's bedroom light was still off but Vicky was sure she saw the curtains twitch. She let herself in, closed the door and stood for a while staring at her reflection in the hall mirror. She turned her head to get a closer look at her mangled ear and scarred cheek. She'd almost grown used to her scars, thought it would be some time yet before she was completely dispassionate about them, and she knew that it was the first thing anyone saw when they looked at her. She took the glove off her left hand and removed the silicone gel sheets. She counted the blisters that had appeared since she had applied the sheets. Nine. That was a lot. She clenched and unclenched it. The skin had tightened. It wasn't painful, just uncomfortable. She would have to pop the blisters and treat them with TCP and antibiotic ointment before she went to bed. And apply moisturising lotion to the scars on her face. She looked at her reflection again, then turned so that she could only see the right-hand side of her face in the mirror. She smiled. She did look pretty, from that side anyway. She turned to look at the left-hand side and her smile became fixed. It seemed as bad now as when she had first left the hospital, though Dr Adams had said the scars were diminishing week by week. She wished that were true but in her heart of hearts she believed that he was only telling her what she wanted to hear.

She went upstairs, treading softly so as not to wake her mother.

37

Vicky's phone buzzed to let her know she'd received a text and it woke her up. She sat up, ran her hands through her hair and picked up the phone. She didn't recognise the number. LAST NIGHT WAS FUN. WE SHOULD DO IT AGAIN. She smiled as she realised it was from Matt, then she frowned. She didn't remember giving him her number. Had Farmer given it to him? Matt had said that they'd talked about her, but it didn't seem like the sort of thing Farmer would do.

She got up and showered, then put moisturising lotion on her scars, dressed and went downstairs. Her mum was already up and had a cup of tea ready for her, along with freshly made toast.

'Eggs?' asked Barbara.

'I'm okay. Toast is fine.'

'Most important meal of the day.'

Vicky laughed. 'Mum . . .'

'Check on Baxter, will you? He's in the sitting room and he's gone quiet, which probably means he's chewing something.'

Vicky went into the sitting room but there was no sign

of the dog. Then she heard a scuffling from the conservatory. 'Baxter? What are you doing?'

The dog was lying next to the wicker sofa and he sat up and looked at her, his tongue lolling from the side of his mouth. 'What have you got there?' asked Vicky and Baxter's tail twitched guiltily. Vicky went into the conservatory and looked down at Baxter. He was chewing on the TV remote. 'Are you serious?' she said, picking it up. She waved it under his nose. 'It's plastic. Why are you chewing plastic? How does that even taste good?' She took it back into the sitting room and put it next to the TV. Baxter followed her, tail wagging, and they went back into the kitchen.

Vicky sat down at the kitchen table and Baxter flopped down at her feet. Her mum sat down opposite her and sipped her tea. 'So you were right about Matt. Very good-looking.'

'Excuse me?'

'The young man who dropped you off last night. I'm assuming that was the Matt from the bar who was taking you for a pizza.'

'You were spying on me! I thought you were asleep.'

'A car pulled up. Of course I look to see who it is. I am in the Neighbourhood Watch, you know.'

Vicky laughed. 'You are terrible.'

'He did look very handsome.'

'He didn't get out of the car. What were you using, binoculars?'

She held up her hands. 'If you don't want to talk about it, that's fine. I understand.'

'Mum, please . . .' She buttered a piece of toast and smeared it with marmalade as Barbara continued to look

at her, an amused smile on her face. 'Fine,' said Vicky
eventually. 'We had a pizza and some wine and he was
a perfect gentleman. Happy now?'

Barbara beamed. 'As Larry.'

'Larry who?'

'It's an expression.'

'I know.'

'So why did you ask?'

'I was making a joke. Seriously, Matt is just . . .' She
shrugged. She didn't know what Matt was. She didn't
even know his surname. But she remembered the kiss
and the thought of it made her smile. Her phone rang
and she jumped.

'Maybe that's him,' said Barbara.

'Mum . . .' Vicky picked up the phone. It was Farmer.
'Guv?'

'Are you up, sweetheart? Bright eyed and bushy-tailed?'

'Yes, I guess so.'

'My car's playing up again. Bloody ridiculous, I paid
two hundred quid to get it fixed and it still won't start.'

'I left my car at Dowgate again.'

'Is that a problem?'

Vicky sighed. Yes, it was a problem. All he had to do
was call for a cab, but instead he wanted her to get a cab,
collect her car, drive to pick him up and take him to the
station. It made no sense at all. But he was her boss and
she wanted to keep in his good books. 'I'm on my way.'

She ended the call and realised her mum was looking
at her and shaking her head. 'He's using you as a taxi,
that's not right.'

'His car's in terrible shape. Plus he's teaching me a lot.'

'He can use the bus. Or the Tube.'

Vicky stood up, gulped down her tea and picked up her last piece of toast. 'Love you,' she said.

'Love you, too. And let me know how things work out with Matt.'

Vicky headed out, calling for a minicab as she went.

She arrived at Farmer's house about an hour later. He was on the pavement waiting for her, looking at his watch. He climbed into the passenger seat and fastened his seat belt. 'You took your time,' he said.

'Good morning to you, too,' she said as she pulled away from the kerb. 'To be fair, you could have given me more notice.'

'I thought the car was okay,' he said. 'It was fine yesterday. Today nothing.'

'Sounds like an electrical fault.'

'Do you think?' he said, his voice loaded with sarcasm.

They drove the rest of the way in silence. As they drove up to the station, the pump ladder was pulling out. Farmer wound down his window and called up to the driver, Bob Morris. 'What's happening?'

'Shout in Chalk Farm, they've just gone to pumps four. Warehouse alight.' Morris hit the blues and twos and the pump ladder pulled out.

'Let's get the van and we'll attend,' said Farmer.

'Right, guv.' She parked the car and they went upstairs to collect their gear and back to the van. Farmer grabbed the details of the shout from the office and by the time Vicky was in the driver's seat he had scanned them and gave her directions.

The warehouse was on an old industrial estate, a brick-built building with a flat roof that was well ablaze when Vicky and Farmer drove up in their van. The Dowgate pump ladder was there, along with two pumps from Paddington and another from Soho. Watch Manager Tony Abbey was incident commander in charge of the fire and he beamed when he saw Vicky climb out of the van.

'Vicky Lewis, as I live and breathe, how the hell are you?' he said as he hurried over. He hugged her and patted her on the back.

'Hi, Tony,' she said. She nodded at Farmer. 'You know Des Farmer?'

'Everyone knows the Grouch,' said Abbey.

'Yeah, fuck you too,' said Farmer, opening the rear door of the van. 'How about you put the bloody thing out so we can work out what happened.'

'We're working on it, Des.' Abbey punched Vicky gently on the arm. 'Good to see you, Vicky.'

'You too, Tony.'

He winked at her and jogged back to his pump ladder, where Crew Manager Dave Potter was waiting for him. Potter waved at Vicky and she waved back. One of the Paddington firefighters was pulling the Halligan bar from its rack. Abbey spoke to him and pointed at an emergency exit to the far left of the building where two more fire-fighters were getting a hose ready. Two firefighters were already spraying water on to the roof but Abbey was clearly hoping to attack the fire from inside by getting the hose in through the emergency exit.

The firefighter hurried over to the emergency exit and swung the bar like a baseball bat, trying to dig the point into the gap between the two doors. He failed at the first two attempts but managed it on the third. He pushed the handle to the side and the doors splintered open. He placed the back of his hand against the door to check that it wasn't hot, then turned to check that the firefighters were ready with the hose. They were. He nodded, and pulled open the doors. The men dragged the hose inside. Vicky's breath caught in her throat and she realised her heart was pounding. It was the first fire she'd seen since her accident and she could feel her hands starting to shake. She looked down at them and realised with a jolt that it wasn't excitement she was feeling, it was fear. She stared at her trembling hands, unable to process her emotions. She'd never been scared before. She'd gone into burning buildings without a second thought but something had changed. She could feel the adrenalin coursing through her veins but it wasn't preparing her for action, it was telling her to run, to get as far away from the fire as she could. Her mind was telling her the same thing. Run. Run. Get away.

Farmer clapped her on the shoulder and she jumped.

'Bet you wish you were going in with them, don't you, sweetheart?' he asked.

'Yes, guv,' she said, but she could hear the lack of conviction in her voice.

Smoke was billowing out through a row of skylights in the roof. There was a loading bay off to the right with metal shutters.

Half a dozen spectators had gathered together on the other side of a wire fence and they all had their smartphones out and were recording. 'See if any of the vultures called it in,' said Farmer. 'And let's get a timeline sorted.'

'Will do,' said Vicky. She grabbed her helmet and put it on as she walked towards the onlookers, glad to have something to do so that she didn't have to dwell on the fire. She couldn't understand what had happened. Was it seeing the body in the hostel? Did she now have more understanding of the damage that fire could do? Was she scared of fire now? Scared of being burned? What the hell was wrong with her? She blocked out the negative thoughts and emotions and concentrated on the job in hand.

An ambulance arrived, lights flashing and siren wailing. Abbey went over to speak to the driver and the siren went off.

'Ladies and gentlemen, did any of you call nine nine nine to report the fire?' Vicky asked the group.

A teenager raised his left hand, his iPhone still recording in his right. A Jack Russell terrier was sitting at his feet and the teenager was standing on its lead.

'What's your name?' asked Vicky, pulling a notepad and pen from her tunic pocket. She took down the lad's details. He had been walking his dog and had seen smoke coming from the roof. That had been at about half past eight. She'd asked him if he'd seen anyone hanging around the warehouse. He hadn't and nor had the other onlookers. Vicky took all their names and contact numbers.

Farmer had taken the digital camera from the van and was photographing the warehouse. The firefighters appeared to have the fire under control and the volume of smoke escaping through the skylights had definitely decreased.

The Dowgate crew had another hose ready and Morris was attacking a padlocked chain fastened around the delivery bay door with a Halligan bar. The padlock broke and Morris pulled the chain away. He checked the temperature of the metal door, then pulled it open. The firefighters went in with the hose. Vicky could feel her heart pounding. Before she would have given anything to be going in with them and doing what she most wanted to do in the world – fight fires. But now . . . now she wasn't sure.

'Okay, sweetheart?' asked Farmer.

'All good,' she said.

38

The firefighters were damping down the inside of the building when a fire investigation van pulled up and parked next to theirs. Jamie Hughes got out of the van. He was wearing full firefighting gear and carrying his helmet. He waved at Vicky, then went to the rear of his vehicle and opened it. A spaniel jumped out, its tail wagging excitedly. It wasn't Watson, this one was bigger and older and brown and white. Hughes clipped a lead to the dog's collar and went over to Vicky and Farmer. 'We've had a couple of warehouses torched in the last month so we're putting a dog in first,' said Farmer. 'It can sometimes save time. In a building like this where there shouldn't be any accelerants, the dog can often be quicker than us at spotting something that's not right.'

'Do you want to come in with me?' Hughes asked Vicky. 'See how it works.'

'Sure,' she said. She looked across at Farmer and he nodded.

They went in through the delivery bay door. 'I keep her on the lead so we can control where she goes and what she sniffs,' said Hughes. 'Her name is Marple, by the way.'

'After Miss Marple?'

'Exactly.'

He took the dog around the inside of the warehouse. She was excited and clearly happy to be working. 'If she spots anything she'll sit and stare at the area where she smells an accelerant,' said Hughes. They spent the best part of an hour checking the building but there was no reaction from Marple. They went back out. Farmer was smoking a cigarette and talking to Tony Abbey.

Hughes loaded the dog into the back of the van and closed the door. 'Right, I'll leave you and Des to it,' he said. 'But I don't think you'll find the fire was set. It'll be a stray cigarette, maybe an electrical fire.'

'Des says never to have any preconceptions,' said Vicky.

'Each to his own,' said Hughes, taking off his helmet. 'So do you fancy a drink some time?'

'Sure. I'll probably be in the Steelyard later with the guys.'

Hughes looked uncomfortable. 'I meant, somewhere else. You know. Away from the job. A Chinese maybe.'

'Dinner?' She saw his face fall at her reaction, but he had caught her by surprise. Drinks with the team after work were the norm in the brigade but he clearly had more in mind than that and she hadn't been expecting him to ask her out.

'It doesn't matter,' he said. 'Forget it. Sorry.' He hurried around the side of the van, climbed into the driving seat and drove off.

Farmer had caught the tail-end of the conversation and he grinned at her. 'Don't say a word, guv,' she said.

'I was just going to say make sure you get photographs of all the windows and entrances,' he said.

'The dog didn't find anything,' said Vicky.

'I didn't expect it to,' he said. 'The other warehouse fires were nothing like this, and stuff had clearly been moved out before the fires. This one has been empty for a while. From what I've seen, the place isn't exactly secure. I did a walk around and there's a window that looks suspect at the back. Looks to me as if kids have been breaking in. Did Jamie find anything?'

'He was only watching the dog,' said Vicky.

'That's the problem with using our four-legged friends,' said Farmer. 'There's a tendency to rely on their noses instead of your own eyes. But for a quick run-through of a large scene, they're useful enough.'

Farmer took Vicky back inside the warehouse and they spent three hours checking it out. Farmer was right. There was a window at the back that had been prised open and they found evidence that someone had been drinking cans of extra-strong lager and smoking cannabis. There were no scorch marks to suggest exactly where the fire had started and there was a lot of water damage that made it even more difficult. But the electrical circuits all seemed fine and there was no evidence that the fire had been deliberate. Farmer's best guess was that a smoker had started the fire accidentally but there was no direct evidence to prove his hypothesis.

They put their equipment in the van and Vicky drove back to Dowgate. They were about ten minutes away from the station when Farmer's phone rang. He answered it and had a quick conversation before ending the call. 'Change of plan,' he said. 'Clapham.'

'Clapham?'

'You've heard of it,' he said. 'South of the river.' He waved his hand. 'I'll give you directions, don't worry.'

Vicky headed for the Thames. 'What's the job?' she asked.

'You'll see when we get there,' he said. He sat deep in thought, only speaking to give her directions. Eventually he had her park next to a terraced house near Clapham Common Tube station. They got out and Vicky went to the rear of the van to get their gear but Farmer told her not to bother. 'This isn't official,' he said. 'Just tunics and helmets, we won't be needing photographs.'

'What do you mean?'

'It's not our case,' he said. 'We're just having a look-see.'

Vicky followed him along the pavement to where a SOCO van had been parked. The fire engines that had attended were long gone, but as always they had left plenty of evidence behind – a smashed front door, a broken window and water everywhere. A uniformed PC in a fluorescent jacket was standing guard at the door but he stepped aside and saluted as soon as he saw the jackets and helmets.

Farmer went through to the kitchen and Vicky followed him. She recognised the Scene of Crime Officer – it was Garry Harding, the man Danny McGuire had introduced her to. He was wearing a white paper suit with the hood up, protective gloves and shoes and a facemask. He grinned when he saw her. 'You drew the short straw today, huh,' he said, nodding at Farmer.

'What does that mean?' asked Farmer.

'I met Vicky when she was out with Danny at a meth lab,' said Harding.

'I know, I sent her,' said Farmer. 'So what's the story?'

'The body's been taken away, what was left of it,' said Harding. 'The fire was well alight by the time your guys got here and they couldn't get in for more than an hour. Just bones and charred flesh, pretty much. Her name is Jayne Chandler. Jayne with a "Y". Looks like a simple laptop fire, but the victim's a young blond so I know you'll never let me hear the end of it if I didn't let you know straight away.'

'Who was out for the brigade?'

'Dale Robertson. He's just gone.'

'And Dale thinks . . .?'

'Computer caught fire. Which is what I think. Because that's what it is. But I know you have a thing about dead blonds. You do still have a thing about dead blonds, don't you?'

'If they die in a fire, yes.'

'Oh, is this like the cases in your bedroom?' said Vicky.

Farmer flinched as if he'd been struck. He looked across at Vicky, barely able to conceal his anger and he stared at her for several seconds. Vicky looked away, lost for words. She'd spoken without thinking and she could see that Farmer was livid. Eventually, Farmer looked back at Harding and forced a smile. 'You didn't tell Dale you were going to call me, did you?'

'Why would do I do that? You think I want him bending my ear?'

'Good call,' said Farmer. 'So if the body was badly burnt, how did you know she was blond?'

Harding chuckled and pointed to the fridge. There were half a dozen photographs of a young blond woman peppered over the door, held in place by fridge magnets in the shape of fruit and vegetables. 'Plus her driving licence was on the hall table.'

Farmer looked around. 'Not much damage downstairs.'

'Yeah, the laptop was on her bed. The fire spread to the second bedroom and up into the attic.'

'Have you got the laptop?'

'What's left of it,' said Harding. He pointed at the kitchen table. The laptop was in an evidence bag and the charger was in another smaller bag. There was another blob of plastic in a third evidence bag, all that remained of a mobile phone.

Farmer picked up the laptop and studied it. It was a misshapen mass of plastic, blackened with soot. 'This was definitely the source of the fire?'

Harding nodded. 'There were no candles, she wasn't a smoker. There's a TV in the room which was damaged by the fire but it wasn't plugged in.'

Farmer put down the laptop. 'Mind if we go up?'

'Knock yourself out.' He grinned. 'Not literally, obviously. Do you want me with you?'

'Your call,' said Farmer. 'It's your crime scene.'

Harding shook his head. 'No crime that I can see, Des. Just a sad accident.'

Farmer flashed Vicky another baleful stare before he went through to the hallway. There was a smoke alarm in the ceiling just outside the kitchen door. 'Did that go off?' he asked.

'Doesn't look like it, but then the fire was upstairs.' Farmer went back into the kitchen and grabbed a chair. He set it down under the smoke alarm, then stood on it and reached up and pressed the test button. Nothing happened. He looked over his shoulder at Harding. 'You okay if I open this up?'

'Be my guest,' said Harding.

Vicky watched as Farmer opened the alarm. He smiled

when he saw the battery and used his phone to take a photograph. 'Have you got a fingerprint kit?' asked Farmer.

Harding pointed at his overalls. 'This isn't fancy dress,' he said. 'Of course I've got a fucking fingerprint kit.'

Farmer waved an apology. 'Do you mind dusting the battery for prints?'

'Are you serious?'

Farmer pulled out the battery and stepped down off the chair. 'Humour me.'

He put the battery on the kitchen table. Harding fetched his fingerprint kit and dusted it for prints. He frowned as he worked.

'Okay?' asked Farmer.

Harding shook his head. 'No, not okay,' he said. 'There aren't any prints. Not even smudges. How the hell does a battery get into an alarm with no prints? Did she wear gloves?'

'They were wiped,' said Farmer.

'You think someone put a dead battery in there?'

'I'm sure of it,' said Farmer.

'Des, that's one hell of a conspiracy theory,' said Harding, shaking his head.

'Give me another theory then?'

Harding shrugged. 'She came in wearing gloves and kept them on when she put the battery in.'

'It's a fiddly job, why wouldn't she take the gloves off?'

Harding sighed and threw up his arms. 'I don't know. Maybe she's allergic to batteries.'

'And that's a more sensible theory than mine, is it?'

Harding grinned. 'Let me get back to you on that.'

Farmer headed upstairs and Vicky and Harding

followed him. There was more water damage on the stairs
and black marks where the hose had scraped the walls.
At the top of the stairs was a bathroom, blackened with
smoke.

The main bedroom was straight ahead, at the back of
the house. Vicky could see the way that fire had spread
from the main bedroom across the carpet, the flames
blackening the hall ceiling and melting the plastic shade
around the single light. The second, smaller, bedroom
was to the right and it had been destroyed. The bed and
an armchair had been reduced to ash while a pine dressing
table had been charred, giving it an alligator skin effect.

The carpet underfoot was soaking wet and squelched
with every step. 'What time did the appliances arrive?'
asked Vicky.

'Just after midnight,' said Harding. 'A neighbour called
it in, but by then the fire was well underway. The back
bedroom isn't really overlooked.'

'Any way of finding out what time she went to bed?'

'Her mobile was in the bedroom but it was very badly
damaged. I can talk to the phone company, get a list of
calls and texts she'd made. Why?'

Vicky shrugged. 'I'm just wondering how fast the fire
spread, that's all. There's a lot of damage here.'

'There was a lot of combustible stuff,' said Harding.
'And you know laptop batteries burn like fuck.'

'It's still unusual for them to burst into flames,' said
Farmer.

'Well, yes, but once they're put on a bed the cooling
fan is a lot less efficient and the battery can overheat. It
does happen. But I accept what you're saying, laptop
fires aren't anywhere near as common as phones or TVs.'

Farmer went into the bedroom. Vicky and Harding followed. There was a thick sludge on the floor and over all the surfaces that hadn't been destroyed where the water had mixed with the ash and soot. All that remained of the bed was the springs in the mattress. A TV on the wall opposite the bed had melted and warped and the built-in wardrobes and the clothes and shoes they contained were a mass of ash. The heat had cracked the windows and the curtains had burned to nothing.

'So what do you think, Garry?' asked Farmer.

'She left the laptop on the bed and she fell asleep. The laptop overheated and the battery burned and she was incapacitated by the fumes. Because the fire was upstairs and at the back of the house it had plenty of time to burn and spread. It took your guys a while to get the fire under control and by then . . .' He shrugged.

'Did Dale get here while they were fighting the fire?'

'He was quick off the mark. They were just putting the fire out when I got here and he'd been here for a while.'

'So you came in together?'

Harding nodded. 'As soon as they said there was a body we both came up. He took his photographs but left all the sampling to me. The body was well burnt and it was only when I went down to the kitchen that I saw she was a blond and thought of you.'

'I appreciate that.'

Harding laughed. 'I knew you'd find out anyway so I figured I might as well go through it with you while it was fresh rather than having to look at my notes down the line. So you're still on this serial-killer thing?'

'This is number nine in London, Garry.'

'This was an accident. She was in the wrong place at

the wrong time with the wrong laptop. You're barking up the wrong tree.'

'The batteries?'

'She would have been dead upstairs long before the smoke reached the alarm.'

'True. But if the alarm had gone off then a neighbour might have heard it and called nine nine nine and the appliances would have got here sooner.'

'She'd still have been dead, Des.'

'Yes, but there might have been enough left of the body to carry out a decent post-mortem. As it is, we don't know if she was dead or alive when the fire started.'

Harding shook his head. 'Don't you have enough on your plate without looking for phantom serial killers?' he said. 'It is what it is.'

'It's my time I'm wasting,' said Farmer. 'Are you okay if I take some photographs?'

'Sure,' said Harding. 'I'll be filling out my report in the kitchen. Let me know when you're done and I'll leave with you.'

'I appreciate this, Garry. Thanks. By the way, do you remember that hotel fire in Kilburn a while back? It was abandoned but there were homeless people living there.'

'Sure. That was where you got burned, wasn't it?' Harding asked Vicky. She nodded but didn't say anything.

Farmer nodded. 'That wasn't your case, was it?'

Harding shook his head. 'I was on days when it happened. I don't know off the top of my head who handled it for us, but I'll find out for you.' He groaned. 'Please don't tell me you think your hypothetical serial killer was behind it.'

'Thought hadn't crossed my mind,' said Farmer.

Harding went downstairs. Vicky looked over at Farmer. 'Guv . . .' she said.

'Not now, sweetheart,' he said brusquely. 'We'll talk about it later. Right now I've got work to do.'

39

Des spent more than an hour taking photographs with his phone before telling Vicky they were done. She followed him outside to the van. Vicky could see that he was angry, so she said nothing as he lit a cigarette and took a long drag. 'What the fuck, sweetheart,' he said eventually. 'Seriously, what the fuck have you been playing at?'

'Guv, I'm sorry.'

'What did you do? Search my house?'

'It wasn't like that.'

'How is not like that? When the fuck did you go in my bedroom?'

'When I carried you home, that night you were drunk.'

'And while I was passed out, you did what? Searched my house? What the fuck, Vicky?' He shook his head angrily.

'I didn't search your house,' she said patiently. 'You wanted water, I went looking for the bathroom.'

He shook his head in disgust.

'I wasn't snooping. I opened the wrong door, that's all.'

'And when you saw it wasn't a bathroom, what did you do?'

'Oh come on. What would you have done?'

'I'd have shut the door and gone about my business.'

'The hell you would. You'd have done exactly what I did.'

'Snoop?'

'I had a quick look, that's all I did. I saw the crime-scene pictures, the cuttings, the photographs. And the map.'

'How long were you in there?'

'Not long. I was . . . intrigued.'

'Intrigued?'

'It's a pretty impressive display. A lot of work has gone into it. I wondered what it was, that's all.'

'It's private, that's what it is,' he said. He stared out of the side window. 'Private business.'

'Private investigations, that's what you mean. You're looking into cases, in your own time. Cases like this Jayne Chandler fire. Am I right?'

He took another long drag on his cigarette and then blew smoke up at the sky. 'I've no choice,' he said eventually 'The powers-that-be say I'm crazy.'

Vicky laughed. 'I have heard it said, that's true.'

'I mean batshit crazy,' he said. 'They told me to drop them, told me that the cases were closed and I was to leave them alone.'

'What sort of cases?' she asked. 'Garry said the Chandler fire was one of yours. What did he mean?'

'Why do you care?'

She pulled a face. 'If you care, I care.'

'If that's the only answer you've got, you're as crazy as I am.'

She smiled. 'Maybe that's it.'

'You really want to know?'

'Sure.'

'Fuck it,' he said. 'After work. You can see for yourself. But you say not one word to anyone, do you understand?'

Vicky nodded. 'Yes, guv.'

'To anyone,' repeated Farmer.

They got into the van and Vicky drove them back to Dowgate. The pump ladder was already back in position. Two of the firefighters had left their boots and leggings by the rear doors, ready for the next shout. Vicky parked the van and she and Farmer climbed out. Watson came bounding over and Vicky squatted down to pat him and let him lick her face. Farmer grimaced.

'You're not a dog person, are you?' asked Vicky.

'Horrible things,' said Farmer.

'What about cats?'

Farmer grunted and shook his head.

'I guess you're just a people person,' said Vicky. Jamie Hughes walked over, holding a copy of the *Evening Standard*. 'Ah, the lady of the hour,' he said. Watson went over to him, his tail wagging furiously.

'What do you mean?' asked Vicky, standing up.

'You haven't seen the paper?'

Vicky shook her head. 'Human spontaneous combustion not being a thing?'

Hughes frowned. 'What?'

'I spoke to a journalist about human spontaneous combustion not being a thing.'

'Well that's not what she wrote. Hero firefighter sidelined, that's what she wrote.'

'Sidelined?' repeated Vicky.

'Says you hate being in fire investigations but that you've been blocked from going back into firefighting.'

'That's not what I said,' protested Vicky.

Farmer grabbed the paper and ran his eyes over the article. 'So you're wasting your time in fire investigations, are you?'

'I never said that.'

'The journalist says you did.'

'Then she's lying. Or mistaken.'

'So it's fake news, is it? It says here the brigade has assigned you to investigations since you returned to duty despite you asking to go back to your station.'

'I didn't say that.'

'And it says you'd rather be up a ladder than sitting behind a desk.'

'I definitely didn't say that,' protested Vicky.

'Well, that's what it says here.'

She peered over his shoulder at the article. 'None of that is in quote marks. She's paraphrasing.'

'There is one quote there. "I just want to do my job and hopefully one day get back to fighting fires." Did you say that?'

'I guess. But it's true. Everyone knows that I want to get back to firefighting.'

'But this makes it sound like you've been exiled to Siberia.'

'I can't help that. But that's not what I said.'

'For fuck's sake, sweetheart, I told you to put her straight about spontaneous combustion, not cry about being in the wrong job. You make us look like a bunch of arseholes.'

'Guv, that's not fair.'

He thrust the paper at her and stormed towards the entrance.

Vicky opened the paper and read the article in full. The only quote the journalist had used was the one Farmer had read out. There were photographs of the hotel fire in Kilburn, the Dowgate station and a fire investigation van. The only picture of her was the one all the newspapers had used at the time of the fire, taken just after she had joined the Fire Brigade, her posing in front of a fire engine. It was a good picture, so good that her mum had paid to have it blown up and framed and had hung it with pride on the wall. Now it only served as a reminder of how she used to look, before the accident. She looked so pretty back then, fresh-faced, her eyes sparkling, thrilled to be doing the job she had always wanted to do.

'To be honest, I thought it was a good piece,' said Hughes. He tapped the paper at the bottom. There was a photograph of a dark-haired bearded man and Vicky realised it was Stefan, the man she'd rescued. 'They even got a nice quote from the guy you pulled out of the building.'

'Pushed him out, you mean. Before I came a cropper.'

Vicky looked at the caption under the photograph. 'Stefan Petrescu: Vicky Lewis saved his life in hotel fire.' Vicky scanned the article and found a quote from the man: 'She saved my life that night. I will always be grateful. Because of Vicky Lewis my wife has a husband and my children have a father.'

'Don't worry about Des,' said Hughes. 'There's a reason they call him the Grouch.'

'Yeah, you said. His sunny disposition.'

'He'll get over it.'

'I hope so.'

'Haven't you realised that his bark is worse than his bite? That's what Watson always says.'

Watson barked as if echoing his point and Vicky laughed.

'See, even Watson agrees,' said Hughes. He smiled at her but she realised there was no warmth in his eyes. She wondered if he was still unhappy about the way she'd turned down his offer of a meal.

'Jamie, about the Chinese thing.'

'It's fine. I get it. It was unprofessional of me, I'm sorry.'

'It caught me by surprise, that's all.'

He held up a hand to cut her off. 'No need to explain, I was out of order.' He bent down and patted the dog, then whistled and walked off, the dog sticking to his heels. Vicky wanted to call after him but she figured that might just make the situation worse so she turned and headed inside. As soon as she got back to her office Vicky sat down and phoned India's mobile. She answered immediately. 'So how did you like the piece?' asked the journalist.

'I didn't see anything about spontaneous combustion.'

'We're waiting for a quote from the coroner on that, but my news editor thought there was an article in you working for the investigation unit.'

'You might have told me what you were going to do.'

'It was all a bit frantic and we had a deadline,' said India. 'But I thought you came over really well. You're a hero, Vicky. People should know about you.'

'Well, I'd have preferred a lower profile, to be honest,' said Vicky. 'But I was interested to see that you tracked down Stefan. That must have taken some doing.'

'It wasn't that hard. The Romanian community is fairly tight-knit.'

'So where is he these days?'

'Still squatting with his wife and kids.'

'I wouldn't mind saying hello to him,' said Vicky.

'Are you serious.'

'Why not? Where can I find him?'

'How about this?' said India. 'I'll take you to him and we'll get a photograph. Deal?'

Vicky thought about it for several seconds. She wasn't happy about being in the paper again, but at least she would have the opportunity to make things right with Des Farmer. And she really wanted to talk to Stefan. 'Okay, why not,' she said.

'After work?'

'I'm pretty busy today. What about first thing the day after tomorrow?'

'Sounds like a plan. Can you come to our offices in Derry Street? Just off Kensington High Street. I'll make sure Stefan is here.'

'See you then.' Vicky put down the phone and leaned back in her chair. If a journalist had tracked down Stefan so easily, why hadn't Willie Campbell tried to talk to him? An investigator was supposed to talk to as many witnesses as possible, and Campbell didn't appear to have even tried to contact Stefan. And if he had done, he would have known that the squatters hadn't tampered with the electrical supply. And if the squatters hadn't, then who had?

40

Vicky thought that the newspaper interview might have put Farmer off taking her home, but at finishing time he knocked on her door. 'Ready to go?' he asked.

'Sure.'

They went down to her car and he sat in silence as she drove to Bethnal Green. She found a place to park and Farmer took her into the house and upstairs to his flat. He let them in and opened the spare bedroom door and stepped to the side so that she could go in first. She stood in darkness until he flicked the light on. She blinked as she tried to focus, then jumped as he closed the door behind her with a dull thud.

'Other than Willie Campbell, you're the only other person who's ever seen this,' he said from behind her.

'Willie was helping you?'

'Not really helping, but he let me talk it through with him.'

She folded her arms as she stood looking at the collection of photographs, reports and newspaper clippings interlined with threads of different colours. 'What did he think?'

'He thought I was seeing patterns where there weren't any.'

Vicky nodded as she scanned the pictures and cuttings.

'So, first impressions?' asked Farmer.

'You're as nutty as a fruitcake,' she said. She turned and grinned at the way his face had fallen. 'Joke.'

He jerked a thumb at the door. 'If you're not going to take this seriously, you can fuck off.'

'I'm taking it seriously, guv, don't get your Calvins in a twist.'

'I get my underwear from Marks and Spencer,' he said.

'As I know all too well, remember?' said Vicky. She turned back to look at the display. In the centre of the wall facing her was a map of the United Kingdom. There were fifteen pins in the map, eight in London, three in Leeds, two in Manchester, one in Edinburgh and one in Belfast. She was fairly sure the Edinburgh and Belfast cases had been added since she was last in the room. A thread ran from each of the pins to a separate display of pictures, cuttings and Post-it notes covered with scribbles. She counted the pins. 'So fifteen cases, all fires,' she said. 'And all women victims.'

She walked up to the map. Underneath each pin was a small card with a date on it. The first date was under the pin in Manchester. November 2011. The most recent was in Camden. The victim was a pretty blond called Diana Hewson. All the London dates were within the past three years.

'So you think these fires are connected?' asked Vicky.

'I don't think. I'm sure.'

She walked to the left and studied the pictures and cuttings of a house fire in Bayswater. According to a fire brigade spokesman quoted in the *Evening Standard*, a cigarette dropped down the back of a sofa had started the blaze and the owner of the flat, a thirty-five-year-old woman, had died from smoke inhalation. Farmer had managed to get a photograph taken during the post-mortem and it made gruesome viewing. All the hair had been burned off, the flesh was charred and the teeth were exposed down to the roots. Vicky shuddered.

A photocopy of the initial fire report was pinned to the left of the *Evening Standard* cutting. Vicky pointed at the signature at the bottom. 'You were the investigating officer?'

'I was pretty sure it was an accidental death when I first got there,' said Farmer, walking over to stand next to her. 'Cigarette falls down the back of the sofa, smoulders, smoke incapacitates the victim, fire takes hold. It happens all the time. One in three fire fatalities involve cigarettes.'

Vicky scanned the report and the conclusion. 'You said it was a cigarette fire. That was your conclusion.'

'It was. No question. But then I attended the post-mortem.' He pointed at another report pinned to the wall. It was from the coroner. Vicky read the typewritten report and then frowned. 'I don't see the problem,' she said. 'Death by asphyxiation, body burned from the fire, smoke in the lungs, which suggested she was still breathing as the fire burned.' She shrugged. 'That's exactly what you'd expect to see, isn't it? She falls asleep with a lit cigarette, the cigarette ignited the sofa, the smoke knocks her out, the fire kills her.'

'And why didn't she wake up when the fire started?'

'Because she was . . .' She leaned forward and scanned the report. 'Ah. She hadn't been drinking.'

'And the cigarette was a regular cigarette. No drugs.'

'She was tired and fell asleep?'

'So tired that a fire didn't wake her up?'

She turned to look at him. 'So what are you saying?'

'I'm saying that she was unconscious when the fire burned her.'

Vicky frowned and looked back at the post-mortem report. 'There's no suggestion she was knocked out. No physical trauma other than that caused by the fire.'

'I think she was drugged.'

'There's no mention of drugs in the system.'

'Because the coroner wasn't looking. Why would he? It was a cigarette fire, he'd check for alcohol but there was no evidence of drug-taking so he wouldn't bother.'

'But you think she was drugged?'

Farmer nodded. 'Rohypnol, maybe. Even a bog-standard sleeping tablet.'

'Couldn't the coroner test for that?'

'I asked but he said he didn't have the resources.'

'It was down to money?'

'He said it would be a waste of time. He said it was cut and dried. An accidental death.' He took a pre-rolled cigarette from his tobacco pack and lit it. He blew smoke at the ceiling. 'We had a bit of a set-to.'

'A fight?'

'He was being an arsehole. I might have pushed him. I was escorted off the premises. I tried to get my bosses on side but they agreed with the coroner so the body was cremated and that was that.'

Vicky folded her arms and looked at a head-and-shoulders photograph of the victim. She was blond with high cheekbones and pale blue eyes, probably in her mid-thirties. 'Pretty,' she said. She moved across the display, seeking out photographs of all the victims. All were blond. The youngest was a teenager, the oldest was in her mid-forties. 'So you think there's a killer targeting blonds?'

Farmer blew smoke but didn't reply.

'Sometimes you can see patterns where there are no patterns,' said Vicky. 'What do they call it?'

'Confirmation bias,' said Farmer. 'The tendency to interpret new evidence as confirmation of one's existing beliefs or theories. You sound like Willie.'

'You see the point, though? You think there's a killer killing blond-haired women. So you look at those cases where a blond died in a fire and you think they're connected.'

'I don't think they're connected. They *are* connected.'

'Or they appear to be because you're concentrating on those victims that fit your criteria. You might find a similar pattern if you looked at elderly Asian men, for instance. Or pensioners in their eighties. Most fire victims are eighty and older, aren't they?'

Farmer sighed. 'Two-thirds of all fire deaths are over seventy, yes. And one-third have mental health issues. But these women weren't in their seventies. They weren't elderly or infirm, they weren't mentally ill, they were all in the prime of their lives.'

'And they all died in fires that looked accidental?'

Farmer nodded. 'And there's something else they have in common. See if you can spot it. It took me a while.'

'Something in common? With the victims?'

Farmer shook his head. 'The crime scenes.'

Vicky turned back to the display. She went over to the details of the Manchester victim. Her name was Sophie

Bone. There were half a dozen photographs around a news report clipped from the *Manchester Evening News*. One was a head-and-shoulders shot. She was blond and in her twenties. There was a view of the outside of the house, and several shots from the inside. Sophie had died on her bed in a fire that had started while she had been smoking heroin. She lived at her parents' house but they were on holiday. The coroner decided she had been smoking heroin, burning it on strips of silver foil. Chasing the dragon. She had been using a candle to ignite the heroin and the coroner figured she has passed out and the candle had fallen on to the bed.

One of the photographs was a close-up of a smoke alarm, a battery-powered model.

She looked at the case linked to Belfast. Clare Knight. A student. She lived in a small bedsit not far from Queen's University, where she was in her final year. There was a washing machine in her bathroom and she had put a load of washing in before she went to sleep. The circuit board had ignited and a laundry basket containing more clothes had caught fire and by the time the fire brigade had been called, Clare was dead. There was a photograph of a badly burnt body on what was left of a single bed. The room had been full of books and magazines and a large vinyl record collection, which meant it had burned quickly and fiercely. Again there was a close-up of a badly burnt smoke detector. It was open and the batteries were clearly visible.

Vicky quickly scanned all the photographs on the wall. In each group of photographs there was at least one of a smoke detector. She turned to look at Farmer. 'They all had smoke alarms?'

'There's hope for you yet,' said Farmer.

Vicky frowned. 'But if they had smoke alarms, how come they were overcome by smoke?'

'A good question.'

'Were they working?'

'And another good question. We'll make a fire investigator out of you yet.'

'So what's the answer?'

'No. They weren't working.'

'Had the batteries been removed from any of them?'

Farmer shook his head. 'Nope. There were batteries in all of them. But they were dead.'

'All of the victims had smoke alarms with dead batteries?'

Farmer flashed her a tight smile. 'Still think it's confirmation bias at work?'

'When the batteries in smoke alarms die, the alarms beep,' said Vicky. 'You have to ignore the beep for days and it's annoying as hell. Most people replace them but some idiots just pull the batteries out.'

'You're getting there,' said Farmer. He took a pull on his cigarette.

'So you're saying what? Someone disabled the smoke alarms?'

'You've got it,' said Farmer.

'Someone removed the batteries and replaced them with dead ones? Then set the fires?'

'Bingo,' said Farmer.

'Did you check the batteries? For fingerprints?'

Farmer grinned. 'Yes, I did. Want to take a guess at what I found?'

'The batteries had been wiped clean?'

His grin widened. 'Clean as a whisker. Now who the hell wipes batteries before putting them in a smoke detector?'

'No one,' said Vicky.

'A killer,' said Farmer. 'A killer who wanted his victim to die in a fire without an alarm sounding.'

Vicky rubbed the back of her neck. 'Wow,' she said.

'Yup.'

She turned to look at him. 'But that's hard evidence? Why haven't the cops started an investigation?'

'I spoke to a mate at the Met and he reached out to Homicide and Serious Crime and they spoke to the chief and I was called in and given a serious kicking for ignoring the chain of command. I was told that I was wasting my time and the Met's and that I was to drop the investigation. Except they didn't call it an investigation. A wild goose chase were the words he used. Wasting the brigade's time and resources. I was to cease and desist with immediate effect.' He grinned. 'That was about six months ago.'

Vicky folded her arms. 'That doesn't make any sense at all,' she said. 'There's clearly a killer who is targeting blond women and using fire to cover his tracks. It's a serial killer. No question.'

'Thank you,' said Farmer. 'But your opinion counts for nothing in the grand scheme of things.'

'But why doesn't the chief see it?'

'Because he's always hated my guts, for one. Because if the press gets a hold of the story there'll be a panic, plus add to that I'm saying that at least fifteen fatal fires were classified as accidents when they were actually murders. That makes the brigade and the police look incompetent.' He took a long pull on his cigarette. 'But at the end of the day, he simply doesn't believe me. He thinks I'm imagining things. We have more than three hundred fire deaths a year, he thinks that I'm guilty of confirmation bias. I only look at the cases that fit my hypothesis. He doesn't give a shit that I went through every single fire death in the UK over the past ten years. I looked at every one and the only ones on the walls are the ones I'm certain about.'

'So what are you doing?' asked Vicky. 'You've clearly not stopped.'

'I work on it on my own time,' he said. 'I did ask my opposite numbers for them to dig out any similar cases and I got a couple before the chief found out and put his foot down. I've got a few mates who'll help me on the QT but I can't get anything officially.' He shrugged. 'I know I should just knock it on the head, but I can't. There's a killer out there and he's getting away with it and if I don't do anything then he'll carry on getting away with it.'

Vicky turned back to look at the map. 'You've found fifteen but there could be more,' she said quietly.

'No way of knowing,' he said.

She put her head on one side and frowned. 'This could just be the tip of an iceberg. There could be a lot more.'

'Like I said, there's no way of knowing. But I'm sure they were all killed by the same man.'

'Or woman,' said Vicky.

Farmer shook his head. 'I don't think a woman would do this,' he said. 'Women kill, there's no doubt about that. And there have been female arsonists. But I think he's using the fire to cover up his kills and I think he's using fire because he wants to destroy any physical evidence.'

'You think he's raping them?'

'Raping them. Or doing something that could identify him. So he sets the fire and kills two birds with one stone. He makes the murder look like an accident and destroys any evidence.'

'The perfect crime?'

Farmer flashed her a tight smile. 'If it was the perfect crime it wouldn't be plastered over my walls, would it?' He handed her an envelope containing photographs that he'd taken that afternoon and several photocopied sheets and gestured at the display. 'Make yourself useful while I go get us some beers.'

41

Vicky was putting photographs of Jayne Chandler's house on the wall when Farmer returned with two cans of lager. Among the details he'd given her was a copy of the initial report by one of the investigators who had been on the night shift. Dale Robertson had joined the investigation team a few months before Vicky. They had only really crossed paths when shifts changed over and he always greeted her with a nod and a curt smile. Other than when Farmer had introduced him, he hadn't said a single word to her. Vicky had the impression that he resented the fact that he had waited several years to join the team but she had apparently waltzed in with next to no training. 'Does Dale know you're looking at this case?' she asked. She ran a yellow thread from the report to the pin on the map, marking the position of Jayne's house in Clapham.

'Hell no,' said Farmer, putting his can of lager down on the table.

'Garry's helping you?'

'He thinks I'm mad, but he humours me.'

She waved at the map. 'Have you shown him this?'

'I don't want word getting out. I trusted Willie, but . . .' He shrugged.

'But the evidence you've got here, cops like your friend must realise the significance?'

'No one likes being second-guessed, do they? If I'm right, they're wrong.'

'So why does Garry help you?'

Farmer shrugged. 'Because he's a pal. And I think he's hoping that eventually I'll realise I'm wrong.' He took out his tobacco pack and began to roll a cigarette.

'But you're not wrong, are you?'

'I don't think so, no. But my bosses say that I'm to drop it, so I have to stay below the radar. And that means not mentioning it to Dale, right?'

'My lips are sealed.'

'I'm serious,' she said. 'I don't want you talking about this. To anyone.'

Vicky's eyes narrowed. 'You think it might be an investigator who's doing this?'

Farmer held up his hands. 'It could be anybody,' he said. 'But whoever it is clearly knows a lot about fires. He knows how to set them without being discovered, which means he could well be a firefighter. Or an investigator.'

Vicky looked back at the map. 'And the first was in 2011?'

Farmer nodded. 'Manchester.'

'So he started in Manchester and moved to London?'

'They started in the north and then moved south, yes,' said Farmer. 'Three in Leeds. It could be that he realised if he stayed up north there was more chance of him being found out.'

'And Edinburgh. And Belfast.'

'I've just found those two,' said Farmer. 'It would be easy enough for him to visit another city.'

'Yes, but it takes time, doesn't it? To stalk and to plan? Which means a fireman's shift system would suit him, right? Four days on and four days off.'

Farmer smiled thinly. 'That had occurred to me.'

Vicky frowned and looked at the three pins in Leeds. 'Danny Maguire was in Leeds.'

'That had also occurred to me, sweetheart. But Dale has family there. And he used to work in Glasgow which isn't that far from Edinburgh. People move around.'

She took a sip of lager. 'I was thinking about the smoke alarm thing.'

'Yeah?'

'Yeah. I get what you're saying, that the dead batteries are a common link. He takes out the batteries and replaces them with dead ones so that no one is surprised when the smoke alarm doesn't go off.'

'That's what I figure, yes.'

'But that would mean he's targeting women with smoke alarms and that wouldn't make any sense at all. No one would do that. If anything, he'd be targeting women without alarms because that would be easier.'

'But there's no way it's a coincidence, you can see that. The dead batteries are all the same brand. The odds of that being a coincidence are . . .' He shrugged. 'Astronomical.'

'But that's what I mean. You've been using the dead batteries as a way of linking the cases, and you've come up with fifteen, right?'

Farmer nodded. 'Sixteen, including the latest.'

'The point I'm making is that there could be cases where there were no smoke alarms. If he killed them and started a fire to cover his tracks, it wouldn't be on your radar because you're only looking at cases with non-functioning smoke alarms.'

'I get that, but this is a way of narrowing the cases down.'

'Exactly. But by doing that, you could be underplaying the scope of what he's doing. You've got sixteen cases. There could be sixty. Or even more. This could be way, way bigger than you think.'

Farmer ran a hand through his hair. 'I agree, but it would take for ever to go through every single fire death in the UK. By looking at those with dead batteries, I'm able to see the wood for the trees.'

'Yes, but you don't have to look at the whole forest. He has a type. Women who live on their own. Not too old, not too young. And blond.'

Farmer shrugged. 'It's a big enough job as it is,' he said.

'The more cases you have, the more likely it is you'll find a link. A pattern. And if you can find the pattern, you can find the killer.'

'Maybe. But it's taking me all my time just to look at the ones I have.' He finished rolling his cigarette and slipped it between his lips.

'So I'll help. I'll do the legwork.'

He waited until he had lit the cigarette and taken a drag before answering. 'If the powers-that-be find out you're helping me with this, there'll be hell to pay. You know that.'

'Don't care,' she said. 'This is important. There's a killer out there and somebody has to stop him.'

'So you believe me?'

Vicky turned to look at the map and nodded slowly. 'Yes, guv. I do.'

42

Vicky was working with her door closed but that didn't seem to worry Farmer. He opened it without knocking and popped his head round. 'How are you doing?' he asked.

'I'm getting there,' she said.

It had been a busy shift. A car had burst into flames on a piece of waste ground in Stoke Newington in what was almost certainly an insurance job, a housewife had been badly burnt in a chip-pan fire in Ealing and there had been an electrical fire in a lap-dancing club in Mayfair that seemed to have attracted far more appliances than was necessary. Farmer and Vicky had spent as much time driving in the van as they had at the fire scenes and they had been in such a rush there had been a stack of paperwork to do when they got back to Dowgate, all of which Farmer had dumped on her. 'Rank has its privileges,' he'd said, though to be fair he had made the coffees.

The car fire had definitely been set, with a piece of rag thrust down the filler neck, but the owner was claiming it had been stolen by joyriders. The fact that he was well behind on his payments and the dealer he'd bought it from was threatening to seize the vehicle suggested otherwise.

The chip-pan fire had been awful. A housewife had left the pan on the cooker to attend to one of her three young children, and had gone back to the kitchen to find the pan was on fire. She'd panicked and did the worst thing possible – she threw a bowl full of washing-up water into the flames. The water vaporised almost immediately and produced a boil over, ejecting the burning oil and water vapour out of the pan and into a large fireball. The woman had burns over her face and arms and her clothing had caught fire. By the time the fire brigade got there the kitchen was ablaze, though the woman had managed to crawl into the hallway. The ambulance arrived soon after the appliances. The woman would live but she was very badly burnt.

The fire in the lap-dancing club had been caused by a faulty circuit board controlling the lights and sound system. The club had recently paid for an overhaul of their wiring and clearly something had gone wrong, but Farmer had discovered that it wasn't human error responsible for the fire, but vermin error. A small mouse had crawled into the equipment looking for food or shelter and had caused a short circuit.

It had been a busy day and Vicky was looking forward to going home. But Farmer clearly had other ideas. 'So, there's someone you need to meet,' said Farmer.

'Business or pleasure?'

'Peter Mulholland. He's a Met SOCO, he was on duty the night of your fire.'

'It's my fire, is it now?'

'Do you want to come or not?' said Farmer gruffly. 'I thought I was helping.'

Vicky stood up. 'Sorry, guv. Thanks.'

'I'll see you down by the car.'

Vicky thanked him again, feeling bad that she hadn't been more enthusiastic. He was helping and he didn't have to.

When she got down to the car, Farmer was already waiting, wearing a raincoat over his uniform. Vicky had pulled on her coat. 'So where are we going?' asked Vicky, as she started the engine.

'Marylebone,' said Farmer. 'The Prince Regent pub.'

'Got it,' said Vicky. She pulled out of the car park.

'So this has got two engines, right?' asked Farmer as they headed west.

Vicky nodded. 'There's lithium-ion battery pack that has a range of twenty-three miles. And a turbocharged one point five litre three-cylinder petrol engine.'

'Rear-wheel drive?'

'Sure.'

'Top speed?'

'More than one fifty.'

'How fast have you have gone in it?'

Vicky chuckled. 'I did one twenty once, but don't tell anyone.'

'Naughty girl.'

'I didn't buy it for the speed. I bought it because of the way it looks. It's so bloody cool.'

'It's got a style of its own, that's for sure. What's it like on a regular run, fuel-wise?'

'About eighty miles to the gallon. Less than thirty if the battery's dead.'

'Not great.'

She smiled. 'I didn't buy it for the fuel economy either. So what can you tell me about this Peter Mulholland?'

'Old school, like me,' said Farmer. 'He's been doing forensic work for more than twenty years, due to retire in a year or two, I think. Bit of a health nut, still plays lacrosse for a seniors' team.'

'Isn't that a girls' game?'

Farmer looked across at her. 'For fuck's sake don't say that to Peter.'

'I'm just saying, that's the game girls play in public schools, throwing a ball around with a net on a stick.'

'Yeah, well, the way Peter tells it, lacrosse was invented by the Iroquois Indians who used sticks with nets to throw around the heads of their enemies. He's from Manchester and it's a big butch game up there.'

'I'm sure it is,' said Vicky.

She drove to Marylebone and Farmer guided her to a parking space a short walk from the Prince Regent. It was a Victorian pub with gold-framed mirrors, lots of dark-wood panelling and extravagant chandeliers. Peter Mulholland was sitting at a corner table, a large leather briefcase at his feet. He had thick grey hair and a sharp angular face that broke into a grin when he saw Farmer walking towards him. He stood up. He was wearing a light grey suit, a white shirt and a tie with crossed lacrosse sticks on it. Mulholland shook hands with Farmer then turned to smile at Vicky.

'This is Vicky, Vicky Lewis,' said Farmer, sitting down at the table.

Mulholland shook hands with her. She saw his eyes narrow when he saw the scars and her mangled ear but the smile stayed genuine as they shook. 'Des has told me a lot about you,' he said.

'All good, I hope.'

Mulholland wrinkled his nose. 'Fifty-fifty, I'd say.'

Vicky's jaw dropped but then he grinned and she realised he was joking. She grinned back. Farmer nodded at the bar. 'You know the rules – the newbie gets the drinks,' he said.

Vicky looked at Mulholland expectantly. 'Vodka tonic,' he said. 'Ice and a slice.' He sat down next to Farmer and they both smiled up at her.

When Vicky got back to the table the two men were looking at an LFB file on the table. She sat down and they all clinked glasses.

'Peter can't take anything out of the office but he's got a memory like a steel trap,' said Farmer. 'I was showing him what Willie had done, report-wise.'

'To be honest there isn't much to remember,' said Mulholland. He took out a dozen or so photographs from the file and spread them over the table. 'Willie was there from the get-go and he had all the hard work done by the time I turned up. The squatters had jerry-rigged the electricity supply and it was an old building.' He shrugged. 'If it had been a new building with a decent sprinkler system then it would have stayed confined to the bar.'

'Did you speak to any of the men living in the hotel?' asked Vicky.

'No. Why?'

'One of the men told me that they didn't have electricity.'

Mulholland tapped one of the photographs of the consumer board. 'You can see the remains of the wiring there. And it was definitely the point of origin. I saw that with my own eyes.'

'What about other points of origin?' asked Vicky.

Mulholland frowned. 'What do you mean?'

Farmer put down his glass. 'Vicky was at the top of the hotel,' he said. 'She saw fire there. And the floor collapsed below her which means the second floor had been alight and burning for a while.'

'So the fire spread from the bar to the second floor? Nothing unusual about that, especially given the nature of the building. If it had been steel or concrete we wouldn't be having this conversation. Some of those walls were lathe and plaster, and several layers of wallpaper over that.'

Farmer nodded. 'But she also discovered fire on the fourth floor, at the back of the hotel.'

Mulholland looked over at Vicky and she nodded. 'It was well alight.'

'Nobody mentioned that to me,' said Mulholland.

'You didn't look through the upper floors?' asked Farmer.

'There were health and safety issues,' said Mulholland. 'By the time I got there the place was pretty much destroyed. And as I said, Willie was there first and he seemed satisfied that the fire had started in the bar. You know how easily fires start when people start messing around with the electricity supply.' He sat back in his chair. 'There were no fatalities so it wasn't a priority. You think there was something else going on?'

'I'm thinking three points of origin, Peter,' said Farmer. 'Maybe more. Sorry, mate.'

'How did Willie miss that?'

'I don't know. I'll talk to him, obviously. But I wanted to see what you had to say first.'

Mulholland put his hands in the air. 'I don't know what to say. It looked pretty straightforward to me, from what I saw. I suppose I should have had a more thorough look around but Willie is one of the best, I assumed I could rely on him.' He pointed at the photograph of the consumer board. 'You can see for yourself that they tapped into the consumer board and that there was a fire there. That's what I said in my report.'

'And you weren't wrong,' said Farmer. 'That was definitely a point of origin.' He shrugged. 'It's just that now, with hindsight, we're thinking that maybe there were several points of origin. And I take your point, with the upper floors pretty much destroyed, getting up there would be problematic.'

'So what, vandalism?'

'Who knows? If the fire was set then whoever set it wanted it to look as if it was a consumer-board fire and your average vandal doesn't bother doing that.'

Mulholland looked pained. 'So you're thinking it was a professional job?'

Farmer shrugged. 'I'd be guessing, mate. But the building was demolished pretty sharply, and it was listed, which wouldn't have happened without the fire.'

'It wouldn't be the first time that a building has been torched to get around planning restrictions,' said Mulholland. He flicked through the LFB report and frowned. 'It's a bit light on witness statements, isn't it?'

'Willie probably thought the same as you. Open and shut.'

Mulholland looked across at Vicky. 'And he didn't talk to you?'

Vicky shook her head. Mulholland cursed under his

breath and took a long pull on his vodka and tonic. 'But I was in hospital,' she said.

'What do you want to do, Des?' asked Mulholland, sitting back in his chair.

'I'll talk to Willie, see what he has to say,' said Farmer. 'But you could maybe have a look to see if there have been any similar cases – fires that were set that started in consumer boards and spread quickly.'

'Insurance jobs?'

'Not necessarily. It's the method I'm interested in rather than the reason.'

'I'll check,' said Mulholland and drained his glass. 'It might take some time, but I'm on it.'

Farmer finished his drink and both men looked expectantly at Vicky. She sighed and stood up. 'My round,' she said.

43

Vicky set her alarm to wake her at six, but after she'd showered, treated her scars and dressed, Barbara was already up and scrambling eggs and a cup of tea was waiting for her on the table. In the sink was a bunch of flowers that her mother had brought in from the garden. 'How do you do that?' asked Vicky, sitting down. Baxter scratched at the kitchen door and Barbara let the dog in.

'Do what, honey?'

'No matter what time I wake up, you're always up before me.'

'It's what mothers do,' said Barbara, putting toast on the table.

'You're amazing,' said Vicky.

'I'm just a mother. So where are you off to so bright and early? Not chauffeuring that horrible man again, are you?'

'No, I'm off to see a journalist,' said Vicky, buttering a slice of toast.

'A story about you? That's nice.' She put Vicky's eggs in front of her and then sat down. 'Now eat up.'

'I know, most important meal of the day.' Vicky dug her fork into the eggs. Her mum did make the best scrambled eggs. 'You know, mum, I may never leave here.

You take such good care of me.' Baxter woofed and pawed at her leg, wanting food, but Vicky ignored him.

'Nonsense,' said Barbara, though she beamed with pleasure. 'You'll find a nice young man one day. Maybe you already have. How is Matt?' She began arranging the flowers in a crystal vase.

Vicky shook her head. 'Don't go there, Mum.'

'I'm just saying, grandchildren would be nice. My clock is ticking.'

'You don't even know what that means.'

'I know exactly what it means. I'm not getting any younger.'

'None of us are.'

Barbara opened her mouth to speak but Vicky raised her fork. 'Let me eat in peace, Mum.'

Barbara pretended to zip her mouth closed, but she smiled as Vicky tucked into her eggs.

It took Vicky half an hour to drive to Kensington. She parked at a multi-storey close to the offices of the *Evening Standard* and walked into reception and asked for India Somerville. The receptionist was a young girl barely out of school who stared at Vicky's scars with undisguised horror. Vicky turned her head so that her hair covered her left cheek. The receptionist forced a smile and asked Vicky to take a seat.

India appeared five minutes later, wearing the same red coat and carrying the same Louis Vuitton bag as the first time they'd met. They shook hands and India gestured at the doors. 'Stefan sells the *Big Issue* so we thought it might make a good picture of you in the street with him. My photographer's with him in Kensington High Street, so we'll do it there if that's okay with you.'

'Sure,' said Vicky.

They went outside and down Kensington High Street. 'I should have asked you to bring your helmet.'

'To hide my scars?'

India stopped. 'God, no, that's not what I meant. Oh my God, I'm sorry. Really, that's not what I meant at all.'

Vicky felt suddenly guilty for making the journalist feel so uncomfortable. 'Sorry,' she said.

India reached out and touched her arm. 'I just mean to show you were a firefighter. Pictorially. I wasn't trying to hide anything.'

'I'm just a bit sensitive, obviously,' said Vicky. She shrugged. 'I should think before speaking sometimes.'

'Vicky, your scars are there because you saved a man's life. Like he said in my article, because of you a wife has a husband and his kids have a dad. You don't have to hide anything.'

'Okay, thanks. And I'm sorry for taking it the wrong way.'

India smiled, then impulsively stepped forward and hugged her. Vicky felt her cheeks redden and wasn't sure how to react. She patted India softly on the back.

Eventually India stopped hugging her and they walked along Kensington High Street to where a young black man in a leather bomber jacket and laden down with two bags of camera equipment stood next to a big bearded man in a long coat. Vicky smiled as she recognised Stefan and he grinned when he saw her and came barrelling down the pavement. He was holding a stack of *Big Issue* magazines and they bounced off her back as he hugged her, hard enough to knock the wind from her. 'You are my hero,' he said. 'My hero.'

'Thanks, Stefan,' she said.

He let go of her and turned to India. 'Thank you for bringing her,' he said in heavily accented English. He looked back at Vicky. 'I never had chance to thank you before so now I thank you.' He transferred the magazines to his left hand and put his right hand over his heart. 'I thank you now, from my heart.'

A small dark-eyed woman with her hair covered with a brightly coloured headscarf came up, holding two small boys by the hands. Like Stefan she was wearing a long wool coat that had seen better days. The two children were wrapped up in black wool jackets and padded trousers. 'This is my wife, Maria,' said Stefan.

Vicky smiled down at her. 'Pleased to meet you, Maria,' said Vicky.

Maria smiled up at Vicky but her eyes widened when she saw the scars on her cheek. Then she frowned. 'Was that the fire?' she whispered.

Vicky nodded.

'My lady, I am so sorry,' she said. She let go of the child on her right and reached for Vicky's hand, then pressed it against her own forehead. 'I thank you with all my heart.'

'It's okay,' said Vicky. 'I was just doing my job.'

'You gave me back my husband,' she said. She kissed the back of Vicky's hand. 'Thank you.'

India was watching and scribbling in a small notebook. 'Right, let's get that picture, shall we?' She looked over at the photographer. 'This is Delmar, he'll be taking the pictures.'

Delmar nodded curtly as he adjusted his lens. 'How about Vicky and Stefan stand together, and we'll do the family shot later,' he said.

Stefan stood next to Vicky, clutching his magazines to his chest.

'Okay, big smiles,' said the photographer.

Vicky smiled and tilted her head to the side so that her hair covered her scarred cheek. The photographer clicked away. 'Stefan, maybe put your arm around Vicky,' he prompted.

Stefan did as he was told and gave Vicky a squeeze.

'Good, perfect, now big smiles,' said Delmar. He took a dozen or so shots and then asked Maria and her children to join in. Stefan and Maria stood either side of Vicky and the children in front. Delmar nodded enthusiastically. 'Terrific,' he said, and began snapping away.

Vicky tried to keep her right side towards the photographer and it was clear from the way he was aiming his lens that he was happy not to shoot her scars.

After a few minutes he stopped shooting and India went over to talk to him. He held the camera out and began showing her the pictures he'd taken.

Vicky turned to look at Stefan. 'Stefan, when you were living in the hotel in Kilburn, did you take electricity from the mains?'

He frowned, not understanding the question.

'Did you take electricity?' she repeated. 'Power? In the hotel?'

'You mean steal? We not steal anything.' He folded his arms defensively.

His wife leaned over and spoke to him in Romanian. He answered, gruffly. Maria turned to Vicky. 'We never took electricity. It is illegal. In England you can stay in a

Stephen Leather

house and the police can do nothing. But if you steal the gas or the electricity they can throw you out. So we never took electricity.'

'What about anyone else staying there?'

She shook her head. 'No one would steal electricity. Why do you think we did?'

'They think the fire started near the electricity meter. In the bar.'

She shook her head again. 'We didn't go in the bar. We stayed upstairs. Always upstairs. We didn't want anyone looking in the windows at us. Many people do not like Romanians. Sometimes we have problems.'

'And you didn't have electricity upstairs?'

'No. No electricity. We use gas cylinders to cook.'

'What about charging your phones?'

'We did that outside.'

'Did anyone from the police or the fire brigade come to talk to you about the fire?' asked Vicky.

Stefan and Maria shook their heads.

'Are you sure?' asked Vicky. 'No one?'

'Sure,' said Maria.

'Yes,' said Stefan. 'Sure.'

India came over, beaming. 'Everything okay?' she asked.

'All good,' said Vicky. She looked at her watch. 'I need to be going.'

'Thank you so much for agreeing to do this.'

'No problem, but can you do me a favour?'

'If I can.'

'Can you quote me as saying I love working for the investigation team, they're a great bunch of professionals who do fantastic work. Maybe something that investigators save more lives than firefighters.'

India looked pained. 'Did your bosses not like the piece I wrote?'

'They felt that maybe I was not being supportive enough of the unit,' said Vicky. 'If you could redress the balance in the next article, you'd be doing me a favour.'

India nodded. 'Not a problem. And thanks again.'

They shook hands and Vicky headed back to the multi-storey to get her car. Her phone rang as she got into the driving seat. It was Farmer. 'Yes, guv.'

'Where are you, sweetheart?'

'On my way in. What's up?'

'You got anything on tonight?' he asked.

'In what way?'

'I thought maybe we could take a run out to see Willie Campbell. He's not answering his phone and we could do with asking him a few questions.'

'I'm up for that.'

'Great. And you can drop me home afterwards?'

'Sure.'

'It's a date then.'

'A date?'

Farmer sighed. 'It was a joke.'

'Ah, right, guv. Hilarious.'

44

Farmer knocked on Vicky's door and pushed it open. 'You good to go?' He already had a coat on over his uniform.

Vicky looked at her watch. She'd been so busy updating her recent cases that she hadn't realised her shift was over. 'Yes, guv.'

'Let's head off then.'

Vicky picked up her jacket and followed Farmer down the stairs to where she'd parked the BMW. 'Where are we going?' she asked as she climbed into the driving seat.

Farmer grunted as he lowered himself down. 'This is so bloody low on the ground,' he complained.

'Sorry about that,' said Vicky. 'Would you like me to get you a cushion?'

He looked across at her, eyes narrowing. 'I've been noticing a tendency for you to be sarcastic lately,' he said.

'I can't think where I picked that up,' she said. 'I'll try to be less so. Where are we going?'

'Hackney,' he said. 'Head north.'

'Something you need to know,' she said as she started the engine.

'That sounds ominous.'

'I went to see that journalist this morning.'

'You didn't kill her, I hope.'

Vicky chuckled as she edged the BMW out of the car park. 'No, I wanted to meet the guy I pulled out of the fire. She'd found him.'

Farmer looked over at her. 'What did he have to say?'

'They never touched the electrical consumer board. He was definite about that and so was his wife.'

'They could be lying.'

'They could be, but I don't think they were. The wife had a good point. If you're just squatting, the cops stay away. But if you start stealing electricity it becomes theft and that's a criminal matter. So they said they never tampered with the board.'

Farmer nodded. 'That's interesting.'

'Isn't it? And no one ever tried to talk to them, after the fire. Not the cops and not Willie. There are only two witnesses quoted in Willie's report and they were passers-by.'

'But he did speak to the person who called nine nine nine?'

'That was one of the passers-by. He saw flames through the window and made the call. And he stayed there to watch while the fire brigade attended. Turns out he was an off-duty community support officer. The thing is, that journalist had no trouble tracking down the guy I pulled out, so why didn't Willie?'

'It's a good question, and one we can put to him when we see him.' He pointed ahead. 'Hang a right there.'

Farmer gave her directions to Campbell's house. His knowledge of London's roads was impressive and Vicky was starting to think that he was right, it was better to know where they were going rather than relying on the satnav. It was the same with taxis – a black-cab driver who had done the Knowledge and knew every street and landmark in the City was always going to get you to your destination quicker than a minicab driver who was following a route on his iPhone.

Campbell's house was a neat semi-detached with roses growing in the front garden. The driveway was empty so Vicky pulled in and parked in front of the garage. Farmer walked up the path and rang the bell. The garage had glass panels along the top. Vicky stood on tiptoe and peered in. 'No sign of a car,' she said.

'Probably playing golf,' said Farmer. He rang the bell again and then stood back to look up at the bedroom windows. He took out his mobile phone and called Campbell's number again. It went straight through to voicemail.

A middle-aged woman weighed down with full Waitrose carrier bags turned into the path of the house next door. 'Are you looking for Willie and Ann?' she asked, peering at them through thick-lensed glasses.

'Are they out?' asked Farmer.

'They're in Spain,' she said, putting down her carrier bags and pulling her keys from her handbag.

'Holiday?'

'A long holiday,' she said. 'They've bought a villa out there.'

'Nice,' said Farmer.

'Lovely place it is,' said the woman. 'Four bedrooms, terrace, pool. And it's on a fantastic golf course.'

'Willie loves his golf,' said Farmer. 'So when will he back, do you know?'

'I'm really not sure. Ann said they were planning to

spend the winter months out there and the summers here.' She put the key in the lock. 'They're doing the right thing, that's all I can say. I'd be out in Spain like a shot if I could.' She disappeared inside with her shopping and closed the door behind her.

'That's interesting,' said Farmer.

'He didn't mention he was moving abroad?'

'Sure, he always said he wanted to retire to Spain but he said he'd have to sell up here first.' He pulled a face. 'Maybe he came into money.'

Vicky's eyes narrowed. 'You're not thinking what I think you're thinking?'

Farmer wrinkled his nose. 'I'm a suspicious bugger, I know, but let's not go counting chickens.' He looked at his watch. 'Right, are you okay to drop me at home?'

'Of course. What's happening with your car?'

'It's in the garage again. I've told them they'd better put it right this time or there'll be hell to pay. We've got four days off now so I'm going to make sure it's done properly.'

'You should threaten to burn the place down. That'd get their attention.'

Farmer wagged a finger at her. 'See now, that's not funny,' he said. 'But you know, you might have a point.' He gestured at the BMW. 'Okay, so home, James, and don't spare the horses.'

Vicky tugged her forelock. 'Aye, aye, sir.'

45

Vicky looked around, panting for breath. The whole room was ablaze now and her body was bathed in sweat under her tunic and leggings. She bent down and grabbed the injured man under his armpits but he was too heavy and no matter how much she strained she couldn't lift him. She released her grip and hurried around to kneel down next to him. Her mask was misting up and it was as if she was looking through a thick fog. She wiped the visor with the back of her glove but it didn't make any difference. The injured man forced a smile. It was her father. He was wearing his helmet but no breathing apparatus and every breath he took was an effort. 'Don't worry, sweetheart, you did your best,' he gasped.

'I'll save you, Dad, don't worry.'

Her father smiled. 'I'm so proud of you.'

In the distance she heard a siren kick into life. 'They're coming, Dad. They're coming to save us.'

Her father shook his head. 'No, sweetheart, it's too late. You have to let me go.'

'Dad, no!'

The siren got louder and louder, then the sound changed. It was her mobile ringing and it jerked her awake. She lay on her back, panting for breath, then groped for her phone. Farmer. She frowned. Their run of four shifts had come to an end and she was now off-duty for four days. 'Yes, guv,' she said.

'Wakey wakey, rise and shine,' said Farmer.

'What's up?'

'You're going to prison, sweetheart.'

Vicky ran a hand through her tousled hair. 'What are you talking about, guv? We're off for four days, remember?'

'I think I know who burned you. He's behind bars now. Peter Mulholland got back to me with a name and he fits the bill. Can you pick me up? I'll have breakfast ready. And wear your uniform.'

'Okay,' said Vicky. She showered, dealt with her scars and dressed in her uniform.

By the time she went downstairs her mum was already in the kitchen. She frowned when she saw what Vicky was wearing. 'I thought today was an off-day,' she said.

'It was. The guv's called me in.'

'Well you can have a hot breakfast before you go. Surely you've got time for that?'

'He's cooking again, Mum.'

Barbara raised her eyebrows. 'He's a bit of a strange one, your guv'nor.'

'Tell me about it,' said Vicky.

Forty-five minutes later she was outside Farmer's house, pressing the buzzer. He let her in and by the time she walked into his flat he was placing a fried egg on an overflowing plate. 'I'm out of baked beans so I went with tinned tomatoes,' said Farmer. 'And you'll have to butter your own toast.'

'No problem,' said Vicky slipping off her jacket. As

they tucked into their breakfasts, Farmer explained what was going on. 'Remember the police investigator, Peter? He came back to me with a name, a guy currently behind bars for setting four fires for money. He was caught watching a fire he'd set in south London but they found enough evidence in his house to link him to three more. And his technique of choice was to make it look as if the electricity supply or gas supply had been tampered with.'

'Like in the Kilburn hotel?'

'Exactly like the Kilburn hotel,' said Farmer. 'Peter says we should go and have a chat with a Mr Michael Walsh, so that's what we're doing.' He waved his knife at her plate. 'How's your egg?'

'Perfect.'

Farmer beamed at the compliment and they both tucked in. When they'd finished Farmer put the plates in the sink and grabbed his coat. She led the way downstairs and Farmer pulled the door closed behind them.

'I've no idea how to get to Wandsworth Prison, and I've got a perfectly serviceable satnav,' said Vicky as she sat behind the wheel.

'Sweetheart, they rot your brains,' said Farmer, fastening his seatbelt. 'I know the way.'

'Whatever you say.'

Farmer was as good as his word and he gave her clear instructions to cross the river and drive south. It took just over an hour to reach the prison and another fifteen minutes to find a parking space where Vicky was at least hopeful that her BMW wouldn't be vandalised.

'So what do you know about Wandsworth?' he asked as they walked up to the main gates.

'Not much,' admitted Vicky.

'It's what they call a Category B men's prison,' said Farmer. 'It's the biggest prison in the UK but its main claim to fame is that Ronnie Biggs escaped from here in 1965.'

'Ronnie Biggs?'

'Good grief, girl. The Great Train robber. Don't tell me you've never heard of Ronnie Biggs?'

'Before my time. Sorry.'

He looked across at her and frowned as if he thought she was winding him up, but then he shrugged. 'Anyway, they were hanging criminals here until 1961. They did a hundred and thirty-five in all, and if it was up to me they'd be doing it still.'

'Right,' said Vicky, unwilling to be drawn into a discussion of the pros and cons of capital punishment. 'And this guy we're coming to see. What's his story?'

'Like I said, his name's Michael Walsh, and he confessed to starting four fires that investigators originally thought were electrical faults.'

'So why didn't the cops connect him to my fire?'

'Because that happened while he was out on bail, and because, as Peter said, the LFB view was that it was misadventure. It was blamed on squatters tampering with the electricity supply. The other three fires were outside London. One was in Brighton, another in Bristol, and the first one he confessed to setting was in Manchester where his mother lives.'

'And who paid him?'

'Different people each time. He said he was on a dark website where firestarters met to talk about their addiction and he was approached there. Money was paid into his account and the cops followed the money trail. In each case, it was either an insurance job or a developer trying to circumvent planning regulations. Walsh gave up the names and cooperated with the detectives. That's how Peter tells it, but let's get it from the horse's mouth before we jump to conclusions. And this has to stay on the QT, you understand that? What we're doing goes against all rules and policy. Mum's the word.'

They walked in through the visitor's entrance and joined a queue to talk to a prison officer standing behind a thick sheet of protective glass. The walls were dotted with posters about items that were prohibited in the prison and the penalties for trying to smuggle in contraband.

'We're here to see Michael Walsh, I'm told he's on B wing,' said Farmer when he reached the front of the queue. He held out his LFB ID and the officer motioned for him to slip it under the security glass. 'I'll need the lady's ID, too,' he said. Vicky pushed her ID after Farmer's. Her hair fell away from her injured cheek and the officer flinched, but then recovered his composure and forced a smile. He checked their names against a list of approved visitors, then handed back two prison IDs to clip to their uniforms.

'Do you have any weapons?' asked the prison officer.

'Just my rapier-like wit,' said Farmer. It was clear from the look on the officer's face that he was in no mood for humour so Farmer smiled an apology. 'No,' he said.

'Have you been here before?'

'No,' said Farmer.

The prison officer pointed at a set of sliding glass doors to his left. 'I'll open these doors, you walk in, and the doors will close. You pass through any mobile phones you have to my colleague, and she will give you a token so that you can get them back when you leave.'

Farmer smiled and nodded and the officer pressed a button to open the doors. They stepped through and the doors rattled shut. The female officer seemed as humourless as the first so Farmer and Vicky said nothing as they handed over their phones and received blue circular numbered tokens in return. A second set of doors rattled open and they walked through into a corridor where there was an airport-style metal detector. They put anything that might set it off into plastic trays and walked through. Another prison officer was there to greet them, a big woman with close-cropped hair and the forearms of a weightlifter. She introduced herself as Ms Collier and made no move to shake hands, instead twirling a set of keys on a chain with her right hand. 'This way,' she growled and led them down a corridor past several identical doors. She turned left at the end of the corridor then stopped at the second door. There was an alarm above it and a plastic sign that said INTERVIEW ROOM.

The officer opened a door to an interview room and showed them in. There was a single Formica-topped table that was bolted to the floor with four plastic chairs around it. 'Take a seat and I'll have someone fetch Mr Walsh for you,' she said, and closed the door.

Vicky looked at Farmer in surprise. '*Mr* Walsh?'

'Everyone has to be shown the right amount of respect these days, less their fragile egos are damaged,' said Farmer. 'Have you seen a prison cell? Even in an old Victorian prison like this they have their own TVs, PlayStations and a choice of meals.'

'Still, you wouldn't want to be here, would you?' said Vicky.

'I always figure if you can't do the time, don't do the

crime,' said Farmer. 'But with the judges we've got, these days, it looks as if they bend over backwards not to send people away. Anyway, don't get me started on crime and punishment. I'm of the "eye for an eye" school. Now, when they show in Mr Walsh, let me do most of the talking.'

'No problem.'

'This guy loves fire, so he's going to be staring at you. Just to warn you.'

Vicky frowned. 'What do you mean?'

Farmer rubbed his own cheek. 'The scars, sweetheart. How often do you think he gets to see the results of his handiwork, close up? Try not to react, yeah? Just let him look.'

'Okay.'

He frowned. 'Have I upset you?'

Vicky hesitated. He had upset her, but she knew that he was only telling her the truth and she had to respect his honesty. 'I'm fine, guv.'

'It's a way of getting to him,' he said. 'He'll have all his defences up so we need any advantage we can get.'

'I understand.'

The door opened and a man wearing a prison sweat-shirt and baggy blue tracksuit bottoms stood at the threshold. He was middle-aged, plump and pasty-faced with a greasy comb-over that did little to conceal his bald patch. He had pale fleshy lips like strips of raw fish that emphasised the yellowness of his teeth. A prison officer appeared behind him. 'In you go, Walsh, we don't have all day.' The officer was well over six feet, broad-shoul-dered with a thick moustache and a crew cut. The hair, and his ramrod straight back, suggested a military career before he'd joined the prison service.

Walsh shuffled in. He stole a quick look at Farmer, then averted his eyes.

'Sit down, Walsh,' said the officer. 'They won't bite.'

'I don't want to talk to anyone,' muttered Walsh. Vicky thought there was a trace of a Scottish accent.

'Then don't talk, just listen to what they have to say. Now stop pissing around and sit down.'

Walsh sat down on the chair facing Vicky and Farmer as if he feared it was going to electrocute him. He folded his arms and stared at the floor.

'Do you want me to stay, sir?' the prison officer asked Farmer.

'I think we're okay,' said Farmer.

The prison officer nodded. 'I'll be outside. Just ring the bell when you're done.' He left them and pulled the door closed. Walsh linked his fingers and continued to stare at the floor. 'How are you, Michael?' asked Farmer. Walsh ignored him. Farmer let the silence drag on for at least a minute before speaking again. 'My name is Des Farmer, I'm with the London Fire Brigade.'

For the first time, Walsh looked up and he stared quizzically at Farmer. 'You're a fire investigator?'

'Yes, I am.'

Walsh nodded slowly. 'You must love your work.'

'It has its moments, yes.'

Walsh looked over at Vicky and his eyes widened when he saw the damage to her face. He licked his fleshy lips as he stared at her.

'Do you know who this is, Michael?' asked Farmer quietly.

Walsh continued to stare at Vicky's scarred face.

'Michael?'

Walsh looked at Farmer, then shook his head slowly. He had his fingers interlinked and his thumbs were digging against each other.

'Her name is Vicky Lewis. Say hello, Vicky.'

'Hello, Michael,' said Vicky.

'Vicky is a fireman,' said Farmer. He shrugged. 'I'm not supposed to say that, am I? Firefighter, that's what she is. She fights fires.'

Walsh was staring at her left cheek. She moved her head slightly so that the hair fell away from the ear, giving him a better view. Walsh licked his lips.

'She fought the fire that broke out at a hotel in Kilburn, six months ago. You were out on bail for the fire you set in Wimbledon. The one that got you ten years for manslaughter.'

'Involuntary manslaughter,' said Walsh, still staring at Vicky.

'That's right, you didn't mean to kill Mrs Hemmings. Wrong time, wrong place. You like setting fires, don't you, Michael?'

Walsh nodded. 'It's a sickness. That's what the psychiatrists say.'

'You've done it since you were a kid?'

Walsh nodded again. 'Always.'

'Played with matches? Set fire to things in your house?'

Walsh was nodding continuously now, his head going back and forth like a metronome.

'But you got your obsession under control, didn't you? You don't set random fires any more, do you?'

Walsh sat back, crossing his arms defensively.

'Now you do it for money, don't you? That sort of kills two birds with one stone, you get paid and you get your rocks off, as they say.'

Walsh clamped his jaw tight. Vicky could see a vein pulsing in his forehead. Farmer smiled. He reached slowly into his pocket and took out his disposable lighter. Walsh stared at it, then licked his lips. Farmer flicked the wheel and the lighter ignited. The flame was an inch long and it flickered as Farmer moved his hand from side to side. 'I'm guessing they don't let you have matches or lighters in here,' said Farmer. 'What with your track record and all.' He let his thumb slip off the fuel lever and the flame disappeared. Walsh leaned forward, a pleading look in his eyes.

'Don't be coy, Michael,' said Farmer. 'You pled guilty, remember? You didn't have any choice really, did you? Not with all the stuff they found in your garage. And there was CCTV footage of you watching the fire. That was a mistake, Michael. But then you know that. If you hadn't stayed to watch, you might well have got away with it.' Farmer shook his head and he looked across at Vicky. 'You know, virtually all arsonists want to stay and watch their handiwork. That's what leads them to get caught.' He looked back at Walsh. 'I know you didn't mean to kill Mrs Hemmings, any more than you meant to hurt Vicky. Just wrong time, wrong place.'

Walsh looked down at the floor.

'Same MO, Michael. It was you. You understand MO? *Modus operandi.* The fire in that Kilburn hotel was set in exactly the same way as you set the fire that killed Mrs Hemmings. You made it look as if it was a consumer-board fault but there were other points of origin. What did you use, Michael? The old pack of Quavers trick? Diesel sprayed on toilet paper? Firelighters?'

Walsh kept his eyes averted. His left leg had started to tremble, a sign of the tension he was feeling.

'And three other fires that you set, for money. The cops knew about the three others but for some reason they didn't spot the similarities with the hotel fire in Kilburn. But you set that fire too, didn't you? While you were out on bail?'

Walsh said nothing.

Farmer flicked the wheel on top of the lighter and it ignited again. Walsh stared at the flame and licked his lips.

'You're a rarity, Michael. A firebug who gets paid for it. How lucky are you?'

Walsh said nothing.

'The four jobs you were convicted of were insurance jobs. You were very cooperative with the detectives, weren't you? Told them who'd paid you and how much and even showed them where the money was. I guess that's why you got a relatively short sentence, isn't it? It pays to cooperate. Michael. That's the way the system works. You help the police and the CPS go easy on you in court.'

Walsh closed his eyes and bit down on his lower lip.

'Come on, Michael. What's the point of doing this if you don't get the credit? It was never about the money, was it? I mean, I'm sure the money came in handy but it was always about the fires, wasn't it? The smoke, the heat, the flames?'

Walsh opened his eyes and glanced over at Vicky, then back to the lighter. Farmer slipped his thumb off the fuel lever and the flame vanished.

'Here's the thing, Michael. You pled guilty to starting the four fires that the CPS charged you with. But that means the Kilburn hotel fire is still there. When are you due out? Four years if you keep your nose clean? Five, maybe? I might be retired by then, but even if I'm not I'll still be around and I'll make sure that the day you're released there are a couple of cops at the gates who'll arrest you and charge you with what you did at Kilburn. I've got the evidence, Michael. It's open and shut.'

'You can't say that,' said Walsh. 'You don't have any evidence.'

'There was evidence at your house,' said Farmer. 'There was diesel and you don't have a car or anything else that requires diesel. And you had firelighters but no open fire.'

'I have a barbecue.'

'And you had lighter fluid for that. Who uses lighter fluid and firelighters to get a barbecue started?'

'I like to be sure,' said Walsh.

'I bet you do,' said Farmer. He flicked the lighter and moved the flame from side to side as Walsh stared at it.

'I know what you're suggesting,' said Walsh.

'Enlighten me,' said Farmer.

'I like to be sure when I'm lighting my barbecue, that's what I meant.'

Farmer shrugged. 'That's what I thought you meant. I didn't mean to suggest anything else.' Farmer sat back and folded his arms. He smiled at Walsh but said nothing. Vicky realised he was waiting for Walsh to fill the silence. As Farmer and Vicky continued to stare at him but not say anything, Walsh continued to look increasingly uncomfortable. Eventually he broke the silence. 'I want to go back to my cell.'

'No problem,' said Farmer. 'But you need to realise that if we don't resolve this, you'll be serving your full sentence and you'll be arrested when you leave. I guarantee that.'

'I'm not confessing to something I didn't do,' said Walsh.

'No one is asking you to do that, Michael.' He let the lighter go out and then leaned across the table so that his face was only inches from Walsh's. 'I've looked at the files, I've checked the evidence, and I know you set the Kilburn fire. It's the same MO. You were out on bail. You had the opportunity, and once I start looking I'm sure I'll be able to put you in the area. The one thing I don't know, the one thing I need to know, is who paid you to set the fire. If you tell me that, Michael, then I can get the fire added retrospectively to your guilty plea. No one was killed, though obviously Vicky here was badly burnt. But she's not one to bear grudges, are you, Vicky?'

Vicky's eyes widened and her mouth fell open. 'What?'

'You wouldn't be planning to sue Michael? Not if he confessed.'

She didn't understand what he was getting at and frowned in confusion.

'It's not about money, is it?' said Farmer. 'If Michael were to admit to what he did, you wouldn't sue, would you?'

She shook her head, still confused but playing along with what he obviously wanted her to say. 'Of course not.'

Farmer looked at Walsh, nodding. 'See, Michael. It's a win-win situation. You tell us what happened, who paid you to torch the hotel, and you don't serve one extra day behind bars and Miss Lewis here doesn't take all your assets off you. Your house, for instance. You own that, don't you? Well, if Miss Lewis sets her lawyers on you, how long do you think it will stay your house? You've got lawyers, haven't you, sweetheart?'

Vicky nodded. 'Yes, guv.'

Farmer continued to stare at Walsh as he slipped the lighter back into his pocket. 'There you go, Michael, that's from the horse's mouth. You play ball with us, and we'll play ball with you.' He leaned back in his seat. 'But if you fuck us around, Michael, we will royally fuck with you. You can see the damage the fire did to her face. The fire you set. Can you imagine how much that's going to cost to put right? Tens of thousands of pounds, I'd say. Hundreds maybe. Say you don't put your hand up to the Kilburn hotel fire. Say we arrest you when you leave jail and we charge you again and they find you guilty? And they will find you guilty, Michael, because by then I'll have all the evidence I need. So you'll be back in prison and Miss Lewis here, well she'll set her lawyers on you. And they're Rottweilers, aren't they, sweetheart?'

Vicky nodded. 'Yes. Rottweilers.'

'And by the time they're done with you, you won't have a penny to your name, Michael. And when you do eventually get out, you'll be homeless and penniless. Is that what you want? Seriously? Is that what you want?'

Walsh said nothing. He was staring at Vicky's scars but when she turned to look at him he looked away and stared at the floor.

'Fine,' said Farmer. He placed his palms on the table and pushed himself to his feet. He pressed the bell and the prison officer opened the door. Vicky stood up and Farmer stepped to the side to let her go out first.

'Have you got a number?' asked Walsh, still staring at the floor. 'A phone number?'

'Sure,' said Farmer. He pulled out his wallet and took out a business card.

'Not you,' said Walsh, looking up. 'Her.'

'Why do you want her number?' asked Farmer.

'I'm not talking to you,' said Walsh. 'I don't like you.'

'You're not getting her number, Michael. That's not what this is about.'

'It's all right,' said Vicky. She took the card from him and scribbled her mobile number on the back. She gave it to Walsh. 'If you want to tell me the truth, call me,' she said. 'But any funny business and I'll report you to the governor.'

Walsh nodded as he stared at the number. He licked his lips and they glistened under the overhead lights.

'We're done here,' said Farmer.

They left the interview room, Walsh's eyes still glued to the card.

46

Vicky didn't speak until they were driving back to north London. 'You're sure he did it, guv?' she asked eventually. 'He's the one who torched the hotel?'

'I'm sure, but being sure and proving it are two completely different things,' said Farmer. 'It's his MO, and there aren't that many firestarters for hire out there. Most of them are too stupid, for a start. They almost always get caught eventually, usually because they stand around to watch things burn.'

'But you think he was paid to set fire to the hotel?'

Farmer nodded. 'I'm sure of it. But it was six months ago so getting new evidence is going to be difficult to say the least. We rely on CCTV footage to place people and no one keeps footage for six months. We could start looking for witnesses but people's memories are bad at the best of times. After six months . . .' He shrugged. 'Needle in a haystack.'

'So what's the plan?'

'The plan? We let Walsh stew. The deal we've given him is a no-brainer. If he takes it he wipes the slate clean. He doesn't serve any extra time and he can't be done for it down the line. If he does admit to it, he gets nothing added to his sentence, so it's all upside. Providing you don't set the Rottweilers on him.'

'I don't have Rottweilers.'

'I thought your lawyer got you millions after what happened?'

'The owners used a law firm but I just gave them my bank details. Actually I didn't even do that. My mum did it while I was in hospital.'

Farmer rubbed his chin. 'That was nice of them,' he said.

Vicks phone rang and she took the call on hands-free. It was Matt. 'Busy?' he asked.

She looked across at Farmer who was pretending not to listen. 'Day off, but still busy-ish.'

'Fancy Ronnie Scott's? I've got tickets.'

'I need to eat,' said Vicky.

'Dinner and Ronnie Scott's it is, then,' he said.

She laughed. 'I fell into that.'

'My treat,' he said.

'No, we'll go Dutch.'

'Nah, I hate Dutch food,' said Matt. 'Cheese and tulips. That's all there is to it. How is that a cuisine?'

She laughed again. 'How about we meet at Mildreds in Lexington Street?'

'I'll book.'

'You can't book. It's vegetarian and it's first come, first served.'

'Suddenly Dutch food is starting to sound attractive.'

'What time's the jazz?'

'Nine-ish.'

'So I'll see you outside Mildreds at seven.'

'It's a date.'

'Actually, it's a time, but you were close.'

He was still laughing when she ended the call.

Farmer was looking at her with a sly grin. 'Don't ask,' she said.

'I wasn't even listening.'

47

Vicky drove home, parked outside and hurried in. 'What's the hurry?' called her mother from the kitchen.

'Flying visit!' shouted Vicky as she rushed up the stairs. 'I'm going out for dinner.'

'With Matt?'

Vicky stopped in her tracks. 'Now how would you know that?'

'I'm a mother. We know stuff. Now hurry up and don't keep him waiting.'

Vicky shook her head in amazement as she headed up to her bedroom. She grabbed a dress from her wardrobe, one with long sleeves to hide her glove as best she could. She didn't have time to deal with her blisters, she just changed into the dress, combed her hair and put on fresh make-up. She ordered a minicab and rushed back downstairs where her mother was waiting.

'Calm down,' said her mother, giving her a hug.

'I'm late.'

'He'll wait.'

Vicky looked at her watch. 'Gotta go.'

A white Prius pulled up outside and she climbed into the back.

Matt was waiting on the pavement when she arrived at the restaurant. He gave her a hug and a soft peck on her good cheek. 'You weren't joking about no reservations,' he said. 'But I've put my name down and there are three couples ahead of us.' He looked through the window and saw a waitress taking two men into the main part of the restaurant. 'Make that two.'

'It makes more sense for them, I guess,' said Vicky. 'They don't have people not turning up, and you know you can always get a table if you're prepared to wait. Anyway, I'm sorry I'm late, I was with Des and I left myself short of time. I haven't showered or anything.'

'You look great,' he said. 'I haven't showered either so we're even.'

Vicky grinned. 'You look great, too.' He did. He was wearing a Ted Baker jacket and Versace jeans and his hair was glossy and combed back. He smelled good, too. 'What's the aftershave?'

'Hugo Boss,' he said.

'Des says I can't wear perfume, he says it interferes with his sense of smell.'

Matt laughed. 'Des is an idiot,' he said.

Another couple were being shown to a table and four people were getting their coats to leave.

'Looks like we're on,' said Matt. Five minutes later they were sitting at a corner table with menus. The waitress was in her teens with clear unblemished skin and long blond hair that almost reached her impossibly slim waist. The position of the table meant that Vicky's scarred cheek was on show so she kept her head tilted slightly forward so that her hair covered it.

Vicky ordered the classic burger – smoked tofu, lentil,

piquillo pepper, in a focaccia bun with relish, rocket, red onion and tomato.

Matt studied the menu and shook his head. 'I'm a carnivore,' he said. 'I'm lost.'

The waitress laughed. 'Do you like Mexican food? Have the black turtle bean and squash burrito. It comes with iceberg lettuce, cheddar cheese, sour cream, salsa and guacamole – there's so much going on you won't even notice there's no meat.'

'Sounds like a plan,' said Matt, handing the menu back to the waitress who gave him a beaming smile before heading off to the kitchen.

'Do all the waitresses fall in love with you?' asked Vicky.

'They just recognise someone else who works in the hospitality industry,' he said. 'Professional courtesy.'

'So your devilish good looks and charm have nothing to do with it,' said Vicky.

Matt laughed and reached over to touch her hand. 'I'll take that as a compliment,' he said.

The waitress returned with their bottle of wine and showed the label to him with an expression on her face that suggested his opinion mattered more than anything in the whole wide world. He nodded and she went to work with a corkscrew.

'So, busy day?' Matt asked Vicky.

'A weird day all round,' she said. 'Des took me to see an arsonist who might have started the fire that I was burned in.'

'Are you serious?'

'Looks like it. We're trying to persuade him to confess.'

'Why would he do that?'

'Des is talking about a deal. He owns up to setting the fire but doesn't get any extra prison time. That way we'll get confirmation that the owners of the building had it torched.'

'Why would they have burned their own building?'

'So they could rebuild. It was listed. So I spent a big chunk of the day behind bars.'

'With several hundred men who haven't seen a woman in years. Nice.'

The waitress finished extracting the cork and poured a little wine into his glass. He gave it to Vicky. 'You can do the honours,' he said.

She sipped the wine and nodded her approval but the waitress only had eyes for Matt. It was only when he smiled at her that she poured wine into their glasses, then she flashed him a toothpaste commercial smile and walked away.

Vicky shook her head and chuckled.

'Stop it,' said Matt, grinning. 'So, you still set on getting back to fighting fires?'

'I thought I was, but now I'm not so sure.'

'What do you mean?'

'I don't know. I was at a fire and I was . . . I don't know . . . scared is the only way I can describe it. And I threw up when I saw a body that had burned.'

'That's not surprising. I'm sure I would, too.'

'Yes, but I've always been able to put any fear aside when I'm doing the job. The training kicks in and you do what you have to do.'

'It's probably like riding a bike,' said Matt. 'If you do go back to firefighting, the fear will go.'

'I hope so.'

'Though Des always says fire investigators save more lives than firefighters, overall.'

She grinned. 'I bet he does.'

'What he means is that you guys identify the causes of fires and so that stops people making the same mistakes. That saves lives.'

'I guess so.' She sipped her wine thoughtfully.

Their food arrived and again the waitress only had eyes for Matt. She was tempted to give the girl a kick but realised that Matt wasn't actually discouraging her attentions. He smiled at her and thanked her as he looked into her eyes for a second or two longer than necessary. Only after she had walked away did he look down at his food. 'This looks like one hell of a good burrito,' he said. 'And your burger looks tasty, too. You might well change my opinion on veggie food.'

'I'm happy to eat meat, but I like vegetarian occasionally,' she said. 'I don't think I could eat it all the time.'

'Bacon,' said Matt.

'Oh yes. Bacon.'

She tucked into her burger. Matt narrowed his eyes and put down his knife and fork. 'I've had a thought,' he said.

'They won't give you bacon here,' she said. 'I tried asking once. Never again.'

He frowned at her in confusion and then laughed as he realised she was joking. 'Funny,' he said. 'No, I mean I had a thought about Des and all the stuff you said he had in his room. Did you ever hear about that American fire investigator, John Orr?'

Vicky shook her head.

'He was a fire investigator in California in the eighties

and nineties. There was a series of fires that killed four people and caused millions of dollars in damages. He investigated a lot of those fires but it turned out that he set most of them. He's serving life in prison.'

'No, Des didn't start those fires. I solved that little mystery.'

'In prison?'

She shook her head. 'No, it was nothing to do with the guy in prison.'

'I'm intrigued.'

'I'm talking out of school, I shouldn't.' She waved her knife at his food. 'Eat.'

'I'm eating. But you can't leave me hanging like this. I'm on tenterhooks. Real, genuine tenterhooks.'

'What is a tenterhook anyway?'

'Now you're changing the subject.'

'I'm not. I just want to know.'

He laughed. 'Okay, how about this? I'll tell you what a tenterhook is, you tell me who started those fires.'

'You're crazy,' laughed Vicky.

'Deal?'

'Yes, fine. It's a deal.'

He grinned and sat back in his chair. 'Okay, then. A tenter is a wooden frame, often in the form of a line of fencing, used to hang woollen or linen cloth to prevent it from shrinking as it dries. They were used a lot in the north of England last century, in the mills. Strictly speaking, on the land outside the mills. And the tenterhooks were the hooks used to hold the cloth in place on the tenter.'

She looked at him, impressed. 'How do you know that?'

'I read a lot. Now spill the beans about the fires. How did you solve the mystery?'

Vicky sipped her wine, then put her glass back on the table. 'Just between you and me, okay?'

'Cross my heart.'

'I'm serious, Matt. I wouldn't want Des to think I was talking behind his back.'

He waved his hands. 'Hey, I'm only joking, if you don't want to tell me, that's fine. I'm sorry, it's just . . . you know . . . interesting. Let's change the subject.'

'No, it's okay.' She leaned towards him and lowered her voice. 'I asked Des point blank.'

Matt's eyes widened. 'Are you serious?'

'It was driving me crazy. I knew there was no way he could have caused those fires and killed those women. So I asked him.'

'And?'

'He took me in and showed me the cases.' She looked around to make sure that no one was listening, and lowered her voice even more. 'Des reckons there's a killer around who kills women and uses fire to cover his crimes,' she whispered.

'Get out of here.'

'I'm serious. He's gathered all sorts of evidence. The fires are different in each case but he's sure it's the same man. He likes blonds.'

'Des?'

'The killer. Are you following this?'

Matt laughed. 'It just sounds so far-fetched. Why hasn't he gone to the police?'

'The police don't believe him. Nobody does.'

'Do you?'

She took a sip of wine. 'Actually, I think I do. The killer clearly knows about fires. You might be right, it might be a firefighter who's doing it, but it definitely isn't Des.'

'That's good to know.'

Vicky smiled. 'Sorry, I shouldn't be talking about work.'

'It's okay, I wish I had something interesting to talk about, but I serve drinks and that's that. I can't remember when I last saved someone's life doing that.' He pretended to think. 'Actually I can,' he said. 'Never.'

They spent the rest of the meal chatting about pretty much anything other than work, then he took her along to Ronnie Scott's where they listened to several top-class jazz acts and drank another bottle of wine between them. They left just after midnight and again Matt dropped her off at her house.

This time when he moved to kiss her she slipped her hand behind his neck and pulled him closer. He kissed her on the lips but she didn't feel much enthusiasm and she wondered if she'd misread the signals. There was a reluctance about the kiss and he was the first to break away.

'My mum's probably not asleep but you're welcome to come in for coffee,' she said.

He flashed his boyish smile. 'I'll have to take a rain check,' he said.

'Are you sure?'

He nodded. 'I've got a beer delivery first thing,' he said. 'But let's do this again. I had fun tonight.'

'Me too,' she said. She wondered if he would kiss her again but he just smiled and nodded so she let herself out of the car. She turned as she walked up the path to the house to see if he would wave but he had already sat back in his seat and was staring straight ahead as the car drove away.

48

Her name was Vicky Lewis and she lived with her mother in Peckham. He had checked the electoral roll and there was no man in the house. The house was a tidy three-bedroomed detached with an integral garage and a small front garden. Vicky's bedroom was at the back of the house, the mother slept at the front. The mother was usually in bed by ten and switched off her light at eleven. Vicky's coming and goings were much less predictable. Usually she drove her expensive BMW but sometimes she arrived home in a cab. She didn't appear to have much of a social life. She was probably self-conscious about her scars. They had a dog. A Labrador. She often took the dog for a walk last thing at night. Dogs were a nuisance. Usually he would steer clear of a woman who had a dog, but Vicky Lewis was different.

She didn't seem to have a Facebook account or use Twitter. Googling her name turned up only the fire that had burned her and her rescue of a family at the Grenfell Tower fire. She had gone into a burning hotel to rescue a homeless Romanian and had been trapped when the floor had collapsed under her. There were no photographs of her burned, all the newspapers had used the same picture taken not long after she had joined the Fire

Brigade, posing in front of a fire engine, her helmet tucked under her arm. The articles on her Grenfell Tower shout were equally dramatic though she didn't appear to have been interviewed as there were no direct quotes from her. He figured another fireman had given the story to one of the papers and the rest had just copied it.

She didn't seem to be a smoker, and neither did the mother. The mother did have a Facebook page but she hadn't used it for more than two years and there were no photographs taken inside the house. That was a pity, but it was no big deal. Every house had something that could be used to start a fatal fire. A television. A laptop. Even a mobile-phone charger. All he needed to do was to ignite them with a blowtorch and stand well back. The girl and her mother would have to be dead, of course. That was the part he was looking forward to. The mother wasn't his type but Vicky most definitely was. He found himself growing hard at the thought of what he was going to do.

49

Des Farmer padded over to the fridge and took out a can of lager before heading to the spare bedroom. He sat down in the armchair and popped the tab of his can, then took a long slow drink as he stared at the map on the whiteboard in front of him. Fifteen cases. Fifteen women dead. All blonds. There was one killer out there, he was sure of that. A killer who understood fire. A killer who knew enough about forensic science to cover his tracks.

The killer left no evidence. Or, at least, any evidence he left behind was consumed by the fire. There was no way he would ever be able to tell who the killer was by examining the crime scenes. There was nothing there that would point to the killer. But there was another way of identifying the killer and that was by working out how he chose his victims. They were all blond, that was obvious. But they were from different cities, working for different employers, with different interests and hobbies. The killer must have moved around, and then settled in London because that was where the most recent cases were. Was he following a career path that took him from city to city? Most of the fires occurred in the late evening. So did he work during the day? And how did he meet the girls? Their backgrounds were so different, how did he cross paths with them? The Internet, maybe? Internet dating? He took another long pull on his lager. And why did the girls let him get so close? There were never any signs of a break-in, which meant that the girls must have allowed him in. Which meant what? That he was in a position of authority? A cop, maybe? A council employee? Someone who could knock on a stranger's door and be invited in without question? A police officer would understand forensic evidence, but then so would anyone who watched CSI. Maybe he was just a good-looking guy. Ted Bundy was one of America's most successful serial killers because he was handsome and charming. Maybe this killer was, too. Maybe he could just walk up to a beautiful girl and start talking to her and get invited into her home.

His doorbell rang and he frowned. He wasn't expecting anyone. He walked into the hallway and picked up the intercom phone. 'Yeah?' he said. There was only static. Farmer cursed. It was probably kids. 'Hello?' he said, then hung up. He had only just sat down and picked up his lager when the intercom buzzed, twice this time. Farmer swore and went back into the hallway. He grabbed at the intercom. 'Who the hell is it?' he shouted. Again there was only static. He slammed the phone back on to the unit. Almost immediately it buzzed again. He opened his front door and hurried down the stairs, muttering under his breath.

He could hear the television on in the ground-floor flat. Probably Mrs Patel watching one of her Indian soap operas. Farmer never complained about the noise of the TV or their kid when he played too loudly, because Mrs

Patel was a sweetheart and at least once a week would bring him up one of her wonderful curries.

He unlocked the front door. There was nobody there. He looked around, cursed, and then turned to go back inside. He heard a noise from the side of the house. 'Is there someone there?' he asked.

There was no reply.

'Who's there?' asked Farmer.

He stepped outside. Was it kids playing a joke? It wasn't Halloween and anyway the local kids knew better than to go knocking on the doors of strangers. He heard a scraping noise and he walked towards the side of the house. As he turned the corner, opening his mouth to speak, he heard a crackling sound. Something pressed against his side and he went into convulsions before collapsing in a heap, his head banging against the wall as he fell to the ground.

50

D es Farmer was heavy. Really heavy. He had to take the stairs one at a time and keep his left hand against the wall to steady himself. Fingerprints weren't a problem, he was wearing blue latex gloves. In fact, he had double-gloved, like the professionals did. With each step Farmer seemed to get heavier and eventually he had to drop him and drag him up instead, grabbing him under the shoulders and going up backwards.

Farmer was unconscious but breathing, spittle dribbling between his lips. He stank of booze and cigarette smoke. The man pulled him across the threshold and kicked the door shut. He took a deep breath, then grinned down at Farmer. 'Right, let's get this show on the road.' He carried him through to the sitting room and dropped him on the sofa.

He went through to the kitchen and got a glass from a cupboard and a can of lager from the fridge. He popped the tab of the can and poured a bit into the glass and the rest down the sink. He shrugged off his backpack, put it on the table, and unzipped the side pocket where he kept the Rohypnol in a small vial that had once contained eye-drops. He poured the clear liquid into the glass and swirled it around.

Back in the sitting room, Farmer blinked his eyes and groaned. He remembered going down to the front door, but nothing after that. He put his hand up to his head and it came away bloody. He groaned again. He rolled over and blinked at the coffee table. His phone was there but it seemed to be miles away. He stretched out his arm and it seemed to extend for ever. He fumbled for the phone and pressed the screen with his thumb. He squinted at it but could barely make out the icons. He pressed the Phone icon and then pressed the button to redial the last number he had called. Vicky Lewis. He lay back and put the phone to his ear. It was ringing.

51

'I could do carbonara,' said Vicky's mum. 'With a salad. And I've a bottle of Chardonnay in the fridge.' They were in the sitting room, waiting for *The Voice* to start. It was her mother's favourite show.

'Sounds great, Mum,' said Vicky. Baxter was sitting at her feet and he woofed softly.

'Or I could do something with the salmon I have.'

'Either, Mum.'

'You know what? How about a salmon carbonara?'

'Is there such a thing?'

'It's a Jamie Oliver recipe.'

Vicky grinned. 'So it must be good. Whatever you do is fine by me. You've never given me a bad meal.'

Barbara laughed. 'Tell that to seven-year-old Vicky,' she said. 'She hates broad beans, carrots, black pudding, lasagne, radishes . . .'

Vicky held up her hands in surrender. 'I get it,' she said. 'I was a picky eater when I was a kid.' Her phone rang and she looked at the screen. It was Farmer. She took the call but the line was dead.

'Hello?' she said. 'Guv?'

No answer.

'Who is it?' asked Barbara.

'My guv'nor.'

'What does he want at this time of night?'

Vicky stared at the screen. 'I don't know. He didn't say anything.'

'He's probably drunk in some pub somewhere and wants you to drive him home.'

'He's not like that.'

'How can you say that? He gets you to drive him everywhere. Hasn't he heard of cabs?'

Vicky called Farmer back but the phone went straight through to voicemail. She left it a minute or so and tried again. Voicemail. 'I think I'd better go around to his flat. There might be something wrong. Can you put a hold on dinner, until I get back?

'Of course. And the salmon carbonara sounds okay?'

'It sounds delicious,' said Vicky, grabbing her coat.

52

He walked in and saw Farmer lying on his back with the phone to his head. He cursed, ran over, grabbed the phone and switched it off. How had he missed the phone? That was careless and he was never careless, he always planned everything down to the last detail. That was why he had never been caught. He took a deep breath and forced himself to relax. He had to be calm. He had to think. He put the phone on the coffee table. Farmer's eyes were closed and from the way he was breathing it looked as if he had passed out again. He knelt down and put his left hand behind Farmer's neck, pulling up his head. He carefully poured the liquid between Farmer's lips then tilted his head back. Farmer swallowed. A reflex action. He poured the rest of the liquid into Farmer's mouth, then let his head fall back on to the sofa. The drug would keep him sedated for several hours, which would be more than enough time for him to do what had to be done.

He took the glass back into the kitchen, washed it and left it on the draining board. He went back into the hallway and opened one of the doors and switched on the light. His eyes widened when he saw the display. He walked into the middle of the room and put his hands on his hips. 'This is good, Des,' he whispered. 'This is so good. I should do something like this.' He pulled out his phone and took several photographs of the display, and then a short video. He walked over to the map and smiled as he studied the pins and the threads that led from them. 'You missed a few,' he said. 'Bristol. And two in Birmingham.'

He went back into the hallway and opened the second door. It was Farmer's bedroom. The man wrinkled his nose at the stink of stale cigarette smoke. 'Fuck me, Des, you really do live like an animal,' he muttered.

He walked around the room. Lots of combustibles. Two overflowing ashtrays. Several disposable lighters. He smiled to himself. This was going to be so easy. Just another smoker who fell into a drunken stupor and set himself on fire.

He picked up a chair and carried it out to the hall. He used it to reach the smoke alarm. He opened it and took out the nine-volt battery. He stepped down, went back into the kitchen and put the battery in a side pocket. He took out a dead battery, inserted it into the smoke alarm and closed it, then took the chair back into the kitchen.

He dragged Farmer into the bedroom and heaved him on to the bed. He rolled him on his back and pulled his right arm so that it was hanging off the bed. He took one of the ashtrays and put it on to the floor a few inches from the dangling hand. He caught sight of his reflection in the mirrored wardrobe and he grinned and flashed himself a thumbs-up.

He had seen a can of lager in the spare bedroom so he put it next to the ashtray. He stood up and looked at the scene. Pretty much perfect.

He planned to set two fires. One in the spare bedroom, one in the main bedroom. If he did it right it wouldn't look as if there were two seats, but simply a fire that had started in the main bedroom and spread to the spare bedroom. The flat had fitted carpets so it would be filled with smoke within minutes. Farmer would breathe in the smoke and die so that even if the brigade attended promptly he'd be dead and the coroner would find smoke in his lungs. The chances of them testing for Rohypnol were slim to none.

He went back to the kitchen and took his spray bottle filled with diesel and a roll of toilet paper. He tore off long strips of tissue and used them to connect the two bedrooms, then sprayed diesel over them. He used some of Farmer's pins to attach toilet paper to his maps and papers, and sprayed more diesel over them, then sprayed the diesel over the carpet and the chair.

To any investigator, it would look as if the fire had started in the main bedroom, spread along the hall carpet and into the spare bedroom. Both rooms were full of combustibles that would burn quickly.

There was a pack of rolling tobacco on a table next to the chair where Farmer had obviously been drinking his lager. He opened it and grinned when he saw there was a cigarette already rolled up. He took it through to the kitchen and took a book of matches from his backpack and put it and the cigarette on the table.

He went back into the main bedroom, picked the biggest butt from the ashtray and put that on the carpet. He sprayed more diesel over the curtains and the carpet, just enough to help the fire spread but not enough to leave any trace.

Farmer's sitting room was untidy, a coffee table scattered with newspapers and magazines, a tunic thrown over the sofa and several pairs of boots under a small dining table. Like the rest of the flat, it smelled rank. There were a couple of disposable lighters on the coffee table but there were enough in the bedroom already. There were wooden blinds over the window and he pulled the cords to close them. The bedrooms were at the rear of the building, which meant the fire hopefully wouldn't be spotted for some time. There was no need to encourage the fire to spread to the sitting room, the bedrooms would do the job.

He went to the kitchen and picked up his backpack. He slung it over his shoulders as he walked along the hall, running through his mental checklist, making sure that he hadn't forgotten anything. He took one of Farmer's disposable lighters and pulled a pillow off the bed and on to the floor. He flicked the lighter and played the flame along the edge of the pillowcase. After several seconds it began to smoulder. He straightened up and took a step back. It continued to burn, giving off plumes of grey smoke.

He walked quickly to the kitchen picked up the cigarette and the book of matches and went into the spare bedroom. He lit the cigarette, took two long drags to make sure it was burning, and then stuck it into the book of matches. He placed it on the armchair, then used a lighter to ignite the toilet paper over the noticeboard displays. It flared up quickly and within seconds several sheets of paper were also ablaze. The threads linking the map to the photographs burned and fell away.

He went back into the hall and lit the toilet paper there,

then tossed the lighter into the spare room and hurried to the front door. He let himself out and walked quickly down the stairs, opened the main door and left the house. Less than two minutes after starting the fire he was walking along the pavement, humming contentedly to himself.

53

V icky parked in the road a short walk from Farmer's house. She called his number again but it went through to voicemail. She walked to his house, wondering why he wasn't answering. She reached his front door and rang the bell. No answer. Tomorrow was a work day, and he hadn't mentioned that he was going anywhere. And he wasn't the sort to be in the pub, Farmer was happy enough to have a drink after work with the guys from the station but from what she knew the rest of his drinking was done at home.

She looked up at the top floor. The lights were off. She frowned. He couldn't be in bed yet, surely. She rang his number. Voicemail. She pressed the bell. No answer. She was starting to get a bad feeling about what was happening, but she could hardly call out the police to say that her boss wasn't answering his phone or his doorbell.

She walked around the side of the house and almost immediately saw the red flickering through the curtains. No, she realised with a jolt. The curtains were on fire.

She pulled out her phone and called 999. She asked for the fire service and within seconds was talking to a brigade operator. 'Fire in a house in Bethnal Green,' she said. She gave the address. 'Listen, I'm a firefighter. Tell control to make pumps two, persons reported. We'll need an ambulance.'

'Is there anyone in the house?' said the operator.

'I think so. My boss is on the top floor, I think. I'll get the people out of the ground floor now.'

'Under no circumstances should you attempt to go inside,' said the operator. 'Wait for the fire brigade to get there.'

Vicky ended the call and ran towards the house. She banged on the front door and rang the bell for the ground-floor flat. A light went inside and a few seconds later the door was opened by an Indian man in his pyjamas. 'What are you doing?' he shouted. 'Why are you banging on my door?'

'There's a fire upstairs,' she said. 'Is there anyone else in your flat?'

The man's eyes widened in panic. 'My wife. My son.'

'You have to get them out now. There's a fire upstairs!'

The man didn't move and his mouth opened in shock.

Vicky grabbed the man by the shoulders and shook him. 'You have to get your family out now! There's a fire upstairs! Do you understand?'

The man nodded and Vicky pushed him back into the hallway. 'Get them outside now!' He pushed open the door to his flat and Vicky followed him inside. There was a kitchen to the right and Vicky ran and grabbed a tea towel. She ran it under the tap, then headed back to the front door. The man was there with his wife and young son.

'Get away from the house, now!' she shouted. 'I've called for the fire brigade, they're on their way.'

He did as he was told, scooping up the little boy and

running with him down the pavement as his wife followed. Vicky looked up the stairs. Her mouth had gone dry and she was having trouble swallowing. She knew all too well what was at the top of the stairs. The flames. The smoke. The heat. She flashed back to the body in the hostel. The pugilistic pose. Was that how she would find Des? Was that how she was going to end up, blackened and burned, lying on the floor with her arms and legs up, her skin split and her head a hairless grinning skull?

She grunted and shook her head, trying to blot out the gruesome images. 'I'm coming, Des,' she muttered under her breath. 'I'm coming for you.' She draped the wet tea towel over her head and ran up the stairs. It was only when she got to the top of the stairs that she remembered that there was a second door there and she grunted in frustration. She felt the door with the back of her hand to confirm it wasn't hot and then kicked it as hard as she could. She felt it give a little. She kicked it again, and again, and on the fourth kick the lock splintered and the door crashed in. Smoke billowed out and she ducked down, then realised she needed to get lower and went down on her hands and knees, coughing and spluttering. She could feel the heat scorching her skin and she gritted her teeth against the pain.

She heard the crackle of flames and shadows flickered on the walls. Her eyes were watering and she blinked away tears. Her heart was pounding and her hands had started shaking. 'Des!' she screamed at the top of her voice. 'Des!'

There was no reply and she didn't expect one. If he were conscious he would have made his own way out. She was going to have to go in and get him. Into the flames. Into the fire. Her whole body was trembling now and she was having to fight the urge to turn and run back down the stairs.

'You can do it, sweetheart,' said a voice. Her father. Vicky looked over her shoulder but of course there was no one there. But her father was right. She could do it. It was what she had been trained for.

She blinked away the tears. Visibility was still just about okay while she was on her hands and knees but the smoke was still stinging her eyes which meant she was also breathing it in. She remembered the carbon dioxide fire extinguisher in Farmer's kitchen and she headed there, clutching the wet tea towel over her mouth. Her eyes were streaming with tears but she found the extinguisher and grabbed it.

She crawled back into the hall and along to the bedrooms. She frowned as she realised that the smoke alarm hadn't gone off. She passed the spare bedroom. The door was open and flames were licking up the curtains. Was that where the fire had started? She pushed the door open wider. The heat was almost unbearable now. There was a pool of flame on the floor and the armchair was burning fiercely. It wasn't papers burning, it was an accelerant. Something inflammable had been poured or sprayed across the carpet and set alight. She looked around. There was no sign of Farmer. She aimed the extinguisher at the armchair and gave it three quick bursts. The fire went out. She crawled forward and sprayed the floor and in a few seconds the fire there was extinguished too, though the air was now thick with choking black smoke. The noticeboard was still burning but two quick sprays with the extinguisher and the flames went out.

She shuffled back along the hall to the main bedroom. The door was open and she could see flames flickering inside. She crawled in, dragging the fire extinguisher with her. Farmer was on the bed, lying face up.

'Des!' she shouted at the top of her voice. 'Des!'

There was no reaction. The smoke layer was only inches above his face and she knew that once he started breathing in the smoke he would be dead within minutes.

Everything was alight in the room. By the look of it accelerant had been spread across the carpet and the curtains and pretty much everywhere. There was no doubt the fire had been deliberately set, the two seats of the fire was proof enough of that. And she had a gut feeling that if she were to take the time to check the batteries in the smoke alarm she'd find they were dead.

She fired two quick bursts from the extinguisher at the carpet around the bed. The flames went out but the carpet continued to smoulder. There was an armchair burning fiercely in the corner. The flames were huge, almost reaching the ceiling. She squeezed the extinguisher's trigger and fired a long burst at the armchair, starting high and moving low. The flames went out but the smoke was thicker and blacker. She was on her knees but the smoke was dangerously close now.

She dropped the extinguisher and grabbed Farmer's arm and pulled him off the bed. He hit the floor with a loud thud, like a dead weight. There was blood on his head but his chest was moving. She slapped his face. 'Guv, wake up!' she shouted but his eyes stayed closed.

She dragged him towards the door. The armchair reignited and was soon engulfed in flames again. The smoke was just three feet from the ground now so she had no time to use the extinguisher. She crawled backwards, dragging Farmer with her.

The wet tea towel fell off her head and on to the carpet but she ignored it. The bed was ablaze now and the fire was getting hotter by the second.

She pulled Farmer out of the bedroom and into the hallway. Her arms were aching and her knees were hurting. She took a deep breath and stood up. The smoke immediately made her eyes water. She bent down and grabbed Farmer under the arms and hauled him up, then she ducked down and threw him over her shoulder. She put out her left hand to touch the wall, kept a hold of his legs with her right, and started walking towards the stairs, holding her breath. Her hand touched the kitchen door frame, then there was a gap, then the frame again. It was four more steps to the top of the stairs, then she continued down, keeping her hand against the wall.

Within a few steps the air was clearer and by the time she was halfway down she could breathe again.

She reached the door and stepped out into the night air, gasping for breath, tears streaming down her soot-stained face. She gritted her teeth as she carried Farmer away from the house. She kept on going until she reached the pavement. The Indian neighbour hurried over and helped her lower Farmer to the ground.

'Is he okay?' the neighbour asked.

'He's breathing.'

The man knelt down and opened Farmer's shirt. He put his hand on the side of Farmer's neck.

'What are you doing?' asked Vicky.

'I'm a nurse. I'm checking for a pulse.' The man

nodded. 'His heart's strong.' He examined the wound on Farmer's head. 'Do you have a handkerchief?'

'I don't,' said Vicky. She pulled a pack of tissues from her pocket. 'I've got these.

The man took several tissues and pressed them against the wound. 'He's going to be okay,' he said.

In the distance they heard an ambulance's siren.

'Where are the pumps?' muttered Vicky.

'Pumps?' repeated the man.

'The fire engines,' said Vicky. As if to answer her, they heard a fire engine siren off to their left. Then another. They were on their way.

Vicky sat back on her heels. Her heart was pounding and she forced herself to breathe slowly and deeply.

'Are you okay?' asked the neighbour.

She nodded. 'I'm fine.'

'Heck of a thing you did there, getting him out.'

She smiled. 'It's my job.' She nodded at the bloody tissues. 'I'll do that,' she said. 'You go and take care of your family.'

He let her apply pressure to the head wound and then hurried over to his wife and son. The ambulance arrived and she let the paramedics take over. They were putting Farmer on a stretcher when the pump and pump ladder arrived from the Bethnal Green station. The crew manager was Terry Jenner and as his crew began unravelling hoses and connecting the pump to a fire hydrant, he came over to her. 'What are you doing here, Vicky?'

'It's Des Farmer's house,' she said. 'They're putting him in the ambulance now.'

Jenner's grin vanished and was replaced by a look of concern. 'Is he okay?'

'I think so,' she said. 'Okay, so the house is empty. Des was in the top-floor flat on his own and I got him out. There's fire in both bedrooms at the back of the flat, but it's probably spread to the front by now. No fire on the ground floor and everyone is out.'

'Good job,' he said. Then he frowned. 'Wait, what? You were in there?'

'I saw fire and went in to get him. He was unconscious on the bed. By the look of it someone had belted him, and I think the fire was deliberately set. Can you ask your guys to take it easy up there? Be nice if there was some evidence I could look at down the line.'

'First priority is to put out the fire, you know that,' said Jenner. 'But I'll tell them.'

'The top door's already open,' she said. 'They can go right in.'

Jenner nodded and jogged over to his crew who now had two hoses fitted. Two firefighters were preparing to go inside and two more were taking their hose down the side of the house.

The ambulance drove away and Vicky turned to watch it go. The fact that they weren't using their lights or the siren was probably a good sign, she figured.

The firefighters with the hose disappeared into the house.

It took them less than five minutes to extinguish the fires and Jenner came over to let her know that other than a bit of damping down to make sure the fire didn't reignite, it was all over. A fire investigation van arrived and Dale Robertson climbed out. He was clearly surprised to see Vicky. 'What the hell are you doing here?'

'It's Des's house,' she said. 'I was just passing by.'

Robertson's jaw dropped. 'No way.'

'They've just taken him to hospital.'

'Is he okay?'

'Should be. Some smoke inhalation, but he wasn't burned.'

'You think it was a careless cigarette?' asked Robertson.

She shook her head. 'I'm sure it wasn't,' she said. 'Someone knocked him out and set fire to his place.'

'How do you know that?'

'He has a nasty wound on his head. Someone belted him. And there were two seats of the fire, one in his bedroom and one in the spare bedroom. The hall carpet was alight too but it didn't look to me as if the fire had spread from one room to the other.'

'You were in there?'

She nodded.

'Bloody hell, Vicky. What are you like?'

'It's your case, Dale. But I can tell you it was set. Oh, and check the smoke alarm, will you. It didn't go off. Can you photograph the batteries that are in there and get them checked for prints?'

'Prints? Fingerprints?'

'Please, Dale, just do it, yeah. I'll explain later.'

'You're not hanging around?'

'I'm going to the hospital to check on Des.'

54

Des Farmer slowly opened his eyes, clearly still in pain despite the painkillers they had pumped into him. He lay looking up at the ceiling, blinking his eyes as he tried to focus.

'Welcome back to the land of the living, guv,' said Vicky. She was sitting on a chair at the side of the bed and he slowly turned to look at her.

He tried to smile but it turned almost immediately into a wince. 'Where am I?'

She smiled and gestured at the monitoring equipment on the trolley next to him. 'Take a wild guess.'

'I know I'm in hospital. Which one?'

'The Royal London. You're being well looked after.'

Farmer sighed. 'My head hurts.'

'There's no lasting damage and your scan was clear. But it looks like you were hit on the head.'

'I feel like shit.' Farmer shook his head and winced again. 'Whoever it was zapped me from behind. A Taser, maybe. I don't think they hit me.'

'Maybe it happened when you fell. Either way it was the killer. The one you've been chasing.'

'How do you know?'

'The way the fire was set. The fact that he switched the batteries in your smoke detector. And the fact that there was enough Rohypnol in you to subdue a horse.'

'Rohypnol? Are you sure?'

'It's definite. They fast-tracked your blood test. Whoever hit you drugged you as well, just to be sure you'd be unconscious. It's the same MO, no question.'

Farmer sighed and stared up at the ceiling. 'Why the hell did he try to kill me?'

'Presumably he knows you're on to him.'

'That's impossible.' He sighed. 'The last thing I remember is going to the front door. Then I got zapped. How did I get out of the flat?'

'I carried you.'

'Fireman's lift?'

'Firefighter's lift, guv.'

'Thanks, sweetheart.'

'Least I could do.'

'You're serious? You carried me out?'

Vicky nodded.

He turned to look at her. 'What were you doing there?'

'You don't remember? You called me.'

He frowned. 'I called you?'

'You didn't say anything. And when I called back your phone was off.'

'I've absolutely no recollection of doing that.'

'That's the beauty of Rohypnol, I suppose.'

Vicky's mobile phone rang and she took it out and looked at the screen. The caller was withholding their number, but she apologised to Farmer and took the call anyway. 'This is Vicky,' she said.

'You the firefighter that got burned?' It was a man, gruff and whispering. She realised who it was immediately. Michael Walsh.

'Yes. How come you're calling me on a mobile?'

Walsh chuckled. 'Anything you can get outside, we can get inside.'

'What do you want, Mr Walsh.'

Farmer's eyes widened when he heard the name. 'Michael Walsh?' he mouthed, and Vicky nodded.

'I've been thinking about what you said. You and that Farmer guy.'

'And?'

'I need you to answer a question first.'

'Okay,' she said, hesitantly.

Walsh took a deep breath, and Vicky could almost hear him licking his lips. 'What did it feel like, the fire?' he asked eventually.

'Hot.'

'Not good enough. I want you to tell me what it felt like, when the flames were all around you and you thought you were going to die.'

Vicky screwed up her face. Part of her just wanted to end the call, but she knew that she needed Walsh's cooperation, and if answering his stupid questions achieved that end then all well and good. 'It was scary, but I'd been trained well. I had a casualty and I had to get him to the ladder. So I did what I had to do.'

'Why didn't you leave him?'

'Because that's not what firefighters do. We rescue people, we don't leave them.'

'Was he heavy?'

'Very heavy,' said Vicky.

'You got him out, but you didn't save yourself. Why?'

'The floor collapsed under me,' said Vicky.

'You fell?'

'Yes, I fell.'

'Into the fire?'

'Yes. Into the fire.'

She heard a slight gasp and realised that Walsh was getting off on the story.

'Mr Walsh, will you tell the truth about what you did? About who paid you? About how you set the fire.'

'Tell who?'

'The police.'

There was a long pause. The silence went on and on but Vicky didn't want to be the one who spoke first.

'You still there?' said Walsh eventually.

'Still here.'

'If I give a statement, can I give it to you?'

'It has to be to the police,' she said.

'But you can be there?'

'I can attend, yes.'

'That's what I want.'

'And I can do that. I can be there when you give your statement. But you have to tell them everything. How you did it. How you got in.'

'They gave me a key to the back door.'

'Who did?'

'The man I met.'

'You need to tell the police that. And how they paid you. And what they told you to do.'

'They wanted the whole building to burn. That's what they wanted. They said they needed it destroyed.'

'Then that's what you need to say,' said Vicky.

'And you'll be there?' She could hear the hope in his voice and it made her shudder.

'Yes, I'll be there.'

There was another long pause. 'Okay,' he said eventually. 'I'll talk to my lawyer.'

The call ended and Vicky realised she had been holding her breath. She sighed. She felt somehow dirty following the conversation, but there was relief, too.

'What's happening, sweetheart?' asked Farmer.

'Walsh is going to talk to the cops.'

Farmer grinned. 'About bloody time.'

55

Vicky managed to find a parking space a short walk from Wandsworth Prison. She looked at her watch. It was just before ten. She had arranged to meet two detectives at the prison, along with Peter Mulholland from SOCO. All three were waiting for her at the entrance.

Mulholland was wearing the same suit and lacrosse tie that he'd had on when she'd met him in the pub with Farmer. And he was carrying his big leather briefcase. He shook hands with her and introduced her to the two detectives. The older of the two was Detective Inspector Paul Rees, his colleague was Detective Constable Maureen Price. 'I've briefed them on my report, and they're up to speed,' said Mulholland. 'I've also offered to open a vein, if that helps.'

'Michael Walsh has been setting fires for a long time, he's good at covering his tracks,' said Vicky.

Mulholland shrugged. 'I should have taken more care,' he said. He shrugged. 'Anyway, at least we get a chance to put it right,' he said, gesturing at the entrance.

They checked in and were escorted along to the same interview room they had used during Vicky's last visit by a cheerful West Indian prison officer. He showed them into the room and then went off to get another chair.

DC Price took a digital recorder from her bag and set it on to the table and placed a microphone on a small stand.

The inspector waved Vicky to a chair and she sat down. Mulholland sat down next to her and put his briefcase on the floor. The guard reappeared with an extra chair and told them that Walsh was on his way.

Five minutes later, a female guard escorted the arsonist into the room. Walsh was wearing a stained prison sweat-shirt and jeans and he leered at Vicky when he saw her. 'Hello, Miss Lewis,' he said. 'Thank you for coming.'

'It's what you wanted,' she said.

Walsh looked around. 'Where is Mr Farmer?'

'He's busy on a case,' lied Vicky. In fact, he was still in hospital, but very much on the mend.

DC Price pressed a button to start the recording and nodded at the inspector.

'This interview is being conducted under caution,' said Inspector Rees. 'We will be recording the interview and will provide you with a copy or a transcript if you require one.'

'Don't need it,' said Walsh.

'That's your choice,' said the inspector. 'Now, you do not have to say anything. But, it may harm your defence if you do not mention when questioned something which you later rely on in court. Anything you do say may be given in evidence. Do you understand that?'

Walsh nodded.

'If you'd please say yes for the recording,' said the inspector.

'Yes, I understand,' said Walsh. 'But before we go any further, I want to be sure that my sentence won't be increased.'

'That's agreed,' said the inspector. 'We have already spoken to the CPS. Providing what you tell us is the truth, and you are prepared to give evidence in court, the offence will be added to your list of convictions and there will be no extra time to serve.'

Walsh nodded at Vicky. 'And she won't sue me.'

'I won't be suing, I promise,' said Vicky. 'I don't need your money, Mr Walsh. I just want justice for what happened.'

Walsh licked his fleshy lips as he stared at her scarred cheek. 'Okay,' he said. 'I did it. And they paid me to do it.'

'Did what, Mr Walsh?' asked the inspector.

'Set the fire. The fire what burned her. I did it. I blow-torched the electrical consumer board after I jerry-rigged a feed from the mains.'

'And why did you go to that trouble of doing that?'

'They wanted me to make it look as if the squatters had tampered with the electricity supply.'

'They? Who do you mean?'

'The guy who paid me. He gave me ten grand, cash. Two grand before, eight grand after I did the job.'

'And what was this man's name?' asked the inspector.

Walsh shrugged. 'He didn't tell me his name. Why would he?'

'But he knew your name?'

Walsh shook his head. 'He knew my nickname. My handle.'

'Your what?'

'The handle I used on the website. There's this website where people who love fires get together to share stories. That's how I met him. He wanted to know if I would do a fire for him and I said, sure. He didn't want to meet, he wanted to pay me with Bitcoins or something but I said fuck that, I wanted cash. I got caught out taking money into my bank before so this time it had to be cash.'

'You were on bail at the time for three other fires?' said the inspector.

Walsh nodded. 'Yeah, and you bastards seized all my money, so I said it had to be cash.'

'And where did you meet this man?'

'Battersea Park.'

'And he gave you ten thousand pounds?'

Walsh shook his head. 'Two thousand pounds. Then I did the fire. Then someone else gave me the rest of the money.'

'So you met two men?' asked the inspector.

Walsh nodded.

'Please answer for the recording, Mr Walsh,' said the detective inspector.

'Yes,' said Walsh.

'And did either of these men identify themselves?' asked the inspector.

'No.'

'Can you describe them?'

Walsh shrugged. 'The first one was about your age. About your size. He wore glasses. He had a hat on so I couldn't see his hair. He had a mole on his neck. I remember that.'

Mulholland bent down and opened his briefcase. He took out a glossy booklet and put it on the table. Vicky realised it was a brochure for the property development company that owned the hotel. Mulholland opened the

386   *Stephen Leather*

brochure to a page on which there was a group photograph of the company's directors. 'Do you recognise
anyone in this picture?' asked Mulholland.

Walsh peered at the photograph, then shook his head.
'No,' he said.

Mulholland gritted his teeth. He turned the page. There
was another photograph there of the firm's security team.
Walsh studied it and then nodded. He tapped the man
standing to the left of the group and grinned. 'That's
him. I knew he was wearing the glasses to change his
appearance.'

Vicky leaned over. It was the firm's head of security.

'And him,' said Walsh, tapping another figure. 'That
was the second guy.'

'You're sure?' asked the inspector.

'Dead sure,' said Walsh.

'For the benefit of the recording, would you name the
two people you have just pointed at.'

Walsh leaned forward and squinted at the caption. 'Neil
Hopkins, head of security. And Alan Muir. It doesn't say
what he does.'

'And just to confirm, Neil Hopkins gave you two thousand pounds to set fire to the hotel in Kilburn, and Alan
Muir paid you a further eight thousand pounds after you
carried out your instructions.'

'Yes.'

'And did either of these two men tell you that there
would be people in the building?'

Walsh nodded. 'They said there were Romanian squatters living there, but they were usually out in the evenings.'

'So they were definitely aware that there were people
living there?'

'Sure. But they were living on the top floor. They never went into the bar, which is where the consumer board was.'

'They weren't concerned about the people living there?'

'No. But they said they would be blamed for the fire.' He sat back and folded his arms. 'So are we good?'

The two detectives looked at each other, then back at Walsh. The inspector nodded. 'Provided you're happy to give evidence in court, I'd say we're definitely good,' he said.

Vicky raised her hand. 'Can I ask a question?'

'Of course,' said the inspector.

Vicky looked at Walsh and he licked his lips. 'How many fires did you set?'

'Three,' he said.

'Why?'

'They wanted the building destroyed. That's what the first guy said. It had to be damaged so badly that they would have to knock it down.'

Vicky looked over at the inspector. 'That's what they did,' she said. 'They've redeveloped the site in a way that wouldn't be possible with a listed building. That's why they were in such a rush to pay me off.'

The inspector nodded. 'Interview terminated at . . .' He looked at his watch. 'Ten forty-five.'

DC Price gathered up the digital recorder. Vicky and Mulholland stood up.

'I want her to come to court,' said Walsh.

'I'm sorry, what?' said the inspector.

Walsh gestured at Vicky. 'I want her in court when I give evidence.'

The inspector began to protest but Vicky cut him off with a wave of her hand. 'I'm okay with that.'

Walsh grinned and rubbed his hands together.

Vicky left with the detectives and Mulholland. They collected their phones and gathered together on the pavement outside the prison. 'He'll be a good witness,' said the inspector. 'We'll bring in Hopkins and Muir and I'm guessing we won't have any problem getting them to roll over on their bosses. They were clearly acting under orders, I doubt they had much to gain financially.'

Vicky punched the air. 'Finally. Thank you so much.' She patted Mulholland on the back. 'Thanks, Peter. You don't know what this means to me.'

'Someone's going to have to talk to Willie Campbell,' he said.

'He's coming back from Spain next week,' said the inspector. 'We'll be at the airport to meet him. He's got a lot of explaining to do, obviously.'

56

Vicky parked on the street and walked to Dowgate station. Jamie Hughes was throwing a tennis ball for Watson and the dog was running up and down excitedly. 'He looks happy,' said Vicky.

'He's easy enough to please,' said Hughes. 'Not like some people I could mention.' He flashed her a sarcastic smile.

'Bloody hell, Jamie, I just didn't fancy dating you, no need to bear a grudge.'

'But you're okay to go out with Matt the barman?'

'How do you know about that?'

'Everybody knows. Why? Is it a secret?'

'I had a pizza, it's no big thing.'

'I could have taken you for a pizza.'

'You didn't offer me pizza.'

'If I had done, you'd have gone?'

Vicky laughed. 'I think that ship has sailed,' she said. 'But if it makes you feel any better, Matt did ask me first.'

Watson returned with the tennis ball and Hughes took it from him. 'So how's Des?' he asked.

'On the mend.'

'What the hell happened?'

'He doesn't want me to say.'

'Well, thank you very much.'

'It's not me, Jamie. It's Des. He's been chasing up some cases and it looks like it came back to bite him on the arse.'

'What cases?'

Vicky sighed. 'What bit of "he doesn't want me to say" don't you understand?'

Hughes held up his hands in surrender. 'Fine,' he said. Watson barked for the ball and Hughes threw it.

'It's not you, Jamie. He doesn't want anyone to know. But between you and me, someone set fire to his house so he's going to be staying with me for a while.'

'Why would anyone set fire to Des's house?'

Vicky sighed. 'He's on the trail of a killer who's been using fire to cover his tracks. He wants me to pick up some evidence he left in his office. But Jamie, mum's the word, okay?'

'Of course,' he said. 'Give Des my best, yeah. I hope he's up and around soon.'

'I will,' said Vicky.

Hughes went over to Watson and took the ball from him while Vicky went upstairs to Farmer's office. She sat down at his desk, deep in thought. She had been there for less than a minute when the door opened. It was Danny Maguire. 'I thought I heard someone here,' he said.

'I'm just picking something up for Des.'

'How is he?'

'He's okay, but his flat is a write-off.'

'How did it happen?'

'Dale's got the case,' said Vicky. 'What does he say?'

'He says it's ongoing, but Des is a smoker, and you know . . .' He shrugged.

'It wasn't an accident, Danny,' said Vicky.

'What?'

'Remember that case I was asking you about? Samantha Stewart? It's connected to that. Look, best we don't talk in the office. I'll see you downstairs in the bar in five minutes.'

Maguire nodded and left, closing the door as he went. Vicky closed the desk drawer and sat back in Des's chair. She didn't like lying to her colleagues, but she didn't have any choice. The killer had tried to kill Des and would almost certainly try again. And when he did, Vicky's life would also be on the line.

She sat for a few minutes then went to the gym, where Bob Morris was on an exercise bike, listening to music on his iPhone. He took his earphones out when he saw Vicky. 'What can I do you for, darling?'

'I want to borrow a couple of pieces of kit, on the QT.'

She told him what she wanted and he frowned. 'What the hell do you need that for?' he asked.

'It's a surprise,' she said. 'Are you okay with it? I'll get everything back to you tomorrow morning.'

'No problem, we've got spares. But if you get caught, it's on you.'

'Deal,' she said, patting him on the back.

57

Matt looked over at the table where Vicky was deep in conversation with Danny Maguire and wondered what they were talking about. He had been in the stock-room when they turned up so he hadn't served them, but he had caught Vicky's eye a couple of times and she had smiled and waved. She was dressed casually in a sweatshirt and jeans and a long scarf wound around her neck so he figured it was her day off.

After fifteen minutes Maguire drained his glass and left. Matt took the opportunity to pop over to the table.

'How are you doing?' he asked.

'Good,' she said.

'I sent you a text.'

'I'm sorry. I've been rushed off my feet and my battery died.'

He picked up the empty glass. 'So I heard Des was in a fire,' said Matt. 'Is he okay?'

'He's in hospital. But he's out today.'

'What was it? An accident?'

'Someone set fire to his flat.'

'No way.'

She lowered her voice and leaned towards him. 'Des

reckons it was the killer. He thinks the killer found out what he was doing and wanted to stop him.'

'Are you serious?'

'That's what it looks like, Matt. Why else would anyone set fire to his flat?'

'No idea. My God. So what happened?'

'I dragged him out. Just in time.'

'Wow. What, the flat was on fire and you went in?'

Vicky nodded.

Matt smiled. 'You can't help but be a hero, can you?'

'I don't think I was being heroic. I just needed to get him out.'

'Fireman's lift?' Vicky nodded and Matt grinned. 'Sorry. Probably easier carrying him down than up, though being unconscious wouldn't help.'

'He's not getting any lighter, that's a fact,' said Vicky. 'But at least this proves his killer theory, doesn't it?'

'You think?'

'Hell yeah,' said Vicky. 'Now he's got the *Evening Standard* interested and they're going to do a story on the whole thing. Remember that reporter who did the story on me? India? She's really interested. She says she'll do a front-page story on it and that'll get the cops fired up. She's going to interview me and Des tomorrow.' She looked at her watch. 'I'd better be going. I've got to pick him up.'

'Not literally?'

'Ha ha. In the car.' She drank the rest of her wine and put down the empty glass.

'Always the chauffeur,' said Matt. 'You should tell him to get an Addison Lee account. Or a bloody bike.'

'He's staying with me for a few days,' said Vicky.

'This gets better and better,' laughed Matt.

'His flat is a mess, it'll be a while before he can move back in.'

'So he forced himself on you? He's unstoppable, isn't he?'

'It's okay. My mum has gone on holiday with her sister so there's plenty of room.'

'You'll be waiting on him hand and foot,' said Matt. 'You know what he's like.'

'What can I say?' Vicky stood up. 'He's the guv.'

'You're too bloody good to him,' said Matt, picking up her empty glass and standing up. 'So, fancy a pizza or something over the weekend?'

'Or something?' she said.

'I thought I'd leave my options open,' he said. 'Saturday?'

Vicky grinned. 'Saturday,' she said. She looked at her watch. 'I've got to dash.'

'Give my regards to the Grouch,' said Matt.

'Will do,' said Vicky. She headed for the door as Matt took her glass over to the bar.

58

By the time Vicky got to the hospital, Des Farmer was waiting for her, sitting on his bed with his bag packed. 'You're late,' he said. He looked at his watch and shook his head.

'To be fair, we didn't have a time fixed,' said Vicky. 'Anyway, how are you?'

'Hungry,' he said. 'The food's crap here.'

'I'll cook something when we get home,' she said. 'Well, I say cook, I mean I'll reheat something my mum left for me.'

'Or we could order pizza.'

'Yes, we could order pizza,' she said, picking up his bag. 'Are you good to go?'

He nodded and stood up. He took a deep breath and Vicky took his arm. He shook her off. 'I'm not an invalid, sweetheart.'

'Sorry.' She walked with him to the lift, and down to the ground floor. She found him a seat in reception and went off to get her car, but by the time she returned with the BMW he was standing outside, his bag at his feet, as if he feared that at any moment he might be dragged back inside.

She helped him into the car and put his bag in the boot.

'How about we pick up a pizza on the way.'

'What is with you guys and pizza?'

'What do you mean?'

'That's what Matt's offering me over the weekend.'

'He's a pretty boy, isn't he?'

'And charming. Don't forget charming. Guv, did you tell anyone about being zapped and drugged?'

He frowned. 'The doctors, you mean?'

Vicky shook her head. 'Anyone from Dowgate?'

'Just Dale.'

'But no one else?'

'Dale likes to gossip so I assume everyone at Dowgate knows now. Why do you ask?'

Vicky shrugged. 'No reason. Just wanted to know.'

59

He heard the car coming down the road and he hugged the shadows. He was standing at the side of the house. The house was in darkness. He had his backpack slung over his shoulder and he was wearing blue latex gloves and a dark coat with a black wool beanie hat.

The car turned into the driveway. The flash BMW that she'd bought with her compensation money. The headlights were blinding but he caught a glimpse of someone in the front passenger seat before he ducked back into the darkness. The garage door rattled up and he frowned, wondering what was happening, then realised she must have used a remote to open it. She drove slowly into the garage and the door closed behind it. He waited, breathing slowly and evenly. When she didn't reappear he assumed there must be a connecting door from the garage to the house and that she'd gone inside. He'd heard the dog bark for a while and then it fell silent.

He heard voices in the kitchen. Her voice, and a man's. He hadn't seen the man's face but he knew it was her boss, Des Farmer. The one they called the Grouch. The kitchen light went off and everything went quiet. He peered around the side of the house. The sitting-room curtains were drawn but he could see that the lights were on. He waited, shifting his weight from side to side to keep his circulation flowing. It was getting cold and his breath was feathering in the night air. Ten minutes passed and he checked again. The sitting-room lights were off.

He walked slowly across the lawn and looked up at the rear of the house. Vicky's lights were on. Then the bath-room light went on. She must have been showering. Or doing whatever it was she did to her scars. He waited. The bathroom light went off. Five minutes later Vicky's bedroom light went off. He assumed the dog was upstairs with Vicky but he had a contingency plan for the dog if it was still downstairs.

He went around to the front of the house. All the upstairs lights were off. The house was in darkness. He walked quietly to the rear of the house again, sat down and waited. He needed them to be in a deep sleep and for most people that happened about an hour and a half after they went to bed.

He kept checking his watch as time crawled by. His heart was racing, he wanted to get inside the house and get it over with, but he knew that he had to be patient. There were two people inside, Vicky and her boss, and if either heard him breaking in then it would all be over. One woman he could overpower easily enough, but to be sure of overpowering two people he would need them asleep.

He checked his watch. Ninety minutes had passed. He stood up and rolled his shoulders, then did some stretching exercises to get his muscles working again. He took a few deep breaths, then walked around to the front door. He checked the lock and smiled to himself. A Yale. Easy enough to pick and he'd had plenty of practice. He had a set of picks in his backpack and knew from experience that it would take less than a couple of minutes to open it. As a fall-back position he had a glass-cutter but he would prefer to get inside without causing any damage.

He checked the garage door but it was down and locked. He went back along the side of the house. An upstairs window was open slightly, the glass was frosted so it was probably a bathroom. There was a drainpipe running up by the window and he tested it. It was metal and looked as if it would bear his weight.

He carried on around the side of the house and to the kitchen door. He tried the handle but it was locked. To the right was a conservatory with sliding doors on to a small terrace. He stepped on to the terrace and gently pushed the glass door. It slid open. He smiled to himself. It was his lucky day.

He took a small foil-wrapped package out of his pocket. Inside was a piece of raw steak. He'd never yet met a Labrador that couldn't be won over by a treat. He slipped inside and pushed the door closed behind him. He stood for a while, steadying his breathing. There was a wicker sofa and a wicker chair with matching cushions, a glass-topped wicker coffee table and dozens of assorted potted plants. Beyond the sofa was another sliding door, this one leading to a sitting room. The curtains were drawn and a small patch of moonlight illuminated the threshold, but the rest was in darkness.

He tiptoed around the wicker sofa and stepped into the darkened living room. All he could make out were dark furniture shapes. He figured the door to the hallway would be to the left and he looked over that way, blinking his eyes as he tried to see. That was when the light flicked on.

60

'Hello, Matt.' Vicky had been sitting in the armchair for the best part of an hour before she had heard the door to the patio slide open. She had left it unlocked, figuring that whoever had attacked Farmer would also be after her. She had the thermal-imaging camera that she had borrowed from Dowgate and she had watched as the figure had stood in the conservatory, listening.

It was only when the figure had stepped across the threshold into the sitting room that she knew for sure that it was Matt from the bar. Matt who had kissed her. Matt who been the perfect gentleman. She had suspected, of course. But it could just as easily have been Jamie Hughes or Danny McGuire. Or anyone from Dowgate. Everyone now knew about Farmer's obsession with the serial killer, and that he had been attacked in the flat. The truth was, she had hoped it was anyone but Matt. She liked him, she really liked him. But the Matt she thought she knew wasn't the real Matt. He wasn't Matt the potential boyfriend or Matt the man she could settle down and have children with. He was Matt the arsonist. Matt the killer.

He had taken an involuntary step back when she had switched the light on and she had smiled at his confusion.

He had crept into her house thinking that he was the attacker and she was the victim and had been blindsided by the role reversal.

'I'm guessing you're not here to bring me chocolates, are you?' She scowled when she saw the piece of steak in his hand. 'And you were going to drug my dog? Like you drugged your victims. You bastard.'

'What's going on, Vicky?' He tossed the meat back into the conservatory. He was wearing gloves, she noticed. Blue latex gloves.

'I think I'm the one who should be asking you that, Matt.'

'You set me up? All that crap about the interview, you made it up?'

'No, the interview's real enough. The *Standard* wants to do a story. You set yourself up, Matt.'

Matt took off his backpack and put it down on the floor.

'What is that, your rape kit?' she asked. 'Everything you need to start a fire and make it look like an accident?' She smiled thinly. 'Des always says there's no such thing as accidents. Just actions and consequences and some-times those consequences lead to bad things happening.' She put the thermal-imaging camera down and stood up.

Matt said nothing. He squatted down, unzipped his backpack and pulled out a stun gun. He pressed the trigger as he straightened up and blue sparks arced between the two prongs. 'I'm sorry it's got to end like this, Vicky,' said Matt. 'It's not what I planned.'

'What's your plan? Burn me alive?'

'The smoke will kill you while you're unconscious. If you'd been asleep you wouldn't have felt a thing. Same with Des. Now . . .' He shrugged. 'This will hurt a bit but you'll still be unconscious when you die.'

She sneered at him contemptuously. 'That's the plan? Stun me and then kill me?'

Matt grimaced. 'I'm afraid so.' He pressed the trigger again and sparks arced.

'I'm not sure how that's going to work out, Matt,' said a voice at the far end of the room. Matt whirled around to see Farmer in the hallway, holding a Halligan bar. He was hefting it in both hands. 'Lovely bit of kit, this,' said Farmer. 'Nine pounds of hardened steel and you can do so much with it. You can force open doors and windows, break padlocks, take the hinges off doors, breach drywalls, secure ground ladders, use it as a foot brace on a roof, lift up manhole covers, shut off gas meters, remove battery terminals, prop open car bonnets, you can stab ventilation holes . . . the list goes on and on. Oh yes, and I forgot, you can use it to beat the shit out of a cowardly serial killer and rapist.'

'It's over, Matt,' said Vicky. 'Just accept that. Please.'

Matt looked at Farmer and shook his head. 'I should have used the stun gun longer. None of this would have happened if you hadn't phoned her.'

'Should have, would have, could have,' said Farmer. 'You're just too clever for your own good. You should have just killed me when you had the chance, but with you it's all about proving how clever you are.'

'But you're not half as clever as you think you are, Matt,' said Vicky. 'You gave yourself away. I thought maybe it was you because you were the only one I told about Des's off-the-books investigation. But you confirmed it in the bar. When you said that Des was unconscious.

Nobody else knew that, Matt. We hadn't told anybody, but you knew. You knew because you were the one who attacked him and drugged him. And we knew it was only a matter of time before you tried to finish the job. I still hoped it wasn't you, I really wanted you to be for real.'

Matt turned to look at her, still holding the stun gun. 'I was never for real,' he said. 'You must have known that.'

'You were just using me to find out what was happening in the investigations team?'

Matt sneered at her. 'What, you thought I was attracted to you? Have you seen yourself in the mirror lately?'

Farmer took a step forwards and Matt turned to look at him and pressed the stun gun trigger again. Vicky took out her mobile phone. 'I'm calling the police. It's over.'

Matt transferred his stun gun to his left hand and reached into his jacket pocket with his left. It reappeared holding a small can of pepper spray. He rushed towards Farmer, spraying the corrosive liquid over Farmer's face.

Farmer staggered back and Matt continued to spray. The Halligan bar fell from Farmer's hands and clattered on the floor. Farmer put both hands up to his face to protect his eyes but Matt carried on spraying. Even on the other side of the room the fumes stung Vicky's eyes.

She ran towards Matt but he heard her coming and raised the canister. She put her gloved hand over her face just as he pressed the button and she managed to block some of the spray but not all. He kicked her in the stomach and she staggered back, coughing and spluttering. The phone fell to the floor.

Matt turned back to Farmer, this time using the stun gun. He rammed the prongs against Farmer's side and pulled the trigger. Farmer went into convulsions and his legs collapsed underneath him. He fell on top of the Halligan bar.

Matt tossed the pepper spray on to a chair and grabbed at the Halligan bar. He pulled it but Farmer was too heavy.

Vicky's eyes were streaming with tears. Even with her hand up the spray had got to her and she could barely see. There was a crystal vase containing the flowers that her mum had brought in from the garden and she fumbled for it. She tipped out the flowers and poured the water over her face.

Matt twisted around and grinned when he saw what she was doing. 'Clever girl,' he said, standing up. He held up the stun gun and pressed the trigger. Blue sparks crackled. 'You are making this so much more difficult than it needs to be,' he said. 'Just let me put you to sleep then I can start the fire and get the hell out of here.' He smiled. 'I might even put you and the Grouch in a compromising position. That'd get them talking back at the station, wouldn't it?'

He pulled the trigger again, and stepped forward. Vicky raised the vase. She would only get one chance. If he got her with the stun gun then it would all be over. He stopped, waiting for her to throw. From the confident way he was grinning, she reckoned he figured he could duck in plenty of time. And he was probably right. Then she remembered his injured knee, the injury that had kept him from being a firefighter. Left or right? Her mind raced. Left. His left? Her left?'

He grinned as he sensed her hesitation. 'Come on, Vicky, throw the bloody thing and then we can get this over with.' He pressed the stun gun trigger again and she flinched. Farmer was still on the floor, unconscious and breathing heavily.

She raised the vase, faked that she was going to throw it at his face and then hurled it with all her strength at his left knee. He wasn't expecting it and the crystal vase hit his knee hard. There was a splintering crack that suggested the kneecap had broken and he screamed in pain. He didn't go down but he transferred all his weight to his right leg and he cursed loudly.

Vicky ran towards Farmer. She grabbed the end of the Halligan bar but Farmer was just too heavy. She knelt down and started to roll him over but then she heard Matt limping up behind her. There was a crackle from the stun gun and she threw herself to the side. The stun gun missed her by inches and Matt cursed.

Vicky rolled over and crawled into the hall. Matt followed her, dragging his injured leg after him. She got to her feet and staggered along the hallway to the kitchen. Matt followed, grunting each time he moved his left leg.

Vicky burst into the kitchen and looked around for something to use as a weapon. A knife. She ran to the knife block but then saw the fire extinguishers. She grabbed the bright red carbon dioxide cylinder, and pulled out the safety pin, breaking the tamper seal. She turned and pointed the black horn at Matt and pulled the trigger. He was only a few feet away and the freezing carbon dioxide hit him full in the face.

His face and shoulders were covered in the white spray and he swallowed some, making him cough and retch. He waved his arms around but Vicky kept the spray going and soon he was covered in it, unable to see and barely able to breathe. He stumbled backwards and yelped as he put his weight on his left knee. Opening his mouth to scream let in more of the freezing foam and he began to choke.

Vicky released the trigger, upended the cylinder and slammed the base into Matt's face, enjoying the crack of his nose shattering and the way the foam on his face turned a frothy red. Matt hit the wall and slid down it, covered in pink foam. Vicky stood looking down at him, her breath coming in ragged gasps. She raised the cylinder again. She wanted nothing more than to smash his head to a pulp.

'Best not, sweetheart,' said a voice to her right. Farmer had crawled into the hallway and he was blinking up at her. He pulled himself into a sitting position and wiped his streaming eyes with his sleeve. 'Let the boys in blue do their job, yeah.'

Vicky put the fire extinguisher down on the floor. 'I suppose you're right, guv.' She went back into the sitting room and picked up her phone. She dialled 999 and the operator answered almost immediately. 'Do you need the police, the fire brigade or an ambulance?' asked the operator.

Vicky took a deep breath and smiled. 'Just send all three,' she said.

CR